Charlotte's Locket

by
Susan Siracusa

Strategic Book Publishing and Rights Co.

Strategic Book Publishing and Rights Co.
12620 FM 1960, Suite A4-507
Houston, TX 77065
www.sbpra.com

ISBN: 978-1-61897-543-0

Design: Dedicated Book Services, (www.netdbs.com)

'Know that love is truly timeless.'
Mary M. Ricksen

FOREWORD

'1697
Mill Cottage, Littleham
I feel compelled to write my story, in the hope that one day in the future, it will be discovered and read, although I wonder if believed. What happened to me that sunny afternoon in the garden of Mill Cottage was so fantastic—so unreal—it seems like a dream, a beautiful dream.'

I paused and dipped my feathered quill into the little clay pot of ink upon my desk, gazing momentarily out of the tiny lattice window at the driving rain. *Such a dreary November day!* The light was poor, and what little I received from the flickering candle beside me strained my eyes. I knew I must continue, even if I became blind in the attempt. To me, it would have all been worthwhile.

Chapter One

'The early morning sunlight streamed in through my bedroom window, dancing upon my sleeping face, as it flickered through the leaves of the large tree outside my flat. The rays of sun grew stronger and succeeded in their endeavor to awaken me. I groaned and turned away from the window, pulling with me the pretty floral lemon quilt that matched the curtains and décor of my small, but comfortable, bedroom. I opened one eye and squinted at the small digital clock beside my bed, which informed me in shiny, bold red numbers that it was 10:37am. My heart raced for a moment, but then I realized, with a warm and satisfied feeling, that today was Monday, and I was on a week's vacation from work. I turned over again, and faced the sunlight, now obscured by the window frame, that had moved away from my face. I stretched and flopped back against the pillow, my long auburn hair glinting in the morning light as it lay across the lemon floral pillowcase.

I was 25 years old and still single after a succession of disastrous relationships, which had made me increasingly wary of getting involved ever again with the male species. I had shunned any man that showed the slightest interest in me, becoming something of a recluse. I was the 'Ice Maiden' of the Accounts Department, in the small office of *Thomas Denbridge & Sons.* My female colleagues had all but given up on me, no longer asking me to join them on 'girly nights out' in town. I had become an embarrassment to them, and a good candidate for the local shrink. It didn't bother me. I was happy. Men were problems I could quite happily do without. I had my own flat, my own income. I could pay my bills, cook, unblock the sink, mend a fuse, and change a light bulb. Who needed men?

Slipping on my fluffy yellow slippers and unhooking the dressing gown from the back of the door as I left, wrapping its softness around me, I padded along the passage to the bathroom. As I passed the front door, the clanging of the noisy letterbox startled me. I watched a succession of envelopes scatter haphazardly upon the mat. The postman was no longer a welcome arrival. I could foresee the contents in my hand without looking—a bill or two, leaflets advertising loans, junk mail from the local shops, and maybe an unscrupulous company telling me that I had won a prize in their lottery, which I had supposedly entered at one time, but had no recollection of doing so. Throwing the pile down upon the kitchen table, I picked up the kettle to fill, and sighed heavily as the water gushed into the plastic container, before I snapped the lid shut. *What could I do today?* I definitely needed to get some shopping done, clean the flat a bit, I suppose, and then take a walk around the new shopping mall that had recently opened in town. *No. Not the shopping mall.* That usually involved buying unwanted clothing to cheer myself up and consequently spending money I could easily put to better use.

I made myself a cup of coffee and sat down at the little table, sipping the comforting brew while eyeing the pile of unopened envelopes before me. Reaching out, I picked up a familiar brown envelope and tore it open, Water rates reminder. I was going to pay that this week. Another was addressed to a *Mr. J. Harper*, the flat's previous occupant. I tossed it to one side. With no forwarding address, it was destined for the bin. The usual loan advertisements followed, until I reached the last in the pile. A plain brown envelope with a name stamped in red across the top: *T. J. Elliot & Sons, Solicitors.* My heart started to beat faster. *What had I forgotten to pay? Was someone suing me?* I could think of nothing that would engage the wrath of a solicitor, and I checked again to see if it *was* addressed to me. The name *'Miss Emily Howard'* was plainly stated on the front. I fingered the ominous brown envelope and very hesitantly unsealed it, withdrawing the neat white folder paper within. Slowly I opened it up, and read the contents with baited breath.

'Dear Miss Howard,

I am acting on behalf of your late uncle, Mr. James Herbert Howard of 14 Edmonton Street, London. I have information that is to your advantage and would ask you kindly to contact Messers. J. Morgan and Co., 46 High Street, Banbury, Tel. 01325 667671 for an appointment as soon as possible. I have passed all subsequent information on to Mr J. Morgan.

Kind regards.
Thomas J. Elliot.'

James Howard? The name rang a bell deep in my subconscious—one of those uncles that you only ever met at weddings or funerals. They hugged you like a lost child, told you how much you had grown and then they disappeared—back into oblivion—until the next family reunion. *Something to my advantage?* I had no idea what that could possibly be, unless he had left me some money. *Why should he?* I didn't know him well, if at all. I pondered over the possibilities as I sipped my warm coffee, re-reading the letter over and over again.

The doorbell rang, and I jumped. Putting down the intriguing letter, I went to the door. Checking that the chain was still in place, I slowly opened it. I recognized the caller as the young man from down the corridor, Sam. We had passed one another frequently in the hallway, exchanging pleasantries, but nothing more. I unlatched the chain. He stood there staring at me, before dropping his eyes down to my cleavage, poking out of my nightgown. I pulled the gown tightly around myself, feeling uncomfortable, and tucked my uncombed hair back behind my ears.

"Can I help you?" I asked, a little irritated at being scrutinized in such a way. Sam flicked back his dark blond hair from one side of his face, blushing profusely, before opening and closing his mouth in an effort to speak.

"I—I—was wondering if you had any tea to spare?" he stammered. "My mum is visiting me today, and I don't have any." I resisted the urge to say, '*Why don't you buy some?'* He looked so pathetic; I couldn't help but feel sorry for him.

"Hang on a minute. I'll go and look," I said, leaving him standing there while I returned to the kitchen and opened a cupboard. There, tucked at the back, was a foil packet of tea bags. God knows how long they had been there. It had been a long time since I had any visitors, and they were probably well past their sell-by date. "Here." I said, handing him the packet and managing a weak smile, out of pity.

"Thanks," he replied, remaining at my door and shifting from one foot to the other nervously. I sensed there was more to come, and waited with apprehension. "I was wondering if you would like to come out with—"

"No thanks!" I interrupted, and slammed the door in his face. "Not in a million years," I said out loud to myself. *Not in a million years.*

You are probably thinking by now that I am a cold-hearted bitch, and I don't blame you in the least. I did once have a heart—a big heart that loved everyone and everything. Over time, it was worn away by unscrupulous men—everyone from husbands who had deemed me good mistress material to general lying, deceitful individuals. I had given my all to those men. Now I had nothing left. I trusted no one—loved no one—and that was how it was going to be. This '*Ice Maiden'* was impenetrable.

Turning back to the letter that had just been delivered, I was curious as to what information these people had that could be to my advantage. Banbury was only a short bus ride away. I could get my shopping done at the same time. Picking up the piece of paper, I carried it with me to the phone on a nearby table. I cautiously dialed the number and requested an appointment from the stern-sounding woman on the other end of the line. She informed me that the only available appointment that day was for 1pm, otherwise it would be next week before Mr. Morgan could see me. I didn't think I could contain myself until next week, so I gratefully accepted the 1pm slot. Looking at my wristwatch, I was horrified to see it was nearly midday already, and ran into the bedroom to dress. I chose a black skirt and jacket with a red top. It was smart, sophisticated and complemented my auburn hair, which I tied back into a neat bun, secured by a matching red scrunchie.

The bus ride into town was, as usual, noisy and crowded. I had to stand part of the way and held onto a rail, jostled by a pair of male school kids who swore frequently, telling one another what they would like to do to Justin Carter in Year 10 in no uncertain terms. I glared at them. This was where it all began. *God help the next generation.*

I got off the bus at the Red Lion pub. From here there was a shortcut between two department stores that led out onto the main High Street. It didn't take me long to locate the premises of *Messers. F. Morgan and Co.* A small indiscreet green door sandwiched between a photographic shop and a confectioner's, led me to a steep staircase that opened out into a small reception area. It was not difficult to tell that this had once been someone's private house, and I was now seated in his or her bedroom.

An elderly gent sat opposite me, rubbing his hands together in an agitated manner. I wondered what had brought him to this place, and a tall woman emerging from an adjoining door soon enlightened my curious mind.

"Here we are, Mr. Lewis," she said, handing him a folded piece of paper. "I've taken a copy of your wife's death certificate, and Mr Morgan will be in touch shortly regarding the Will." The elderly man rose unsteadily from his chair and thanked the woman before making his way to the door. I felt touched by the man's sadness, *what would his life be like from now on?* The love of his life gone, leaving him to grieve alone with no purpose to his existence—soon to be shipped off to '*God's waiting room*' at a local nursing home, by uncaring and selfish relatives, who waited like vultures for the inevitable. I thought about my own parents, tragically killed in a car accident when I was seven. They never experienced old age. *Maybe that was a good thing in this day and age—maybe not?* The tall woman turned to me.

"Miss Howard? Mr Morgan will see you now," she announced, smiling. I got up and followed her into the next room. Seated at a huge antique desk surrounded by piles of files and papers was Mr. Morgan. A large gentleman, to say the least, who struggled to stand upon my entrance, before holding out a welcoming hand.

"Miss Howard, please sit down," he said, gripping my hand tightly and gesturing to a nearby chair with the other. I smiled and seated myself, a little intimidated by the grandeur of his office and the man himself. Mr. Morgan shuffled through some papers on his desk, muttering to himself, before taking hold of a file and expressing satisfaction at finding it. "Ah! Here we are!" he exclaimed loudly as he opened up the file and examined the contents. It seemed like forever, as I sat and watched him twirling his grey moustache, while he absorbed the information. I felt like shouting at him to hurry up and tell me what it was all about. I waited patiently for him to finish reading. At last he looked at me over the top of his gold-rimmed glasses. "Did you know your uncle?" he asked.

"No, not really. I think he was at my Aunt Clara's funeral, but I can't be sure." He returned his attention to the file momentarily before snapping it shut.

"Well, my child. You were obviously favoured by your late uncle," he said, leaning towards me across the desk. "And I can see why." His smile turned into a leer as his eyes dropped to my bust. I sat further back in my chair, the feeling of wanting to leave his office right then and there was overpowering, but I fought hard to control my anger.

"So did he leave me anything?" I said stiffly and to the point. Mr. Morgan was shaken from his lecherous stupor and sat upright, coughing to disguise his indiscretion.

"Yes, indeed," he replied as he opened a drawer of his desk and took out a large brown envelope, which he proceeded to cut open with a silver letter opener, before emptying the contents onto his desk. A huge bunch of rusted keys clattered onto the desktop, together with a yellowed piece of folded paper. I looked at the pile before me in amazement, totally lost for words. Eventually I found my voice.

"He left me a bunch of keys?"

"It appears so, but not just any ordinary bunch of keys," he replied, opening up the file again and reading aloud from its contents. "Your uncle has left you, in his Will, a house known locally as Mill Cottage, with land of approximately one acre and a small outbuilding." He stopped to observe my reaction before continuing. "The cottage is situated in the village of Littleham, down in the County of Kent. I have the deeds to the cottage, if you wish to examine them." I shook my head, unable to form rational words and reached out, in a daze, to pick up the folded piece of paper. "That came with the keys," Mr. Morgan informed me, "You may find it a little…*strange*." I found the whole scenario strange, *what could get any more bizarre?* As I carefully unfolded the brittle paper, I wondered how old it would have had to be to get into this state of decomposition. Inside, written in fading black ink, were six lines of writing. At first it was difficult to decipher the words, but I soon grew accustomed to the writing.

'To you, dear child, I leave this place.
Go hither there. Do make haste.
Seek the garden. Seek the pear.
For old Mill Cottage will still be there.
The time is present. The time is past.
Decide on two, the third's your last.'

The hair on the back of my neck stated to bristle. Looking up at Mr. Morgan, I had to ask the question.

"Was my uncle sound of mind when he died?"

"We have no reason to think otherwise," came the reply.

"I don't understand," I said, baffled. "The third what?" The gentleman struggled to his feet yet again and smiled apologetically.

"I'm sorry I have no further information. I am merely passing on your uncle's last wishes."

"Yes, of course," I replied, gathering up the keys and note before placing them back into the brown envelope. Mr. Morgan handed me the deeds to the cottage, shook my hand, and bid me farewell.

I left the offices of *Messers F. Morgan and Co.* and wandered up the High Street. The weight of the keys in my handbag reminded me that what I had just experienced was not a dream, and that this matter had to be dealt with in reality.

Purchasing only enough food for the night's dinner, I made my way home. My mind was far from being focused on the trivialities of shopping for groceries. There were far more important things to digest. I had so many questions to ask, and yet no one to ask them to. The poem—or whatever it was—intrigued me, yet at the same time it unnerved me. It had an ominous ring that worried me.

Once home, I searched through the kitchen drawers for a road map of Kent, eager to see where exactly my cottage was located. Spreading it out on the floor, I got down on my hands and knees and tried to find the town or village of Littleham. It was not an easy task, and I had all but given up when I spotted it, in tiny print, in the middle of nowhere. *This is definitely a job for Betsy*, I thought to myself, noticing the absence of a nearby railway station or, I suspected, any national bus route. Betsy was my pride and joy—my little red sports car, bought by me and paid for on my 21st birthday with money put in trust by my parents. She was garaged nearby, and used probably only three or four times a month. It was far easier to get the bus to town, as the parking was atrocious, and I used the same method for work.

Getting up from the floor, I suddenly felt light-headed. The room started to spin, and my vision blurred. I grabbed hold of the back of a chair and waited until everything steadied itself. I soon realised that I had not eaten any breakfast—merely a cup of coffee—before I rushed out. Lunch had also gone uneaten. No wonder I felt like this. Chastising myself for being so stupid, I made some sandwiches and a bowl of hot vegetable soup. It was now well past 4pm, and I ate hungrily.

That evening, I planned my journey to Littleham. It looked pretty straightforward, and I estimated it to be around 70 miles or so away. The nearest large village was Offenham. Once there, I could ask the way to Littleham, if need be. I was thankful that I had a week off of work. It couldn't have worked out better. I smiled to myself—life was definitely improving, and not a man in sight. *Perfect!*

Just before I turned in that evening, I gathered up all the necessary road maps, my scribbled instructions on how to get there, and the brown envelope containing the keys and odd note. The bunch of keys had left rust debris on my coffee table from where I had examined them earlier. There were three in all—large iron keys covered in a thick layer of rust that flaked off readily when touched. Those definitely would not fit on my key ring, I thought, smiling to myself. *Maybe I could get the locks changed to a modern-day Yale key?* Taking one last look at the poem, and still being none the wiser, I tucked it into the envelope. It would probably make sense once I had seen the cottage. With that last thought, I slipped under the soft duck down quilt. Exhausted from the events of the day, it was not long before sleep cradled me in its warm caress.

It was still dark when I awoke with a start, in the early hours of the morning. My heart was pounding crazily in my chest as I looked around the room with wide, staring eyes. Perspiration ran down my face and neck, and my nightgown stuck to my damp body. I was terrified. It took me several minutes to realize that I had been having a nightmare—a nightmare about my little cottage. My mind had transformed my inheritance into something resembling Dracula's castle. Evil spirits dwelled within. Witches, chanting my poem, approached me with outstretched gnarled hands and pointed fingernails, beckoning me to enter—if I dared.

I switched on the bedside lamp and glanced at the clock. 3:37am. Lying back down onto the pillow, I fought to stay awake, not wanting to return to my fate within the cottage. Stupid, I know, but dreams can provoke such powerful images. It was at times like this that having a strong male body to cuddle up to would have been very comforting, if only to alleviate my own foolish fears. I finally drifted off just before dawn, my enthusiasm for the forthcoming trip to Littleham somewhat thwarted. That emotion had been replaced by an impending sense of doom.

Chapter Two

I awoke a few hours later, as warm sunlight filtered into my room. The bad dream from last night, still clear in my mind but no longer so intense, occupied my thoughts. Today I made sure I had a hearty breakfast before venturing out. I needed my strength for the long journey ahead, and subsequent hunt for Mill Cottage. As I walked around to the garage, I saw Sam coming the other way. He lowered his eyes as he passed and muttered an unenthusiastic greeting. I acknowledged it guiltily, the tea bag incident still fresh in my mind. Maybe I had been a little harsh. *I must learn not to inflict my antagonism on every male I met.* A polite refusal with a believable excuse would have sufficed.

The motorway seemed to go on forever. I stopped at every service station en route and had some refreshment. Whether this was a subconscious action, to delay my journey and eventual arrival at my destination, remains uncertain. I was feeling anxious, and a queasy sensation in the pit of my stomach did nothing to allay my reservations.

It was around 11:30am when I turned off the motorway and headed towards Offenham. The road was now a single lane and required more concentration, due to the sharp bends and blind corners. Many T-junctions were devoid of signposts, and only by consulting the map spread out on the adjacent seat did I know which way to turn. The overhanging trees arched over the road, meeting their counterparts on the other side and giving a tunnel effect, cutting out the light significantly. I hadn't passed any cars for at least three miles and began to feel lonely and isolated. I pulled over to the side of the road and consulted the map again. According to this, I was on the right route, and the village was somewhere along this road.

I switched off the engine and got out of the car to stretch my legs. Walking over to a nearby gate I noticed several sheep in the field, grazing idyllically on the lush green grass, their distant 'baas' the only audible sound around, apart from the occasional bird chirping in the hedgerow bushes. There were no houses in sight, but in the distance, I could just make out the steeple of a parish church tucked away in some sleepy backwater. It could have been 400 years ago. The timeless scene would have been the same, its beauty unspoilt by modern man—for now, anyway.

I returned to my car, and carried on driving along the leafy lane. Before long, a few small cottages appeared on the roadside, and a sign in big red letters on the grass verge informed me I was entering the village of Offenham and cautioned me to '*drive slowly*'. I soon found myself in the main village. If this was a large one, I couldn't imagine what a small village consisted of. There couldn't have been more than eight houses, including a pub, bank, grocery store, bakers and a quaint tea room. All the buildings were at least 200 years old. The windows had been updated on all but a few with white plastic frames, but the doors remained the original. Most of them were now coated in various paint colors instead of raw wood, which in my opinion, would have looked better.

Wandering along the pavement, I was amazed at how quiet it was. The only sign of life appeared to be an elderly gent who passed me on his ancient bike, tinkling his bell and smiling politely. I returned the greeting with a cheerful nod. Peeping discretely into the pub windows as I passed, I noticed that no one was there. The grocery store was deserted, and the tea room empty. *Where was everyone?* The contrast to Banbury was astonishing. Beginning to feel thirsty and in need of sustenance, I decided to venture into the tea room. After all, the notice on the door did say it was '*open*'.

A bell attached to the door clanged noisily on my entrance, and I cringed, feeling like I had dropped a saucepan near a sleeping baby. Within seconds, an elderly woman appeared from behind a screen. She wore a black dress and full white apron, her grey hair tied back into a severe bun. The word '*Victorian*' sprang to mind.

"Aft-noon, me dear," she said in a thick country accent, and pulled out a nearby chair.

"Hello," I replied, sitting down obediently. She presented me with a piece of card on which was handwritten the tea shop's menu in quaint Old English writing. Busying herself behind a counter, she eyed me suspiciously, as I looked over the menu and decided on a steak and kidney pie.

"Chipped or boiled?" she asked, referring to the type of potatoes I wanted.

"Chipped."

"Cabbage or peas?"

"Peas."

"Tea or coffee?"

"Coffee please," I replied, feeling a little uncomfortable with her rapid-fire questions.

She disappeared behind the screen once more, leaving me to sit and survey my surroundings in silence. Everything in the place was dated around the early 1900s. An assortment of china tea pots balanced precariously on varnished wooden shelves. Decorated plates adorned the walls, and a huge Aspidistra plant dominated the far corner, sitting majestically in an ornate green china pot on a pedestal. I remembered my late grandmother having one just like it in her drawing room—one of the many beautiful items cleared out for next to nothing after her death, and now probably fetching hundreds of pounds in antique shops countrywide. *If only we knew.*

I glanced wistfully out of the large shop window. *How could they make a living here with such sparse trade?* It was the height of summer. The tourist season was in full swing, *so where were all the people?* Maybe they hadn't found this hidden gem on the map. After all, it wasn't exactly easy to find.

"Here you are me dear." I jumped as the old woman placed a plate of piping hot food before me. It smelled wonderful, and

I picked up my knife and fork eagerly. "Just passing through?" she enquired, standing in front of me with folded arms.

"Yes. I'm on my way to Littleham," I replied before taking a large bite of the delicious pie.

"Littleham, you say?" I nodded, my cheeks bulging with the delicacy within. "There's nought there, me dear. Used to be once, when I was a child, but not now." I swallowed my mouthful and questioned her further.

"There must be something there—a cottage perhaps?" The old woman thought hard and shook her head.

"Just a couple of derelict cottages and some ruins, I believe. Why do you ask?"

I proceeded to tell the old lady about Uncle James, his Will, and my inheritance. I left out the bit about the poem, sensing she already thought I was a little unhinged. She listened attentively, nodding now and again. Finally, she shook her head in disapproval.

"You've been had there, me dear. I know this cottage of which you speak. It is nothing more than a shell of its former self, uninhabited for years now." My heart sank. *What on earth was my uncle thinking to play this sick joke on me? What had I done to deserve his wrath?* I pushed the rest of my dinner aside, my appetite suddenly diminished. *I had come all this way—but for what?* "You can go and see for yourself if you like," continued the old lady, saddened by my disheartened face. "It's not far from here. Take a right by the pub and then a right again at the crossroads. You'll find Mill Cottage down there on the left—about 50 yards or so." I smiled feebly and sipped my cold coffee. I had come all this way, so I might as well see what a white elephant I had inherited. Again a man had let me down. *Was there no end to my misery that they even taunted me from beyond the grave?* I paid my bill and thanked the old lady for her directions. She smiled at me, more out of pity than friendship, as I left her tea room and made my way back to Betsy.

Following her directions, I thought I probably could have walked it, but with no pavement on either side of the lane, it was a bit treacherous if a car did happen to come my way. I completely missed it on my first run. After about half a mile I turned around and made my way slowly back along the lane, scanning the woods for signs of any buildings. I thought I saw a bit of pinky-grey brickwork through the trees and pulled over as far as I could upon the verge. Stumbling through the dense undergrowth, I caught my jeans on the many brambles that entwined their prickly barbs around all that was green, and scratched my head on a protruding branch, whose twig-like tendrils seized hold of my hair and seemed to want to hold me captive. Cursing, I carefully unravelled my hair from its grasp and painstakingly picked my way through the undergrowth, finally arriving at a small clearing.

The sight of the cottage before me brought tears to my eyes. The old lady had been right. It was nothing more than a ruin. Its crumbling walls reached up to the open sky. The roof was long since gone, and the door, hung by a single hinge, rotted against the faded moss-covered bricks.

"Brilliant! Just brilliant!" I shouted. "Thanks, Uncle James. Just what I've always wanted—a dump!" I kicked the half-hung door angrily, and the remaining hinge gave way, sending the door slithering down onto the ground. It was then that I noticed the worn plaque sunk into the decomposed wood. Rubbing the grime from its surface I could just read the name imprinted on the metal. Jasmine Cottage. *Jasmine Cottage?* This wasn't my cottage. I sat down on a nearby tree stump, looking about, bewildered. Then I remembered the old lady's words, 'Just a couple of derelict cottages.' *So where was the other one?*

Getting up, I wandered a few yards this way and that, before venturing down a narrow pathway—mostly overgrown, but at one time well trodden. I could hear water running somewhere ahead of me, and I negotiated the track cautiously, looking back over my shoulder frequently as I went, anxious not to lose my way in this wilderness. It didn't take me long to locate the source of the running water. A small, clear stream meandered its way over green boulders and disappeared down a steep incline. I followed the stream uphill, slipping occasionally on the wet stones. And, suddenly, I saw it. There it was. My cottage.

My first impression was one of relief. It still had a roof! In fact it still had, in a fashion, everything, including filthy glass in the windows. The cottage had not been lived in for many years, which was blatantly obvious, and it had fallen into a severe state of dilapidation. Pulling back the ivy from where it obscured the window, I tried in vain to see inside, but it was as dirty inside the glass as it was out—and dark. Moving around to the door, I could see it was still firmly attached to the frame and hinges. It was a good, solid door that had withstood years of use—how many years; it was difficult to say, but at least two to three hundred, if not more.

There were three downstairs windows to the front and two upstairs, which were only partially showing, under the rampant ivy that almost completely covered the roof and chimney. Despite its pitiful exterior, I couldn't help visualizing how it once must have looked—clean, crisp white paint on the brickwork, sparkling windows, roses around the door, and a plume of smoke from the chimney rising into the sky from the welcoming roaring fire within. Heaven.

Taking the rusted keys from the brown envelope, I hesitated on the step, worn into a deep hollow from footsteps over time. Memories of last night's dream came flooding back, and I shivered, feeling a chill creep up my spine that momentarily paralyzed my muscles. I told myself not to be so stupid. It was just a dream—the mind playing tricks after reading that poem. Removing a spider's web gingerly from around the keyhole with a twig, I inserted one of the large keys into the hole and tried to turn it in the lock. It turned neither left nor right, even with more force applied. The second key inserted, I again fought hard to turn it within the lock. It gave a little and, for a moment, I thought it would work, but nothing happened.

"It has to be this one then," I said aloud, changing the key to the last on the bunch. I wiggled it about in the lock and turned it this way and that. I was determined to get the door open, and my patience began to wear thin. Forcing it to the right, with my shoulder up against the door, I gritted my teeth in a last ditch attempt to get the damn thing open. Without warning, the key shot over to the right with a loud clunk, and the door sprang open, taking me with it. I cried out in surprise, and then in horror, as a thick web wrapped itself around my face. I hated spiders, and the thought of one now embedded in my hair was enough to send me into a fit of frantic flapping, to remove its sticky web and contents from my face. My heart racing, I eventually calmed down. I rubbed my hands down my jeans in disgust, hoping that all traces of the offending creature were now removed. Not wanting to repeat the performance, I took hold of a large stick and waved it in front of me like a magic wand as I entered the dark interior of the cottage.

I could have done with a torch, as I strained my eyes to see where I was. The door had opened up straight into a room. A shaft of dusty light, from the window where I had removed the ivy, enabled me to see the interior. The room was bare, apart from a large stone fireplace on one side with a rusted grate. Beneath me were large uneven flagstones of various sizes covered in years of grime; to such an extent that fungus grew in several wide gaps between the stones. Turning away, I saw another wooden door leading from the room and tentatively pushed it open. It was even darker inside this one, the window offering hardly any light at all. For what I could see, it was similar in layout to the first room—same flooring, only this one had a narrow door leading off it—not on ground level, but raised up on a step. The stale, dusty air began to irritate my lungs, and I started to cough, but my curiosity at that point was far more overwhelming than any concern for my health, so I pressed on. Sliding up the latch on the door, I pulled it open.

A staircase stretched upwards and rounded a bend. A little window to my left gave me just enough light to see that the stairs were wooden and rotten in places. *Did I dare go up?* I was beginning to feel my bravado ebbing away fast as I stared up into the darkness. The loud pounding in my chest didn't help. Maybe it was the fast diminishing daylight, the fact that I was totally alone, or the sudden overwhelming feeling of despair that made the decision for me. I hurriedly turned, running back through the rooms and out of the door into the fresh, sweet air, slamming the door shut behind me.

Driving back into Offenham village, I decided to stop off at the tea room again, partly because I wanted something to eat and drink, before setting off on the long journey home. More importantly, though, I wanted to ask the old lady some questions about the cottage. She was there, peering through the window, as I parked opposite her shop. A smile broke out on her face, as she saw me get out of the car and walk across the road towards her. Opening the door as I approached, she greeted me warmly.

"Did you find it?" she asked, with a slight hint of concern in her voice.

"Yes, I did—eventually," I replied before sitting down at a table near the window.

"Can I get you anything, me dear?"

"Yes, please. A coffee and one of those sticky buns with icing," I said, pointing to some cakes perched temptingly on a stand on the counter. "It wasn't in too bad a state, really, considering the time that it's been empty," I said. "Not as bad as the other one, anyway."

"Jasmine," the lady said, knowing which one I was referring to. I sipped the hot coffee.

"Tell me about Mill Cottage. When you were young, and it was lived in." The old lady sighed and pulled up a chair, for a moment lost in thought, as she transported herself back to her younger years.

"I must have been about seven or eight," she began. I listened attentively. "I lived here in Offenham then as I do now. My brother Charlie and I used to go and play with the children of the family there. There was Mabel, my best friend, and her sister Flo."

"What year was that?" I asked, taking out a small note-book and pen from my bag.

"Must have been about 1942. I remember the war had be-gun and, soon after, the children were sent away to some-where in Wales. I never saw Mabel again, but I heard sev-eral years later that she had died of pneumonia."

"What was the cottage like then?" I asked quickly, trying to change the subject, as I noticed her faded eyes start to glisten.

"Much like any other around these parts. I remember Mrs. Holley was a keen gardener. She had beautiful flowers in the garden. I can see them now."

"And Mr. Holley?"

"Never saw much of him. I believe he was quite ill and spent a lot of time in bed upstairs." I remembered the wind-ing staircase behind the latched door. "He sometimes used to open the window and shout at us to be quiet if we became a little rowdy," she recalled, smiling.

"Did you ever go inside?" I continued, licking the icing off of my fingers.

"Only into the kitchen, if it was raining. Mrs. Holley gave us milk and jam tarts she had made herself."

"What happened to the Holleys?"

"Mr. Holley passed away eventually, and his wife went to live with her daughter, Flo, in Devon."

"Who had the cottage after them?" I urged, eager for more information to add to my notebook.

"I don't know, me dear. After that, I never had cause to visit the cottage again." The room fell silent as I finished off the remainder of the sticky bun. "You could look at the deeds of the cottage. That would tell you," the old lady added as an afterthought. *Of course! The deeds! The document that I had left behind in my Banbury flat. Damn it!*

Glancing at my watch, I was horrified to see it was nearly 5pm and quickly got up from the chair.

"Sorry. Have to go. Long drive back home to Banbury," I said apologetically. "How much do I owe you?"

"Don't go worrying yourself 'bout that. It was nice to talk to you—eh—what's your name?"

"Emily. Emily Howard."

"Well, Miss Howard. Safe journey home now, and maybe you will come again to Offenham?"

"Yes, I expect so," I replied, smiling. I drove off, waving to the lonely figure in the doorway. I should have asked what her name was.

On the long journey home, I thought of nothing but the little cottage in the woods. It had captured my imagination, and I was hungry for any information that could help me piece together who had lived there over the years, and why it was called *Mill Cottage*. I was also annoyed at how freaked out I had been, about going upstairs, and pondered over who I could get to come with me on any further visits to my inheritance. I could think of no one, although Sam's name crossed my mind for some inexplicable reason.

It was after eight by the time I walked wearily up the stairs and unlatched my door. I threw everything down upon the sofa and went into the kitchen. Last night's washing up still littered the countertop and sink. I searched for a clean cup in which to make some hot chocolate. I really should have made myself a decent meal, but I was too tired. Even making a drink was an effort. Setting the steaming cup down on the coffee table, I went over to my desk and pulled out the deed document from the drawer. The envelope contained a couple of large sheets of aged paper, with typed solicitor jargon and ink-penned names in fancy writing. It took a while to understand what I was actually looking at, having not seen a deed document before. I skimmed over the jargon and got straight to the interesting parts.

There was my uncle and some woman who appeared to be the last occupants—also the Holley's of whom the old lady spoke. Further back it was passed down through several Howerd family members. I read on, totally astounded, as to the wealth of information it contained. Finally I reached the section listing some of the earliest inhabitants of Mill Cottage, and froze as I read one particular entry.

'Hannah Mary Howerd to Emily Ann Howard and Samuel Howerd for no exchanged sum. 15th day of June 1696'.

Chapter Three

The last thing I remember thinking was about my namesake. The next thing I knew, I was waking up with a start the following morning to the doorbell ringing. I sat up stiffly, rubbing my neck that had suddenly gone into a spasm, due to the unusual sleeping position on the sofa. Blinking from the bright light of the nearby lamp, I felt disoriented until the doorbell rang again and spurred me into some form of muddled responsiveness.

Stepping over the deeds strewn on the floor, I staggered to the door and opened it up. The chain was unattached, forgotten in my exhausted state the night before. Sam stood before me, clutching a box of tea bags and smiling nervously.

"Hi," I muttered, staring wide-eyed at the box. "You didn't need to do that."

"I wanted to repay my debt. You okay?" he asked, frowning at my dishevelled state.

"Yes. Fine. Fell asleep on the sofa last night," I replied, laughing uneasily. I took the box from him. "Thanks for these."

"You really ought to take more care of yourself, you know," he continued, his voice changing to one of serious concern. The hairs on my back started to bristle.

"What are you, my doctor or something?" I blurted out angrily before I could stop myself.

"Maybe one day. I'm a medical student at Southwood University," he informed me, turning to go. I bit my lip. *Why do I always see the worst in men?*

"Sam, look. Why don't you come in for a coffee? I'm just making one."

"You sure?" he replied anxiously, not wanting to ruffle my feathers any further. I held open the door and smiled warmly. It would be nice to talk to someone. *Just forget he's a guy*, I thought as I gestured for him to sit on the sofa while I made our drinks.

When I returned ten minutes later with two hot coffees, I saw that Sam was deeply engrossed in reading the deeds. He looked embarrassed and put them down on the table abruptly as I entered.

"Sorry. Just being nosy. Interesting stuff, though. What is it—a house? Must be old, with that kind of history behind it." I sat down next to him and picked up the deeds. Before long I was giving him a full account of how I came to be in possession of the cottage, and I told him of my trip yesterday to Littleham. He was fascinated by my description of the property, genuinely interested in the old lady's account of her childhood memories, and he laughed when I told him I had been too scared to go upstairs. I was beginning to warm to this easy-going guy. He was caring, funny, and like the brother I never had—none of the heavy romantic rubbish to get in the way. He was a good friend, nothing more, and for that I was thankful.

"I notice there is an Emily here," he said, pointing to the name near the bottom of the list.

"Same surname, too—with Howard spelt with an '*a*,' and not an '*e*,'" I told him excitedly.

"That's a coincidence."

"Kind of spooky."

"Isn't it just…" he replied, in deep thought. As he finished off the remainder of his coffee, he turned to me, flicking his fringe back away from his face, in a way that had me itching to get out a pair of scissors from the kitchen drawer. "Are you going to go back down there again this week? Starting tomorrow, I have three days free. If you like, I could come with you—keep you company—protect you from the evil spirits that dwell within!" he said, making ghostly noises and accompanying arm movements. I threw a cushion at him, and we laughed over my foolish behavior. I had contemplated returning to Littleham tomorrow, and taking Sam with me was a comforting proposition. I readily accepted his offer. "I'll bring a large torch," he said, smiling as he left. "See you at nine then?"

"I'll be ready," I replied, shutting the door behind him.

I was ready and waiting long before nine the following morning, having gotten up ridiculously early in anticipation of the return journey to Littleham. Sam arrived on the dot, fully prepared for all eventualities. I don't know what he expected to encounter, but it was reassuring, nonetheless. He was comfortably dressed in jeans, a lightweight jumper, sturdy walking shoes, and a raincoat. I was similarly dressed, although my shoes were stylish white trainers, and a raincoat hadn't entered my mind. My hair was tied back into a ponytail with a pretty silver band, and I had gone to extra lengths to ensure my face was free from blemishes. *Why?* I asked myself. *Did I find him attractive?* No. *Was I trying to make an impression?* No. *Was I hoping something might come of our friendship?* No. *Was I an idiot?* Yes, probably.

The drive down to the village went so much faster with Sam in the passenger seat. By the time we turned off of the motorway, we had devoured two packets of Maltesers, a bag of creamy toffees, half a canister of Pringles and drunk nearly two litres of mineral water. He had told me his life story. I, in turn, filled him in on my past, although I purposely omitted some aspects of my dodgy relationships. He was easy to talk to, and a fun kind of guy. I never thought I would ever be able to think of any guy as being fun after all the bad experiences I had. Sam was unlike any guy I had ever met.

As we entered Offenham village, Sam let out a low whistle.

"It's going to be really hard to find a parking place here. So much traffic," he said, smiling sarcastically across at me. I laughed, knowing just what he meant, and pulled over to the side of the road. We both got out and stretched our legs. "What do you do for fun around here?" asked Sam, looking up and down the road.

"Come on. I need to find the parish church," I said, starting off up the road.

"That wasn't exactly what I had in mind," mumbled Sam as he followed me along the narrow footpath.

It wasn't difficult to locate the church. Its steeple could be clearly seen above the rooftops. We entered through the old lynch gate and found ourselves on a pathway leading up to the church doorway. On either side of the path, gravestones were set haphazardly among the uneven grass. They were all shapes and sizes and dotted among them were larger tombs dedicated to entire families. I reached into my pocket and pulled out a photocopy of the deeds that I had done yesterday.

"Well, we found the villagers. Pity they're all dead!" said Sam jokingly as he bent down to read an inscription on a highly polished black granite stone.

"Here," I said, ignoring his jovial remarks. "Take this and see if you can find anyone on it." Sam took the paper and looked intently at the names and dates.

"I doubt if they will be around this area of the graveyard. Look at these dates," he said, pointing to several stones close by. "Died 1967…1972…1981. We need to look around the older parts, like over there." I followed Sam across the grass, stepping respectfully over the mounds as I went. It was a difficult task, and I'm sure I accidentally walked over several of the dearly departed.

We split up, Sam wandering off to the left as I kept to the right. I didn't need the paper to remind me who I was searching for. Their names were emblazoned on my memory. After some minutes, I heard Sam shout out,

"Found one. Two points to me." Hurrying over to the direction of his voice, I found Sam standing triumphantly by a stone, looking very pleased with himself. "*James Edward Holley, husband of Mary Ann Holley. Died December 18th, 1947.*" I stood for a moment, visualizing a grumpy, ill old man shouting out of a window to the children below to be quiet, his long-suffering wife trying to calm the high spirits of the youngsters and failing miserably.

"Keep searching," I told him, continuing my quest off to the right. The stones were getting increasingly harder to read the older they became. Parts of the names and inscriptions were worn smooth by time and inclement weather. Sam had disappeared from view among some yew trees. I shivered as a cloud passed over the sun, plunging the graveyard into a somber shadowy state. Then the cloud released the sun from its grasp, and the graveyard was once again illuminated by a cheerful yellow glow. I began to feel disillusioned as I wandered aimlessly among the crumbling unreadable stones. I heard footsteps behind me and looked up, suddenly afraid.

"Any luck?" asked Sam.

"No, not really. It's so hard to read most of them," I replied, sighing with a mixture of relief and disappointment.

"Yeah, I know what you mean. Have you checked those out against the church wall?" I looked over to where he was pointing and saw five stones bunched together crookedly against the wall of the church—an area I had not yet investigated. I shook my head.

We walked over and managed to read the first stone's inscription, even though some of the letters were missing.

"William Howerd, late of this parish, who departed this life 15th June 1688, aged 52." I read loudly.

"This one's a Howerd too," remarked Sam, moving on to the next stone. "*Charles Howerd* aged something—can't read it—and *Hannah Howerd, died, aged 44.*"

"Must be a family plot," I said, moving past Sam to read the others. The name on the end stone caught my eye, and I went straight to it. *"Here lieth the body of Emily Howerd of this parish, who dyed 7th October 1752, aged 87"*

"So you found her—the elusive Emily. That was who you were hunting for, wasn't it?" I nodded, lost in thought, as I tried to imagine what she must have looked like.

"There must be something very disturbing about looking at a gravestone with your name on it," said Sam.

"It isn't *my* name, this has an 'e' in the surname, not like in the deeds."

"I know, but it's still kind of creepy." Sam sighed and turned to look around. "Did you notice that so many of the graves were children—many dying before their fifth birthday? Probably just from a cold that turned into an infection or pneumonia."

"That's why they had so many children then. They knew at least half wouldn't make it," I replied sadly, still gazing at Emily's stone. We stood in silent contemplation for a while.

"That's strange," remarked Sam suddenly.

"What is?"

"Look at how old Emily was when she died." I looked at the age but couldn't see what Sam meant.

"She was 87. So what?"

"Most people in those days didn't live beyond 55. You can see that by reading the other stones. Emily was 87. Doesn't that strike you as odd?" asked Sam, curiously.

"Maybe she was a healthy individual. You know, jogged around the block every morning, went to yoga classes, and ate organic veg," I said, laughing. Sam's dry sense of humor was starting to rub off on me.

"Very funny," replied Sam, taking my arm casually and steering me back down the pathway to the gate. "I'm starving. Can we eat yet?"

We had lunch at the pub in the village. Our only companion was an old scruffy-looking man, with a dog, huddled up in a corner hugging a pint of beer. The man was muttering to himself, and it was painfully obvious from his demeanor that he was well and truly drunk. Avoiding all eye contact with him, for fear he would stagger over and start some bizarre conversation, I edged closer to Sam and engaged him in a discussion about illnesses in the 17th century. Having eaten our fill and replenished our energy levels, we left the pub to make our way back to Betsy.

Sam was eager to see this wonderful cottage that I had told him so much about, but as I pulled over onto the grass verge, he looked over at me wondering why I had stopped.

"It's through the woodland a little way," I explained as I got out of the car. Sam collected his torch and started singing 'The Teddy Bears Picnic.'

"If you go down in the woods today, you're sure of a big surprise." I sensed he was becoming a bit uneasy with the surroundings.

As we made our way through the dense undergrowth, I could hear Sam's curses behind me as he encountered the brambles and hazardous low branches. I smiled to myself and told him not to be such a baby, to which he replied with more unmentionable oaths. Before long, we arrived and stood together before Mill Cottage.

"My God! Is that *it*?" said Sam, his mouth hanging open in astonishment.

"Yes. Isn't it beautiful?" I replied, my eyes sparkling with excitement and anticipation.

"It's a dump!" cried Sam. "You've brought me all this way to see this—this—," his voice trailed off, unable to find the words. I helped him out.

"This wonderful enchanting place?" He shot me a look as if I'd gone mad.

"This condemned ruin more like. My God, Emily! There's nothing you can do with this that a bulldozer can't fix."

"It isn't that bad, really. It isn't!" I cried. "It needs cleaning up a bit, but…" Sam had started to walk off in the direction of the car. "Where are you going?" I yelled after him.

"If we leave now, I might just get back in time to catch the beginning of '*Die Hard*,' called back Sam, continuing to fight his way back through the woods.

"But you haven't seen the inside yet!" He came to an abrupt halt and turned around.

"Are you kidding? The whole place could fall down at any second."

"It's stood for hundreds of years, for goodness sake. It's not going to fall down the minute you walk in it. Besides,

I went inside last time," I pleaded, almost in tears. Sam scoffed and flicked back his fringe. "Will you stop doing that!" I shouted angrily "It's getting on my bloody nerves!" We stared at one another defiantly. Sam shocked at my sudden offensive outburst, and I seething with resentment over his negative attitude. It was Sam who spoke first after a long period of strained silence.

"Okay. I'll take a look inside your cottage, if it means that much to you," he said softly, returning back to where I stood, shaking with pent-up emotion. "Just don't insult my hair again, deal?"

"Deal," I said, stifling a smile.

Grating the huge key around in the lock, I carefully pushed the door open. Sam stood close behind me, peering over my shoulder apprehensively. I picked up my 'web whacking' stick from where I had left it and handed it to Sam.

"You might need this," I said, stepping aside.

"I might need my brains tested too," he replied, as he gingerly entered the darkened room. He switched on the torch in his hand and a powerful beam illuminated the immediate surroundings. Swishing the torch this way and that, he walked across the room. "How long did you say it had been empty?" asked Sam, before going into a fit of coughing.

"I don't know exactly. My uncle moved in about 1964, according to the deeds, but the solicitor gave me an address in London where he died recently."

"No one's lived here for years. Look at the state of it!" exclaimed Sam, flicking the beam of light onto a doorway.

"I didn't see that door last time!" I cried excitedly. "Open it up!"

Taking a deep breath, Sam unlatched the door. It creaked eerily as it swung back into another room. Windows to the back of the house cast a yellow shaft of light across the room. A large stone sink sat underneath. Its bottom, I noticed, grimacing, was covered in an assortment of long dead creepy crawlies. Some dirty wooden cupboards lined the walls, and a broken chair lay crumpled on the cold stone floor.

"And here we have the kitchen," announced Sam, putting on a voice. "Spacious, but in need of a little updating. Notice the unusual rustic style storage cupboards and authentic stone sink, an attractive feature point in this much sought after home."

"Shut up, Sam!" I cried, walking back into the other room. "I want to see upstairs."

"Ah! The boudoir. Aren't I the one supposed to be dragging *you* up to the bedroom?" asked Sam, his eyes twinkling mischievously in the torchlight. I ignored the innuendo and strutted through the doorway to the adjoining room.

"It's through there," I said, tapping on the raised latched doorway.

"Go on, then," said Sam, grinning, "After you."

"You have the torch. I'll follow you." I replied, stepping back nervously.

"Women! Cowards, the lot of them," remarked Sam as he opened the latch and shone the flashlight up into the darkness. I swear he hesitated for a moment before cautiously ascending the wooden staircase. I followed a few steps behind him, when he rounded the bend and came to a sudden stop, with a look of horror on his face.

"What? What is it?" I stammered, clutching the crumbling plaster. Sam staggered back against the wall; still staring shocked at something in front of him.

"Oh my God, Emily! It's a skeleton. Don't come up. It's too awful!" I cried out in fright before bursting into tears, my limbs unable to move. I sat down on the stair, mortified. Sam just stared at me in amazement, flashing the light on my pale, tear-stained face. He looked guilty. "Hey, Emily. I was only joking. There's nothing there. Just an empty room," he said, his voice filled with concern, as he joined me on the stair and put his arm around my shaking shoulders. "You should have seen your face though. *Priceless!*" That just about did it. I lashed out at him with my fists, thumping him repeatedly on his chest in a fit of rage and humiliation. "Whoa! I'm sorry, okay?" he cried, defending himself from the unexpected onslaught.

"Why did you do it? Why?" I sobbed, exhausted now from my tirade.

"I don't know. It's just my crazy sense of humor, I guess. I can't help it," he said, pulling me closer against his warm body. I suddenly came to my senses.

"What are you doing?" I yelled, springing apart and standing up shakily on the stair.

"Comforting you?"

"I don't need any *comforting*, thanks." Sam raised an eyebrow and sighed heavily. Holding out his hand, he nodded up the staircase.

"Come on. Come and see the room. It's really quite quaint." I looked up at him questionably. He read my thoughts. "There's nothing there, honestly. I'm sorry for scaring you." I declined his hand and made my way around the bend into the upstairs room.

He was right. It really was quite '*quaint*,' as he put it. A stone fireplace dominated the room, but it had been partially bricked up. An old 1930s-style heater sat in front of it. A couple of built-in wardrobes occupied the spaces on either side. One had its door missing. An opening from this room led us into another bedroom of similar size. This one had no fireplace, no wardrobes—nothing, in fact, apart from the remains of a dead mouse on the floor by the window. We stood for a while, contemplating the room and its stark emptiness.

"Do you feel it?" I asked Sam suddenly. He turned and looked at me blankly. "Can you feel the wretched loneliness and despair in this room?"

"It's probably where old man Holley died," said Sam, walking over to the window. He tapped loudly on the window and shouted out to some imaginary children below. "Be quiet, you little brats. I'm trying to sleep!" One look at the expression on my face told him he was skating on very thin ice. "I'll tell you what I do feel," he said quickly.

"What's that?"

"Bloody cold! It's freezing in here." said Sam, thrusting his hands deep into his pockets.

"No! It's something more than that. Something very distressing happened here once. I can feel it."

"Come on. Let's go and have a look at the back garden. You're giving me the creeps." With that, Sam marched out of the room and back downstairs. I followed in hot pursuit, not wanting to be left alone in the empty room that harboured so many memories. Using one of the other keys in the bunch, Sam managed to open the back door in the kitchen with surprising ease.

The back garden was, putting it plainly, a jungle! Years of neglect had transformed it into a wilderness of weeds, long grass, and overgrown trees.

"A project for '*Ground Force*' if ever I saw one!" laughed Sam. I was looking at how far the ivy had managed to climb over the cottage when a loud yell from Sam, off to my left, distracted me. "Shit! That hurt!"

"What's the matter?" I asked, finding him hopping madly on one foot among some tall grass, in obvious pain.

"Bloody rock! Didn't see it," he cried, falling down onto the ground and untying his shoe.

"Let me look," I said, helping him pull off his shoe and thick woollen sock. A small gash on the side of his foot was oozing a steady trickle of blood. Sam groaned and lay back on the grass. Typical man, I thought, the least little thing. "You'll live," I said, wiping the blood away with a large green leaf. "Go and wash it in that stream over there." Sam looked up at me in horror for suggesting such an unthinkable task.

"No. It's okay. Look. It's stopped now." I shook my head in despair and threw him his sock.

"So where is this big bad rock then?" I asked, getting up and searching the flattened grass. I soon found the small offending item protruding out from the undergrowth and brushed aside the weeds. "It's got some writing on it. Look!" I exclaimed, kneeling down.

"What's it say?" mumbled Sam, tying his shoc "Got another sucker!"

"It looks like just one word—JA, and then something else—maybe an E or S?" I called back.

"Probably the family pet or even a headstone for a baby. I don't know!" shouted back Sam irritably, before scrambling to his feet and warily taking a few steps forward. I stood up. The thought of someone's baby buried in my back garden was a little upsetting, but I suppose it might not have been particularly uncommon years ago. "Can we go now? I'm tired, hungry, and my foot hurts like hell," he moaned. I sighed and went over to Sam. If truth be known, I was rather tired too, and lunch seemed like hours ago.

"Can you make it back to the car, or shall I ring for an ambulance?" I asked sarcastically.

"I'll try," he replied feebly, giving me a pitiful look that was supposed to make me feel sorry for him. It didn't work.

Driving back into Offenham, I noticed that the tea rooms were closed, so we went back to the pub where we had dined earlier. The landlord greeted us warmly as we entered, as if we were old friends. The place was busy this time. There were three people in this time, plus the dog. I skimmed over the menu and handed it to Sam across the table. He appeared to have other things on his mind, but difficulty in expressing what they were. Finally, he managed to blurt it out.

"Why don't we stay down here tonight? It's late, and you're tired. I'm sure the pub has a couple of rooms for the night if I ask him." I stared at him across the table, a thousand thoughts invading my mind—none of them pleasant. Before I had a chance to answer, he hurriedly continued. "After all, we don't have to get back for anything, and tomorrow I could give you a hand pulling down some of that ivy from the cottage, if you like?" *This is crazy*, I thought. I hadn't really known the guy for five minutes, and here we were contemplating spending the night together! Well, not actually '*together*', but you get my drift. For some reason, I didn't put up much of a fight. Sam didn't appear interested in me in that kind of way, and I certainly had no romantic feelings for him, so what harm would it do staying on in a couple of rooms for the night? I agreed to his suggestion, thankful that I did not have to endure the long drive home that night. Sam went over to the landlord and had a word with him as I studied the menu and decided on a ploughman's lunch with cheddar cheese. He returned, looking a little edgy.

"Everything okay?" I asked as he sat down next to me.

"Do you want the good news or the bad?" he replied, avoiding my eyes. I suddenly had a bad feeling that the '*good*' news part would be equally as bad.

"Go on," I said, bracing myself.

"We can stay here tonight, no problem, but they have only one room vacant as the other one is being decorated."

"Well. That's it then," I cried, my mind made up. "We go back tonight."

"But it's a twin room! You know, two separate beds—not joined together."

"I'm fully aware of what a *'twin'* room is, and the answer's no!" Two of the customers glanced over, hearing my raised voice. The landlord stared at me intently as he dried a glass from behind the bar. I felt like I was in a goldfish bowl.

"Think about it, Emily," whispered Sam, lowering his head towards me. "Imagine us being in an airport departure lounge. Our planes been delayed several hours, and we have to spend the night on the floor. We sleep as best we can next to one another until the morning. We spend the night together sleeping. We don't '*sleep*' together. It's a play on words, and this isn't any different." I tried to find a logical argument in this scenario, but I couldn't. He was good—damn good! My hesitant reply gave him the answer he wanted, and he returned to the bar to confirm the arrangement. I sat, stunned, wondering how I had managed to get myself into this situation when another bombshell hit me. "Right. All done. I've signed the register, and they will bring the meals up to the room. You just need to sign in, only the landlord's a bit of a prude about room sharing, so I've told him you're my wife," said Sam, walking away quickly to avoid the fallout.

"You told him *what*!" I hissed loudly, arriving at the bar. The landlord interrupted any further verbal outcry from me.

"Mrs Warren, if you could just sign here," he said sweetly, pushing the register towards me and waving a pen expectantly. I had no alternative but to go along with this charade and reluctantly signed the name '*Emily Warren*' in the place indicated. He handed Sam the keys, who turned to me and smiled roguishly.

"Come along, darling."

"Don't push it!" I growled back under my breath, as I followed him up the staircase to our room.

The room was small, clean and nicely decorated. The only problem was the beds! They were pushed together, giving the impression of a double bed, and I brought it to his attention immediately.

"What do you want me to do?" cried Sam, getting a little tired of my constant complaining. "Push one over there by the door and prevent us getting out? Give it a rest, Emily!" With that, he stormed off into the adjoining bathroom and slammed the door. *We are behaving like an old married couple,* I thought, flopping down onto the bed by the window. *Thank God it wasn't for real, and we wouldn't have to go through the inevitable divorce.* Sam came out of the bathroom, and I went in. A frosty atmosphere prevailed between us, with neither of us making an effort to converse amicably. When I came out several minutes later, he was sitting cross-legged on the bed, tucking into a chicken curry. The TV was showing the final scenes of '*Die Hard*', and my ploughman's lunch was deposited on the adjoining bed.

I ate it in silence, pondering how Sam had gone from being a virtual stranger to my husband in the space of one day! It was surreal and—when I thought about it—quite comical. He was probably right, though. I did need to loosen up a bit and not take life so seriously.

"You okay with that bed?" I asked, trying to break the ice.

"Unless you would rather be by the door ready to escape," replied Sam, without taking his eyes off the TV.

"No, it's okay. I have the window this side to jump out of," I said, dissolving into giggles. Sam looked over at me and smiled, our feud forgotten.

Taking off my shoes and jeans only, I slid underneath the covers. I was probably going to be too hot wearing my sweater in bed, but I could remove it later in the night, undetected. Sam took off his jeans and then his sweater. At that point I looked away, wondering what else he intended to remove, but breathed a sigh of relief as he stopped there and climbed into bed. I reached up and pulled the cord dangling over the bed, plunging the room into pitch darkness. For a while we lay there, reminiscing about the day's events, our conversation slowly diminishing, as we grew sleepy. Finally Sam turned to me, his voice full of concern.

"You're not considering moving down here, are you?"

"No. Of course not. I have my job in Banbury."

"That's good," he replied. "It's a hell of a long way to come to borrow some tea bags."

Chapter Four

Awakening from the night's sleep, I slowly adjusted my eyes to the early morning light through the curtains, and stared at the sleeping man, whose face was inches from mine. For a moment, I didn't remember where I was, nor who this person I was '*in bed with*' could possibly be. Then it all came flooding back. I rolled over to face the other way, feeling awkward and embarrassed. Noticing my discarded sweater and bra strewn on the floor, I wrapped the quilt tightly around my bare shoulders and contemplated how I was going to get dressed in front of Sam. It felt like the aftermath of some drunken one-night stand.

I could hear the rustling of the bed covers behind me as Sam stirred and yawned loudly. I listened, my heart racing. *This is awful.*

"Morning, sweetheart," said Sam cheerfully.

"Morning," I replied apprehensively, staring at the window. I could hear him move closer to me across the bed, and I stiffened in anticipation as to what he would do next.

"Sorry it wasn't quite the honeymoon you would have expected," he said affectionately.

"I wasn't expecting anything. I thought I made that clear."

"Crystal," he replied, laughing. I turned over and faced him. My hair, tangled and messy, fell over the covers. His own hair, equally tousled, made him look somewhat endearing.

"I expect it's the first time you've slept with a woman and didn't...*you know?*" He smiled to himself and looked up at the ceiling in deep thought.

"Actually, it's the first time I've slept with a woman," he said, looking over at me to observe my reaction, which was, of course, surprise.

"Oh, really! I would have thought you medical student types had them queuing up."

He propped himself up on one elbow and looked deeply into my eyes before delivering the next sentence.

"I mean, it's the first time I've slept with a '*woman'*." It took a while for the penny to drop. I'm not the brightest bulb in the lamp when it comes to hints.

"Oh!" I eventually replied, "I had no idea."

"Anyway, you don't mind if I use the bathroom first? I'm dying for a pee," he said, throwing back the cover and picking up his jeans.

"No. Go ahead," I said, still reeling slightly from his unexpected revelation. I suppose I should have picked up on it earlier. The signs were there, but I was just too dumb to notice. I had nothing against gays. There was one in my office at work, come to that, and he was a real sweetheart.

Picking up my clothes hurriedly from the floor, I got dressed and sat on the bed, waiting for Sam to emerge, which he did a good ten minutes later, looking clean and tidy, with his hair nicely combed. My own efforts were not nearly as impressive, *but who cared?*

"Shall we have a hearty breakfast here before we start?" asked Sam as he opened the bedroom door for me.

"Good idea, but let's have it across the road, at the tea room, if it's open. I want you to meet the old lady there."

"Okay. That's fine by me. Lead the way, Mrs Warren," he replied, giving me a wink. I smiled at the irony of that statement.

The tea room showed an '*open'* sign in its window, and I was happy to get another chance to talk to the old lady, and to introduce Sam as my friend. Stepping inside the shop, I thought for a moment I had entered the wrong premises. The whole interior of the shop had changed. Gone were the little wooden shelves housing the dainty teapots. The china plates had been replaced by paintings done by local artists, and the counter was now a shiny stainless steel refrigerated cabinet, displaying doughnuts, sandwiches and salads. Even the tables and chairs were different.

"Everything's changed," I whispered to Sam, "It's all—*modern*."

"Perhaps they had it refurbished?"

"What, since I was last here? They couldn't have," I cried, sitting down on a plastic chair.

"Are you sure it was *this* tea room?" asked Sam. "Maybe there's another one."

"No, there is only one here. This is definitely the same one I visited before." A door to the back of the counter swung open, and a blonde lady in her thirties entered, dressed casually in jeans and a blue blouse.

"Morning, love. What can I get you?" she chirped, drying her hands on a tea towel.

"I'll have the full English breakfast please," said Sam, looking across at me. I just sat there in a mesmerised state, unable to answer. "Make that *two* full English breakfasts and a couple of coffees, too, please," continued Sam. The lady gave me a puzzled look and smiled uneasily, before going behind the counter to make the coffees from an Italian espresso machine.

"That's not her," I said quietly.

"I gathered that," replied Sam, studying the menu. "Hey. I thought you had a steak and kidney pie when you came here last? It's not on the menu. Look." I took the menu and scanned down the meals. He was right. This was getting ridiculous, and I had to sort the mystery out.

"Where's the old lady that was serving here a couple of days ago?" I called out, ignoring a gentle kick from Sam under the table. The woman turned and frowned.

"I don't have an elderly lady helper, love. It's only me here, and sometimes my husband helps out when I need to get some stock in."

"But I saw her here. I spoke to her the other afternoon!"

"Not here, love. I don't open in the afternoons. I close at 12 noon," she said, walking over and setting down two large mugs of coffee.

"How long have you been here?" I asked, unable to comprehend what she was saying.

"Must be nearly five years now." She replied after a moments thought.

"Who had it before you?"

"I bought it from a man who had to give up working due to ill health"

"And before that?" I said in a demanding voice that, I could see, was starting to irritate the woman.

"Lord knows. I came from outside the village and don't know anything about the history of the place. Now, if you'll excuse me, I have some cooking to do." With that, she disappeared through the door, and I was left questioning my sanity.

"I think I'm going mad!" I exclaimed, running my hand through my hair in desperation.

"Perhaps you dreamt it? You know dreams can seem very real sometimes," offered Sam, trying to alleviate my confused state of mind by suggesting a rational explanation.

"It wasn't a dream, Sam!" I cried. "It was *real.*"

Our breakfasts arrived, and we ate in silence, during which time the door of the tea room opened and an elderly man entered and sat down nearby. The blonde woman reappeared almost immediately and greeted the man.

"Morning, Jack, love. How are we today?" she said, approaching his table.

"Not so bad. The old back's playing me up, though," he replied in a gruff voice.

"Aw, that's a pity. The usual, is it? With two slices of toast?"

"Aye, lass, and don't go sparing on the butter this time," he called after her. I stared at him. He might have lived around these parts for many years and know something.

"Excuse me," I began. Sam hissed at me across the table to '*leave it'*, but I ignored his pleas and carried on. "Forgive me for asking, but have you lived in the village for long?"

"Aye, lass—for more years than I care to remember. Came here as a wee tot back in—oh, I don't know now. Me memory's not so good." I estimated he was in his late eighties or early nineties, so we were talking around 1915 or so.

"Do you remember who owned this tea room then?"

"Emily!" shouted Sam from behind me, beginning to get embarrassed by my questioning. I shot him a warning look and returned my attention to the old man again.

"Aye, that I do remember! She was a friend of my mother's—now what was her name? Flora? Fiona? No, Frances. It was Frances. Aye, that was it."

The blonde lady retuned and put down a plate of toast and marmalade on Jack's table. She hovered nearby, curious as to where this conversation was heading.

"My mother, God rest her soul, used to send me to buy some homemade scones from her. Ten scones for two half-pennies they were, and tasted wonderful," he thought for a moment as I waited for him to continue. "She always made me a glass of lemonade. *Real lemonade,* not the rubbish you get these days, lass."

"What was the shop like then?" I asked, eager to learn more about the shop's history.

"Teapots!" cried the man, remembering, "She loved collecting them—had them all over the place. When I grew older, I fixed her up a couple of shelves to put them on." The color began to drain from my face as I asked the inevitable next question.

"What was she like?"

"I used to be quite frightened of her at first—reminded me of a stern school mistress, with her hair done up like it was, in a tight bun on top. She was always in black after her husband died. Aye, I can remember her clearly standing there with her arms folded, saying, "Be off home with y'now, Master Jack, and no eating them there scones on the way, mind." I turned excitedly to Sam, who was sitting low in his chair biting his nails nervously.

"That was her! That's the old woman I saw here two days ago! She had teapots on shelves too!" I exclaimed, overjoyed that at last someone corroborated my story. The room fell silent. The old man leant forward in his chair towards me and grasped my hand.

"Frances died in 1997, lass. I went to her funeral. It can't have been her you saw."

"It was her! It was!" I screamed hysterically, standing up. "The teapots were on shelves over there! I saw them. And over there," I cried, almost in tears, "there was a large plant on a stand."

"I'm sorry, lass. Was Frances Howard a relation of yours?" I stopped dead and glared at the old man.

"Frances *what*?" Before he had time to answer, Sam was on his feet and had come around the table to me. Putting a reassuring arm around my shoulder, he said gently,

"Okay. That's it. Come along, Emily. It's time we were getting you back home."

"Don't patronize me!" I yelled, pushing off his hands. Sam turned to the shop's owner and whispered apologetically,

"Sorry about this. She's not well." The blonde woman nodded understandingly as Sam guided me over to the door. "Now, be a good girl and stand there while I pay the bill." I opened my mouth to rebel, but the look on Sam's face told me to rethink. I stood quietly by the door, looking out into the street in a daze.

"You have your hands full there," whispered the woman as Sam paid for the breakfasts.

"Tell me about it. Last week she swore she was abducted by aliens, and the week before that? Well, you don't want to know."

"I really admire the work you carers do. I wouldn't have the patience."

"Thank you," replied Sam smiling, "I do my best."

"What were you talking about?" I asked Sam as he opened the shop door for me to go out.

"Nothing to worry your pretty little head about," replied Sam, grinning impishly. It was almost a year later that I finally got it out of him what had been said.

Holding my arm securely, Sam marched me down the road, looking over his shoulder frequently, until we were out of sight of the tea room's window.

"Let go of me! I'm not an imbecile!" I cried, wriggling free of Sam's grasp.

"Just shut up, and get in the car," he ordered. Fuming, I undid the car latch and got in, slamming the door noisily behind me as Sam sat down heavily in the passenger seat.

"Is it just me, or is there something funny going on here?" I said, turning to face a rather bewildered Sam. "First, I get this weird little cottage, and then I find one of its previous residents has my name and now, to top it all, I appear to have met a woman the other afternoon who died in 1997, and she made me a steak and kidney pie!"

"Wow! A ghost that cooks you meals. That's really cool!" laughed Sam.

"Be serious for once in your life!" I cried, feeling tears prick the backs of my eyes. Sam leant over and took hold of my hand, his face kind and caring as he squeezed it reassuringly.

"I believe you, Emily. How else would you have known about the teapots and the old woman's description if you hadn't actually *seen* her? This whole thing scares the shit out of me, I can tell you."

"Glad you came?" I asked, smiling.

"Ecstatic!" replied Sam "So what now? Back to the cottage for a spot of DIY?" For some reason I didn't feel like returning to the cottage that day. My enthusiasm had gone off the boil. I just wanted to be somewhere warm, safe, and away from here.

"I want to go home," I said as I started up the engine.

"That's the most sensible thing you're said all day!" remarked Sam, fastening his seat belt.

The drive home was quiet and the mood somber—a stark difference to yesterday's happy journey down to Littleham, but then a lot had happened since then. I tried to make sense of everything, but my mind refused to accept that I had encountered a ghost from the past, although no other logical explanation was apparent.

It was after 3pm when I parked Betsy back into her garage. I felt tired from the long journey, and exhausted from puzzling over what had transpired. Sam had slept most of the way home, leaning uncomfortably against the window on his bunched up raincoat.

"We home yet?" he muttered sleepily as I turned off the engine.

"Safe and sound," I replied, getting out and waiting for him to gather up his belongings. Arriving outside my flat door, I turned to Sam and threw my arms around him in an affectionate hug, much to his surprise.

"Hey! Stop trying to seduce me. I'm not that kind of guy!" he laughed as I let go and stood back, feeling a little foolish.

"Thanks so much, Sam—for everything."

"Let's just say it's been '*educational',*" he replied, pulling a comical face.

"See you around, then?"

"Sure, babe. Take care." With that, he walked off up the corridor to his flat at the far end.

In a funny kind of way, I missed Sam being around. The flat suddenly felt very lonely, as I extracted a frozen meal for one out of the freezer, and left it on the counter to defrost. He had rekindled my faith in men and the fact that life could be a lot of fun with them, despite the complications—regarding his sexuality—of this particular relationship. I had learnt to trust a man again.

Lying in bed that night, I found it difficult to sleep. One thing that was becoming increasingly clear in my mind was that I was meant to have this cottage. It was my destiny, and the powers that be were going all out to make sure of it. *Am I related in any way to Frances Howard? Could Emily, now lying long dead in Offenham's parish cemetery, be a very distant ancestor? How can I find out?* I turned over and hugged the pillow. *Sam will know. I'll ask him tomorrow.*

I went into town early the next morning to get the week-end's shopping. I couldn't believe it was Friday already—my week's holiday already drawing to a close. I could just imagine the conversation in the office on Monday. *'Hey Emily. What did you do on your week off?' 'Oh, nothing much—inherited a cottage, married a gay guy, and had lunch with a ghost. Pretty mundane, really.'* I smiled to myself. *They would never believe me.* Passing the local library in town, I hovered outside, debating whether to go inside and find out some information on tracing family ancestors. Curiosity got the better of me, and I went in. Having no experience in this kind of thing, I wandered aimlessly up and down the aisles until I found a couple of books called '*Researching Your Ancestors*' and '*Where Do I Come From?*' Sitting down on a hard wooden chair, I flicked through the pages. Within a short time, I realized I needed to do one of two things: A) Go to London and visit the public records office; or B) Go online to the various web sites, which are available to help aid the search. I took and pen and a piece of paper from my bag (formerly the back of my shopping list) and scribbled the site addresses down. I didn't have a computer at home, but maybe Sam did. Failing that, I could use the office computer. I imagined that this, however, would become quite a lengthy process and would not be possible to do with the boss passing by every four minutes, making sure we weren't using it for anything remotely enjoyable.

Back at home, I unpacked the shopping and stored the items away in the appropriate cupboards. I put the tins in neat little rows, labels to the front and descending in size to the front of the shelf. The fridge was equally regimental. You could tell I was unmarried and childless. Stopping in front of the mirror in the hall on my way out, I checked to see if I was presentable—a pretty pointless task considering Sam wasn't the least bit interested in me, and never would be, but he always made such an effort with his appearance that I felt obliged to do likewise. I tapped lightly on the door of number thirty-eight and waited. He wasn't returning to university until tomorrow, so hopefully he was in.

I heard footsteps from within, and the door opened to reveal Sam, still dressed in his pajamas with a loosely-tied pale lilac robe over them.

"Oh God. Sorry. I didn't mean to wake you," I said apologetically. "I'll come back another time."

"No. It's okay, Emily. Come in. I was just making some tea." A male voice from within the room suddenly echoed out into the corridor.

"Is that the delightful Emily? Bring her in, Sam. I'm dying to meet her." I wanted to turn and run, but Sam opened the door wider and stood aside, bidding me to enter. Cautiously, I stepped inside and was introduced to a younger curly-haired lad on the sofa, who was also still in his pajamas.

"Emily, this is Toby—my friend," said Sam, enjoying seeing me squirm uncomfortably, the color in my face turning a shade redder with embarrassment. Toby jumped up and, taking hold of my hand, planted a tender kiss upon it.

"Enchanted," he murmured. "I've heard so much about you that I feel I know you already. Please come and sit," he said, patting the sofa. I looked at Sam with an expression of desperation, but he purposely ignored it and went off into the kitchen to make the tea, leaving me in the company of Toby and my inhibitions. Thankfully, Toby chatted away constantly, enabling me to give him the once-over without having to make polite awkward conversation.

He was slightly younger than Sam. His brown hair was such a mass of tight curls that I couldn't quite decide if it was natural or permed. Cute freckles dotted his high cheekbones. All he needed was a bright red ribbon to complete his transformation into a living porcelain doll. Sam arrived with a tray of mugs and cookies, and set it down on a small table in front of us, before squeezing himself down on the sofa next to me. I was sandwiched between the two men with no means of escape and felt like the proverbial gooseberry.

"What've you got there?" asked Sam, noticing the piece of paper I was clutching in my hand. Before I had a chance to answer, he took the slightly damp item from me and surveyed the writing upon it.

"Baked beans. Eggs. Bread. Fruit—"

"The other side," I interrupted quickly.

"Ah! Web sites. I think I know where this is leading."

"I was wondering if you had a computer?" I asked, looking around the room but not seeing one. Toby leant over and whipped the paper from Sam's hand.

"Of course he has one. It's in the bedroom," he cried excitedly. "Come on. Drink up, Emily darling. We have work to do. This is *so* interesting."

It turned out that Toby was quite knowledgeable regarding ancestor hunting, having traced his own family tree back several generations, and discovering that one had been a famous knight who had an eye for the ladies. *The inherited gene must have gone adrift on this occasion,* I thought to myself, smiling. I gave him all the information I knew regarding grandfathers and great-grandfathers—where they lived and who married whom. Sam, in the meantime, lay stretched out on the bed, unconcerned that I had his lover's full attention, and had shut him out of our cozy tête-à -tête. *How different men's relationships were to women's*, I thought. If I had been this absorbed with another woman's boyfriend, she would have scratched my eyes out by now, and accused me of flirting with '*her'* man. I had to admire their maturity and indifference in such matters.

We started tracking back the history of my uncle first, as Toby had a feeling that he was somehow connected. It was a complicated process and not one I would have managed to achieve on my own accord. It was a good two hours later when, after several blind alleys, he discovered a path. Sam had fallen asleep, and his gentle snoring was rudely awakened by my sudden cry of joy.

"That's it! That's her!"

"What is?" mumbled Sam, sliding off the bed and coming over to where we sat bunched together closely on a couple of chairs.

"Listen to this! Frances Howard had a son called James. I bet that was my uncle, which would make her my *grand-mother,* as my father and James were brothers. I never got to meet her, and now I have. Isn't that fantastic?" I stopped to catch my breath, my eyes wide with excitement.

"Yeah, but not surprising," replied Sam, yawning. "I bet if you traced Emily's father back a bit more you would find a few more connections with the ever-expanding Howard mob."

"You really think so? This is so exciting! What was your father's name, Emily?" cried Toby, his fingers flying rapidly over the computer keys. I could hear Sam groan and leave the room, muttering something about food, and the lack of it.

"Maybe I should go?" I told Toby as I stood up, but he wouldn't hear of it, and pulled me back down onto the chair. I knew that my mother's father's name was Albert, and he married a Joan. From that, Toby found out his father's name, which was John. He had been born in 1864. The census of 1871 showed young John, aged seven, living in Northwood with his brothers, sisters and parents—John and Mary Howard.

"Pizza anyone?" A large plate containing a sizzling cheesy pizza was thrust in front of us.

"Thanks, Sam," said Toby, taking a slice, hardly tearing his attention away from the screen. I got up and joined Sam on the edge of the bed, feeling guilty for commandeering his boyfriend for such a long time and, consequently, ruining his day. After all, it was of no personal interest to him. We sat munching our way through several slices of pizza, discussing what university life was like, when Toby let out a cry.

"My God, Emily! You *are* related to the Howerds of Littleham!" I jumped up and joined Toby on the chair.

"According to this, John Joseph Howerd, born in 1731, was your great-great-great-great-great-grandfather, whom Emily gave the cottage to in 1751." Toby sat back in the chair. Mission accomplished. To me, though, the mission was only just beginning.

Chapter Five

Returning to work on Monday morning, I felt like a different person. The past week's events had mellowed me into a much more socially acceptable individual. My fellow office workers did not know quite what to make of the new and improved Emily. Simon, the resident homosexual, was a little unnerved by my sudden ability to converse with him on a much deeper level. I had no intention of telling them the reason for my curious transformation. Watching their faces made it so much more enjoyable. I felt an inner contentment, as if a large burden had been lifted from me, and I knew that I had been assigned a purpose in life—to take care of Mill Cottage as so many loving owners had done before me. Now, as its new owner, it was my turn.

I couldn't wait for the week to finish, so that I could go down to Littleham and start working on the cottage's restoration. With the ivy removed, the windows cleaned and the inside rejuvenated, it would look so much more like home. Sam had returned to university, along with Toby, and I missed him being around. Before he left, he presented me with a large box of mixed spring bulbs to plant around my cottage, for when I next went down that way, which he anticipated would be sooner, rather than later.

The weekend finally arrived, and I spent much of Saturday doing the usual boring household chores. The shopping trip into town included additional items on my food list, as I intended to make up a picnic basket to save me humiliating myself in the tea room again, or sitting alone in the pub with the landlord inquiring about the marked absence of my so-called '*husband*.'

As I had planned on an early departure the following morning, I had gathered in the hallway a heap of essentials to take with me. These included a broom, dustpan and brush, glass cleaner, cloths, scrubbing brush and a bucket. For the outside, I had purchased some gardening gloves, a spade, pruning shears, a weeding knife and a trowel. It was going to be a long, tiring day tomorrow, and I turned in early in preparation for the task ahead of me.

Sunday morning dawned sunny and bright and, after a light breakfast, I loaded up the car and set off down south. The journey was not nearly as enjoyable as when Sam accompanied me, but I compensated for this by playing my CD at full volume, and singing along to *Texas'* greatest hits. It was nearly 11am when I pulled over onto the grass verge outside the cottage and began the arduous job of unloading Betsy, after changing into some old jeans and sweater. It took several trips back and forth before everything was deposited outside the cottage, the last being the picnic basket and box of spring bulbs. Sitting down in the long grass, I took out the flask from the basket and poured out a coffee into the small plastic cup provided.

It was so peaceful. The sunlight flickered through the canopy of leaves above me, while birds twittered and went about their daily business, unseen in the abundant foliage. A rustling in the grass behind me caused me to turn around nervously, only to be confronted by an inquisitive hedgehog, its noise twitching erratically as it got a whiff of my ham and cheese sandwiches. Before I had a chance to reach into the basket, he had scuttled off through the undergrowth, probably to assemble an army for an attack on the wicker basket, as soon as the enemy was out of sight. Sighing, I returned my attention to the cottage. The peaceful serenity of the place had lulled me into a dream-like state, and I looked unenthusiastically at the collection of cleaning implements. *Where do I start? Brush the floors first, or clean the windows?* I remembered how dark it was inside, and thought that a better option was to cut back some of the ivy, so I could actually *see* what I was doing. Picking up the clippers, I walked over to one of the downstairs windows and pulled at the leafy climber surrounding the window. Its thick stem had, over the years, embedded its roots into the brickwork, and all I succeeded in doing was snapping off various sections of the stem, which, in turn, came away with some of the mortar still attached. It wasn't just a case of pulling on one end and the whole lot tumbled down effortlessly. I decided on Plan B—to cut each stem at ground level, thus killing the plant's lifeline. This would make it easier at a later date to remove the dried and dead stems, without tearing down the whole cottage in the process. I did, however, clip away the leaves from the window areas to enable more light to penetrate the gloomy rooms within, although the upstairs ones were out of my reach, and the bedrooms would have to remain shrouded in twilight.

Next, I tackled the filthy windows, which involved getting a bucket of water from the stream, and literally scrubbing them to remove some of the grime accumulated over the years. The inside ones were a little less encrusted. Overall, I was pleased with my efforts, although they were by no means sparkling. I even plucked up the courage and cleaned the window in the cold bedroom, although I didn't spend so much time and effort in there as the rest. Looking over my shoulder anxiously several times, I was convinced someone or *something* was watching me. My energy was starting to wane as I picked up the broom and swept it across the kitchen floor. Almost immediately a cloud of choking dust rose from the floor, like a fog, and engulfed me in its suffocating blanket. Coughing like crazy, I ran outside, throwing down the broom, as a spiral of the murky smog wound its way out through the door and up into the treetops.

Defeated, I flopped down onto the grass, feeling tired and hungry. *This is going to be more difficult than I had previously imagined,* I thought, as I opened up the picnic basket. Signs of frantic gnawing around the bottom of the basket made me smile, and I threw a sandwich into the undergrowth as a reward for the hedgehog's heroic, but unsuccessful, raid. Glancing at my watch, I was surprised that it was already four-thirty. All that time, and I had hardly made any impression on the place. *Perhaps Sam is right. It was just a dump, and far beyond any hope of resurrection to its former glory.* Picking up the box of spring bulbs, I looked at the bright pictures of red tulips and yellow daffodils that adorned the sides of the box. The least I could do was to plant his gift. They would always be there each spring, as a constant reminder of our friendship, and the fact that I did try and make the cottage respectable.

Getting up, I wandered around with the box and trowel, trying to decide where to plant them, and found myself out near the road. Here, several very large trees were scattered about. Some had succumbed to disease and were in various states of decay, while others flourished, their huge boughs supporting higher networks of branches that swayed majestically in the summer breeze. Marvelling at their resilience, I guessed they were at least two or three hundred years old. The sights these trees must have seen, if only they could speak.

One of these trees captured my interest, for high up and way out of reach, there hung from its branches small dark green fruits, which I recognised as pears. The strange poem immediately came to my mind, with its mystifying lines.

'Seek the garden, seek the pear. For old Mill Cottage will still be there.'

Okay, so I'm in the garden. I've found the pear tree, and the cottage is just over there through the trees. It still makes no sense whatsoever. The cell phone in my pocket suddenly sprang to life, and I pulled it out, smiling at the name of the caller.

"Hello, Sam," I said cheerfully. "Guess where I am?"

"Police station? Psychiatric unit? Mental asylum?" asked Sam, laughing. I giggled back. He never failed to cheer me up with his insane sense of humour.

"No. I'm at the cottage, doing some cleaning."

"How's it going?"

"All right," I lied. But he could hear the disappointment in the tone of my voice.

"Didn't I tell you it wasn't worth the effort? You're flogging a dead horse there, Emily."

"Yeah, yeah. I know. Don't rub it in."

"Did you plant the bulbs?" he asked, changing the subject.

"I was just going to, around the base of an old pear tree."

"Great! I love pears!" There was a moment's silence before Sam continued. "Listen, Emily. I have to go to Biology now. Take care, won't you? I'll talk to you later."

"Sure. Bye." I put the phone away. Well, that problem was solved, the pear tree it was!

It was hard work digging a hole around the base. The tree's roots had infiltrated the top layer of soil, making it nearly impossible to gain any depth. The fifth hole I started on appeared a little more promising, as I scraped away the earth with the trowel. My long hair kept falling forward, and I kept pushing it back with my dirty hands, before I remembered a cotton cap and hair band I had in my jeans pocket. Fixing my hair into a ponytail, I then put on the green cap and tucked my hair up underneath it, out of the way. *This is so much better,* and I forged ahead, trying to make the hole deep enough to insert a bulb.

Suddenly, something caught my eye, tangled up in the trowel. It looked like a fine chain of some sort, and I carefully brushed away the soil, but it went far deeper into the ground. I dared not pull on it too hard, for fear of breaking its delicate links. The trowel was a much too cumbersome tool. I needed something finer, if I were to release the chain from the soil's hold, without any damage. I returned with the weeding knife—not ideal, but the only other option available. I picked away at the earth slowly with the knife, and the chain was gradually exposing itself, bit by bit, until I hit upon something more solid.

Some ten minutes later, I was still trying to extract the object from the earth and was growing impatient, but I managed to curb a rougher approach that I would perhaps regret later. Eventually, I got underneath the object and was able to release it from its shallow grave. It was enveloped in a clod of clay that needed further removal, but that was relatively easy, and I soon was left holding a small oval-shaped piece of metal.

It didn't look like much, and was far too badly corroded to see any real detail, although parts of it glinted a yellowy color, which made me think it might be plated gold. The thickness of the metal oval also suggested it was a kind of pendant or locket, and I tried to locate a catch. It was difficult to see, but there did appear to be two slight bumps on one side, indicating a hinge. With this in mind, I struggled to pull apart the opposite side, but with nothing to get a grip on, it was impossible. Not to be outdone, I stood up and positioned the locket in the sun's rays to get a better view and inserted the weeding knife down the side, gently turning it to try and gain access. I fought with it for quite some time, and was on the verge of throwing it down in a fit of temper, when it suddenly relented and sprang open. Inside was what appeared to be a miniature portrait of someone. Sadly, its deterioration over the years had left it badly water-stained and hardly recognizable as a person at all. I couldn't make out if it was a woman or a man, although a small section of hair made me think it was female, but then again, I could have been wrong. I had been looking at the picture for no more than thirty seconds when it happened.

It began with a strange rushing sound in my ears, similar to what you hear as you go under an anaesthetic. This was followed shortly after, by the feeling that everything around me was spinning. I grabbed hold of the bark of the tree as my vision began to blur, and I was plunged into darkness, yet still conscious. The sensation can only be described as being on a roller coaster in the dark, falling endlessly through a black void that had no ending. Terrified and helpless, I suddenly felt an intense pain on the side of my head as it struck the tree and then—nothing.

How long I stayed unconscious on the ground was anyone's guess. It was still daylight, so it could not have been for long—maybe a few minutes? Opening my eyes, I found it hard to focus, and a deep throbbing in my head made me feel slightly nauseous. Several minutes passed before I had gained any normal awareness and vision, but this just made the matter worse. I hadn't any recollection of my surroundings. True, I was in a wooded area, but somehow it just didn't look right. Sitting up, I noticed I was grasping something. I unfolded my hand to reveal the locket I had found moments before—only it wasn't the same. This locket was new. The case and chain were a bright gold, and the picture within was clear and freshly painted. The image of a young, auburn-haired woman stared back at me. Her eyes, deep and penetrating, held a fiery passion. I groaned and put my hand up to my head, as another intense bout of pain shot through it. The streaks of bright red blood, on my hand as I withdrew it, scared the hell out of me, and I began to feel panicky and tearful. Rising unsteadily to my feet, I looked about for the pathway to the road. I needed to find Betsy and get to a hospital quickly. The gash on my head probably needed stitches. I walked in the direction where the road should have been, but only discovered a narrow, muddy dirt track, so I turned back and walked in another direction, totally disoriented. Taking the cell phone from my pocket, I tried to contact Sam, but there was no signal.

The sound of children laughing somewhere in the distance suddenly filled the air, and I breathed a sigh of relief. Where there were children, there were likely to be adults that could help me. I hurried through the trees towards the sound. Stumbling upon a small cottage in a clearing, I stepped out of view behind a large tree. It wasn't Mill Cottage. This one had three upstairs windows, timber-framed, and an untidy thatched roof. A steady plume of smoke rose wistfully up from a stone chimney on one side, indicating that it was lived in. I couldn't understand why I had not come across this cottage before. *Surely I would have known of its existence, being so close to mine?*

A stifled giggle behind me made me turn around. Standing at a distance were two young girls. One was about seven, and the other was younger—maybe four or five? It wasn't their strange, ragged clothing that became immediately apparent. It was their wild, unkempt appearance. Their little faces were dirty and drawn. Thin, skeleton-like arms dangled down by their sides, indicating malnourishment or illness, while dirty hair hung long and loose about their shoulders, covered at the top by grimy white moppet-styled caps. I realized that these must be gypsy children, but they typically lived in caravans and not cottages, and their standard of hygiene was usually much higher than that of these poor waifs.

"Hello," I said warily, offering them a friendly smile. They stood motionless, just staring at me. I must have looked a sight, with blood running down the side of my face. It was, in all probability, this that made them suddenly let out piecing screams and run terrified into the open doorway of the cottage. "It's okay. I won't hurt you," I called after them, but it was too late. They had vanished inside.

I debated whether to run myself, not wanting to be confronted by an angry gypsy father wielding a shotgun. Instead, a woman appeared in the doorway. She was in her late thirties to early forties. She, too, wore a cap similar to the girls and was dressed in a dark brown floor-length woollen dress, with a dirty apron-like garment over the top of it. The girls clung to the folds of her dress like frightened rabbits, while a young boy peered around the wooden doorframe. I took a step forward, out from behind the tree, where I could be seen more clearly, thus ensuring them that they had nothing to be afraid of. Unfortunately, this had the reverse effect, and the protective mother pulled her brood closer to her body, an expression of real fear etched upon her pale, hollow features.

"Don't you be coming no closer now. I have neither gold nor silver here. We are but poor country folk," the woman cried out from the doorway. I stood for a moment, trying to make out what she meant.

Did she think I was out to rob them? My God! Surely I didn't look that bad?

"I'm not going to rob you. I just want to use your phone, if you have one?" I called back, taking another step closer.

"Away with you now!" she hollered back, terrified. This woman was genuinely afraid of me, and a feeling of hopelessness engulfed me. I began to feel faint. The blood loss was starting to affect me, and I dropped to my knees, feeling weak and trembling. Tears started to flow, mingling with the blood to form pink spatters on the bare ground.

"Sam, I need you. Please help me." I pleaded out loud to myself, as my vision darkened and I started to lose consciousness. The last thing I heard was a woman's voice asking,

"You be knowing Master Samuel, then?"

When I regained consciousness some time later, it was dark. I could feel heavy covers on top of me, and I presumed I was in some kind of bed. A creaking sound in the nearby shadows belonged to an old rocking chair, on which sat the woman I had encountered earlier. A fire crackled in a grate at the foot of my bed, its last dying embers giving off enough light to show me that the woman slept soundly. Reaching up to my head, I felt a large wad of cloth positioned over my wound, secured around my head by more strips of cloth and tied at one side. I sat up slowly and tried to acquaint myself with the surroundings. It appeared I was inside the cottage. How I got to be there remained unclear, but I was grateful nonetheless for her kindness. The most sensible thing for her to do was to call for an ambulance and get me treated at the nearest emergency room. Why she had taken it upon herself to treat me with such antiquated dressings was a mystery. The room started to spin, and I lay back down on the bed, still far too weak to attempt going anywhere that night. I would stay until the morning, then thank her for her hospitality and be on my way.

I was awakened at dawn the following morning by the loud crowing of a cockerel outside my window. Sitting up with a start, it took a while for me to gather my senses and whereabouts. The rocking chair sat empty beside the bed. The fire was reduced to a pile of white ash, and it was cold—*really* cold. Sliding off the high bed, I wrapped my arms about myself as I exhaled puffs of warm vapor on every breath, and went over to the window. Frost had made intricate white patterns on the lower panes—even on the *inside*, but I could still see out of the top half. In the garden below, several chickens and cockerels scratched about noisily in the dirt. No one was about, and I looked at my watch to see what time it was. I gasped as I saw it was only 5:35am. No wonder it was so bloody cold. *Haven't these people heard of central heating?*

Shivering, I got back under the covers, and lay contemplating the room. I hadn't noticed it last night, but that wasn't surprising. There was no center light or light switch. The floor was just plain wooden boards without carpeting, and there was a marked lack of any furniture, apart from a large carved chest against the far wall and a small dresser on which stood a large bowl and jug. *How could these people live like this? Maybe they belonged to some weird religious cult that shunned anything modern, like the Amish of North America? That would explain the simple, peasant-style clothes. I need to get out of here before they try to enlist me!*

I must have fallen asleep again for a while because, when I next awoke, the sun was streaming into the room, and a row of little faces were lined up against the wall, staring at me. There were the two girls I had seen yesterday with the young boy, two more boys of six or seven—at least I believed them to be boys, as their hair was as long as the girls, and the only difference between them was that they wore knee-length puffy trousers. Beside them stood a very small girl—no more than two years old. *Just how many children does this woman have?* The boy nearest the door turned and called down the staircase.

"Mother, come quickly, the young Master has awoken." Hurried footsteps on the wooden stairs brought *'mother'* into the room, pulling a heavy woollen shawl closely around her thin shoulders as she came over to me.

"You be feeling better now, I see. You gave me a fair fright yesterday, I can tell you."

"Yes, I feel much better. Thanks. Sorry to be such a bother to you, but I really appreciate you dressing my wound and letting me stay last night," I replied politely, getting off the bed and edging little by little towards the door. The woman grabbed hold of my arm, stopping me in my tracks. She was surprisingly strong, considering her frail frame.

"You be going nowhere, young Master, until you have eaten your fill and have a warm drink inside you. Now, get down them stairs and be seated by the fireside." I obediently descended the staircase, not wanting to appear ungrateful, closely followed by the troop of children and their mother. *Why the hell does she keep calling me 'Master?'* I thought to myself. *Surely that was an old term used for a boy?*

The room at the bottom of the staircase was a cross between a kitchen and a lounge, and resembled the one at Mill Cottage. At one end was a log fire blazing fiercely in a grate, over which hung a black iron pot attached by a chain. To the side was an iron stove. A high-backed wooden bench was placed nearby, with a few cushions scattered upon its hard seat. A large worn table with two candles and three bare chairs were placed across the room on the rough ragstone floor. There were very few other furnishings to adorn this rather bleak abode. *They must be very poor*, I thought, sitting down upon the hard bench, and immediately reaching for a cushion to place beneath me. Some of the children opened the cottage door and ran out into the garden, laughing, while one boy and the little girl stayed nearby, their mournful eyes constantly fixed on me. I couldn't help but feel for these deprived children. *What kind of life did they have, so removed from society?*

The woman took an earthenware bowl from the side and scooped some porridge-like mixture into it, which she offered to me, followed by a spoon. I took it from her. It was really hot, and I set it down to one side to cool.

"Now then. I can't be calling you Master all the time, so I take it you were blessed with a name?" said the woman, as she took a seat beside me.

"It's Emily," I replied. This revelation caused the two children to giggle, and I couldn't for the life of me see why.

"Emily, you say? Now that be a strange name for a boy if ever I heard." I looked at the woman, thinking she was joking, but her face was serious.

"Why do you think I'm a boy?" I asked, surprised.

"Your clothing speaks little of a woman, Master Emily, and what clothing it is! I have never seen such like in these parts." With this, she reached out and ran her hand along my jeans, feeling the texture and material with great interest. "This be a fine weave indeed. Who made you such a fine garment?" I started to laugh. This conversation was getting absurd.

"Surely you've heard of jeans? I mean, *everyone's* heard of jeans, for God's sake!" The woman threw her hands to her face in shock.

"May you be forgiven for taking the Lord's name in vain!" she cried, visibly distraught.

"I'm sorry. I didn't mean to upset you," I said anxiously. The woman got up, and poured some liquid from an earthenware jug into a mug, which matched my bowl. She handed it to me silently, and I could tell she was in deep thought. So was I, come to that, I was wondering how soon I could get out of this madhouse and back into the real world. I sipped the strange drink. It tasted awful, and I made a face as I quickly swallowed a mouthful.

"What *is* this?" I asked, convinced she was trying to poison me.

"Why, it's only mead," she replied, surprised at my reaction.

"I'll stick to the porridge, thanks," I said, taking up the bowl and tentatively tasting the contents. It was edible, and I was hungry, although I was a bit put off by the numerous little black insect-like specks that were mixed together with the porridge. I picked out as many as I could, and lined them up along the edge of my bowl, much to the amusement of everyone watching.

After I had finished, she took the bowl and mug and disappeared into another room. I turned to the children—who had slowly edged nearer to me—and held out my hand in a friendly gesture, which was ignored.

"So, what are *your* names, then?" I asked, smiling, trying to gain their trust. They remained silent and expressionless. "I bet you're called Lucy," I said, pointing to the girl, "and you're Andrew." The trick paid off, and they both called out their proper names in unison. William and Sarah.

"I have no doubt your family will be a-wondering where you are, Master Emily," said the woman as she came back into the room, before stopping to take a look at the wound on my head. "As you be knowing Master Samuel," she continued. "I'll take you there, and he can ride with you safely home."

"I don't think we are talking about the same '*Master Samuel'* somehow," I replied, and then I laughed, thinking of Sam on a horse, and how utterly ridiculous that sounded.

"Be still while I take off the dressing. The blood has ceased to flow now." I felt my head, and the stiff matted hair around the wound. It had dried up all right, but I worried that it may start bleeding again with the slightest knock. I would have to be careful until I reached a hospital.

"I should be going now. I have to get back home. Thank you again for everything," I said, walking over to the door quickly, before she had other ideas.

"You'll be doing no such thing! I fear you have a sickness of the mind, and are in no state to go a-wandering in these woods. You will walk with me to my sister at Mill Cottage, and speak with her son Samuel, with whom I believe you are acquainted."

My ears pricked up at the mention of Mill Cottage. *Could this be the Mill Cottage? If it is, how can someone be living there?* I felt confused, wondering if the woman was right, and that I had sustained an injury to my brain. Then a thought—that's all it was, just a thought, which crossed my mind and was gone—planting, as it went, the first seeds of an unfeasible possibility.

Chapter Six

I was torn between wanting to see my cottage, and its unlikely inhabitants, and wanting to leave this godforsaken place to get back to reality. Common sense was over-ruled, and I elected to accompany her to Mill Cottage, more out of a desire to crush a nagging doubt that refused to go away. I followed the woman, who I now knew as Mary, along a dirt path. We passed a large pen to the side of the cottage, which housed several sheep and two goats.

A familiar stream came into view as I traced Mary's footsteps along its banks, feeling increasingly uneasy as to what I might find—and be forced to believe. Three dogs came barking like crazy towards us as we approached the cottage—two small terrier breeds and a much larger, scruffy gray animal that looked decidedly unfriendly. I saw the thatched roof first, and then the two up and three down windows. There was no mistaking it. This *was* Mill Cottage—or, should I say, what it would have been like some 300 years ago.

My mind felt totally scrambled, trying to comprehend how this was even possible. The very idea that I had somehow been transported back in time was ludicrous. *How could this happen? What could I have done to cause it? No. This isn't happening. There has to be a rational explanation for it all.*

A woman came out of my cottage smiling. She was older than Mary, and dressed in a similar woollen garment that reached down to the ground, only this one was more of a dark gray in color.

"This be Hannah, my sister," said Mary proudly. I held out my hand, but she refused it and did a curtsy-like bow instead. I nodded my head and watched as her eyes moved downwards—over my body—and back up again, her mouth slightly open in amazement. My clothes were obviously attracting a lot of attention, and I began to feel uncomfortable.

"I'm Emily," I said lightly, trying to distract her attention away from my attire.

"Pleased to make your acquaintance, Master Emily. Mary has told me of your injury—and confusion."

"I am confused as to how I actually *got* here," I confessed truthfully.

"And as to your given name also," added Mary. I stared at her, perplexed. *Why won't they believe I was called Emily?* Also this '*boy*' thing was really starting to irritate me. Two young girls appeared from behind Hannah. One held a small baby in her arms, wrapped tightly in a bundle of rags.

"This be Ellen, Hannah, and baby Eliza, I am blessed with two sons also. Master John, whom I summoned yesterday to help carry you to rest, and Master Samuel, my eldest, whom I believe you know of. They be away with their father at the mill, but will hasten to return by noon, I am sure."

Hannah took baby Eliza from her young daughter, and began to undo the laces on the top part of her dress, exposing her large white breasts. I watched, somewhat embarrassed, as she pushed a nipple into the baby's mouth, who fed hungrily. Apart from it being such a natural and spontaneous action, which would be unheard of in public from where I came from—or anywhere else for that matter—it also gave me an idea.

"I am not a *Master;* I am a *Miss,"* I told the women and pulled my sweater up over my head. They stared at me as if I had gone mad, exchanging uneasy glances with one another. Next, I removed my bra and threw it to the ground triumphantly. "There. *Now* do you believe I'm a woman?"

Everyone has, at some point in their lives, done something really stupid that they would rather forget. This was my moment of idiocy. I suddenly heard the distinct sound of horses snorting in close proximity behind me, before a rough male voice shouted out loud.

"I do indeed! And a fine specimen of a woman, at that." I could see Mary and Hannah's eyes focused high over my shoulder, as I stood frozen to the spot, wishing the earth would swallow me up. Mary reacted first, stepping forward and throwing her shawl around my shoulders. I turned slowly around, the color rising to bright crimson in my cheeks and my heart thudding like crazy. Three men—I don't do things by halves—dismounted from their horses and stood, admiring the view.

"This be Charles, my husband," announced Hannah, going forward and touching the older man—and owner of the lewd comment—on the shoulder. He was fairly short and stocky, with a full beard, but had a kind and fatherly face. Next to him stood a well-built teenage boy—maybe sixteen or seventeen, with long, curly sandy hair that rested on the shoulders of his fit, muscular frame. John grinned at me in silent contemplation, obviously remembering holding me in his arms yesterday, which thankfully I had no recollection of. It was the far gentleman that disturbed me the most—a tall, brooding figure, his long hair matching his eyes, that were as black as night. He reminded me of Cathy's Heathcliff in *Wuthering Heights*—a swarthy, gypsy-like man, who I instantly disliked. He was introduced to me as Samuel.

"Clothe the woman before she catches her death," said Charles sympathetically, taking the reins of all three horses and walking them around the back of the cottage.

The two brothers walked into the cottage, Samuel bending his head low under the door as he entered.

"Come," said Hannah, taking my hand. "I will find you some clothes that are more suited to you." Picking up my discarded sweater and bra, I followed Hannah into the cottage, past the two men who sat drinking by the fireside, and up the narrow staircase that I knew so well. It was strange to see the bedroom and cottage furnished, however sparsely, and I sat on the edge of the hard bed, thinking, as Hannah rummaged through a large oak chest.

"Are you Hannah Howerd?" I asked uneasily, recalling the names on my deeds.

"I am that," she replied. "Why do you ask?" I thought for a moment before asking the next question. I didn't really want to hear the answer, but the evidence was now so overwhelming, I had to know for sure.

"What year is this, Hannah?"

"Why, dear child. Have you forgotten?" she replied, concerned.

"Please. Just answer my question."

"It is the year of our Lord, 1696," she answered casually, taking out a long brown dress from the chest and laying it out on the bed. "Here, this be fitting you just fine, indeed."

I suddenly felt so alone. I wasn't supposed to be here, talking to these people, involved in the day-to-day lives of my long dead ancestors, who were now as large as life—and very much alive—in front of me. It wasn't right. It wasn't meant to happen. What scared me the most was how I was going to get back—*if it is possible to get back?* My real life seemed a million miles away from here. Sam was a million miles away. I wanted to go home. *Oh God! How I want to go home!*

"Emily? Emily!" cried Hannah. I was lost in my own thoughts and was startled by her cries. "Are you not feeling well?" she asked, "You have gone quite pale."

"No, I'm fine," I lied as I picked up the dress. *Does she honestly expect me to wear this?* I supposed I had to go along with it for now. It would give me a little time, to try and work out how to get back to where I belonged. She left me to change into the garment, which was rough, itchy and a little tight, but I managed to button it up. I found it had a pocket in the skirt, and I took the locket from my jeans and tucked it safely away in there. The locket, I believed, was my passport home—if only I could remember how.

I wasn't used to having material flapping around my legs. It felt strange, and I walked up and down a few times to get accustomed to the movement. My hair was only partly secured in the hair band, so I took it off and let my hair swing loose and free. I wished I had a comb, as it was so dreadfully matted. I wished even more for a mirror to survey the damage to my head, but that would probably worry me more, and I had enough problems to cope with.

Lifting my skirt a little, I descended the staircase cautiously, each footstep echoing loudly on the bare wooden boards. The room fell silent as I entered. Everyone was staring at me. I checked the dress, fearing I had put it on back to front, but it appeared to be fastened correctly. Mary broke the uncomfortable silence.

"Now you are a *real* woman. Come sit with us and take a drink, Miss Emily." Moving over to the only available chair around the table, I sat down between Charles and John, which, unfortunately, was directly opposite Samuel. I could feel his deep penetrating eyes watching me intently although, when I met his gaze, he looked away.

"Have you got any milk?" I inquired innocently, as Hannah went to pour me some of that mead stuff, which I had tasted and disliked earlier. The room erupted into laughter at my strange request.

"My dear girl. Are you still a child in arms that you require such nourishment?" said Charles, wiping the mead from his beard with the back of his hand. I blushed profusely at being the center of their amusement, and fixed my eyes on the table, feeling somewhat foolish.

"Give the woman milk, if that's what she so desires," Samuel's clear, distinct voice filled the room, and the frivolity ceased immediately.

"I'll fetch her some," said Hannah meekly, leaving the cottage. Samuel rose from the chair and went over to the fireplace, where he stood with one hand upon the beam, watching the flames dance between the logs in silence.

"So, Miss Emily, where have you travelled from?" inquired Charles, breaking the icy silence. "Samuel has no knowledge of you, although I am told you called out for him in your moment of pain."

"It's true. I don't know *this* Samuel. Where I come from, I know of a Sam. He is a good friend of mine—nothing more." Why I found myself adding the last unnecessary declaration surprised me. It was really none of their business.

"Where *is* this place you come from?" urged Charles, leaning forward.

"Yes, tell us, Miss Emily," said John eagerly, full of curiosity. Hannah arrived with the milk at that awkward moment. I was relieved because I didn't have an answer—at least not one that they would understand, anyway.

"Maybe Miss Emily cannot remember too well. You should not worry her so, Charles. She will tell us when she is good and ready—is that not so, Miss Emily?" said Mary kindly.

"Yes, my memory is not so good," I lied, taking a sip of the warm milk. It was not cow's milk, for sure. *Maybe goats?* I thought, taking another curious sip. Hannah watched me as I drank, noticing my hesitation.

"It's sheep's milk, if you be a-wondering," she said, as if reading my thoughts. Samuel turned around and stared at me, as I sat motionless with a mouthful of this alien milk bulging in my cheeks. Not having anywhere to spit it out, I was forced to swallow it. The actual taste was not unpleasant—just the mere thought of its origin.

Charles stood up, scraping his chair noisily on the stone floor.

"Time for us to return to the mill. See to it that our visitor is well cared for, and that a bed is made ready for her stay. Mary must not be troubled with such burdens."

"Yes, sir," replied Hannah, doing a small curtsy and casting Mary a worried glance. John was excited at the prospect of me living with them. He had obviously developed a crush on me that I found quite endearing. His brother, Samuel, was less enthralled and strode from the cottage, his dark eyes blazing with anger. An argument followed as they mounted their horses outside, between him and Charles, which made it apparent that I was not welcome in their home. I looked at Hannah, who just sighed and cleared away the mugs. This was evidently an everyday scenario between father and son, and I was curious to know why Samuel found my presence in his home so unbearable.

Mary returned home to *Jasmine Cottage* to see to her children, which gave me the opportunity to question Hannah on a few unexplained points. She handed me a bucket containing an unknown mushy substance, before I had a chance to ask, and bid me to follow her outside to an enclosure around the back, containing five filthy grunting pigs, which waded in their own excrement and stank to high heaven. I stood at a distance with my hand over my mouth as Hannah, oblivious to the stench, proceeded to tip the contents of her bucket into a trough. She held out her hand for my bucket, which followed suit, causing a writhing mass of squealing flesh as they fought over the food.

Next were the chickens, where the same buckets were used to transfer grain, collected from a sack against the cottage wall. I hurried after her, hitching up my dress and stumbling over the hardened muddy ruts in the caked ground. Jeans would be so much more suited to this terrain, but '*when in Rome'* —as the saying goes. A lull in the loud squawking of the feeding frenzy enabled me to begin my intended conversation, with a certain amount of trepidation.

"What did your husband mean by burdening Mary, is she ill?" Hannah turned to me and smiled weakly. Years of constant hardship and worry had etched deep lines over her face, and I wondered how old she actually was. She looked around 60, but with such young children, I could be off by at least 20 years.

"My sister is dying, Miss Emily. She grows weaker everyday, and I fear the Lord may take her soon."

"What's wrong with her?" I asked quietly.

"Her heart is tired. Our mother had the same sickness. We just wait and pray."

"What about the children after…" my voice trailed off, as a lump came to my throat.

"They will come to me as my own." replied Hannah; surprised I should have to ask that question. *Of course. What am I thinking?* I did a quick calculation, which would make Hannah the mother of eleven children—all crammed together in a two-bedroom cottage. It didn't bear thinking about. Then again, this wasn't my problem. Hopefully I would soon find my way home, leaving them to live their lives as God intended.

Hannah returned to the cottage, with me following behind like a faithful puppy, another question on my lips, but the confidence to ask it severely lacking.

"I'll be upstairs, preparing the bed for you, Miss Emily," she said, and disappeared through the latched door to ascend the narrow stairway. "You will sleep with the girls, but have the comfort of your own bed." I thought about the sleeping arrangements momentarily. If the girls and I had one room and Hannah and Charles the other, *where did the boys sleep?* Hitching up my skirt I went upstairs to help Hannah, and found her on her hands and knees rolling out a thick mattress, stuffed with straw, from under the bed. I took hold of the other end and dragged the heavy item across the floor to the far corner. I shuddered to think what manner of creepy crawlies had made their homes within the confines of this mattress, and thought about the night ahead with increasing unease.

"Where do the boys sleep?" I asked, unable to contain my curiosity a moment longer.

"They be out in the barn, with the horses," replied Hannah casually, handing me the corner of a large cotton sheet that we placed over the mattress and roughly tucked underneath. A heavy woven blanket and a hard pillow were added from the chest, to complete my bed for the duration of my stay with this intriguing family. Hannah sat down on the edge of the large bed to rest. Her breathing was heavy and labored, after such little physical exertion, and I doubted that *her* health was not without its problems.

"John is a cheerful, likeable lad," I said lightly. "You wouldn't think that he and Samuel were brothers. They are so different in looks, as well as temperament." Hannah shot me a troubled look, which told me I had perhaps said something rather sensitive. "I'm sorry. I shouldn't pry. It was just an observation," I added awkwardly. Hannah sighed and looked over at the window. Her hands grasped each other tightly as she fought to control her feelings. I waited, anticipating that she wanted to tell me something, but found it somewhat distressing.

"Samuel is not born of Charles," she said finally. "I was with child before I met him."

"Oh. Were you married before?" I asked innocently. Hannah got up and went over to the window, running her slender fingers along the dusty sill.

"If I were, I would not have had to endure the shame and ridicule that such a condition brought forth." I frowned at this last comment, not altogether sure what the context of her words meant. She turned and looked at me, a sadness in her eyes that signified a burden she had carried for many years.

"I walked to the village on my own that day," she began. "Mother had warned me of such wrong doing in these parts, but I was young and foolish. By the time I left to return home, darkness had fallen. I was alone and frightened, but knew the way, and hastened my journey home." She returned to the bed then and sat down next to me. I took hold of her hand and encouraged her to continue her sorrowful tale. "I did not see or hear him approach, and I was thrown to the ground easily. I tried to fight him off, but he was too strong for me, and he—he—" she cried, unable to continue, and sobbed into her apron.

"It's all right. I understand," I whispered quietly. "These things happen. It's not your fault. I take it that Samuel is the result of this incident?" She nodded, wiping away the tears.

"He was believed to be a local gypsy man, a renowned thief and murderer. My father hunted him down and killed him for the evil deed that he had bestowed upon me." *That would account for Samuel's dark and swarthy looks,* I thought, *and possibly the ill temper that was so apparent. Does he still hold a grudge against the family that killed his father? Surely not? He has been well cared for and loved, despite his ill-fated conception.* "I was acquainted with Charles, through my father, soon after. We were betrothed. He agreed to bring up Samuel as his own, to spare me the dishonour. He is a good man—a kind man, Emily." I squeezed her hand reassuringly and smiled. "I must away now and prepare a meal. The men shall return soon," she said, getting up and hastily drying her eyes. "Please do not tell Samuel of which we have spoken. He would be sorely displeased to know his past had been told of to a stranger."

"No, of course not," I said honestly. I had no intention of getting on the wrong side of this disagreeable man. I seemed to be doing that quite well as it was.

I helped Hannah with the meal. It was a simple meat stew, with no potatoes or vegetables to accompany it. It was obvious from her reply, when I questioned her, that this was the standard diet, and that eating vegetables with a meal was unheard of—if they were grown for consumption at all. A large lump of homemade bread was placed in the center of the table, along with some cheese and an earthenware jug, containing the dreaded mead. The two candles were lit, and a lantern hung in the window. Logs were added to the fire, and the sudden spurt of flames warmed the chilly room within minutes. Young Eliza was fed and put to bed, while Ellen and her sister Hannah played quietly by the fireside with a simple doll—the likes of which I had seen before, in an antique shop, costing many hundreds of pounds. The way they pulled roughly at its hair made me cringe, and I wanted to rescue it from its fate.

The cozy atmosphere was disturbed by the sound of horses outside. Hannah's mood changed instantly from one of calm to heightened anxiety, and I myself felt my heart pound louder within my chest. The door swung open shortly after, and John bounded into the room first, greeting his mother warmly and smiling shyly at me. Charles followed, shutting the door behind him, against the raw wind that had picked up, momentarily fluttering the candle flames upon the table. I stood motionless, watching the door.

"I told Samuel to secure the horses well tonight in the barn. I feel a storm is coming upon us," Charles informed his wife, as she ladled out some of the stew onto a dish. Hannah beckoned the girls and I to the table to receive our share. I sat down next to John, and the girls returned to the bench by the fire with their dinner. Hannah recited a little prayer of thanks, and we began our meal in silence. The meat, whatever it was, appeared a little tough, but I was hungry and chopped at the meat with my spoon and knife, thankful for every morsel that I managed to separate from the stringy lumps.

Suddenly, the door was thrust open, and a gust of wind rushed through the room, extinguishing one of the candles. Samuel slammed the door shut, causing the other candle to sputter and die, plunging the room into semi-darkness. At that moment, a vivid flash of lightning lit up the interior, and illuminated our rigid positions around the table. A loud clap of thunder terrified the young girls. John took his dinner and went to comfort them over by the fire, as Hannah re-lit the candles from a fire taper. Samuel took off his coat and threw it over the back of the bench, before sitting down at the table, opposite me. He roughly pushed his empty plate across the table for his mother to fill, which she did so without delay. I kept my head down and only acknowledged Hannah with a quiet 'thank you' when she handed the girls and I mugs of milk to drink.

Having finished his meal, Samuel sat back in his chair and sipped the mead, his gaze fixed to the tabletop in silent contemplation. I watched him guardedly, remembering Hannah's story and feeling a certain amount of pity for this poor soul, whose very existence troubled him so. I was so absorbed in my thoughts that I didn't realize he had looked up, and had now fixed me with a stare that chilled my spine.

"What is it, woman?" he growled, slamming down his mug noisily. "Why do you stare at me so?"

"I'm sorry. I didn't mean to be rude," I spluttered nervously.

"Leave her be, Samuel, she means you no harm," said Charles anxiously.

"I want to know what this woman finds so interesting about me," continued Samuel, fixing me with his black, piercing eyes. His eyes moved over to his mother, who hung her head guiltily and gave him the proof he needed. In a fit of rage, he stood up and flung the chair across the room. "She told you, didn't she?" he shouted. "That I am her bastard son, whose father was nothing more than a murderer and common thief, condemned to die like a mad dog, for giving into temptation from this whore!"

Whimpering cries from baby Eliza, which drifted down the stairs, broke the stunned silence. The shouting had awakened her from her peaceful sleep. Ellen and Hannah sat huddled up against John, too petrified to cry. I was too traumatized to speak. I had never seen such bitterness and pent up anger unleashed from a man, and he hadn't finished yet.

"Did she also tell of Charlotte? My wife to be, who on the eve of our marriage took it upon herself to elope with her lover, whose child she bore, leaving me standing at the altar waiting for her to come? You can gloat over my wretchedness and condemn me to hell, for I am forever cursed by my father's wrong doing!"

"GET OUT!" yelled Charles, as his wife collapsed, sobbing in despair.

"Gladly," hissed Samuel, in my face, as he turned to take his coat from the bench. Somehow I managed to find my voice, and stood up, choked with emotion.

"Samuel, you're tearing this family apart. They love you so much. How can you treat them this way?" I pleaded, but he wasn't listening—he tore down the lantern from the window, before disappearing out into the night.

I lay, unable to sleep for ages that night, upon my lumpy mattress, just staring relentlessly up at the beamed ceiling. The moonlight cast flickering shadows about the room from the waving branches outside. I had only been here a couple of days, and already I found myself caught up in this family's personal problems. My interference could change the whole outcome of history, which had already been written. The storm had passed. A far greater one, however, would begin to brew if I didn't return home soon.

Chapter Seven

It was barely light when I slipped out from beneath the warmth of the woollen blanket, into the freezing room. Quietly gathering up my jeans, sweater, and shoes, I crept past Ellen and Hannah, sleeping soundly in the large bed, and down the wooden staircase. My heart was in my mouth at every creak of the stair that my bare feet made. I felt so guilty running out on them. They had showed me nothing but kindness, but I couldn't stay any longer. I was becoming too involved.

Once outside, I breathed a sigh of relief and headed off in the direction of the road—or muddy track, as it now was. It was so cold. My thin sweater did little to ward off the freezing mist, which encircled me and begged me to stay. Taking the locket from my jeans, I tried to recall what I was doing at the moment my transition occurred. All I could remember was standing by the pear tree and opening the locket with the weeding knife, which I no longer had with me. My searched for the pear tree was in vain. In fact, there was a marked absence of any reasonably large trees in the area. Standing there, alone among the bushes, I was surprised to hear a distinct cough close by.

I turned to see Mary's older daughter, Elizabeth, eyeing me inquisitively.

"Why are you wearing your funny man clothes again, Miss Emily?" she asked. Smiling, I went over to her and took hold of her cold white hands.

"I couldn't find my pretty frock this morning," I lied, "so I had to put on these." She appeared to accept my simple explanation on that subject and went on to another.

"Why are you outside? What are you looking for?"

"Actually, I'm trying to find a tree—a pear tree," I said, hoping that she would know of its whereabouts. The child looked up at me with her large, innocent eyes. I noticed, with concern, the dark shadows that had appeared underneath them since we last met.

"What is a pear tree?" she asked, tucking her long tangled hair behind her ears.

"Well, it's a big tree with long green fruits, that grow on it at the end of the summer, and you—well, you can eat them or cook them."

"My father planted some trees before the Lord took him to heaven. He said that one day they would be tall, and we would have lots of these fruits of which you speak."

"Do you know where these trees are?" I asked excitedly. Elizabeth held my hand tightly and, without speaking, led me along a pathway beside Jasmine Cottage, to a patch of open ground. We stopped in front of some small leafy sticks.

"Here are father's trees," she announced proudly. The trees were no more than two feet high. I don't know quite what I expected, but this wasn't it. "Will they grow tall, Miss Emily, like father said?" asked Elizabeth, gripping my hand.

"They certainly will, my darling—as tall as a house," I replied, not having the heart to tell her that it would take hundreds of years for them to reach that height. Suddenly Elizabeth broke into a fit of coughing, which shook her pathetically thin body, and left her gasping for breath. I ushered her back to the cottage and told her to keep warm and have plenty of hot drinks.

"I will get the fire started. Mother is still sleeping," she told me as I left her at the door. Choking back the tears, I walked back along the path, leaving this poor child and her family to their fate.

Standing by the little pear tree, I took a deep breath and opened the locket easily. The young woman stared back at me from within, and I pondered her identity, while I waited for the magic to happen. A minute passed, and nothing occurred. Two minutes, then three. Nothing. *What am I doing wrong?* I waved the locket about frantically in the air, feeling a growing sense of panic overwhelm me. I was sure this was what I did before. *Why isn't it working? Why aren't I back where I belong?* Tears of despair flowed down my cheeks as I collapsed on the ground. *Am I destined to stay here for evermore?* The thought filled me with dread, and I cursed the day I inherited Mill Cottage.

"Miss Emily! Come quick! I cannot wake mother!" screamed Elizabeth, running along the path towards me. I got up and hurriedly brushed away the tears.

"It's all right. I'm here. Don't cry," I said, taking her hand in mine. We hastily returned along the path to the cottage. I ascended the stairs to the bedroom nervously, passing Elizabeth's younger sister Mary on the way, crouched down upon the stairs, her pitiful cries echoing around the silent rooms.

The boys, William, Joseph and John were just inside the bedroom, pressed up against the wall, trying to be brave and manly, but their tear-stained faces told me they had failed to keep their emotions in check, and I thought nonetheless of them for showing that they loved their mother. Little Sarah was curled up on the bed, her arm draped around her mother, not really understanding what had happened, but frightened and bewildered by the reactions of the others. I swallowed hard and slowly approached the bed where Mary lay. Her face was white, her lips were a greyish-blue, and her hair, wet from perspiration, flowed over the pillow. One lock was tightly clasped in Sarah's tiny fingers. There was no mistaking the look of death upon her face. She had gone.

"Your mother is at peace now," I said quietly "She is with your father in heaven." Elizabeth came forward and knelt beside the bed, her hands clasped together as she started to recite the Lord's Prayer faultlessly. The boys joined in as I stood there, head bowed, with tears streaming down my face. Never before had I witnessed something so moving. I bent down and scooped Sarah from the bed, untwining her fingers gently from the lock of her mother's hair that she held on to so desperately. She weighed next to nothing and I easily carried her in my arms. "Come on, children. Let's go and tell your aunt the sad news," I said gently, while moving out of the room and carefully negotiating the narrow staircase. "William, take care of your sister Mary," I said, as we got to the place on the stairs where she still sat crying quietly.

We slowly walked to Mill Cottage. Sarah held on to me securely, her hands tightly clenched around my neck as I carried her effortlessly. The other five children walked silently beside me, trying to come to terms with their loss. The sound of horse's hooves made me look up, and it was with dismay that I saw Samuel mounted before me, his black cloak flapping in the cold wind as he stared down unsympathetically at the sorrowful collection of children before him.

"These children," I began, "have just lost their mother and are in need of a new home." I almost added, *'And this woman is in desperate need of a hug',* but he would never have understood. He dismounted from his horse and, handing the reins to John, walked purposefully over to me. I held Sarah closer to me as he approached, fearful of this unpredictable man. Taking hold of Sarah, he prised her away from me and set her down upon the ground unceremoniously, prodding her in the back roughly to tell her to walk on. "The girl has just lost her mother!" I cried, shocked at his heartless attitude.

"But not the use of her limbs," he retorted, his black eyes blazing into mine. We stood there for a few moments, glaring at one another, before I pushed past him and ran to catch up with the children. Within seconds he was beside me again, uttering further abuse. "Why do you not return to your family, woman? Did you bestow great sadness and tragedy upon them, as you have done upon us, that they were forced to cast you out?"

"Mary was dying before I got here!" I whispered back venomously. "And, believe me, if I could return, I would—thankfully, but it seems that fate has brought me to you—I mean, to your family." I corrected myself quickly, realizing my unintentional error.

"Do not talk to *me* of fate, woman! I—," before he could continue, Charles came running along the path, holding his arms out to embrace the children. Their sad little faces told him what he had dreaded.

"I am so sorry, Charles," I said. "She must have died during the night in her sleep. I don't think she was in any pain." Charles nodded, understanding, before gently guiding the children into the cottage. Almost immediately, a loud wail of despair arose from Hannah as she met the children in the doorway. Charles turned to Samuel.

"Ride to the village and summon the undertaker. We will prepare her body for his arrival." Samuel mounted his horse and turned it around, throwing me a look of hatred as he dug his heels into the beast's side, and galloped off at great speed. I watched him go, his black hair and cloak flying out behind him, and wondered if fate did, in some way, send me here for a purpose.

I stayed behind with the children all morning while Charles, Hannah and, I presume, Samuel dealt with the necessities over at Jasmine Cottage. I could sympathise with them, remembering how I felt when I lost my own parents and they, in turn, could sense that I understood their feelings. Elizabeth's persistent cough was starting to really worry me, especially when little Sarah also started to give the occasional cough. I tried to remember the conversation I had had with Sam in the village pub, about why so many young children were buried in the village graveyard. *Isn't there an illness called consumption or TB, as it is known today, that was spread by coughing?* I wish I had paid more attention now. *How was I to know back then that I was soon to be thrust among the very individuals of whom we spoke?* I knew I was vaccinated against this disease in childhood, and therefore it posed no threat to me, *but what of these poor souls?* With no medication, their outlook was most certainly bleak.

"I'm tired, Miss Emily. Can I go to bed?" whined Sarah, sitting heavily down on a chair next to me.

"It's only mid-morning, sweetheart. Are you hungry for some porridge now?" I asked, knowing she had refused it earlier, like her sister.

"I'm not hungry. I want to sleep," she insisted, climbing onto my lap and winding her thin arms around my neck.

"I'll take her up," said Elizabeth quietly, from the bench by the fire, "I also am feeling a need to rest." I anxiously watched the two sisters disappear up the staircase. Elizabeth's breathing was heavy and laboured as she climbed the stairs behind Sarah, racked by another fit of coughing. I jumped up suddenly and called up to Elizabeth.

"Let Sarah sleep in my bed on the floor. Don't sleep with her. Keep away from her, and when you cough, COVER YOUR MOUTH!" It may be too late for these girls, but I was sure as hell going to try and protect the others.

Going outside, I found the boys and forbade them to go upstairs to see their sisters. They slept in the barn, so were relatively safe from contamination. That just left the girls—Mary, Ellen, Hannah and baby Eliza, and—of course—me. If I could make Charles move out to the barn for the time being, the girls could share the big bed with their mum, Hannah. Eliza had her wooden cradle next to the bed. I had no idea where I was to sleep, but that wasn't important right now. Eliza awoke crying, and I picked her up, just as Charles and Hannah arrived back. She took the baby from me without a word and went inside, her eyes red from weeping. Catching hold of Charles's arm, I led him over to the stream. Sitting him down, I explained my fears and the consequent plans I had made to prevent further spread of this deadly virus.

He was an intelligent man and listened intently to my every word. When I had finished, he looked at me, puzzled—wondering, no doubt, how I had come by such knowledge of this illness and its confinement.

"I will do what you ask, child," he said finally, "but how are you able to attend to the sick without endangering your own life?" Various explanations went through my mind at that point, but none feasibly possible to a 17th century man, so I purposely avoided the question.

I spent much of the late afternoon and evening upstairs with Sarah and Elizabeth. The older sister had taken a turn for the worse, so I sat on the edge of the bed, wiping her brow with a wet cloth as she developed a fever. I felt so helpless. If only I had some antibiotics, or whatever was required to treat this disease. If only I could return, then maybe I could get hold of something that would save them. Sam would know what to do, I was sure.

I could hear Samuel's voice downstairs. His tone suggested that he was, as usual, in an argumentative mood, and although I could not hear the topic of conversation, I was certain that my name was mentioned more than once. The aggressive exchange of words eventually ceased, leaving silence to prevail. Shortly after, footsteps on the staircase warned me of someone approaching. The bedroom door creaked open a little, to display Hannah Senior holding a shaking candlestick. She dared not enter any further into the room. Instead, she held out the lighted candle for me to take.

"Come down and eat with us, Miss Emily. You have had nothing all day. I fear your strength will fail you." She was right. I had badly neglected my own needs, and I was now hungry and exhausted. Placing the candle beside the bed, I checked Elizabeth again, and pulled the cover up over a sleeping Sarah, before going downstairs for some nourishment.

Charles was sitting at the table, his head bowed. His hands tightly clasped a large mug of mead. He acknowledged me briefly, and then returned to his somber thoughts. Samuel was over by the fireside cleaning a gun, neither looking up nor speaking as I sat at the table.

"How are the girls?" asked Hannah quietly, as she spooned some meat onto a dish from a large black pot.

"Elizabeth has a fever," I told her, "but she is sleeping now."

"And Sarah?"

"She is also asleep." Hannah set the plate down on the table, and passed me some bread, before wearily sitting down next to me. "Have *you* eaten?" I inquired, picking up the spoon.

"I have taken some bread earlier. I feel little need for food at this time."

"You must eat! Tell her, Charles. She must keep strong."

"GO ON…TELL HER, CHARLES! DO AS THE WOMAN SAYS!" cried Samuel suddenly, from the bench, in a mocking tone. I glared over at him, disgusted at his outburst. *Has the man no feelings at all?* I wanted to give him a mouthful, but it would only have upset his parents further. Their day had been traumatic enough as it was, with Mary's death. I finished my meal in silence, my temper bubbling precariously just below the surface. One more word from Samuel would be all that was needed for me to boil over.

Charles got up to retire for the night. After kissing his wife affectionately on the head, he headed towards the door, gently squeezing my shoulder as he passed.

"Fetch me from the barn if the sickness worsens," he whispered to me, before opening the door and closing it quietly behind him. Hannah cleared away the plates and she also went to bed, leaving me alone with Samuel.

I went over to the other bench and sat down by the fire, which was now reduced to a red glow among the wood ashes, but still radiated out comforting warmth into the room. A strained silence prevailed, before Samuel put aside the gun and reached for his mug of mead. He glanced up at me momentarily, before casting his eyes to the dying embers.

"Say whatever is on your mind that ails you, and be gone," he muttered. I thought for a moment, and decided to say what was on my mind.

"I was like you once," I began tentatively. "Men treated me badly and let me down continually, I hated all of them… I *loathed* them. Then someone brought me to my senses, which made me realize that I couldn't go through life being forever bitter and resentful. Some relationships just weren't meant to be—just like yours and Charlotte's."

"What do *you* know of Charlotte and I? How dare you sit there and judge what should or should not have been?" retorted Samuel angrily.

"Forget her, Samuel," I continued. "Life is too short to bear a grudge. I believe there is someone out there for you—someone kind and loving—who won't leave you standing at the altar. Your birth has nothing to do with who you are, or who you should become. You are a person in your own right—one who, deep down, needs to love and be loved, just like anyone else." He stared at me, stunned, and in that instant, I thought I saw his eyes soften. But it was short lived.

Throwing the last remnants of his mead into the fire, he stood up, towering over me menacingly as I cowered, hunched up on the bench.

"Don't ever, *EVER* talk to me of love again. Just stay out of my life, or I shall remove you from it—permanently." With this dire warning, he picked up the gun and stormed out of the door, leaving it wide open to the elements. My heart pounding, I went over to close the door after him. I doubted if any of that had sunk in, but I felt better having gotten it off my chest. It would give him something to think about tonight, as he lay on the warm straw in the barn. Thoughts of the warm straw reminded me that I had nowhere to sleep, and after checking the girls—that thankfully were none the worse—I curled up on the hard bench and placed a cushion under my head. The fire was now extinguished, thanks to Samuel's contribution, and I shivered as the cold enveloped me and made me shake uncontrollably. It was the tiredness only that enabled me to fall asleep so readily, as my last thoughts drifted disturbingly to Samuel asleep in the barn.

Awakening from my slumber early the following morning, I was surprised, yet pleased, that Hannah had evidently come down in the night and covered me with a warm blanket. I would probably have awoken much earlier without its comforting warmth. Moving slowly and stiffly to an upright position, I rubbed my aching neck and stared in dismay at the pile of cold ash in the fireplace. I knew where everything was to get the fire going and, clutching the blanket around me, proceeded to attend to it. It took me a little longer to kindle it than I imagined it would have taken Charles or Hannah, but a welcome flame eventually leapt up from a log, causing me to cry out a joyful, "YES!" in response.

I checked on the girls upstairs next, anxiously going over to Elizabeth first, who was barely awake. Her fever seemed to have decreased since last night, and I breathed a sigh of relief. Turning to Sarah, I stared in disbelief at the empty bed. She hadn't come down, so there was only one place she could be. I went across to Hannah's room and quietly opened the door. Sure enough, there was Sarah, snuggled up to her new mother in the bed, along with her sisters. I doubted that Hannah was aware that she had crept in, but there didn't seem any point in removing her now. I closed the door softly and returned downstairs to make some porridge. As I waited for the mixture to warm, I opened the door and went outside. It was a bright, but chilly, morning. The sun was just appearing through the trees, casting its warm glow down upon the nearby stream. Sitting down upon a large log, I was greeting by Jas, the hairy wolfhound, who bounded up to me, jumping up and licking me excitedly as I tried to retain my balance. This friendly mutt was always pleased to see me. *Samuel should take a leaf out of his book,* I thought, smiling. I remembered the rock with the carved, unreadable name that Sam had accidentally stumbled over. It must have been 'J-A-S' —the stone having been placed to mark the poor dog's grave.

My mind wandered back to Sam. It seemed ages since I last saw him, and the likelihood of ever seeing him again was growing increasingly remote. I was destined to end my days here in the past, with a family that were all in grave danger of dying before the year was out and their son, who desperately needed treatment for depression before he killed someone—namely, me. Reaching into my jeans pocket, I took out the locket and flipped it open. *Who is this woman? Could it be Charlotte? I dare not ask Samuel. Maybe Hannah would recognize her?* The sun came out from behind a cloud and bathed me in its warm embrace, striking the locket in my hand and the portrait of the mystery woman.

Within seconds, I began to feel dizzy, and a blinding white light followed by total darkness engulfed me, as I was sent spinning and turning through a black void, falling faster and faster into its depths, but never reaching the bottom.

I shut my eyes tightly, praying for the nightmare to end, which it did as suddenly as it had began. My first thoughts were that I had suffered some kind of blackout, as I slowly opened my eyes and found myself to be lying face down on the ground. My heart and head were thumping in unison, as I sat up and looked about me. My eyes fell upon the derelict ruins of Mill Cottage, covered in ivy, and the realization of what had just happened hit me. I had returned to the future.

Chapter Eight

Rising to my feet, I slowly approached the cottage. Pushing open the wooden door, I stared into the room where, just minutes ago, I had been preparing the family's breakfast over an open fire. Now there was just a cold, empty room—no table with its candlesticks, no bench with its pretty handmade cushions, and no roaring fire in the grate. They were all gone, along with the family that I had grown so fond of these past few days. Now they were just ghosts of the past… dead and long forgotten.

I should have been feeling ecstatic to have finally found my way home. It was what I wanted, so why did I feel this emptiness inside—this *sadness*? Walking back outside, I went over to the food hamper. After all this time, the sandwiches and fruit had gone bad and needed disposing of quickly, as did the stone cold coffee in the flask, now covered by a furry green slime. I made my way back to the road, in deep thought, with an armful of cleaning accessories, stopping to pick up the discarded weeding knife and box of opened bulbs by the huge pear tree. *Elizabeth's little twig. She would have been so proud!*

I suddenly remembered Sam and reached into my pocket for the cell phone, which now showed a strong, clear signal. Dialling his number, I was immediately transferred to voice mail and left him a message to phone me back urgently. He did, just as I was loading the last of my stuff into a rather dirty-looking Betsy.

"Emily!" Sam's panicky voice screamed at me from the other end of the line. "Where have you been? I've been ringing your cell phone for ages, and calling your flat leaving messages. Why didn't you reply? I was on the verge of phoning the police and reporting you missing!"

"Sam, something happened. I need to talk to you," I interrupted.

"What?"

"I can't say on the phone. Are you home?"

"I'll be home next weekend. We can talk then," he replied abruptly.

"NO! No, I need to talk to you *now,*" I cried down the phone. I could hear the bewilderment in Sam's voice.

"Okay, but you will have to come to the university. Are you still in Littleham?"

"Yes, I can take a turn off the motorway and come down to you. Not sure how long I'll be, but I'm coming." I assured him.

"It's Wordsworth Hall, second floor, room 2020. Just ask if you can't find it." I hung up before he could ask me any awkward questions. This definitely wasn't something I wanted to discuss over the phone.

Driving back into the village, I hesitated at the turning that took me to the motorway. The left hand indicator blinked expectantly as the car sat motionless in the road. The loud hooting of a car horn behind me made me jump, and I thrust the gear into first and drove forward into the High Street, waving apologetically to the confused driver behind me. After parking the car, I walked purposefully along the pavement and up the side street to the little parish church. I needed to confirm my fears.

Searching frantically among the old gravestones, I finally came upon a group, clumped together and hardly visible under the ivy that had invaded the area. A lump rose in my throat as the name, *Sarah Howerd, aged 2* screamed out at me from one of its crumbling faces. The next read, *Elizabeth Howerd, aged 8* and, *Oh my God!* There was *Charles and Hannah Howerd* too, over by the church wall.

Tears streamed down my face as I turned away and stumbled blindly over the uneven ground. I must have caught my foot in a stray bramble because, the next moment, I was sent sprawling across the ground and came to an abrupt halt against a gravestone, grazing my arm on its rough edges.

"Damn it!" I cried, getting back on my feet cautiously and throwing an annoyed glance at the stone as I did so. My heart gave an enormous thud, as the words emblazoned on the stone hit me like a sledgehammer.

'Here lieth the body of Samuel Howerd. Departed this life December 16th 1696. May he at last find peace.'

I gave out an anguished cry and sat back down on the grass in shock. He was to die the same year that I was there. *Did he pass away from contracting the TB? Or something more sinister?* Whatever it was, the thought of him dying stirred unsettling feelings within me, alongside a determination to return and save the life of this troublesome man.

I arrived at the university as night began to fall and, after some directional advice, I finally found myself outside of a door numbered 2020. I knocked and stood back, biting my lip, not relishing the conversation that was to follow. The door opened, and Sam's familiar face stared back at me defiantly. He found it hard to be angry with me for long. The fact that no harm had befallen me soon overcame his earlier displeasure at my inability to return his calls.

"You found me, then. Come in. Excuse the mess," he said hurriedly, clearing a spot on the end of his bed. "Coffee? Tea? Vodka?"

"Coffee would be wonderful! It's so good to see you again. I thought I never would." Sam looked at me, puzzled, and filled the kettle.

"So, come on, then. Tell me what you've done this time," said Sam, laughing. The serious expression on my face told him it was no laughing matter, and he dropped the sarcastic grin. I waited until he had made the coffee, and then gestured for him to sit down, warning him that what I was about to tell him might seem a little '*surreal*', but every word was the absolute truth.

As my tale unfolded, Sam listened in silence, his eyes growing increasingly wider as I told him about the family that once lived in Mill Cottage, and their trials and tribulations.

"... And then I was back here in the future," I said, at long last ending the bizarre account of my journey back in time. Sam just sat there, dumbstruck, his mouth slightly agape as he tried to comprehend what he had just heard. Studying my face intently for a few moments, he frowned, as something caught his attention.

"That's a nasty gash on the side of your face, Emily. How did that happen?"

"I think I fell against the pear tree when everything went dark. It was pretty bad at the time, but they cared for me well."

"You hit your head?" Sam said slowly, and I could see where his thoughts were heading.

"Sam, I'm not making this up! It really happened!" I cried in dismay at the uncertainty in his voice.

"Come on, Emily. Get real. You were just knocked unconscious, had a vivid dream, and then you woke up '*seemingly*' back here."

"No! No! That's not true! Why don't you believe me? I *was* in 1696. I was!" Sam raised his eyebrow and took a sip of coffee.

"Time travel just isn't possible—not yet, anyway. Maybe someday in the distant future." He moved closer to me on the bed, putting a caring arm around my shoulder. "Don't you think it's time you saw someone about all these hallucinations, Emily? I can put you in touch with people that can help." I stared back at him, horrified. *My one true friend thinks I am a head case in need of a shrink! God help me!*

An awkward silence prevailed for some time, as I thought over what he had said. *Is it possible that I have imagined it all?* He gave me niggling doubts. Then I suddenly remembered the locket.

"Here, look at this! This is what sent me back to 1696. The sunlight on the girl's face somehow triggers the time switch!" I cried, thrusting the locket in front of Sam's face. He pushed it away, shaking his head.

"Stop it, Emily, for goodness sake. Get a grip."

"Fine. Don't believe me, then," I retorted angrily. "I'm going to return and try and save the family, with or without your help."

"Save the family from what?" asked Sam curiously.

"The consumption that is slowly killing them all." Sam laughed at the ridiculous statement.

"How the hell can you do that?"

"Medicines, antibiotics, painkillers…I don't know. What is it they treat sufferers with?"

"They use a concoction of 4 or 5 different antibiotics over a course of 6-9 months. They aren't available over the counter. It's a prescribed drug." Sam informed me. "So you would have to bring them all back with you and admit them to hospital!" Sam was trying hard not to laugh. I stood up, tears pricking the backs of my eyes. I was humiliated and knew he was right. I had no hope of curing these people. I could only try and prevent the spread of the disease. "Where are you going?" asked Sam as I went to leave.

"Back home to my flat, of course. Where do you think?"

"Emily, don't go back down to the cottage anymore. Sell the place. Get rid of it. It's making you ill." I smiled at him and opened the door, ignoring the last comment intentionally.

"Bye, Sam."

On the long journey back home in the dark, I contemplated the situation. I understood and forgave him for not believing my story. If it had been the other way around, I doubted I would have supported him either. The details of my experience were far too real to be passed off as a dream or an illusion, and I was absolutely convinced that what I experienced was fact, not fiction. I *had* met the Howerd family and confronted their troubled son Samuel. I *had* lived, for a while, in 1696.

Opening the door to my flat, late that night, I dumped everything in a heap on the floor and went to have a shower. It was heaven to at last wash the dirt and dried blood from my hair, and put on my comfortable dressing gown. *The wound has healed up nicely*, I thought, as I studied it in the mirror for the first time. I must have looked quite a state while I was there, though. Making myself a hot drink, I flopped onto the sofa, exhausted. Looking around my room, I found myself comparing the luxuries I possessed to the bare necessities that the Howerd's had in their home, and felt a sense of guilt. Every item I owned I could, if I wanted to, live without. There were far more important issues in life, I had discovered, than materialistic belongings. Sighing, I dragged myself off to bed. It was back to work tomorrow, and I seriously doubted my ability to concentrate on the job at hand. I couldn't discuss this with anyone there. If Sam had wanted to refer me to a psychiatrist, my work buddies would have me institutionalized on the spot.

Turning over, I gazed up at the ceiling, unable to sleep. My thoughts wandered to Samuel, not for the first time that day. There was something about that guy, other than his deplorable nature, that struck a chord. He was like a challenge—a seemingly impossible task, you might think, but one that I wanted to undertake despite the consequences. I refused to believe that I felt anything else for this intolerable man, with his long dark curls and fiery passion. I wanted him to find peace with himself *before* he died.

As soon as I walked into the office the following morning, I knew that it had been a bad idea to come in. My mind was totally shot to pieces, and I found it hard to focus on anything at all. The boss noticed my lack of enthusiasm and, by Wednesday, he had called me into the office for a friendly chat.

"Why don't you take a couple of weeks off, Emily? Perhaps whatever is troubling you will be sorted by then, and you can return to work in a more *productive* mood?" he suggested sympathetically. I decided to accept his offer, knowing I was of no use to anyone here in my present state of mind, and collected my things eagerly. I was now free to return to Mill Cottage. This time, I would go prepared.

Over the next two days I gathered together a few essentials for myself, and a bagful of non-prescription drugs like painkillers for fever, cough syrup, antiseptic, and various creams and ointments. I also visited a charity shop and purchased an assortment of long dresses, shawls and boots that were plain, although I did also buy one rather beautiful silk dress in a deep blue, which I would keep for best, if such an occasion arose. Everything was packed into a brown leather carryall for its journey back in time. I wouldn't be taking my cell phone this time. Instead, I added to the bag a small digital camera, intent on taking a few discrete photos, to prove to Sam that I was telling the truth and not going insane. I also left a note under his door for when he returned, telling him where I had gone and that I would return with proof sometime in the near future.

The next few days brought atrocious weather, with heavy grey skies and torrential rain. It was pointless going down there, as I now realized the sun played an important part in my transition. Without it, I wasn't going anywhere. I began to get anxious as the time passed, wondering what might have happened in my absence. *How were Sarah and Elizabeth? And Samuel?* He must have missed me being around, but then again, he was probably glad that I had left. *It will be interesting to see his reaction on my return*, I thought, smiling to myself.

Tuesday, thankfully, dawned bright and sunny with clear skies. After having a good breakfast and a last cup of coffee, I slipped into my newly acquired long dress. It was a simple design, in dark green cotton with a sash that tied around the back. Even so, I looked overdressed compared to Hannah's plain frock, but it would have to do. I added a knitted cream shawl and brown boots to finish off the *'look'*, feeling like I was about to play the part of an extra in some period drama. Fortunately, no one was around to see me as I put the leather carryall into my car and hastily slid into the driving seat, tucking the long gown under my legs so as not to interfere with the pedals. I placed the locket safely into a holder by the gear stick, and began the long journey to Littleham once more.

On arrival, I parked Betsy well off the road among some bushes. I didn't know for sure how long I would be away and secured it well with a safety steering lock. Not wanting to be too near Mill Cottage when I '*appeared*', I walked a little way along the road, grasping the carryall in one hand and hitching up my dress with the other, until I found a suitable place. Looking up into the sky to locate the sun's direction, I clasped the carryall tightly to my body and slowly opened the locket, tilting it slightly to catch the sun's rays upon the portrait. Although I knew now what to expect, the actual experience never failed to take my breath away, and scare me half to death, leaving me nauseous and light-headed for several minutes after. A small price to pay for such a unique experience.

I tentatively approached Mill Cottage and saw John sitting on the doorstep, looking pensive, as he toiled with a stick, prodding it repeatedly into the muddy ground. He looked up and saw me almost immediately, throwing his stick in the air as he ran over, flinging his arms around my neck and hugging me so tight I could hardly breathe.

"Miss Emily, you have returned to us! Why did you leave us? Where did you go?" I smiled at the lad warmly, ruffling his tousled brown hair affectionately.

"I'm sorry, John…I had to go somewhere important, but I'm back now!" I replied, not wanting to elaborate on my disappearance too much. "How is everyone? Sarah, Elizabeth…are they well?" John's face took on a more somber expression and his eyes dropped to the ground.

"The Lord has taken them both, Miss Emily. They cried out for you in their final moments. You should have *been* here. You should have comforted them as they departed this life." Tears welled up in my eyes at the thought of the two girls crying out for me, their call going unanswered. I pulled John towards me in an embrace, as the tears flowed freely onto his hair. There are no words to describe what I felt at that moment.

"Where's Hannah?" I finally asked, wiping away my tears on the corner of my shawl. John nodded towards the cottage, and I went inside, adjusting my eyes to the dim light within. Hannah sat by the fire, staring unseeingly into the flickering flames, her hands tightly clasped upon her lap. She was unaware of my presence, and I was able to observe her in the fire's glow. Such sadness and despair etched upon her pale features. It tore at my already broken heart. "Hannah," I called softly. "It's me, Emily." She raised her head slowly and looked at me for a moment, before returning her gaze to the fire in silence. "I'm so sorry," I choked. "I didn't mean to leave you…I *wouldn't* have left you, if I had known that…" My voice trailed off. Nothing I said was going to bring back the girls. I turned and went back outside, the guilt weighing heavily upon my shoulders. "Where's Charles?" I asked John.

"My father is up at the mill, but Samuel is around by the barn, if it is him you seek." Having given me this unwanted piece of information, he wandered off to join his sister Mary, over by the stream.

I stood there for a minute, unsure of what to do. I wasn't the family's favorite person at the moment, and Samuel would probably tear me to shreds. *Dared I go and see him? Or wait until he encounters me?* I decided to get it over with. I was already upset, and he couldn't make me feel any more wretched than I already did.

Leaving my carryall by the door, I walked cautiously around to the back of the cottage. A large barn with a straw roof nestled among the trees close by. Outside, on a stool, sat Samuel. It looked like he was shaving, judging by the flat blade he wielded in one hand. He moved it expertly down the side of his face, before swishing it about in a bowl on the ground. *Perhaps this isn't such a good idea,* I thought, as the knife glinted menacingly in the sunlight. Against my better judgment, however, I walked nearer to him, watching him intently through the trees as he completed the task at hand, and threw away the water from the bowl. I must have trodden on a small twig at that point, as a loud '*snap*' beneath me caused me to freeze on the spot, my heart in my mouth. Like a wild animal, his acute sense of hearing latched onto the sound, and he immediately spun round, finding me easily, despite my green dress, which I had hoped would camouflage me against the bushes. I think I took him by surprise, because he just stared at me for a while, before going inside the barn. His reaction unnerved me, as I was fully prepared for a confrontation. Not to be outdone, I took a deep breath and followed him into the barn.

Inside, it was gloomy and musty. Shafts of intermittent light shone through holes in the walls, enabling me to see that the barn was stacked from floor to ceiling, with hay and straw. A rough ladder reached up to a higher platform where more straw was stored. Several woollen blankets lay strewn among the bales, and I guessed it was where the boys and men slept. It was quiet—too quiet. Suddenly, the barn doors slammed shut. My heart pounding wildly, I tried to see in the dim light if anyone was there, *or is it just the wind?*

"Hello?" I called out nervously, "is anyone there? Samuel, is that you?" No one answered. "Samuel! I know you're in here. Stop playing around," I cried out again, my voice showing signs that I was growing increasingly alarmed. Without warning, I was grabbed from behind. An arm went across my neck, forcing my head back, and I felt the cold blade of a knife pressed against my throat.

Chapter Nine

A familiar voice growled low and threatening into my ear as I struggled, unsuccessfully, to distance myself from the blade. I couldn't believe he would actually hurt me, but now was not the time to speculate.

"Why do you return to us? Have you not brought enough misery to this family already, or is it your intention to kill us all?" I tried to reply, but I could only utter a few inaudible sounds, before he dropped the blade and spun me around to face him, one hand securely holding onto a clump of my hair. With his face only inches away from mine, I was forced to look up into his dark eyes. For a moment, I was totally distracted as to what I intended to say. Our close proximity appeared to unnerve him also, and he pushed me roughly away, causing me to stumble and fall backwards onto a heap of straw.

"I went to try and find help to cure the girls of the illness that threatened their lives!" I cried, still lying in a crumpled heap on the ground.

"You succeeded in your venture, I see," he replied sarcastically.

"There is no cure, Samuel, but the spread of the disease can be prevented by keeping the affected person away from other people. Does anyone else show any signs, like coughing and fever?" I asked, getting up rather awkwardly from the floor and becoming tangled in the folds of the long dress in doing so. Samuel watched me thoughtfully, enjoying my humiliation and also the large amount of flesh I was unwittingly exposing. Once upright, I straightened my dress and brushed off the straw erratically in an effort to hide my embarrassment. "Well? Is there anyone?" I asked again, trying to sound unperturbed by the effect this guy was having on me.

"My mother has had the cough these past weeks, and I have heard her speak of Eliza having a fever, although it is of no concern to me what ails them…or whether they live or die."

"You don't mean that! How can you say such awful things?" I said, shocked at his callousness.

"I speak it because it is true," he replied angrily.

"You speak it because you are afraid to show that you care! All this hatred and bitterness in you is just a charade. I can help you, Samuel…I *want* to help you." *Why?* I asked myself at this point, *was it because I was beginning to feel something other than friendship for him?* I had an overwhelming desire to hold him in my arms and comfort his tormented soul until all the hurt had melted away. I wanted to say it. I wanted him to know how I felt, but it would have been absolute madness on my part to reveal my true feelings.

"I have heard enough of your foolish sentimentalities!" shouted Samuel, striding towards the door of the barn and throwing it open.

"Where are you going?" I demanded.

"God forbid, woman, you are *not* my wife, therefore I am not obliged to state my intentions to you."

"I know, but—" I began.

"Is it your intent to be here on my return?" He interrupted, untying the reins of his horse from a low branch.

"You are not my *husband*, so I am not obliged to reply to that question." I said, smiling mischievously. He was not amused. "Yes, I'll be here," I added solemnly.

"Then I shall endeavor to go out of my way to avoid your company," he said seriously, before mounting his black stallion and riding off through the trees. I felt as if a knife had just stabbed me through the heart. I wandered back to the cottage feeling dejected. *Maybe I was trying too hard? Maybe, if I avoided him, he would come looking for me?* All the enthusiasm had been sucked out of me, and I couldn't really care less at that moment. Men were just as insolent in 1696!

There was no sign of Hannah inside. The children had also disappeared, so I sat down at the table and poured myself a mug of mead from the large jug by the fireside. I was thirsty, and as this was the only substance available, I had to endure its taste although, surprisingly, I was beginning to grow accustomed to the unusual flavor.

My somber thoughts were disturbed by the arrival of Charles who had, it appeared, been informed of my return. There was something different about him. The sparkle had gone from his eyes, and his mood was disturbingly morose. He joined me at the table with a drink.

"I fear for the life of my wife and baby. They will not see out the end of the month," he told me when I inquired after his health. "This disease will take us all, of that I am certain. May God spare us undue suffering, so that we will pass quickly and be at peace." I reached across the table and laid my hand on his before an idea came to me.

"Is there anywhere the children can go?" I asked softly. "An aunt, maybe? Or an uncle that lives some distance from here? Somewhere they could stay for a while until this disease has passed?"

"I have a sister and a niece that live in Edgebarton, some 20 miles from here. I have not spoken with her in many months, but I am sure, given the nature of my request, that she would take them in until it is safe to return home."

"Then we must get them there as soon as possible!" I cried, and was about to say that I would drive them there in my car, but I bit my lip just in time, avoiding any unnecessary questions regarding the meaning of the word '*car*'.

"I will prepare the cart for the journey. It will take us near on four hours to arrive, so make sure the children have nourishment and warm clothing," said Charles, before hurrying around to the barn.

"Where *are* the children?" I called after him.

"Behind you!" he replied. I turned around and was surprised to see all six children lined up, awaiting direction.

They had obviously been listening in on our conversation and approved our decision.

"Is it true we are going away to stay with Aunt Elizabeth, Miss Emily?" Asked William, eagerly.

"Will Miss Isabelle be there? I *like* her. She is so pretty!" cried Mary.

"You will travel with us, Miss Emily? Please say you will!" begged Ellen, hopping about on one foot excitedly. I smiled at their flushed faces and ushered them inside.

"Come along now, you must all have something to eat and pack some clothes for your stay. Yes, Ellen, I will be traveling with your father, and I'm looking forward to meeting your aunt… and this *Miss Isabelle*." I took John to one side and asked him quietly about his mother. He informed me that she had moved into her late sister's cottage with Eliza, as not to spread the sickness, and would only let his father attend to her. With John's help we managed to rustle together some bread, cheese, milk and half a cooked chicken, which had been roasted a few days before and was now somewhat dry. I dreaded to think of the amount of bacteria that had accumulated on the bird, but John assured me that it was good to eat and added it to the table. Needless to say, I avoided this particular delight, as my immune system would have freaked out.

After we had all eaten our fill, I helped the girls' sort out some clothes to take, while John took care of the boys' needs. It didn't take us long, as each girl only possessed two frocks—one cotton and one woollen, a shawl, nightdress and mop cap, plus a bonnet for church. All this was easily packed into a small wooden chest and loaded onto the back of the cart, which Charles had brought around to the front with his and John's brown horses in harness.

"Get into the cart, everyone. Emily, you will ride up front with me," said Charles, taking my hand and helping me up onto the bare wooden board that served as a seat. I called to Joseph to fetch me one of the cushions from the bench.

The thought of bouncing up and down on *that* for four hours brought tears to my eyes! "I must see to my wife and child before we leave," whispered Charles. "I will not delay our journey long."

"Of course you must," I replied. Watching him go, I felt saddened that this kind and caring man had to endure such hardship, with even more grief soon to be bestowed upon him, as his much loved wife and daughter would soon be cruelly taken away.

The excited chatter from the children waiting in the cart reached a crescendo, and I was forced to raise my voice a little to quieten them down.

"You sound like our mother, Miss Emily!" William laughed from the back.

"I wish you *were* our mother," said Mary wistfully.

"Don't say that! You have a wonderful mother who loves you all very much," I replied sternly.

"But she is going to die soon, isn't she? Just like Aunt Mary did, and Elizabeth—*and* Sarah," wailed William. The cart fell silent. I didn't need to reply. They all knew what was coming. Charles reappeared from the cottage and walked slowly towards us, his head bowed. I watched him approach, fearing the worst.

"What is it?" I asked shakily, "Has she…?" He shook his head.

"No, but her condition has worsened. I cannot leave her alone at this time. She is too frail."

"Who will take us then, father?" asked Mary, almost in tears. John stood up and leapt to the ground.

"Shall I fetch Samuel, father? He can handle the horses as well as you." I stared at him in horror. *What was he saying? He would never agree to it—not once he saw me here!*

"Yes, John. Hasten and bring your brother here, quickly!" urged Charles. John ran off in the direction of the mill, while I sat there feeling increasingly nauseous. *This is all going horribly wrong.* I suggested to Charles that I stay behind and tend to Hannah, but he wouldn't hear of it, and so I resigned myself to what was going to be an interesting confrontation when Samuel arrived.

It seemed like an eternity before I finally heard the sounds of a fast approaching horse, and Samuel's black stallion galloped to an abrupt halt beside the cart, causing the horse to rear up and nearly throw John to the ground as he clung onto his brother's cloak. *Here we go*, I thought. *Five...four... three....*

"WHAT THE HELL IS *SHE* DOING HERE?" shouted Samuel, dismounting from his steed.

"Miss Emily will be accompanying you and the children to Edgebarton," stated Charles calmly. "They are all ready to go, and if you leave now, you will arrive before nightfall."

"I will not travel in the company of this woman!" raged Samuel. "Either she remains here, or I will decline your request."

"Look...I think it's better that I stay here." I interrupted, beginning to climb down from the cart.

"You will do no such thing. Stay where you are!" demanded Charles, clearly at the end of his tether with his rebellious son. A hostile argument followed for several minutes, which would have resulted in them coming to blows, if it hadn't been for John's interference.

"Why does Samuel dislike you so, Miss Emily?" whispered Mary, as she clung onto my sleeve protectively. I shrugged helplessly. Even I was at a loss as to the extent of his revulsion for me. Finally, a compromise was agreed upon. I was to travel in the back of the cart, on the floor with the children, and John was to ride up front with Samuel. He clearly was still not happy with this arrangement, but John made him relent, if only for his father's sake. I clambered into the back of the cart with my cushion, and sat down between Joseph and William on the dirty floor, smiling apologetically for causing so much disruption to their travel plans. With a loud shout from Samuel, and the crack of a whip, the horses lurched forward, and we began the long and uncomfortable journey to Edgebarton.

There wasn't much to see for the first hour—mile upon mile of thick woodland lined the thoroughfare on both sides. I would have nodded off, if it hadn't been for the numerous deep ruts and small rocks that littered the road, causing the cart to veer sharply and bump over frequent obstacles along the way, throwing me violently this way and that. It was a good two hours or more before Samuel steered the tired horses into a small inn just off the road, where he handed the reins to a man and disappeared into the tavern without speaking. John saw to the horses and followed his brother inside, leaving us alone and cold in the back of the cart, as the sun dipped low behind the trees. It would be dark within the hour, and I did not relish undertaking much more of this journey along these treacherous lanes. I took off my shawl and laid it over Mary, who was now sprawled out across my lap, sound asleep, and looked longingly into the small latticed windows of the inn. A roaring fire inside flickered its welcoming red and orange glow onto the glass, and the sound of men's lecherous laughter and merry chatter echoed out through the half-open door, into the descending cold night air. We waited patiently for over half an hour, and I was just on the verge of going inside to fetch them, when John appeared and handed me a large warm loaf and a bottle of red wine.

"It's all they had," he said. "It will warm you up for the rest of the journey." I took the food hesitantly. *Surely he didn't expect the children to drink the wine? Did he want us to all arrive in a drunken stupor? What kind of example would that set for Elizabeth?* I broke off segments of the crusty loaf and shared it around to those who were still awake.

"I'm thirsty," whined Joseph, eyeing the bottle in my hand.

"Only a little sip then," I replied, removing the lid and holding the bottle to his parched lips. I took several mouthfuls myself after, hoping that the strong aroma would wear off before we arrived. Samuel joined us soon after, staggering slightly as he climbed up and took hold of the reins. I eyed him nervously, hoping that he was still sober enough to control the horses, and that we wouldn't all end up face-down in some muddy ditch along the way.

Thankfully, the second part of the trip was much shorter. Within half an hour we were on the outskirts of Edgebarton. The lighted lamps in the windows of cottages grew in number as we approached the town, their beacons of light casting an eerie glow through the descending fog, but they were a welcome sight for the weary traveller. The horses took a sharp turn to the left, through a tall gate, and along a cobbled path. I strained my eyes to see through the fog as Samuel brought the horses to a gentle stop in front of a large stone building.

"Are we there?" I inquired eagerly from the back.

"This is our aunt's house," replied John, jumping down. "I will knock and tell her of my father's request for lodgings." With that, he disappeared through the fog, whereupon a rapping of a door knocker could be heard, followed shortly after by squeals of delight as a door was opened.

A low, mumbled conversation followed as John told his aunt of the family's demise.

"For goodness sake! Bring them in at once before they catch their death!" cried a woman's voice that I took to be Elizabeth's. Relieved, I woke up the children and handed them down to John, one by one, and he took them inside. I was left standing alone in the cart, debating which was the easiest way to get down without any assistance.

"Are you getting down or what?" Asked Samuel impatiently, as he stood by the side of the cart.

"If you were a gentleman, you would help me down," I said wearily.

"If you were a lady, I might oblige," he replied dryly, making eye contact with me for the first time that evening.

"What's that supposed to mean?" I asked indignantly.

"I thought that was obvious," he sneered, before walking away into the house.

"Arrogant bastard," I muttered under my breath, as I scrambled to the front of the cart and carefully negotiated my way down, tearing my dress slightly on a rough splinter of wood and cursing him even more.

Upon entering the house, it was immediately apparent that these people had money. The furnishings and draperies were in stark contrast to the bare squalor of Mill Cottage. Charles' sister had done well for herself—*maybe married into money?* Whatever it was, the children would benefit greatly from their stay here. I watched the happy family reunion from a quiet corner by the door, until John saw me and dragged me into the limelight.

"Aunt Elizabeth, this is Miss Emily," he said proudly, thrusting me in front of his aunt for her inspection. She wasn't what I expected. A small lady of ample girth, with round rosy cheeks and a friendly smile. I liked her instantly and smiled back, as she bobbed her head in acknowledgment, before extending her chubby hand towards me.

"Delighted to make your acquaintance," she said hesitantly, the smile vanishing from her face, as she stared at me for a moment with a puzzled expression. Her eyes wandered questionably over to Samuel and back again.

There were footsteps on the staircase behind, which drew our attention to a young lady that descended them elegantly. She was about my age. Her long blonde hair cascaded in soft ringlets over her milky white shoulders, and her beautiful pink satin dress clung to her equally beautiful body. I needed no introduction. This was most certainly the infamous *Isabelle*. Samuel stepped forward immediately and bowed graciously to her. This gesture was returned with a curtsy and a shy, flirtatious smile. I can safely say, from that moment, I took a firm dislike of the girl for all the wrong reasons. Her mother turned to introduce her to me, whereupon the young woman cried out in astonishment, and her slender hand rose to cover her perfectly formed red lips.

"I do beg your pardon, Miss Emily," she said sweetly, her vivid blue eyes open wide like saucers, "but for a moment I thought you—"

"Isabelle, my dear," interrupted her mother nervously; "I think it is time to get the children to bed after their long journey. Could you show them to their rooms while I prepare some supper for us?"

"Certainly, mother," replied Isabelle, as she went to usher the children up the staircase.

"I'll come and help you, Isabelle," I called after her. "They may settle quicker with a more familiar face." She smiled back down at me and beckoned for me to follow. There was something puzzling me, and I needed to get Isabelle on her own in order to clarify a few points. The children had woken up, and were now racing excitedly around the top floor of the house, as I helped Isabella collect fresh linen and prepare the beds.

"Who did you mistake me for—downstairs in the hall just now?" I asked her when we were alone.

"I thought Miss Charlotte, Samuel's intended, had returned. You gave me quite a turn, I can tell you," she explained, laughing as she handed me the corner of a heavy tapestry bed cover.

"Am I similar, then, to this Charlotte?" I asked curiously.

"Why, Miss Emily, you are the very image of her, if I say so myself. Has not Master Samuel mentioned it to you?" I shook my head and reached into my pocket, bringing out the gold pendant that resided there. I opened it up and handed it to Isabelle.

"Is *this* Charlotte?" She seemed to recognize the pendant immediately and looked at me in surprise.

"Yes, this is her. Where did you get this, if I may ask?"

"I found it," I replied honestly. "Buried in the ground." Isabelle dropped the bedclothes and sat down heavily on the side of the bed.

"I was with Miss Charlotte, in town, when she had this painted. It was to be a wedding present for Samuel. On the day she disappeared, she left it for him on the table at Mill Cottage." Isabelle had a faraway look on her face. "It was such a shock for everyone."

"What happened? Why did she disappear?" I urged, joining her on the bed.

"They say she was with child, the father being the son of some wealthy gentleman down from London, whom her affections were bestowed upon most ardently. Unable to tell Samuel the reasons for her change of mind, she ran away with her lover, and neither have been heard of since. I am ashamed to say that my feelings were ones of elation, on hearing that they would not be betrothed, for I have always carried a torch for Samuel Howerd—at least since our childhood—in the hope that, one day, he might think of me as someone other than just a mere acquaintance. No one was more pleased to see him tonight than I. Please do not think badly of me, Miss Emily, for I cannot lie to my heart." I smiled weakly at her, but could not find the words of comfort she desperately wanted to hear from me.

We continued to make the beds in silence. My mind was all over the place, piecing together bits of the jigsaw, and coming to terms with Isabelle's confession. So, that would explain why Samuel couldn't bear to be near me—I reminded him too much of the woman he loved...and lost. As for Isabelle, and her plans for seducing her childhood sweetheart from under my nose, it just wasn't going to happen! I was thankful that we would be returning to Littleham after supper, and any temptation that Samuel might feel for this beautiful blonde temptress would be thwarted. The claws were well and truly out!

Getting the overtired children to bed had proved to be a much more difficult task than first anticipated. It was almost 10pm when we finally joined Elizabeth, Samuel, and John around a large oval table in the dining room. Isabelle made a beeline for the seat opposite Samuel, while I took the remaining vacant chair, next to John, at the far end. From here, I could observe the reactions of both parties without being too obvious.

"Why didn't you tell me?" I hissed quietly into John's ear.

"Tell you what?" asked John, taking a sip of white wine from a delicate glass.

"That I was Charlotte's double."

"Double?"

"Yes, you know, her twin, exact look-alike... replica of her!"

"Ah, that," he replied, getting the gist of what I was implying, and glancing nervously at Samuel, whose attention was captured by Isabelle's rendition of her trip to London earlier in the year. "Samuel forbade me from telling you. He has his reasons, no doubt, and I for one do not question his motives," whispered back John, "I'm sorry Emily."

"It's all right. I understand."

I tucked in hungrily. The roast ham was delicious, as was the large selection of cheeses, cakes and biscuits adorning the table. The warmth from the roaring log fire was making me feel drowsy, and I looked at the clock on the mantelpiece, noticing that it was now well past eleven.

"We will have to be leaving soon, Elizabeth. It will be the early hours of the morning before we arrive home as it is," I said, ignoring the dismayed look on Isabelle's face.

"My dear girl, there is no way I would let you travel back home tonight. Highwaymen would accost you before you had ridden three miles in these parts. No. You and Samuel must stay here tonight. I will hear no more about it. More wine?" Isabelle's smug face made me want to throw the wine over her immaculate dress, and push her perfect, doll-like features face down into the dish of sticky marmalade. Jealousy, I discovered, made you think in strange and mysterious ways!

Chapter Ten

It was Aunt Elizabeth's ludicrous idea that I should share a bed with Isabelle that night. Suddenly the back of the cart seemed so much more appealing. The one good thing was that I wouldn't have to lie there all night, worrying if Samuel was embarking on any moonlit excursions down the corridor to her room. If he did, he was in for one heck of a surprise.

Isabelle graciously loaned me one of her white cotton nightshirts, and I crawled into bed beside her, exhausted from the day's journey. I had hoped that she would fall asleep quickly, and I wouldn't have to indulge in polite conversation until the early hours. *How wrong I was!* Starved of young company to express her feelings to, she took this opportunity to unburden her pent-up emotions and tell me all about her infatuation with Samuel. I lie there watching the mesmerizing flicker of the candle on the bedside table, as she droned on and on about the love of her life, and how she intended to one day become his wife. Little did she know that my affections were also centered on the same raven-haired individual, who slept under the same roof as us that night. I'm not sure if I fell asleep, or if Isabelle eventually stopped talking, but the next thing I knew, it was morning.

Looking at my watch, concealed under the long cotton sleeve of the nightshirt, I realized with horror that it was gone ten o'clock, and the empty space beside me told me that my love rival was already downstairs. I hurriedly dressed, and used the bone-handled hairbrush I found on a nearby dresser to make myself presentable. From the window I could see the children playing happily on the lawn outside, and I desperately hoped that my attempt to change their future would save them from an early grave.

Upon entering the dining room, I found Elizabeth seated by the window sewing.

"Ah! Good morning, Miss Emily. I trust you slept well?"

"Very well, thank you," I replied before sitting down at the table. "Where is everyone?" I asked nonchalantly, taking a piece of freshly baked bread from a platter.

"Well, Master John is feeding the horses. The children, as you hear, are playing outside, and I do believe that Miss Isabelle is taking a turn around the garden with Master Samuel." The knife I was holding clattered noisily to the floor. "Such a handsome couple. I have high hopes that we may indeed hear of an engagement before the year is out," she mused, smiling contentedly to herself. I suddenly lost my appetite and pushed the plate away from me. "Perhaps you would care to try some *tea?* A small packet was sent to me by an acquaintance in London just recently. He runs a coffee house there and told me this new drink was becoming very popular, although I fail to see its appeal."

"I think I'll just get some fresh air. Maybe it will give me an appetite," I said, before standing up and opening the door to the garden.

The fresh air that greeted me was very welcoming. I felt as if I was slowly suffocating inside. I walked down across the lawn and under an archway, which brought me to a small, enclosed square with beds of lavender. In the center stood a stone statue of a woman, holding a large urn, and smiling angelically up to the heavens. A second archway led me to another secluded square that was surrounded by a high hedge. This one had a small pond in the center and a stone seat to the side. I stood for a moment, idly watching a lone goldfish circle the perimeter of the pond, when the distant sound of feminine laughter came to my ears from somewhere in this maze of intricate gardens. I followed the path through a narrow alleyway of tall hedgerows, which eventually thinned out, enabling me to see through to the other side.

Another bout of flirtatious laughter rang out nearby, unmistakably that of Isabelle's. Passing through a gap in the hedge, a vivid splash of pink satin caught my eye in the adjoining square, and I ducked back behind the foliage—out of sight, but still able to observe the couple clearly. There, on an ornate stone seat, sat Samuel with Isabelle. His arm was casually draped along the back of the seat behind her, as she sat daintily on the edge, talking to him in low sensual tones, her blue eyes transfixed on his as she spoke. I could not hear what she was saying from my vantage point, but their body language told me they certainly weren't discussing the weather.

As I watched the romantic scene unfold before me, I began to question my motives for interfering in this love affair. *I shouldn't even be here, for heaven's sake. I had no right to try and change what was meant to be.* Isabelle was probably destined to marry her childhood sweetheart, and my presence here was just complicating the issue. *But wait! What am I thinking? Isn't Samuel supposed to die within the year?* Therefore, his relationship with Isabelle will be very short-lived, if it exists at all. It had been my intention to somehow prevent Samuel's death. If I did this it would allow him to continue his relationship with her, and eventually marry. If I let Samuel die, as fate intended, Isabelle wouldn't get to have him and regretfully, neither would I. Samuel leaned forward, and tenderly removed a stray ringlet that had fallen over her eye. It was strange to see him display affection, and even stranger to see him smile. My heart was aching for those strong hands to touch *me* with such fondness, and I knew then that there was no way I could stand by and watch him die. I was going to have to outwit this cunning vixen, and hopefully persuade Samuel that she was *not* the woman for him.

Isabelle moved closer along the seat and tilted her pretty head, as Samuel encircled his hand behind her slender neck, and drew her towards him. *My God! He's going to kiss her!* As if pushed by some invisible hand, I burst through the hedge upon the unsuspecting couple. Isabelle cried out in fright, and Samuel looked at me as if I'd gone mad.

"Ah! Here you are," I said, as if I had only just discovered them. "Elizabeth told me I would find you in the gardens."

"Did she also tell you to intrude upon our private conversation?" snarled Samuel, his black eyes flashing in the sunlight.

"I'm sorry…it's just that I hate eating alone," I said apologetically.

"Is Elizabeth there?" asked Samuel coldly.

"Yes."

"Then you have your companion," he replied bluntly, turning back to Isabelle, who was looking slightly shocked at his discourteous attitude towards me.

"Perhaps we *should* return to the house, Samuel, I am a little cold," said Isabelle, standing up and linking her arm through mine. "Come, my dear Emily. Let us go and taste some of Mama's tea. It really has the most extraordinary taste." She stopped and looked over her shoulder. "*Do* come along, Samuel. If you behave yourself, we will let you join us." She giggled, squeezing my arm affectionately. I smiled broadly at the priceless expression on his stunned face. This was going to be easier than I thought.

Isabelle and I indulged in the delights of Aunt Elizabeth's homemade bread and expensive tea, which was kept in a silver caddy on the dresser. Samuel, in the meantime, sulked on a wall just outside and refused to take breakfast with us. I asked Elizabeth if I could take some cheese and bread rolls with us for the journey home, as I knew he would be in need of some substance long before we reached Littleham. She obliged willingly by wrapping several items up in a piece of cloth and tying it securely.

"I will also give you a blanket for the journey. That cotton dress will do little against the cold wind. I trust you have warmer garments at home, now December is upon us?" The word '*December*' sent a chill through me, as I recalled a certain gravestone's inscription.

"Actually, no, I haven't," I said, after a moment's hesitation. I thought of my other flimsy dresses within my carryall, not having accounted for the weather turning colder, but even if I had, how would I have found thick woollen evening dresses in charity shops? Elizabeth sighed, went to a drawer within the dresser, and took out a small box. She handed me five strange looking coins from it. I had no idea of their value and looked at her, mystified.

"There is enough there to purchase two warm woollen frocks—three, if you are not particular. Get Master Samuel to take you with him to Greenham, when he rides again to town. I'm sure he will oblige." *I'm sure he won't*, I thought, glancing out of the window at the solitary figure perched on the wall. I thanked Aunt Elizabeth for her generosity, and safely tucked the coins away in my pocket, along with the pendant.

"I think it is time for us to leave," I said, standing up. "Thank you so much for letting us stay, and for the food. I—*we* really appreciate it."

"You are both most welcome to visit with us when you so please, Miss Emily. Master Samuel too, he will be a welcome distraction for Isabelle, for that I am sure." Mental note to self—*stay away from Aunt Elizabeth's house at all costs.*

"We will. Thank you," I said, smiling insincerely.

"And I will visit with you and Charles at Mill Cottage, when the sickness has passed," said Isabelle excitedly. "I am sure Master Samuel will once again enjoy the pleasure of my company." *Not if I can help it,* I thought, going over to the garden door and beckoning to the children. It was harder than I thought to say goodbye to them. Each one took it in turns to give me a hug, and by the time I got to John, I was close to tears.

"Goodbye, Miss Emily. Take care of father for me, and give my love to mother. You will send word to let us know when…?" His voice trailed off.

"Of course I will," I said, hugging him close and kissing his soft sandy hair, as a tear wound its way down my cheek.

I always hated goodbyes. Samuel bowed politely to his aunt and then turned to Isabelle, who was holding a lace handkerchief tightly in her delicate white fingers, and was trembling with emotion. I watched intently as he bowed to her and then took hold of her hand, gently raising it to his lips, before kissing it softly on the back. His eyes looked deep into hers from under his thick black lashes. In all probability, he would never see her again—one way or another.

Once outside, I scrambled quickly up onto the front bench of the cart and reached over the back for my cushion. Samuel was unable to show his disapproval in front of his aunt and Isabelle, and I found great comfort in smiling deviously to him, as he passed around the front of the horses to take his seat up beside me. The contemptuous look he shot me conveyed his thoughts, and I knew I was in for a turbulent ride home to Littleham.

As predicted, a stony silence prevailed for the first ten minutes of our journey. I didn't really mind. Finally being rid of the irritating Isabelle, and sitting close to Samuel, far outweighed the distinct lack of communication between us—for the time being, anyway. The sun went behind a large cloudbank, and I suddenly felt the chill of the wind through my thin dress. Taking hold of the blanket that Elizabeth had given me, I placed it over my legs and tucked it underneath. Sighing loudly to signify my boredom, I reached for the cloth bag containing the cheese and bread rolls.

"Want something to eat?" I inquired casually, waving a roll in front of him. He looked straight ahead, ignoring my futile attempt to gain his attention. "You must be hungry by now. How about some cheese?" Still no response—not even an icy stare. I began to feel exasperated by his refusal to speak to me, and my temper finally flared. "Look, Samuel. Whether you like it or not, we have to spend the next four hours together, and some civil exchange of words would be much appreciated, or do you intend to ignore me the whole journey?" I waited for some kind of response, but none came, and so I tried another tactic that I felt sure would prompt a reaction. "I *know* why you hate me. It's because I look so much like Charlotte, isn't it?" The horses were immediately reined in and brought to an abrupt halt. *Success, at last!*

"Who told you that?" he demanded angrily.

"Ah! It speaks!" I said sarcastically, but then instantly regretted being so flippant. His hand reached over and took hold of a handful of the thin cotton material around my neck, tearing it as he pulled me forcibly towards him.

"I SAID, WHO TOLD YOU?"

"It was Isabelle, she told me everything," I blurted out, reaching up and covering his hand with mine. "It's all right. I do understand how you feel, but I'm *not* Charlotte. I'm Emily, and I would never—"

"GET OUT!" he yelled, wrenching my hand away.

"What?"

"GET OUT OF THE CART." I looked at him in astonishment. *Why would he want me to get out?* Jumping down from the bench, he came around to my side in a flash and clasped me roughly about the waist, pulling me from the cart like a sack of potatoes. I was thrown down on the roadside, before he returned to the cart to collect the blanket, which was duly hurled on the ground beside me. "Littleham is that way," he said, pointing up the road ahead, before getting back onto the cart and gathering up the reins.

"You can't leave me here!" I cried, scrambling to my feet in a panic.

"Watch me!" he shouted back, as he commanded the horses to go. I stood there, shocked, as the horses gathered speed rapidly up the dusty road, and took Samuel away into the distance.

"Samuel, come back!" I cried helplessly, as I watched him disappear around a bend and out of sight.

At first, I was fuming that he would be so inconsiderate as to leave me here, miles from anywhere, and then I blamed myself for being foolish enough to open my big mouth in the first place. If I had kept quiet, I would still be on the cart. I picked up the blanket and looked back down the road, and then up it. There wasn't a house in sight—just miles upon miles of countryside and dark woods. I remembered Elizabeth's words of warning; '*Highwaymen would accost you before you had ridden three miles in these parts.*' I suddenly felt very alone and frightened. This was 1696. I couldn't just hail a taxi. Thieves and murderers were rife, and a woman walking alone would be easy prey. I could be raped and left for dead, and no one would care—not even Samuel. I debated whether to turn back and return to Edgebarton, but I would have to explain everything to Aunt Elizabeth and—worse still, have Isabelle defend her beloved Samuel and blame me. *Or I could go on and see what lay ahead. Surely that inn we stopped at on our outward journey was not too far away?* I decided to go for the inn, and began walking along the edge of the road. Stupid, really, I was hardly going to be run down in the rush hour traffic.

The quietness was somewhat unnerving, and I kept thinking that someone was lying in wait for me behind a tree. I didn't have much money on me, but they might take the locket. *My God, if they took that, I would be stranded here forever!* Pulling the blanket around my shoulders, I trudged on, turning frequently to look behind me as paranoia set in. Twice I heard the distant sound of horses' hooves, and dived into a ditch as an unsuspecting traveller rode by. I dared not ask for help from these unknown strangers. It began to rain. My torn dress was soon plastered in mud and the blanket about my shoulders grew heavy from the moisture. *Damn you, Samuel Howerd. Damn you to hell for this! You deserve what's coming to you.*

I must have walked for over two hours when I saw, in the distance, a building of some description. I was in such a state of despair by now that I had little energy left in me to muster much enthusiasm. I was wet through. Rivers of water ran down my hair, adding to the already saturated blanket. Shivering uncontrollably, I stumbled the last half a mile to the now recognizable tavern, and the even more recognizable cart that stood unattended outside.

A roaring fire beckoned me from inside, and I blindly pushed open the door, on the verge of collapse. The smoky atmosphere within took my breath away, as I peered through the hazy fog at my surroundings. There must have been about twenty or so men in there, of various ages. Most had had far too much to drink and were loud and boisterous, falling drunkenly about as women in low-cut dresses plied them with more drink, while being lusted over unashamedly by these unsavory characters. The strong smell of ale and perspiration wafted over me, making me feel nauseous, but I was determined to find a certain individual, that was somewhere in this den of drunken vagabonds. Fighting off lecherous advances, from numerous filthy and unshaven men, only added to my already fragile state as I threaded my way between tables and over broken chairs.

Then I saw him, seated in a dark and secluded corner by the fire. Beside him, on either side, sat two wenches—one with her breasts exposed and nibbling his ear, the other with her hand blatantly between his legs. He appeared unresponsive to the women's obvious attempts to arouse him, and stared into his tankard of ale in deep thought. I just stood there, devoid of any rational thought and dripping onto the wooden floor, until one of the women noticed my existence, which wasn't long.

"Ere, Master Samuel. Looks like some beggar woman be a-wanting you," she sneered, running her hand through his black hair possessively.

"This gentleman has no need for the likes of you, so be gone with you!" said the other, looking in disgust at my sodden clothes. Reluctantly, Samuel slowly raised his eyes and cast them upon me, taking in the pathetic creature that stood before him. He didn't appear to be that surprised to see me. It was almost as if he was expecting me. I looked into his deep brown eyes, which had lost their usual hostile blackness, and were now full of remorse. It was this that finally tipped me over the edge, as I only managed to utter six words.

"I want to go home, Samuel," I said feebly, before dissolving into floods of heart-rending sobs.

I felt too weak to discuss the logic behind what possessed him to do what he did. I was just so relieved to see him again, and to feel safe once more. My head began to spin, and I fell forward onto the table, as one of the women caught me and pulled me down onto the seat just in time.

"Fetch her a warm drink while I go and harness the horses," I heard him say to the woman, who disappeared at once, leaving me with my head down on the table, feeling decidedly ill. Shortly after, a hand rested on my shoulder and gently roused me.

"Here you are, miss. Drink this, and don't you be fretting no more," said an unfamiliar man's voice. I looked up to see an elderly man, holding out a pewter mug for me to take.

"What is it?" I asked, taking the warm mug from him and eyeing it suspiciously.

"It's mulled wine. It will do you good," he replied kind-heartedly. I sipped the warm red liquid. It tasted nice, and I thanked him. "You wouldn't have come to no harm, miss. I saw to that."

"What do you mean?" I asked, puzzled.

"I was to keep out of the way and make sure you were in no danger, miss. Those were me orders."

"Whose orders?"

"Why, Mister Samuel Howard's, miss. A fine gentleman and he pays handsomely, too."

"He *paid* you to watch over me?" I said, not quite believing what I was hearing.

"That he did, although I fail to understand why he treated a lady like yourself so badly. A lover's tiff made him behave so foolishly maybe?"

"We are *not* lovers," I corrected him, taking another long sip of the comforting wine.

"Is that so, miss? Mister Howerd was most adamant that no harm should befall you. His concern for your well-being was that of more than just a mere casual acquaintance."

My head began to spin again. This was all too much to take in, and I laid my head back down onto the table. When I next looked up, he had vanished. Another man was now leering at me over the table, muttering obscene sexual requests through his blackened teeth as he pushed coins, for payment, across the table towards me. The stench from his breath was overpowering, and I recoiled in horror, realizing his intentions. Suddenly, the man was dragged roughly from his seat and thrown aggressively against the tavern bar, as a familiar figure in a black cloak growled obscenities at him, which scared him half to death. Samuel then turned to me, and I shrank back into my seat, terrified that I was next in line.

"I'm ready to leave, if you wish to accompany me?" he said calmly. I scrambled out of the seat quickly and followed him across the room. There was no way I was staying in this God-forsaken place.

Once outside, the cold air made me shake violently, and I just wanted to lie down and go to sleep. Samuel didn't question me, as I climbed into the back of the cart and lay down on the wet and dirty floor, pulling the drenched blanket around me. I felt the cart lurch to one side as Samuel climbed up and into the back. He gently pulled the blanket off of me and replaced it with his own dry cloak. I was too exhausted to be sure, but I swear I heard him whisper, 'forgive me,' before he returned his attention to the horses to continue our journey homewards.

Chapter Eleven

I must have slept all the way back, for when I next awoke, it was getting dark, and we were approaching the rough track to Mill Cottage. My head felt like it was on fire from the fever that had now developed, but I tried to put a smile on my face, as I saw Charles waiting to greet us outside. He helped me down, whilst inquiring why I was traveling in the back, to which I replied that it was *my* choice, as I wanted to sleep to pass the time. Samuel took the cart and horses to the barn. I went inside, clutching his cloak to me like a much-loved teddy bear. My first concern was Hannah and the baby. I was relieved to hear that they were no worse, although their condition had not improved, either, which was sadly expected.

Charles was pleased to hear that the children had settled in well, and that his sister and niece were in good health. The pretence that all was well with me begun to take its toll, and I felt increasingly worried that if I didn't get upstairs to bed soon, I would pass out. Making my excuses, I picked up my carryall and went upstairs before Samuel returned, choosing to sleep in Elizabeth's bed despite the poignant memories it held. Taking two painkiller tablets from my bag, I swallowed them without a drink. It would help lower the fever and, hopefully, by morning it would pass. I threw Samuel's cloak over the bed cover to keep me warm, and I crawled thankfully into bed, after discarding the filthy green dress in a heap on the floor.

The night passed slowly. The fever made me delirious, and I had visions of my parents standing in the doorway, of Sam sitting on my bed making fun of me, and later of Samuel lifting my head gently to give me a much-needed drink. Two of the hallucinations were impossible, and the third very unlikely—or so I thought—until I saw an empty mug beside the bed when I awoke, which hadn't been there the previous evening. Sitting up in bed, I felt my forehead. It was still rather on the warm side, but nothing like it was the evening before. Still, to be on the safe side, I would take another two tablets later.

The sound of footsteps on the staircase made my heart pound, and I pulled the cover up around me at the same time, realizing that Samuel's black cloak was missing from the bed.

"Miss Emily? May I enter?" came Charles' voice from outside the door. I breathed a sigh of relief.

"Yes, come in," I called out. Charles peered cautiously around the door.

"I will be going to the mill now, until noon. Hannah has taken a little breakfast and is comfortable, and Samuel has ridden into Offenham village, declaring that there was something he had to do." He shook his head in bewilderment, "I fear I shall never understand my son." My eyes widened as I remembered the churchyard.

"Charles. What is the date today?" I asked apprehensively.

"I do believe it is the ninth day of the month," he replied, a little puzzled. I thanked him and he left the room, confused, and none the wiser for the reason behind my random request. *Seven days...seven days to go before Samuel would be taken from me. How was I ever going to keep him from harm without declaring how I knew of his impending fate?* Getting up, I walked unsteadily over to my bag and took out a dark red cotton dress with black edging, a black shawl, and dry black boots. I did the best I could with the comb, but my hair was now dirty, tangled, and in desperate need of a wash. After tucking the locket and coins away, deep into the pocket of my dress, I descended the stairs.

It was so quiet. I never realised how much I would miss the sound of the children's voices, their shrieks of laughter as they played around the cottage, and the inevitable arguments that followed. Ladling a few spoonfuls of the porridge that Charles had prepared into a bowl, I sat down at the table and wondered what Samuel was doing in Offenham. *Was he sorry for how he treated me yesterday? Did he come to my room last night and give me a drink? Was he actually beginning to care a little for me?* So many unanswered questions. If I could just speak to him and find out how he *really* felt. I pushed the uneaten porridge away and went outside. Although it was dry, a bitter easterly wind blew relentlessly down through the trees, and there was a feeling in the air that snow was not too far off. I went back inside and stood warming my hands by the fire. I really did need to get some warmer clothing soon. I noticed Hannah's cape and hood hanging up behind the door, and I debated whether to borrow it and walk into the village. I wrestled with my conscience for a good ten minutes, before finally relenting and slipping the cloak around my shoulders.

Knowing the village was in short walking distance; I set off down the track. *Maybe I will pass him on his return journey?* I thought, keeping my ears open for the sound of an approaching horse. I didn't see man nor beast in the ten minutes it took me to reach Offenham, and I presumed he was still here, somewhere in the village. I was amazed at how little the village had actually changed over the hundreds of years. The houses and shops were still instantly recognizable, although the merchandise they sold was vastly different. There was a butcher that offered unskinned rabbits and wild feathered fowl, a bakery, an undertaker whose coffins were worked on in the street by craftsmen, a blacksmith with his white hot furnace and a kind of haberdashery, where ribbons and materials could be purchased to make your own garments. I was fascinated and strolled along the street, almost forgetting the purpose of my journey. It was also the busiest I had ever seen it. The place was thriving with people from all walks of life, going about their daily business. Some women were wearing dainty bonnets and carrying baskets. Others looked like gypsies, begging on street corners from passing gentlemen, in their short breeches and frilled shirts.

Dirty children played in the street with tattered clothes, and carts and horses passed up and down the dusty road amid the straw and horse dung. Several horses were tied to posts outside of an inn, and I looked to see if any were totally black, but there were none. A farmer passed by with a flock of sheep, which added to the already heavily soiled street, and I had to tread carefully. A gentleman tipped his hat at me, as he stood to one side to let me pass. I smiled and nodded back. They were so much more polite and respectful in these days. The future wasn't all it was cracked up to be.

I had now walked up as far as the Parish church, and crossed over to examine another group of horses tethered to an iron ring on a wall. One of them was decidedly black, although I couldn't say for certain if it was Samuel's. Peering into the lattice window of a shop nearby, I thought it resembled a kind of café. Several men and one or two women sat at tables, engaged in conversation, whilst drinking small amounts of dark liquid from a cup. *Could this be one of those coffee houses that Aunt Elizabeth spoke of?* Maybe, but Samuel wasn't in there. I sighed and looked around. There wasn't anywhere else he could be. Unless…

I walked back to the pathway that led to the church. The main door was slightly ajar. I could check, but I seriously doubted he was inside. Pushing open the heavy wooden door, I slipped into the church. It was so dark I had to stand for a while at the back, to let my eyes grow accustomed to the light. The smell of lit candles and a heavy mustiness filled the air. I began to make my way slowly down the aisle, between rows of dark pews, harboring one or two lonely individuals praying for whatever tormented their souls. As I neared the altar, a dark shape knelt before it with his head bowed, his hands clasped together as he spoke in low whispers, begging the Holy Father for forgiveness for his sins. Samuel's unmistakable black curls fell forward over his face, and he didn't see me as I knelt beside him on the stone step.

"God will forgive you, Samuel…and so shall I," I said quietly. He raised his head and looked at me in surprise. "I never had you down as the religious type," I whispered with a mischievous grin. "Is this the '*thing'* you had to do?" Without replying, he rose quickly to his feet and strode down the aisle towards the door. I was hot on his heels, as we burst through the door and out into the bright sunlight.

"Emily, just go away. I am not worthy of you," he said wearily, heading down the path. I ran after him and caught hold of his cloak, halting his hasty retreat.

"Samuel, stop it!" I cried. "It doesn't matter what happened before. I forgive you for all the foolish things you have said and done to me. Please, I want us to be friends. Can you at least accept that? Don't shut me out, Samuel, I beg you!"

"I can bring you nothing but grief. Why would you want to befriend me?" he asked, untying his horse from the iron ring.

"Because I care for you, Samuel Howerd. I don't know why, but I do… I have from the moment I first saw you." I let go of his cloak, fearing I had said far too much, and looked away as a tear trickled down my face. My unexpected confession appeared to render him speechless, and it was some moments before he composed himself enough to speak.

"Do you wish to ride with me back home?" he inquired coldly, avoiding my eyes.

"Yes, if I may," I replied, thankful that I wasn't lying face down in a large pile of horseshit at this moment. He mounted his horse and waited for me to do likewise. I had never been this close to a horse, let alone ridden one, and I stared at the enormous beast before me, terrified.

"You *do* ride?" Samuel asked, looking down at me from a great height.

"Er—well, no, actually, but I'm willing to learn. I just need a little help," I replied, giving him a pitiful look.

"Put your left foot in this stirrup," he said as he removed his own foot. "Then hold on to my cloak and pull yourself up behind me." I did as instructed, but the horse moved forward suddenly, and I lost my balance.

"Hold on. I'll try again. Just keep it still," I cried, before clutching hold of a large handful of his cloak and hoisting myself up unceremoniously, swinging my leg warily over the broad animal's back. "Hang on! I've got my dress caught underneath me!" I shouted out, as I tried to pull the offending garment out with one hand, whilst clinging on for dear life to Samuel with the other.

"If you must insist on riding like a man, rather than a lady, then more suitable clothing is best acquired." With that, he dug his heels into the horse's side and cantered off up the street, ignoring my petrified pleas to slow down.

Once out of the village he slowed down to a gentle trot, but I still felt the need to wrap my arms around his waist tightly, which would have been enjoyable in other circumstances. I was so rigid with the fear of falling off that the pleasure was overcome by concern for my own survival. It seemed an eternity before we arrived back home, and Samuel slipped effortlessly from the saddle, leaving me unsupported and clinging onto the horse's mane.

"Samuel, get me down!" I shouted out. He came over and stood smiling at my panic-stricken face.

"You will not learn, if you do not attempt it yourself," he said, taking hold of the reins and standing to the side. "Now place your foot—"

"What foot?"

"Good God, woman. A child has more intelligence than you," he said impatiently.

"Shut up! Just get me down," I wailed, close to tears. Sighing heavily, he took hold of my left foot and placed it securely into the stirrup. His arm encircled my waist as he pulled me towards him off of the horse, which at that point decided to move forward. I fell hard against him, and we both toppled backwards onto the ground in an undignified heap, with him sprawled out on top of me. I broke into nervous laughter, trying to defuse the situation.

"Well, that was the first lesson…can't wait for the second!" I said smiling up at Samuel, whose face was tantalizingly close to mine, but bore a serious expression as he looked deeply into my eyes.

The moment was abruptly ended when we heard cries of despair coming from the near vicinity.

"It's father," said Samuel, scrambling to his feet and running off through the trees in the direction of Jasmine Cottage, leaving me to get to my feet, unaided, and run after him. When I arrived, Charles was sitting on the cottage step cradling in his arms what looked like a bundle of rags, and rocking back and forth, sobbing. I looked over at Samuel.

"Is it Eliza?" He nodded, solemnly running his hand through his hair, unsure of how to handle the situation. I went over, and sitting down next to Charles, put a comforting arm around his shoulder. We all knew it was coming, but nothing compares to the reality of the actual heartbreaking moment. "I'll go up and see Hannah," I said gently to Charles, who nodded and told me that she was asking for me.

"Is that wise?" asked Samuel, a concerned look upon his face.

"Don't worry. I'll be fine," I reassured him. "You stay here and take care of your father. He needs you."

I made my way upstairs and into the front bedroom. The frail white figure that lay in the bed was hardly recognizable as the Hannah I knew. The shock of seeing her so near to death was terribly distressing, but I tried hard to hold it together. She turned her head as I entered and managed a weak smile.

"God has taken my child, but I shall not cry for her. I know that soon we will be together again in a better place, free from this terrible sickness," she said quietly, tapping the bed cover. "Come, young Emily. I wish to speak with you." Sitting down upon the bed, I took her hand in mine. It was ice cold, and I waited while she gathered the strength to speak again. "When I am gone…Charles intends to go and live with his sister in Edgebarton," she began. "We want to leave Mill Cottage to you… and to Samuel, our eldest son."

A severe coughing fit followed as she held a blood-soaked cloth to her mouth. I swallowed hard, fighting back the tears. "I know he has always resented me, but I brought him into this world, and I have always…*always* loved him dearly, despite his wild, impetuous ways." I smiled knowingly, and squeezed her hand tightly.

"And I have always loved you too, mother…despite my inability to show it." We both turned to see Samuel standing in the doorway. I couldn't hold back the tears any longer, and they flowed fast and freely as I buried my face in the bed cover, sobbing my little heart out.

"I love you, Samuel…take care of the children for me… and of Emily. She will bring you much happiness…so much happ—" Her voice faltered and broke off, as her head slumped to one side and her hand went limp. She was gone. When I turned again to the door, he had disappeared downstairs. I was so pleased that he had found it in his heart to declare his love for his mother, so that she died in peace, knowing that he *did* care.

Going back outside, I found that Samuel had to ride into the village and summon the undertaker once again. He had taken with him the pathetic little bundle that was once his sister Eliza. At least there was comfort in the knowledge that they would be buried together. I found Charles over by the stream, sitting on the remnants of a fallen tree. Jas was sitting beside him, his head in his lap, looking up at him with big mournful brown eyes, as if he understood the reason behind his master's melancholy mood and shared in his sorrow.

"I understand you will be joining your sister in Edgebarton?" I said softly, laying my hand on his shoulder.

"Indeed…I shall leave after the funeral. There is nothing here for me now. I cannot abide to linger where memories eat away at my very soul, willing me to follow my beloved to the grave."

"But what about your work at the mill?" I asked, sitting down beside him. "Surely you are needed there?"

"Old Elijah, the mill owner, is in bad health. He told me only yesterday that he can no longer continue. He has a son, Robert, whom he had not seen for over twenty years. He returned for a brief visit two years back, prior to setting sail on the '*Redoubt*'. I hear he has been found aboard another ship, in waters off of France, and has been ordered to return home in haste."

"Then Samuel is also without work?" Charles nodded and sighed heavily.

"Will there be no end to this family's suffering, Emily? What have I done to deserve God's wrath?" he said, putting his head in his hands. The thought that yet another member of his family was about to die made me even more determined to spare this man any further misery.

Samuel returned from the village soon after, with the undertaker following close behind. I watched as they carried Hannah's plain wooden coffin from the cottage, and lifted it up onto the back of the cart, and I couldn't help thinking, *this could be Samuel in a few days time*. The thought of it filled me with dread. I began to wonder *what* he was actually destined to die of. He wasn't ill from the sickness, as he showed no signs of it. It could only be some kind of accident, or the result of an argument that got out of hand. I would have to keep him close by me from now on, watching for any possible dangers that might threaten his life. We were all understandably in a somber mood that evening, as the three of us sat around the table. Samuel had shot a large rabbit earlier on and gave it to me to prepare for dinner. I didn't want to appear unaccustomed to such everyday occurrences, and I took the rabbit gingerly by the ears and hid myself away in the kitchen area, while I dissected the unfortunate bunny as best as I knew how. Not a pleasant task, I can assure you. Charles retired early for the night and returned to his old marital bed upstairs, leaving me by the fireside with Samuel. He was different somehow. I couldn't quite put my finger on it, but he had lost his hostility towards me. There was no angry exchange of words. No withering dark looks or temper tantrums. In fact, there was hardly any interaction at all with me, but I didn't want to push him too much. After all, he had just lost his mother. I, for one, could identify with that.

"Where are you sleeping tonight?" I inquired after a long period of silence.

"The same place I always do," he replied. "Why…where do you suggest?" I decided against being utterly honest with him in my reply, and just shrugged my shoulders, our eyes meeting momentarily in the firelight. I didn't like the idea of him being out in the barn on his own. Anyone could enter during the night. At least inside the cottage I could fasten the door, *but what could I do other then tie him to my bed? Now, there is a scintillating idea, but not practical under the circumstances.*

"So…we are the new owners of Mill Cottage," I said cheerily, trying to make conversation, and distract myself from persistently irrational thoughts.

"It would appear so," came his ambiguous reply, "although I do not intend on sharing it with you alone. The children will be coming home to join us."

"Yes, of course!" I replied. "I wouldn't have it any other way." *Assuming that you are still around by then…God, I hope so. We could all be so happy together,* I thought, staring into the fire as my eyes started to glisten with moisture. *Please God…please don't take my Samuel away from me.* I clasped my hands in silent prayer.

Standing up suddenly from the bench, he put down his mug and turned to me to bid me a polite goodnight. Panic started to engulf me as he went to leave.

"Why don't you take your gun with you?" I blurted out, picking up the firearm from the table.

"Do not be ridiculous, woman!" he laughed. "What should I shoot in the barn? A rat, maybe, for tomorrow's dinner?" I smiled uneasily, and replaced the gun back onto the table. Shaking his head in disbelief, he departed through the door into the night, leaving me anxious and upset. *Perhaps I was being over cautious? After all, it wasn't the 16th as yet, and nothing would happen until then.* I sat back down by the fire, chewing my thumbnail. *Maybe he receives the blow, cut or whatever the horrific event is before then, and only actually dies from the injury on the 16th?*

I felt sick with worry as I paced the floor, trying to allay my fears, but it only made the matter worse, as I knew I couldn't possibly prevent the occurrence without knowing what it was in the first place. Samuel would not tolerate me shadowing him every minute of the day, without some logical reason behind my odd behavior. Exhausted from the day's harrowing events, I crawled up the stairs to bed, but it wasn't until the early hours that I finally drifted off to sleep and had strange, but vivid, dreams involving a bed and a length of rope.

Chapter Twelve

Sitting across the table from Samuel and Charles the following morning at breakfast, I could not help but smile to myself, as I watched him eating his porridge and tearing off handfuls of bread. Last night's dream was still clear in my mind, and my heart pounded loudly as I recalled the intimate details.

"*What* is it, Emily? Why do you stare at me so?" he suddenly declared, looking up. I had not realized that he was aware of my subtle surveillance, and his question caught me off-guard.

"I'm sorry…I did not mean to stare at you. My mind was elsewhere," I told him, feeling the color rise in my cheeks. Charles looked up at me in deep thought, and then at Samuel beside him, but said nothing. The atmosphere was strained until I spoke again. "You need to write to John and Aunt Elizabeth to let them know," I said to Charles. "I will do it, if you give me some paper and a…" I hesitated. *What was it they used in these days?* "Writing implement," I added apprehensively, not wanting to incriminate myself. Both men looked at me in amazement, and I couldn't think why.

"You can *write*?" asked Samuel, as if I had just informed them that I was a brain surgeon. I refrained from replying, '*Why…can't you?*' for fear of sounding too conceited, and reminded myself that these were simple country folk with little or no education.

"Yes…a little," I said nervously. "Someone must have taught me, although I cannot recall who."

"Can you also *read*?" inquired Charles hopefully.

"Yes, I can," I replied. "I can teach you, if you like?" Charles sighed and sat back in the chair.

"I am far too old to understand the complexities of the written word, but Samuel will do well to acquire this knowledge," he said, looking at his son for approval.

"What uses have I for words on paper, when I can speak them just as readily?" he said dismissively. "John is far more the scholar than I. Teach him, if you must."

"I will," I said, annoyed at his reluctance to improve himself, but then I realized it was probably a waste of time and effort, considering what I knew.

Charles got up and went over to a small chest, which was placed on a shelf in the corner of the room. He took it down and brought it over to the table.

"My sister Elizabeth sent this for John some months back. If you can make use of the contents, then I shall take the letter with me to Offenham this afternoon, when I go to meet with the pastor regarding Hannah's funeral on the day after tomorrow." He pushed the wooden box across the table to me, and I tentatively lifted the lid.

Inside was a scroll of parchment paper with a square of blotting paper, a thin ribbon, a red crayon-like object, a feathered quill, and a small earthenware pot with a stopper. *Oh my God!* I thought, staring at the array of antiquities. I wish I had paid more attention in history classes. They watched me, intrigued, as I took each item out of the box and arranged them on the table. Taking the stopper from the pot, I peered inside at the black liquid and carefully placed it to one side. Next I unrolled the paper and, picking up the quill, cautiously dipped it into the ink. The nib that was inserted on the end of the feather was scratchy and awkward to write with. I only managed to form three or four letters before having to refill it from the pot. The letter was therefore much shorter and to the point then I would have liked it to be, but my admirers were suitably impressed with my efforts. Using the blotter, I made sure it was dry before folding it up and moving on to write the address.

"Where do I send it?" I asked Charles.

"Barton House…Edgebarton," replied Charles simply. *No need for ZIP codes, then?* I thought, smiling to myself, as I inserted the necessary information and again blotted it dry. The letter needed to be stuck down with something, and

I picked up the strange red crayon and examined it, trying to think what use it had. Thankfully, Charles came to the rescue. He took the stick and letter over to the fire, where he held the crayon in the flames briefly, before dripping the melted liquid over the joins of the letter, thus sealing it together. *Wax, of course!* Charles tucked the letter into his pocket and finished up his mug of mead.

"I take it the children will not be attending their mother's funeral?" I asked.

"No. It is best they remain at Barton House until arrangements can be made for their return," replied Charles as he was putting on his cloak. "I shall return shortly and expect the animals to be fed and watered," he said, directing the latter to Samuel, who grunted in reply.

I began clearing the table as Samuel got up to go outside.

"I'll help you, if you like? I can feed the chickens, and you can do the pigs," I said eagerly. He stopped in his tracks and turned to me.

"I may be unable to read and write, but that does not make me incapable of doing such a menial task as feeding the animals."

"I know that. I just wanted to help," I replied innocently.

"Then stay out of my way, and go and prepare the meal for tonight. Father has left a brace of pheasants around the back." I cringed at the thought, as he strode off to attend to the pigs, and decided to wash my hair instead.

Finding a large bucket, I went over to the stream and filled it with water. It was ice cold, and there was no way I was going to stick my head in that! So I poured some into the black pot that hung over the fire and waited while it heated up, which took an eternity. In the meantime, I collected some shampoo from the toiletry bag in my carryall and hung around the door, idly watching Samuel tending the squawking chickens, smiling to myself as they got under his feet and he swore at them loudly.

It was so tranquil here. *How could he possibly be in any danger?* Perhaps the gravestone belonged to *another* Samuel

Howerd and I was worrying over nothing. *I mustn't become too complacent,* I said to myself, *for the 16th is still six days away, and until then, I must stay vigilant.* The boiling water brimmed over onto the fire, making it hiss and spit, which distracted me from my pessimistic thoughts. I carefully ladled the hot water into the bucket and struggled with it outside, not wanting to wet the floor. Kneeling down on a patch of grass, I submersed my head into the bucket. The warm water felt so good and I swished my hair about, before unscrewing the cap of my shampoo bottle and adding the creamy contents, making sure the incriminating plastic bottle was hidden back in my bag. The soft water made lather in abundance, and I was soon covered in a mop of foaming bubbles. After rinsing it the best I could in the dirty water, I raised my head and, with my eyes shut tight, felt around on the grass for the piece of cloth that was used to handle the hot iron ladle.

"Looking for this?" I heard Samuel's familiar voice close by. I slowly opened my eyes to see him towering over me, holding out the cloth.

"Yes. Thank you," I said, reaching out to retrieve it.

"Let me, if I may?" he said, kneeling down behind me and gently rubbing the cloth over my wet hair. I was too shocked to speak. Instead, I sat motionless as his strong hands moved back and forth over my head, sending rippling waves of longing through me. "I used to do this for Charlotte," he murmured. "She had hair just like yours." My heart sank like a stone as I realized that his thoughts were elsewhere, and I was just an obstacle for his true desires.

"Really?" I said frostily, snatching back the cloth, "How nice for you." He appeared quite taken aback, as I kicked over the bucket and stomped angrily back inside. *Had this man no regard for my feelings? Was I always destined to live in the shadow of his beloved Charlotte?* The door flew open and banged back against the wall as Samuel entered, his eyes blazing with fury.

"What vexes you so, Emily? That a man cannot do a deed of kindness without such harsh words being bestowed upon him!"

"Why did you *have* to mention Charlotte? How long has it been now…one year?"

"Two," he said defensively.

"Two years!" I screamed in disbelief. "Two years, and she is still on your mind."

"I LOVED HER!" yelled Samuel, banging his fist on the table.

"She left you for another man! A man whose baby she was carrying and you still *love* her? What a fool you have been!" In one stride, Samuel was upon me, and I felt his hand across my face, in a stinging blow that sent me reeling back into a chair. At that moment, I saw Charles standing aghast in the doorway.

"How *dare* you strike a woman in my house!" shouted Charles. "GET OUT!" Samuel turned and left immediately, without a word, leaving me to explain his actions to his distraught father.

"Please don't blame Samuel. It wasn't entirely his fault," I told him, wincing as Charles held a wet cloth to my red cheek.

"A man strikes you, and you defend him? Forgive me, but is this not the action of a woman whose heart rules her head?" I looked up at Charles and bit my lip.

"I will always remind him of Charlotte, won't I?" I blurted out, close to tears, "I just want him to love me for who I am. Is that too much to ask?"

"Oh, dear Lord!" cried Charles, stunned by my revelation. "To hold my son in such high esteem can only bring you unhappiness, and I do not wish that upon you, dearest child. It might be better if you were to direct your admiration elsewhere—to find a more amiable suitor." I could understand what he was saying, but I wasn't going to give up that easily, and I think that Charles was well aware of my misguided intentions. "Come, Emily. I will help you prepare the pheasants," he said, smiling. "There is plenty enough for the three of us."

That night the long-expected snow finally arrived, and I huddled close to the fire with my plate of cooked pheasant and warm milk, avoiding any interaction with Samuel over at the table.

"Emily is in need of some warmer clothing," Charles informed Samuel. "You will take the cart tomorrow and ride into Greenham, so she is able to purchase the necessary garments." It was said in such a tone that it was more of an order than a request, and one that was not to be disputed.

"I have some business to attend to in Greenham, so I will do as you ask," replied Samuel, and I got the distinct impression that he would not have taken me if he didn't have other matters to pursue. It also worried me that he was venturing out of the relative safety of his home, to mix with other associates that I knew nothing of. The town would be full of any number of likely assassins, and I would not be permitted to follow him every step of the way. I suddenly lost my appetite and set my plate to one side.

Charles talked to Samuel for a while about the upcoming funeral of his mother. The discussion involved burials and gravestones, which only added to my anxiety.

"I'm going to bed," I announced, unable to stand it any longer, and took hold of a candle from the table. Charles bid me goodnight and offered me an extra cover for warmth, which I gratefully accepted. "Goodnight, Samuel," I said purposefully. I saw his fingers grasp the handle of the mug tighter, and he nodded in reply, without raising his head for fear that I would see the guilt and shame, which was etched upon his face.

Away from the fire, the rest of the cottage was dark, cold and damp, and I debated about whether to undress or just sleep in my clothes. Peering out through the lattice panes, I could see it was still snowing heavily and wondered if we would, in fact, make it into the town the following morning. *Staying here might not be such a bad idea.* I peeled back the cover and climbed, fully dressed, into the bed, laying the additional blanket over the top. The bed felt wet, and my feet were blocks of ice as I curled up into the foetal position, in an attempt to contain some of the heat. The candle flickered wildly on the bedside table, from a draft that penetrated up through the floorboards, and blew in through gaps in the window frame. I could hear the low drone of Charles' voice talking downstairs, and the intermittent aggravated replies from Samuel, that were unclear and muffled. I would guess that his father was reprimanding him for the incident earlier in the day. I listened as, later, Charles' weary footsteps made their way up the stairs and the door of the cottage slammed shut. The candle slowly burned down, and eventually extinguished itself, long before the two troubled souls finally slept on that cold and snowy December night.

I awoke the following morning to the sound of horses being harnessed below. Wrapping the blanket tightly around me, I shuffled over to the window and made a small clearance in the frosted pane, as clouds of warm vapor from my breath rose up into the room. It was freezing, and I stood rigid with the cold, as I watched Samuel attach the horses to the cart. A good six inches of snow had fallen overnight, but he obviously felt he could make the journey into town. I, however, was not so optimistic.

Charles had already made the fire and prepared breakfast, pointing out tactfully to me that it would be my responsibility after tomorrow, being the woman of the house now. I fingered the pendant deep within my pocket. *Should I just cut and run now? I am a part homeowner, soon to be living under the same roof with a man that despises me, and foster mother to half a dozen kids! When Samuel died…if Samuel died, I will be left to bring them up on my own. How could I desert them and return home? How could I live here without Samuel by my side?* I needed him now, more than anything.

Samuel stood at the door, tapping the frame impatiently with his whip, while I put on my shawl and cape. Crunching through the frozen snow, I climbed up onto the bench, and huddled up against the biting wind, as Samuel cracked the whip and the horses jolted forward unsteadily. It was slow going along the lane, and I felt sorry for the struggling horses.

"Is Greenham far?" I asked, clinging on to the seat as a wheel got momentarily stuck in a drift.

"Near on five miles," replied Samuel, keeping his eyes on the road. The icy wind stung my face, and I put up my hand against the sore red patch on my cheek. My action instigated a response.

"Does it hurt?" he asked softly, casting me a concerned look.

"A little, but I'll live," I said offhandedly.

"I should not have struck you. For that I am deeply regretful."

"Apology accepted, but it was *I* who provoked you."

"Then we are both to blame," said Samuel, smiling across at me. "Your temper too has much to be desired." I smiled back at him. Peace had been restored...*but for how long?*

The rest of the journey passed in silence, and by the time the first signs of civilization appeared, I was frozen to the bone and somewhat sleepy. Hypothermia was beginning to ravage my body. I was so stiff that Samuel had to help me down from the cart, and guide me into a nearby shop. Sitting down at a table, I began to shiver uncontrollably, prompting Samuel to take off his thick cloak and place it around my shoulders.

"Here...drink this," he said, as a young woman with an apron delivered two mugs of a steaming liquid. I carefully sipped the liquid, and the taste was instantly recognizable.

"Chocolate!" I cried in amazement. "It's chocolate."

"You have tasted this before?"

"Yes... well, something very similar," I replied, the color returning to my cheeks. "I didn't think you had chocolate in...." I bit my tongue just in time "In—in this town," I stammered nervously.

"You have never visited a Jocolatte house?" said Samuel, surprised.

"Is that like a *coffee* house?"

"You are able to procure both drinks in this particular establishment, but yes."

The feeling was starting to come back into my toes and fingers, and Samuel and I were actually engaged in a pleasurable conversation! Things were looking up. We finished up our drinks and left to allow our table to be used. It appeared to be a popular place among the better classes, and was in stark contrast to the tavern en route from Edgebarton.

"I have to attend to some business over at The Red Lion," he said, pointing across the street to a scruffy-looking inn. "The shop that you require is further in that direction. You have money?"

"Yes, your aunt was kind enough to give me some," I replied, showing him the assortment of coins from my pocket.

"Very well. I shall meet with you here in two hours." I did not like the idea of him straying into such a seedy establishment, and the unease showed upon my face.

"Is it safe?" I asked as he turned to leave.

"The town has its share of undesirable folk, like many others, but you should come to no harm if you stay within the main street and are prudent with whom you converse."

"No…I meant *that* place," I said, pointing over at the inn.

"My dear girl, I am more than capable of dealing with the odd scoundrel. The fact that you should cast doubt upon me is not only humiliating, but degrading."

"Just take care." I said, not wanting to indulge in anymore discussion concerning his masculinity, or apparent lack of it. I was sure he could take on any number of dubious characters and win. It was the unexpected knife in the back type that gave me cause for concern.

As I walked up the crowded street in this busy and unfamiliar town, the difference between a small country village and a larger town was very apparent, and not altogether pleasant. The thing that struck me most above the noise and the dirt was the smell. A roughly dug out trench ran down the side of the street that carried raw sewage and, because of the snow, this had overflowed onto the road and begun seeping into piles of steaming horse manure. My cloak and dress soaked up this vile concoction, and my boots soon became plastered in human excrement. I stopped and watched, mesmerized as an elegantly dressed lady in a beautiful fur-trimmed cape glided from a perfume shop. She stopped and held a delicate lace handkerchief to her nose, while she waited for her footman to lay a large piece of cloth down upon the slush for her to step onto, before she alighted her coach. Filthy street urchins—some as young as three—besieged everyone in fine clothing, begging for money or scraps of food, only to be pushed to the ground or hit with a cane like disgusting vermin. I had to walk on for fear of gathering up all these unfortunate souls and taking them home with me. Ignoring the frequent cries of, 'Er, Lady, come and sample me wares,' from numerous street vendors, I walked on.

I finally found the clothes shop I was looking for. I was thankful to take refuge inside—away from this strange and frightening world that surrounded me. Scraping my boots on the grid outside as best I could, I entered the shop premises to the sound of a tinkling bell above the door. Almost immediately, an elderly man appeared from behind a curtain, among mounds of different fabrics piled high on the counter. Towards the back of the shop I could just make out, in the poor light, some expensive looking gowns in satin and silk for the wealthier clientele. The man looked at me over the top of his spectacles—summing up, no doubt, my status and ability to pay.

"Good morning, miss," he said dryly. "What manner of cloth are you interested in purchasing?" I looked around at the realms of materials on the counter, some in various types of cotton, some woollen and dark, but none made up into recognizable dresses.

"Do you have any of that?" I said awkwardly, pointing to some dark brown woollen fabric. "Already made up into a dress…I mean, a frock?" I was way out of my depth here, and was terrified of saying the wrong word or using incorrect terminology. Swiftly glancing over my figure, he turned and opened a drawer at the back of the counter, producing a garment that faintly resembled a feminine item of clothing.

It was in dark green wool, unattractive, and had about as much shape as a sack, but it was warm. I reached into my pocket for the coins and laid them on the counter. "How many of these garments can I purchase with these coins?" I said anxiously. The old man leaned over and examined my offering.

"Four groats will buy you three garments likened to these."

"And do I *have* four of these groats?" I asked, feeling somewhat like a young child on the first visit to a sweet shop, with no understanding of the value of money.

"You do, indeed," said the man, giving me a puzzled look, and probably wondering why a woman of my age couldn't count.

"Do you have other colors?" I asked, trying to sound remotely intelligent.

"I have them in black or brown also."

"Then I shall take one of each," I said, smiling. *The black one will be useful tomorrow*, I thought, *and hopefully only tomorrow.* I waited while the clothing was folded and wrapped meticulously in layers of brown paper, before being fastened with a length of string. Handing the parcel to me, he bid me a good day, and I left the shop content with my purchases, however drab.

Checking the time, I saw I still had another hour to kill and carried on walking up through the town. The street veered off into two directions, and I took the right hand fork, which became narrower and almost deserted. The upstairs sections of the houses almost touched one another, as they leaned precariously over the road, shutting out a good deal of the sunlight. I began to feel nervous and alone as I noticed, with growing concern; shadowy shapes that huddled in dark doorways and were watching me pass by with beady, sunken eyes. I remembered Samuel's warning, '*Stay within the main street.*' My heart started to pound as I realized I had strayed from that area, and I turned around to retrace my steps, jumping in fright as a large rat scuttled across my path and vanished into a hole underneath a doorway. Thinking I could hear footsteps behind me, I looked over my shoulder. A man in a long black cape, with a hood obscuring his face was gaining on me fast. I increased my gait and then broke out into a run as panic gripped me. Blinded by tears, I reached the main street and careered headlong into a passing gentleman. My brown paper package was knocked from my hand in the collision, and he kindly retrieved it for me, before some ragamuffin made off with it.

"Can I be of assistance, miss?" he enquired as he handed me my parcel.

"No, but thank you," I replied, looking up timidly at the middle-aged gent. He smiled back at me and bowed politely, as his eyes locked onto mine, holding my gaze for longer than was absolutely necessary. There was something familiar, yet strangely disconcerting, about his eyes which unnerved me. I had no reason to fear him. He had only behaved impeccably towards me. My agitated state was probably to blame for my irrational thoughts. I smiled and bid him good day.

With half an hour left, I decided to explore the left-hand fork. This appeared to be the way most people were heading. I was swept along in the jostling crowds, to a large square in the middle of the town. There was an air of excitement among the throng, with young children sitting upon their father's shoulders and women chattering noisily together. Threading my way through the crowd, I tried to see what all the fuss was about, but it was difficult to see over their heads, and it wasn't until I reached the front of the mass that I discovered the reason behind their jubilation.

A large stone platform rose before me, with steps up on either side. In the center was a large pile of firewood, with a tall wooden pole protruding from its midst. Iron chains and cuffs attached to the pole only confirmed my horrified thoughts, and I turned away to try and escape having to witness this barbaric punishment. The crowd surged forward, and cries of, "Burn the witch!" reached a crescendo, as I heard the sound of an approaching cart nearby. The crowd parted, to make way for the horse as it pulled along its unfortunate victim, and I stared, mortified, at the young blonde girl shackled in the back of the cart. She must have been about my age—very pretty, despite the layers of filthy dirt encrusted on her long, fair hair. A few remnants of clothing hung in torn ribbons about her pitifully thin body, as she sat with her head bowed and silently weeping.

The cart came to a halt at the bottom of the steps, and two men helped her down amid a shower of rotten fruit and vegetables. She didn't protest as the men fastened her thin wrists into the cuffs, and attached the heavy restraining chains about her. I must have been about ten feet away and could clearly see she had no fight left in her, and was resigned to her fate. *I can't watch this! I've got to get out of here!* But try as I might, the pressure of the people against me prevented my departure, and I verged on hysteria as one of the men ignited the pile of wood with a burning torch. The girl suddenly raised her head and looked defiantly into the crowd, before she spoke and cursed them all to damnation.

Just for a moment, her terrified eyes rested on mine, and I mouthed the words, '*God bless you,*' before the smoke increased, obscuring her from my view. As if someone demented, I fought my way through the crowds, pushing and shoving everyone out of my way in my desperation to get as far as possible from this atrocity. Tears ran down my face in torrents, and I felt violently sick, as the smell of burning flesh wafted across the square. The last agonizing screams, as the flames devoured that poor innocent girl, would remain with me forever.

I was already fifteen minutes late when I reached the main street and, clutching my parcel tightly, I ran as quickly as was possible in a long dress on treacherous surfaces. What I had just experienced was not only dreadfully upsetting, but also it brought home to me that disclosing my origin to anyone—even Samuel—could bring about a similar fate. There was no sign of him outside of the inn, but the cart was still tethered to a post, so I knew he hadn't left without me. I sat down on a stone seat near the entrance and tried to calm myself down, trembling this time not from the cold, but from traumatic stress.

Each time the oak door of the inn swung open, I expected it to be Samuel, and began to grow agitated as another ten minutes passed without him appearing. I didn't relish the thought of going inside to fetch him, judging by the rough-looking men that frequented the premises, having not quite got over my last visit inside a 17th century pub. I really could have done without this added anxiety. I paced up and down outside, debating what I should do.

Two men came out. They looked fairly respectable, and I plucked up the courage to approach them.

"Excuse me. Could you tell me if there is a gentleman inside—about thirty years of age, with long black curly hair and a black cape?" I said nervously. The men exchanged uneasy glances with one another.

"Might it be Samuel Howerd that you be looking for, miss?" said one of the men in a broad Irish accent.

"Yes. Is he inside?"

"Aye, that he is, but not in the land of the living, to be sure." The color drained from my face.

"No. NO! This isn't possible," I cried. "It isn't the 16th yet. It *isn't* the 16th of December." I staggered back against the wall, my whole world crashing down around me. I never even got the chance to tell him how much I loved him.

Chapter Thirteen

The two men stared at my shocked face and then smiled at one another, as if enjoying some private joke.

"You can't be knowing young Samuel that well then, miss? He never was one for holding his drink, but seeing as it be his mother's funeral tomorrow, I think you should forgive his over indulgence on this occasion."

"What?" I cried, "You mean he's *drunk*?"

"Aye. What did you think I be meaning, miss?"

"I thought—I thought he was…" I stopped. *Perhaps it would be better not to humiliate myself any further.* I felt like bursting into tears for some reason. Maybe it was the sheer relief of knowing he wasn't dead, or it might have been the fact that I now knew just how strong my love for this man was…and how it would have felt to lose him.

"Come, Padraig. Give me a hand to bring him out," said one of the men, and they disappeared inside.

I waited patiently outside and, before long, the door swung open, and they half-carried Samuel out between them. He could barely stand, and with his eyes tightly shut, he mumbled incoherently to no one in particular. I pointed to the cart, and they heaved him up into the back, and let him drop down onto the floor unceremoniously. I looked over the edge, worried that he might have injured himself.

"He'll be fine in the morning, miss. A good night's sleep is all that he needs, to be sure. Come, Seamus." With that, the two men walked away up the road, and left me standing there, dazed and confused. *Now what? There is no way he can drive the horses' home in that state.* I climbed up into the back and gently shook him.

"Samuel. SAMUEL! Can you hear me?" I said, moving his thick hair away from his reddened face. "Samuel?" He stirred and pushed me away, before lapsing into semi-unconsciousness again. It was no use. I *had* to get him home somehow. I looked over at the horses and reins. *How difficult can it be?* It was a straight road. I only had to follow it. Untying the horses from the post, I took my place on the bench, and gingerly picked up the heavy leather reins in my small hands. My heart was pounding like crazy. Being in control of these two huge beasts...if they bolted, I stood no chance at all. Looking back at Samuel, I whispered, "Wish me luck," and gently flicked the whip as I had seen him do many times before. The horses immediately jolted forward, and I gripped the reins tightly, as they trotted ahead steadily down the street and out of the town. The road narrowed into a lane, and I felt we were going a little too fast, with the passageway so restricted by the snow. I wasn't sure how to slow them down and began to panic, but I found by pulling on the reins and calling out, "Steady," I was ablc to slow their pace.

It was an extremely nerve-racking journey, and I was so relieved when I saw the track to Mill Cottage ahead. The horses seemed to know their way and didn't need any direction from me to turn them, which was just as well, as I hadn't tried that particular maneuver yet. I pulled hard on the reins as we reached the cottage, and they obediently came to a halt, much to my relief. My hands were shaking from the grip on the reins, and my legs felt like jelly as I climbed down from the cart. I searched the cottage and barn for Charles, but he was nowhere about. It looked like it was down to me, yet again, to sort Samuel out.

I tried the gentle approach at first, but soon had to resort to more forceful measures to get him out of the cart. With his arm around my neck, I staggered with him into the cottage. He had no idea where he was or who was with him in his drunken stupor which, in a way, benefited me as I struggled with him on the staircase and led him in the direction of my bedroom. He collapsed onto my bed, and I sat for a moment to get my breath. He looked so helpless as he laid there, his long black hair spread across the pillow, and a peaceful expression on his face. I felt an urge to lean over and kiss him, but resisted the opportunity to take advantage of his predicament.

After taking off his heavy boots, I set about removing his cloak and loosening his shirt to make him more comfortable. That was what I kept telling myself, anyway. The top button of his trousers seemed very tight. With trembling fingers, I gently unfastened it. He stirred at that moment and briefly opened his eyes slightly, trying to focus on the shape before him. He mumbled something, and I leaned in nearer to try and catch what he said. His hand clasped me around the neck and pulled me towards him.

"It's me, Samuel," I said softly, as he stroked the side of my face and gazed into my eyes lovingly. I could feel my heart leaping in my chest, the adrenaline racing around my veins as I lay across him on the bed.

"Charlotte…my darling Charlotte. You've come back to me," he murmured, kissing my forehead tenderly. I froze for a moment but said nothing. He obviously was not aware who it was and continued his caressing.

"Yes, it's me," I replied, feeling guilty for deceiving him, but enjoying the moment far too much to stop his fantasizing.

"Charlotte, I love you so much," he whispered. "Why did you leave me?"

"I'm so sorry, my darling," I whispered back, "I'm here now, and I'm never going to leave you. I promise. I love you, Samuel, more than anything else in *this* world." His lips found mine, and we melted together. I didn't care if he thought I was Charlotte. They were *my* lips he was kissing right now, for the first time—and probably the last. Contented, he fell back to sleep, and I eased my head out from under his arm. Pulling the cover up over him, I pressed a light kiss upon his forehead. "I won't let any harm come to you, my darling," I said quietly. "You and I were meant to be together—and together we shall be, whatever it takes." I left the room and went back downstairs to take the horses to the barn.

Charles returned in the early evening clutching a letter, which he promptly gave to me to read for him. It was from a friend of Elijah, the mill owner, to inform us that he had passed away in his sleep and that his son, Robert, would be arriving shortly. It was Elijah's wish for Charles to give Robert bed and board for the duration of his stay. Charles nodded in agreement to his request, although he knew nothing of this man.

I was preparing the chicken for the evening meal when Charles came into the kitchen.

"Forgive me for not inquiring earlier, but did you purchase the warm garments you desired?"

"Yes, I did. Thank you, Charles. I was able to buy three such garments, and one will be most suitable for tomorrow," I replied, smiling to myself at the spontaneous use of 17th century grammar. I was beginning to belong here.

"Have you seen Samuel since your return from Greenham?" he then asked, somewhat awkwardly. I felt myself blushing and hesitated before replying.

"He is upstairs, lying down…in my bed," I replied, avoiding his eyes. A stunned silence followed, and I quickly rephrased the sentence. "He didn't feel well on our return, so I suggested he rest for a while . . . a bit too much to drink, I fear." Charles accepted my explanation, but there was doubt in his mind.

I had just put the roasted bird upon the table, later that evening, when we heard thunderous footsteps descending the stairs. Charles and I exchanged nervous glances as Samuel burst into the room. His clothes were in disarray and his hair dishevelled.

"How did I happen to be in your bed?" he asked, looking directly at me for an explanation.

"Do you not remember?" I teased, setting him out a plate. He ran his hand up through his hair, trying to recall the morning's events.

"I remember little after arriving in Greenham," he said as he sat down at the table, his eyes burning into mine.

"Then perhaps it is best left that way," I said, smiling sweetly across the table at his bewildered expression. Charles brought the tense moment to a close with a discrete cough.

"I received a letter today, informing us of Elijah's sudden death," said Charles, distracting his attention from me. "We will be having Robert, his son, here as our guest shortly, and I trust you will make him welcome, as he will most certainly be taking over his father's business at the mill."

"Will *he* be sleeping in Emily's bed, too?" smirked Samuel, giving me a frosty glare.

"That will do, Samuel. If you cannot be civil, leave the room!" yelled Charles at his tempestuous son.

The rest of the meal was eaten in silence, with Samuel giving me the occasional puzzled look as he ran his fingers over his lips. *Was he recalling strange unexplainable flashbacks?* It felt good to have one over on the seemingly invincible Samuel Howerd for once. After the meal, Samuel went upstairs to collect his boots and cape. I followed him up purposefully and watched while he dressed and adjusted his clothes, much to his dislike.

"I do not recall the journey home from Greenham," he said, confused, as he fastened his boots. "How did we arrive here if I was so—so—."

"Drunk?" I offered, smiling. He scowled at me and continued,

"Very well. Have your pleasure at my expense!"

"Oh, believe me, I will, and I did." I replied, laughing, which only aggravated him more.

"Just answer the question, woman!" he shouted, standing up and throwing his cloak around his shoulders.

"All right, I will. *I* drove the horses home myself, while you slept in the back," I said proudly.

"Hah! *You* drove the horses?"

"I did indeed. It was not as difficult as I presumed." He looked at me seriously, to try and ascertain if I were merely joking, or if I had really performed this formidable task on my own. He decided on the latter.

"Is there *nothing* the extraordinary Miss Emily cannot do?" he inquired, with a touch of sarcasm.

"I cannot win your heart," I said softly.

"No...you cannot," he replied coldly. "Your lips will *never* have the pleasure of meeting mine in tenderness. You can but dream." With that cutting remark he left the room, unable to witness the large, contented smile upon my face.

I went to bed early that night. It had been quite a distressing day, and tomorrow was not going to be any happier. After laying out my newly acquired black woollen sack of a dress on the chest, I climbed into bed and lay there, visualizing Samuel next to me. I hugged the pillow that his head had laid upon. I could smell him, I could feel him...I could taste his lips upon mine, and I wanted him so badly. It was demoralizing to know he had only shown affection towards me whilst drunk, and then to declare his love for another woman, as he held me in his arms. It broke my heart. I turned away, to stare at the moon through the window, before blowing out the candle. *Perhaps his death will be a welcome release from all this misery?*

The morning of Hannah's funeral dawned dull and overcast. Heavy grey clouds threatened to dispatch their load, be it rain or snow, as we prepared to attend the burial of a much-loved child and devoted mother. The black dress fitted better than expected, and was certainly much warmer than the flimsy cotton ones I had brought with me. Samuel was his usual sullen self during breakfast, but my mind was on Charles. He needed my support today, and I intended to be there for him.

The funeral cortège arrived at the bottom of the track just before eleven. Two beautiful black horses with black accessories and feathered plumes on their heads pulled a cart carrying Hannah's body, and that of her child. The coffin was just a plain wooden box. We were to walk behind the cart, to the church in Offenham, where a short service was to be held followed by her burial. Some other people from along the lane joined Charles, Samuel, and I along the way—all wanting to pay their last respects, and all deeply saddened by the premature deaths.

I was glad, to an extent, that the children were not present. It would have been heartbreaking to see their little faces stained with tears of sorrow. I had only known them for a short time, but felt just as upset and close to tears as the rest. We reached the church and quietly filed inside for the service. Three minutes later, and we would have been caught in a torrential downpour as the heavens opened. I sat next to Charles and gently took his hand in mine, to comfort him during the service. Samuel sat with his head bowed on the aisle side, unable to offer his father any solace. There must have been around thirty people in the church—all complete strangers to me, but they offered me sympathetic smiles whenever I caught their eye. Although the service was short, it was beautifully done. Nothing but praise was bestowed upon Hannah for the short time she had lived on this earth. She was well loved by everyone, and she would have been so proud. Thankfully, the rain had ceased by the time we departed the church, and the sun was breaking through patches of blue sky, shedding some warmth upon the congregation. A plot had been prepared for her burial—up against the church wall, just as I remembered it. William Howerd was there, next to her already, but that was all…for the time being. Samuel stood silently next to me, his hands grasped together as he listened to the pastor reciting from the Bible. I felt uncomfortable. This place held unpleasant memories, and I furtively glanced around at the other mourners.

A man standing some way off under a tree caught my attention. The large black hat he wore was somewhat amusing, and I wondered who he might be. I tugged Samuel's cloak discretely.

"Do you know that man with the funny hat over there by the tree?" I whispered.

"Funny hat?" he repeated, looking in the direction I indicated. I nodded. "No…I am not acquainted with him. Maybe he is a relative from your dubious past?"

"I don't know him," I replied.

"Good...then perhaps we can return to the purpose for which we are here?"

"I'm sorry," I said apologetically, and returned my attention to the coffin as it was lowered into the deep muddy hole in the ground, to rest for all eternity.

Afterwards, Charles mingled with the parishioners and thanked them for their kind words and sympathy. I noticed that the '*funny hat*' man was loitering behind, looking over in our direction frequently, as if waiting for something. Feeling strangely uneasy, I stayed close to Samuel, while he waited for his father to conclude with the well-wishers. As the last person departed, the man made his move and came directly over to Charles, blocking his path.

"Charles Howerd?" the middle-aged man asked politely, removing his hat and releasing a mop of grey curly hair.

"I am he," replied Charles.

"Good afternoon, sir. My name is Robert Spedding. I understand you have been expecting me?"

"Ah. Elijah's son...yes, of course," said Charles, shaking his hand warmly. "This is my son, Samuel. He worked with me at your father's mill." The man held out his hand to Samuel, who took it warily, without smiling. Robert stared at him for a moment, deep in thought, and then he turned to me.

"And who is this delightful young lady, may I ask?"

"This is Miss Emily. She is a guest at the cottage, and shall remain there after my departure tomorrow," announced Charles gently, pushing me forward to greet the stranger. He bowed to me, and I returned the gesture with a small curtsy, as I had seen others do in such circumstances. Taking my hand, he pressed it lightly to his lips.

"Enchanted, indeed," he said softly, looking deep into my eyes. I pulled away. *Those eyes...where had I seen those eyes before?*

We all walked slowly back along the lane to Mill Cottage, Charles in deep conversation with Robert up ahead, and Samuel and I trailing behind.

"I don't like him," I said to Samuel. "I don't know why, but he unnerves me…and I'm *sure* I've seen him before."

"You said you were unacquainted with him before—at the graveside—and now you *know* him?" replied Samuel lethargically, as he picked up a stick from the ground and snapped it in half.

"I think—although I cannot be sure—that I saw him in Greenham yesterday. I bumped into him accidentally." Samuel raised an eyebrow and cast me a weary glance.

"The manner in which you present yourself is of no concern to me. You could do worse."

"What? You think I find him attractive?"

"He is obviously quite taken with you," retorted Samuel, as he threw the sticks away into the trees.

"My God! He is all of fifty years old, if not more!" I cried, "I'm not *that* desperate!"

"Then perhaps you should be, or you will soon find yourself too old to acquire a suitor."

"I'm only twenty-five. There's plenty of life left in me yet," I said, dismayed that he had all but written me off as an aging spinster.

"By your age you should have already been wed and produced seven children, if not more." I laughed out loud at his ludicrous assumptions.

"So why aren't *you* married, then? Isabelle appeared to have your undivided attention whilst at Edgebarton?" I asked cautiously, as we turned onto the track to Mill Cottage.

"You know very well the answer to that impertinent question, and I do not wish to discuss my personal life with you any further," he replied bluntly, walking ahead to catch up with his father and Robert.

Our guest was settled into Charles's bedroom, and was given the grand tour of the cottages and outbuildings, before the evening meal. I had learned that the land on which the two cottages stood was actually owned by the late Elijah Spedding, and would soon be passed to Robert, on the reading of the will in a few days. He sat with his feet up on the table, discussing the mill with Charles, and how he intended to improve on its presently outdated equipment. Every time I passed through the room, I could feel his eyes following me, and I purposely averted my gaze from his unwanted attention. I also noticed that he watched Samuel's movements with interest, but made little effort to converse with him which I thought was strange, as he was also a past employee of his father's.

As this was to be Charles's last night before departing for Edgebarton in the morning, he decided to kill one of the pigs for a special feast, and left the remainder to be salted and stored for us, should food become scarce during the winter months. Robert offered to do the horrendous deed himself, whilst Samuel collected more wood for the fire. Whilst alone with Charles, I decided to ask a few nondescript questions, concerning our new arrival.

"What do you know about this man?" I asked, as I fetched the plates down from the shelf, and began setting four places around the table.

"You say that with concern in your voice, child? I have no reason to doubt that Mr Spedding is a fine, upstanding gentleman. He is soon to come into much money from his father's will." He said the last part as he glanced at me, and I noticed a certain twinkle in his eye.

"But can he be trusted?" I urged, ignoring his failed attempt to lure me.

"Has he acted inappropriately towards you?"

"No."

"Been impolite or disrespectful?"

"No."

"Taken it upon himself to strike you?" I could see where *this* was heading.

"No, of course not, but..."

"Then you are far safer under this roof, with Robert Spedding, than you would ever be with my eldest son. You would be wise to remember that," said Charles, stroking my head affectionately, as a father might a daughter. I sighed and continued to prepare the table, but there was still this niggling doubt in my mind that refused to go away.

The roast pork was delicious. Together with the bread, cheese and red wine, we all fell back in our chairs, fit to burst. Robert was certainly an entertaining dinner companion, and captivated us with exciting tales of his sea voyages around the world. *Maybe I was a little hasty in my opinion of him? He would make someone a desirable husband,* which prompted me to ask him the inevitable question.

"Are you married, Mr Spedding?" Samuel shifted uneasily in his chair beside me.

"No. I am not," he replied, pouring himself some more wine.

"You surprise me, sir," I continued. "You have no children to inherit the business?"

"It would appear so," he answered back, his expression changing to one of insecurity, with a hint of agitation.

"So, why did you choose to go away to sea, instead of working with your father at the mill?" I asked, eager to know more about the past of this intriguing guest, if not to put my own mind at rest from its reservations.

"You ask a lot of questions, young Emily," he commented, casting me a stern glance with his eyes, which had suddenly taken on a much darker appearance.

"I have an inquiring mind," I replied, staring defiantly back at him across the table.

"What you choose to discover is not always to your advantage."

"That depends on whether you have something to hide or not?" I said quickly, without realizing that what I was implying was not only disrespectful to our guest, but also downright rude.

"Emily!" cried Charles, "Apologize to Mr Spedding for your impertinence at once!" I sat back in my chair, the color rising to my cheeks at the humiliation of being reprimanded like a naughty child.

"I'm sorry…that was discourteous of me, to presume you are anything but a respectable and honest gentleman," I apologized, feeling anything but *sorry*. Robert laughed heartily and poured more wine into his mug.

"I accept your apology, Miss Emily, but let me assure you, I have *nothing* to hide." I smiled weakly and collected up the dirty plates, ignoring the disdainful looks coming from Samuel, who immediately followed me into the kitchen area.

"It is evident why you are still unwed, when you treat eligible and prosperous suitors with such contempt!" snarled Samuel, who was close behind me. I dropped the pewter dishes into the sink and spun around to face him.

"Stop trying to marry me off. You are as bad as your father!" I cried. "I have no interest at all in Robert Spedding. I tell you Samuel that man is—"

"That man is *what*, precisely?" interrupted Robert from the doorway. Samuel and I both stood there, stunned, with our mouths open. "If Samuel wishes to continue working at the mill under my ownership, I would think *very* carefully before you respond to that question," said Robert, in a low threatening tone that sent shivers down my spine. I felt Samuel put a strong hand around my waist and pull me protectively towards him. At least now he understood my concerns.

Chapter Fourteen

Robert's eyes dropped to the arm encircling my waist, and he nodded his head, smiling contentedly.

"You have excellent taste in women, Samuel, not unlike myself. I can see *clearly* what attracted you to her," he said, slowly and deliberately. He cast a roving eye over my body, making me feel cheap and dirty.

"Ah! There you are, Robert," cried Charles, poking his head around the door. "I have a fine bottle of brandy. Would you care to join me before we retire for the night?"

"Certainly," replied Robert politely. "I was just telling your son how much I am going to take pleasure in staying here." He left the room to join Charles, without so much as a backward glance. Samuel withdrew his hand at once and stepped aside.

"The man also lies admirably," he said, leaning back against the wall in deep thought. "You would do well to distance yourself from him whenever possible."

"I intend to. Believe me," I said quietly. "And I advise you to do likewise."

"I don't think it is *I* who is the object of his adoration," replied Samuel, giving me a concerned look.

"I didn't think you cared?" I taunted, smiling mischievously.

"Then you underestimate me…although to *care* for someone should not be confused with the concept of *love.*"

"Of course not. Perish the thought!" I cried, turning away to the sink to conceal a grin.

"I bid you, then, a goodnight, Miss Emily," said Samuel as he walked to the door.

"Goodnight, Samuel…and thank you." He turned and smiled. *Was it me, or was there more in that smile than just caring?*

I cleaned the plates and, taking a candle, went upstairs to lay out the straw pallet on the floor that Charles would sleep on tonight, as Robert had commandeered his bed. It would be strange not having Charles here. I had grown to love him as a father, and I would miss him deeply when he moved to Edgebarton. Then a disturbing thought struck me. Tomorrow night I would be here on my own, with Robert, sleeping in the room opposite! *What if he came in to me during the night?* He was a large man—and strong. I would not be able to fight off his advances, and there was no one to hear my cries for help! Feeling increasingly anxious, I crossed the passage into my room and set the candle down on the table by the bed. As Robert evidently thought that Samuel and I were an item, it would not seem strange for my lover to share my bed—to actually sleep with me, you understand, not to *sleep* with me. Memories of dear Sam came flooding back, along with the whole hotel bedroom scenario.

I had not thought about Sam—or my other life, for some time. Now completely absorbed into 17th century life, I had all but forgotten about my other existence. I took off my black woollen dress and folded it up, before placing it at the very bottom of my carryall. Picking up my digital camera, I remembered that I had to take some photos before I returned again, to prove to Sam that this place did exist and was not a figment of my imagination. A piece of paper fluttered to the floor that had stuck itself to the back of the camera. I recognized it immediately. It was the odd poem that came with the deeds of the cottage. Sitting down upon the bed, I read it through again.

'To you, dear child, I leave this place.
Go hither there. Do make haste.
Seek the garden. Seek the pear.
For old Mill Cottage will still be there.'
The time is present. The time is past.
Decide on two. The third's your last.'

It all made sense now. Even the last line, the one that had once seemed so ominous, was now painfully clear. I would only have three chances to travel back in time. On my third attempt, I would no longer be able to return to the future. Therefore I had to decide when I went back home from this, my second venture, whether I wanted to return for all eternity or remain in the future. The answer to that question depended entirely upon Samuel. *If he died, as fate intended, then why should I want to remain here? Why should I want to stay in the future, come to that? There was no one special in my life.* I shivered with the cold and crawled underneath the bed cover. In four days' time, I would have the answer to my question.

The sound of men's voices could be heard, as Robert and Charles made their way unsteadily up the staircase. By the sound of their drunken laughter, they had consumed a fair amount, if not the *entire* bottle of brandy. This was probably Charles' way of dealing with the fact that he had just buried his wife and child. It blurred the reality of it, until he could cope sufficiently without the aid of a bottle. Robert posed no threat to Samuel, as far as I could ascertain. It was I who was in danger of falling prey to this lecherous old man. Tomorrow I would have to speak to Samuel and try and persuade him to sleep in the cottage. Failing that, I would have to move into the barn. Sleeping on warm soft straw next to the man I loved didn't seem such a penance, and I drifted off to sleep with that comforting thought.

The next morning brought about much commotion and activity, as Charles prepared for the move to Edgebarton. Several large chests were loaded onto the cart and secured down for the journey. The horses were harnessed, and I had written down verbal instructions from Charles regarding household chores, the feeding of livestock, and where I could obtain money should the need arise. It was anticipated that John would bring the children home within a few days, if they so desired, although I imagined that life with Aunt Elizabeth and Miss '*Cute Curls*' was far more alluring. It soon became time to say our goodbyes, and I hugged Charles tightly, fighting back the tears. I didn't know if I would ever see him again, but I would never forget him and the kindness he showed towards me. Over his shoulder, I could see Robert staring at us, no doubt wishing it was him on the receiving end of my affectionate embrace. Samuel shook his father's hand and hugged him briefly, before he helped him up onto the bench.

"Give Aunt Elizabeth my regards, and remember me to Miss Isabella," called Samuel, purposely avoiding any eye contact with me, which was just as well.

"Rest assured, Charles. I will take good care of them. They will not go without," added Robert, every inch the considerate gentleman. I felt sick. *If only Charles knew what he had left us to deal with.* "So...now it is just the three of us," Robert said quietly to me, as the cart that carried Charles away rounded the bend and vanished from sight.

"Yes, unfortunately," I said under my breath, and walked past him into the cottage to find Samuel. "I want to talk to you," I whispered, as he sat down on the bench and finished the remainder of his breakfast.

"I am listening," Samuel replied indifferently.

"Not here. Later. Outside," I hissed, as Robert sat down on the bench to join us, uncomfortably close to me. I pulled my green dress out from under his heavy thighs and shifted along, to the far end of the bench by the fire. Robert looked at Samuel, and then to me, as we sat silently together.

"Your father," he began. "Told me of the events surrounding your ill-fated wedding day, Samuel," he said heartlessly. I looked up in horror. This was *not* a good topic of conversation. "Still," he continued, "I am glad to see the untoward occasion has not dampened your ardor. Maybe you will be more fortunate in bringing *this* young lady to the altar?" I felt as if I was sitting on a time bomb and someone had just lit the fuse. A deathly hush fell over the room, and I watched Samuel's face for signs of an imminent explosion. His eyes wandered to the fire, and I noticed his fists clenched tightly, as he fought bravely to control his temper. I felt like smacking the arrogant bastard, right there and then, for bringing up this delicate subject so unnecessarily. Samuel rose from the bench and stood before Robert, looking down at him in disgust.

"I will not waste my breath on one that finds pleasure in other people's misfortune. You were not there to witness my humiliation, and therefore you are in no position to suggest I would wish to repeat such an occasion." After that gallant statement, he turned to me sympathetically.

"I mean to cause you no disrespect, Miss Emily. I am merely speaking my mind."

"None taken," I replied, completely taken aback by his response, which was not only polite, but totally out of character. Samuel left to attend to the horses, leaving me alone with the ill-mannered gentleman. And I use the word '*gentleman*' very loosely.

"Perhaps you should not be too hasty in assuming your betrothal is not without its problems," said Robert as he leaned back, a smirk upon his face. "Maybe an older, more educated man would be more to your taste?" I got up to leave, ignoring his sordid remark. I really had to talk to Samuel about tonight.

I found him in the barn feeding his horse, and went over to stroke the animal, trying to find the right words to use without sounding too promiscuous.

"You wished to speak with me?" Samuel said at last. I fidgeted nervously with the horse's mane.

"It's about tonight." I began hesitantly.

"What about it?"

"I don't want to be alone with Robert in the cottage, and I was wondering if…if—"

"If *what*?" asked Samuel, coming around to my side and unfastening the saddle.

"If…you would sleep with me?" I quickly blurted out. *My God! That sounded terrible!* Samuel stopped what he was doing and stared at me in disbelief.

"Forgive me, but did you just ask me to bed you?"

"I asked for you to sleep with me. It's *not* the same thing." I replied, feeling my cheeks blush a deep red.

"This is most inappropriate, Emily. We are neither united in wedlock nor betrothed, and you stand before me and summon me to your bed? Your request is surely befitting a lady of the night, which I must respectfully refuse."

"No! No, you don't understand!" I cried. "I just want you to sleep next to me, in case Robert decides to take advantage of me. I don't want you to...*touch me*. Just lie next to me. Will you do that for me? I really don't trust him." A long period of silence followed.

"Just to lie next to you?" repeated Samuel at last, looking away from me.

"Yes," I replied. "Nothing more." *Not unless you want to,* I thought, hopefully.

"In my garments?" he inquired seriously.

"If you so wish."

"On *top* of the cover?"

"If you want to, but it's cold," I replied, my heart starting to race. Samuel took off the saddle and hung it on a nail, as I waited with baited breath for his answer. It seemed like an eternity before he spoke.

"Very well. I will do as you ask," he said finally, after much thought. "For the sole reason that I despise the man, and would never forgive myself should any harm befall you, due to my lack of indiscretion."

"Thank you!" I cried, almost wanting to throw my arms around his neck with sheer relief, but that would be pushing him *too* far. Walking back to the cottage, I thought how funny it was that I almost had to beg Samuel to sleep with me. Modern-day guys would have leapt at the chance to get me into bed. I liked the reserved attitude of 17th century men. It was so much more romantic.

Consulting my list of daily chores, I set about feeding the chickens, pigs and sheep. Then there was the cottage to sweep, floor to wash and bread to buy. I had not mastered the art of bread making as of yet. I had the instructions written down, but thought that a daily walk into the village would be more enjoyable than fighting with a lump of sticky dough. Robert had disappeared, having probably walked to the village himself, and Samuel was busy in the barn brushing down the horses. I took a break after an hour and sat down on the doorstep, sipping some warmed milk.

Thinking about what Robert had said earlier, concerning the 'infamous' wedding, I recalled something Charles had mentioned on the day his wife died. *Didn't he bring up the fact that Robert had returned for a brief visit about two years ago? Could it have been around the time of the wedding?* There were many questions I would like to ask Mr Robert Spedding, including the unanswered one about why he went away to sea. I would have to choose my moment carefully.

Robert returned from the village, as I thought, later that afternoon. He handed me a large brown paper parcel and a loaf of bread. The package contained two stiff brown furry rabbits that had been freshly killed, judging from the bright red blood seeping from its mouth.

"I like to pay my way," he informed me. "You can show your gratitude later," he added, with a self-satisfied smirk, and went inside. I was fuming, but refused to let this imbecile get the better of me. Besides, I had an ace up my sleeve for later.

The evening meal was a somber affair, although I was quite pleased with the rabbit stew I had produced, without any help. *Who needs fan-assisted electric ovens when you have a roaring fire?* Robert tried to make conversation, but I found it hard to believe anything he said, and Samuel shot him down in flames at every opportunity, much to my amusement. It was nice to have Samuel on my side for once. I could see a marked change in his attitude recently, and I would have liked to think that *I* had something to do with his transformation. My love for this fiery, unpredictable man had grown so much of late that it scared me. If he was taken from me on the 16th, I would be devastated. *Did I really want to punish myself so cruelly for falling in love with him?* The arrival of Robert posed another threat, *but what possible dispute could he have with a man he had only just met? Unless Samuel provoked him to such an extent that it endangered his life?* This seemed increasingly possible. I would talk to Samuel later about my qualms.

We sat by the fire until late into the evening. I read a small pocket book, which I had found tucked away in a dusty corner while I was sweeping today. It contained love poems and set the mood for the night ahead. Samuel stretched out his long legs across to the bench beside me. I could feel him watching me, and I could almost hear his thoughts as they tumbled around his confused mind. Robert sat next to me, smoking some foul-smelling tobacco in a clay pipe, his fingers caressing the folds of my dress furtively, while he stared intently across at Samuel.

Another hour passed by, and I put the book aside, yawning loudly. It was almost midnight, but no one seemed eager to get to bed. The fire had died down to faint glowing embers, and I got up to light the candles. I had a sneaking suspicion that Robert was waiting for Samuel to leave before making a move on me. I couldn't wait to see his face.

"I'm going to bed. Are you coming, Samuel?" I asked, casually picking up a candle. Robert shot him a startled look, awaiting his response.

"Yes, I am ready, my love," he replied as he got up from his place on the bench. I found it hard to contain my laughter at the expression on Robert's face and hurriedly ascended the stairs, calling out a cheery,

"Goodnight, Mr Spedding," as I went. *Revenge was sweet.*

Samuel and I burst into the bedroom like a couple of giggling schoolchildren and shut the door firmly behind us. We soon composed ourselves as the realisation of what lay ahead dawned on us, and an awkward silence fell upon the room.

"Maybe you could turn away to the window while I—er, undress?" I said as Samuel stood there, staring at me nervously.

"Yes, of course. Forgive me," he said as he turned to the window, embarrassed. "But if I recall, on our first meeting, you had no such reservations in displaying your breasts to me!" Cringing from the memory, I slipped off my thick woollen dress and removed my boots. Charles had given me some of Hannah's clothes, including a long white nightshirt with frilled cuffs, which I hastily put on over my bra and pants. Removing my watch, I placed it with the locket in the side of the carryall and scrambled underneath the covers of the bed, shivering with the cold and mounting anticipation. I turned to face the door and called out softly from beneath the cover.

"All right. I'm in." I listened while he sat on the edge of the bed and took off his boots. More rustling occurred as another item of clothing was removed, and there it stopped. I could hear him breathing rather heavily, but he made no attempt to join me in the bed. After a few moments, I turned around to see what the problem was. The candlelight flickered on his anxious face, as he stood there, rigid with the cold, in his shirt and leggings. "For goodness sake, Samuel. Get in under the cover. I'm not going to bite you!" I said, nodding to the far side of the bed. Sighing, he pulled back the cover and climbed into the bed beside me. It was a very wide bed, and he must have been a good two feet away from me as he lay there on his back, staring silently up at the ceiling. I lay there doing likewise, watching the shadow from the candle dance erratically above us. *This feels so weird!*

"Did you see Robert's face?" I whispered at last, trying to ease the tension. He smiled but continued to stare at the ceiling.

"I think perhaps he understood the situation and shall refrain from any further improper advances."

"Let's hope so," I replied, turning to face him. "I really am very grateful for your support."

"It was indeed a strange request."

"But much more comfortable than a drafty old barn, is it not?" I asked. He did not reply to my question and closed his eyes. *He has the longest eyelashes I have ever seen on a man,* I thought to myself, as I looked at his peaceful face on the pillow. I remembered the way he held me the other day, the way his lips burned into mine with such strength and passion. I longed for him to take me in his arms tonight, if only to keep me warm against the bitter cold. I knew if I attempted to move any closer, he would run like a frightened rabbit. I had to be content. At least I knew he was safe. I turned over and blew out the candle, lying there for ages after, just listening to him breathing deeply next to me. "Sleep well, my darling," I whispered quietly. "Sleep well."

Chapter Fifteen

December 14th dawned bright and sunny. I was awakened early by the sunlight streaming down upon the bed. A mop of curly black hair lay only inches from my face on the pillow, and a heavy arm stretched across my body, pinning me down in the bed. I decided to pretend I was still asleep and let him awake first, to discover where he had roamed during the night. I didn't have long to wait before I felt him stir, and move his arm up around my neck, obviously still not quite conscious. The moment was short-lived, and he suddenly went rigid before retracting his arm quickly and moving over to the edge of the bed.

I began to '*awaken*,' stretching lazily, whilst making soft moaning noises before opening my eyes and looking far across the bed at Samuel's back.

"Good morning," I said sleepily. No reply. "Samuel, are you awake?" Still no reply, so I moved cautiously across to his side of the bed, which sparked an immediate reaction.

"I'll attend to the fire," he cried suddenly, jumping out of the bed. He hurriedly dressed whilst I watched him, propped up on one elbow.

"Did you sleep well?" I inquired while he fastened his boots.

"Yes, very well. It is a long time indeed since I slept upon a bed."

"Good, then you can join me again tonight," I replied, smiling innocently. He stopped what he was doing and stared at me in panic.

"This was not to be a permanent arrangement, as I understood," he said, getting up and moving to the door.

"Just until Robert leaves. After that, you are free to go."

"He could be here *weeks*!" cried Samuel in dismay. I was beginning to feel slightly disheartened and slid out of the bed to confront him.

"Am I really that insufferable that you cannot bear to be close to me?"

"I did not mean for you to feel offended by the manner of my words," he said sympathetically, his eyes dropping to my firm breasts inadvertently beneath the cotton nightshirt. "It is just that I feel *uncomfortable* with one so likened to Charlotte, when it is not her." His eyes returned to my face before he excused himself and descended the staircase. *Perhaps I should cut my hair short and dye it blonde?* I thought to myself in a moment of madness!

By the time I arrived downstairs, the fire was well underway, and I prepared the porridge in the iron pot and hung it above the flames. Samuel was outside, taking his frustrations out on a large log with an axe. We had plenty of firewood stored already, but I left him to work off his pent-up emotions, hoping that by tonight he would be less jittery. I turned to go back inside and stir the porridge, just as Robert appeared through the trees, carrying a gun and three dead pigeons. He followed me inside and threw the birds down onto the table.

"Where did you get the gun?" I asked, eyeing the weapon in his hand nervously.

"I purchased it from the blacksmith in the village this morning," he replied coming over to me. "The wood is so smooth. Do you want to feel it?" He began to run his fingers up and down the gun rhythmically, watching my face earnestly. I suddenly realized what he was implying and turned away, disgusted. He laughed coarsely and took the birds through into the kitchen. After spooning the hot porridge out into three bowls, I set them upon the table, adding some bread and the remainder of the cheese.

I would have to walk into the village today, as there were several items I needed to buy, and I relished the thought of being able to escape from Robert's incessant scrutiny for a while. I asked Samuel if he would care to accompany me to the village, but he declined my offer, in order to stay behind and repair the pig's enclosure. After breakfast, Robert informed us that he would be going to his father's house to make an inventory of his possessions. My mind rested easier. The thought of these two volatile men left in each other's company while I was gone was unsettling. *Anything could happen.* Collecting a few coins from a tankard above the fireplace, I put my cloak around my shoulders and picked up a wicker basket by the door. I felt like little Red Riding Hood on her way to visit her grandma through the woods, but the big bad wolf had gone off elsewhere, and my journey would thankfully be free from danger.

Although it was sunny, it was deceiving. The wind was keen, and I put my head down as I walked briskly along the lane to the village. As usual, the place was busy. I mingled in with the village folk, who were blissfully unaware that they were rubbing shoulders with a time traveler from the future. My basket soon became filled with the items I required, and I still had a few coins left over, which would be put back into the tankard for another errand. We would have to be careful with money until Samuel was, God willing, re-employed at the mill by Robert—not an altogether pleasing prospect, but vital for us to survive. Leaving the village, I walked slowly back along the lane, my thoughts again dwelling on the fast approaching '*Day of Judgment*' for Samuel. My stomach began to twist into knots the more I thought about it, and about how powerless I was to prevent the inevitable. Being so preoccupied with my thoughts, I was startled to suddenly find a man standing in the middle of the lane.

"Robert!" I cried, recognizing him instantly, "What are you doing here? I thought—"

"That is your problem, is it not? You think far too much," he interrupted. I didn't like the tone of his voice, and I felt threatened and very…*very* alone. He walked towards me and stopped a few feet away, with his arms folded and legs apart. *I mustn't let him see I'm scared,* I told myself, but that was before I set eyes on a gun tucked into his wide belt. "You think you were *so* clever last night, enlisting Samuel to protect you. You two are no more in love than you and I, and you never will be."

"You're wrong. We are very much in love!" I lied, my voice wavering.

"So in love that he doesn't take you in the night? The sheets were not soiled. I saw to it this morning." *What kind of man was I dealing with here? A sexual pervert, at the very least!* The Big Bad Wolf had found Little Red Riding Hood, and now the fairy tale was fast becoming a reality.

He walked a few steps closer and stopped. My heart started to pound erratically as I looked about for a way past this madman. The lane was narrow and densely wooded on either side, so it didn't give me much room to avoid his grasp should I make a run for it. I swallowed hard. *Maybe I could distract him with conversation?*

"What do you want from me?" *Stupid question. It was obvious.* He laughed and stepped closer. "Don't come any closer, or I'll scream!" I cried, backing away.

"Who is going to hear you? Not Samuel, for sure." he said calmly, unperturbed by my weak threat. His hand reached down and started to undo the button on his trousers. A bulge strained against the material, demanding freedom. Panic gripped me. Turning, I hitched up my dress and started to run back up the lane. My basket hindered my progress, and I threw it into the bushes, scattering brown paper packages in all directions. The dried and deep muddy ruts were difficult to negotiate at speed in a long dress, and it wasn't long before I was sent sprawling to the ground, as my ankle twisted over sharply on an uneven ridge. Robert's footsteps could be heard getting nearer and nearer as I tried to scramble to my feet, but the pain in my foot was almost unbearable. A large hand grasped the back of my dress and hauled me to my feet roughly, my cries of pain going unheeded as he dragged me into the bushes and pinned me up against the jagged bark of an old tree.

"Please, don't!" I sobbed, pushing away his hand fruitlessly as it pulled up the dress to my waist. I could feel the cold leather of his belt touch my exposed flesh, and I took a sharp breath. He only needed one hand to hold me in place. He was so strong. The other hand fumbled with his trousers, unleashing the beast within. I struggled like crazy as his bristly face scratched against my soft complexion. My mouth was forced into receiving his unwillingly. I closed my eyes. *Should I just give in and let him take me?* My strength began to fail me, as I felt his fingernails dig into the soft flesh of my inner thigh as he prised my legs apart, grunting like some wild pig with saliva dribbling down his chin.

I thought of Samuel. I could hear his voice in my head saying *'Fight, Emily! Fight, my love, for all you're worth!'* With a sudden rush of adrenaline, I thrust my knee up violently between his legs, causing him to buckle over in agony.

"God damn you, Charlotte!" he cried out, loosening his grip on my body momentarily. I took this opportunity to push him over, and he fell face down into the bracken, still moaning from my direct hit. Picking up a small fallen branch, I didn't hesitate as I smashed it down over his head. The moaning ceased. I stood there, shaking like a leaf, my breath coming hard and heavy as I looked in disbelief at the blood-splattered branch in my hand. *What have I done?* Throwing the branch aside, I stared at Robert, lying there on the ground with his eyes closed and blood trickling down the side of his face.

"You called me *Charlotte,*" I said quietly. "You knew her, didn't you?" A sharp pain ripped through my ankle, bringing me back to reality. I had to get back to the cottage—to Samuel.

Limping back along the lane, I gathered up the discarded paper parcels and basket, not wanting to return home empty-handed. My mind was all over the place, trying to piece together Robert's involvement in all of this. I probably never would, bearing in mind the fact that I had just murdered my key suspect. *My God! What was the penalty for murder in 1696?* Then again, no one saw me, and without modern-day forensic evidence, no one would ever know. He was simply a victim of a highway robbery.

It took forever to get back home. By the time I hobbled into the cottage doorway, I felt sick with the pain and collapsed onto a chair, exhausted. On examination, my ankle didn't appear to be broken, just badly sprained, which can be just as excruciating, or so I was once told. I could hear Samuel working about outside, but couldn't face him as yet, and waited for him to come inside as he would—eventually.

"Ah! You are back!" he said happily, as he entered the cottage later and sat down on the bench to remove his muddy boots. "Why did you take so long?" I hesitated in my reply, causing him to look up expectantly.

"I had a fall in the lane on my way back. My ankle is twisted, but not broken."

"Your face is stained with tears! Does it hurt so?" he said anxiously, taking hold of my foot to survey the damage.

"Don't worry. It will soon heal," I told him, feeling guilty for not giving him the whole sordid story. *What would he think of me if I told him the truth? Maybe that I was some kind of psycho who went around battering people to death, and therefore should be burnt at the stake for my sins? 'He deserved it!'* I can hear you scream. That may be so, but I had also lost Samuel the chance of working at the mill again. It would no doubt be shut down indefinitely, with no successor to take it over. Then there was the fact that he called me Charlotte. I dared not mention this, for fear of opening a whole new can of worms, which I had still not yet managed to get my head around myself. I didn't want to bring anymore heartache upon the poor guy. If Robert weren't already dead, he certainly would be, once Samuel found out that he might have had something to do with Charlotte's disappearance. I struggled with my conscience, trying to decide what I should do for the best and decided, perhaps against my better judgement, to keep quiet and appear as surprised as anyone at Robert's sudden disappearance.

A letter arrived in the late afternoon, delivered on horseback by a young boy that looked no older than ten. It was addressed to Mr Robert Spedding. I put it behind the tankard, on the shelf above the fireplace, to wait for all eternity for its deceased recipient. Samuel was still working outside on the pig enclosure, and I felt tempted to unseal it, wondering whom it could be from. It took all of five minutes to convince myself that this might be a *good* idea, as it may shed some light on his past. Taking it down, I carefully unstuck the wax and opened up the single sheet of parchment paper.

It appeared to be from a man who was dealing with Elijah Spedding's Will. He was to attend a reading of the Will, tomorrow in Greenham, at three o'clock. An address was given below that message. I folded up the parchment and reheated the wax over the fire before pressing it together and replacing it behind the tankard. He would never receive his inheritance now. I had altered a part of history—for the good, *or maybe for the worse? Who knows?* There was no turning back. I was responsible for Robert's death and all its future consequences.

Samuel came in just as it was getting dark. He was tired and dirty, but had finally finished repairing the enclosure. I began to ladle out some re-heated rabbit stew when he stopped me.

"Had we better not wait for Robert?" he said begrudgingly. "It would be wise not to provoke him any further." I froze like a statue for a moment before finding my voice.

"Yes…yes of course," I replied, replacing the ladle back into the pot and sitting down.

"I am surprised he has not returned. It is almost nightfall," added Samuel, going out to the sink to clean off some of the grime. I didn't answer. Instead I looked hungrily over at the pot of stew above the fire and wondered how long he intended to wait for our absent guest.

"Perhaps he is staying over at his father's house for the night," I suggested, after nearly an hour had passed and Robert had still not materialized.

"It is a possibility, although I have a doubt as to that being the reason somehow."

"Why?" I asked, nervously fiddling with a spoon on the table.

"I do not know at present—just a feeling..." he replied, watching me intently across the table. "You appear troubled, Emily. Is there anything that worries you?"

"No!" I responded, a little too readily. "I'm just... *hungry.*" Samuel smiled and nodded to the pot.

"Very well. We shall eat. He will have to endure the leftovers, if any remain."

"I'm sure he won't mind." I replied, eagerly reaching for the ladle. *In fact, I was absolutely certain of it.*

As we ate, I mulled over in my mind if Samuel would sleep with me again tonight. With no Robert to protect me from, there was little need for him to stay. I just wanted him close by, although the only possible threat to his life was now eliminated. *Maybe I had inadvertently altered history and Samuel would no longer die on the 16th of December?* It was a pleasing thought, and I felt that a heavy burden had been removed from my shoulders.

As we sat by the fire after dinner, I started to unwind and tried to put the shocking events of the day behind me, but it was difficult. The words, '*God damn you, Charlotte',* kept my mind occupied with disturbing thoughts. Samuel lay stretched out on the bench opposite with his eyes closed, his head resting on a cushion, and his hand spread across his crotch in a sensual way that stirred my imagination. I looked away into the crackling fire, our minds at peace with each other in the quietness and still of the evening, with no one to spoil the magic of these tranquil moments.

Suddenly, out of the tranquillity, came the sound of horse's hooves outside of the cottage. I sat upright and looked towards the window as Samuel stirred and opened his eyes sleepily.

"The wanderer returns," he said, sitting up and stretching. I looked over at him, my eyes wide open and wondering whom it could be at this late hour. “He must have procured a ride back,” said Samuel, going over to the door and unlatching it, while I hovered curiously close behind.

“Samuel! Miss Emily!” A familiar voice cried out from the cart. “It is only I, John, back from Edgebarton.” He jumped down from the cart as I ran over and flung my arms around his neck, hugging him tightly, much to his surprise and embarrassment. It was so good to see him.

“Where are the others?” inquired Samuel, pulling me aside before I suffocated the poor lad in my over enthusiastic greeting.

“They have stayed on. I have much to tell, but first there is a more pressing concern to deal with,” he said, his face taking on a more serious demeanor.

“What’s wrong?” Samuel and I both replied in unison.

“On my journey up the lane, I happened upon a man staggering about on the roadside. I stopped to help the unfortunate gentleman, who was bleeding from a head wound, and I managed to assist him onto the cart.” The blood started to drain from my face as I looked warily towards the back of the cart. With my heart thumping loudly, I listened as he continued his story. “The gentleman was not able to give me his name, but he kept repeating Mill Cottage, and so I brought him here in the hope that you might know of him.” Samuel went immediately to the back of the cart and peered over the edge.

“It’s Robert!” He cried, looking back at me. “John, help me get him inside, and Emily, fetch some warm water and cloths.” I stood there, rooted to the spot, unable to move. “EMILY!” yelled Samuel. “I NEED WATER …NOW!”

Startled, I ran inside ahead of them and filled a pot with water. My hands were shaking violently as I hung it above the fire and threw on several more logs. *This was a nightmare!* They half-carried, half-dragged Robert up the stairs to his room and laid him upon the bed. John came down after a while to fetch the heated water, and told me to come with the cloths to assist them. I reluctantly followed him upstairs into his room. Robert lay, semi-conscious, across the bed. He was unaware of his surroundings and moaned in pain constantly, turning his head this way and that. My eyes wandered to his lower regions, and I saw that under his coat, his trousers were still undone and gaping. It all came back to me in a flash, and I relived those horrifying moments as he held me against the tree. I felt his powerful hands between my legs and his mouth…*his mouth pressing down.*

"For God's sake, Emily. Give me those cloths!" cried Samuel, snatching them from my hands. "What's the matter with you?" I turned and ran from the room in tears, stumbling down the stairs and collapsing onto the bench by the fire, where only a short while ago I sat contented and at peace with the man I loved. John came down first and approached me cautiously, unable to understand my emotional outburst upstairs.

"How is he?" I asked reluctantly.

"He will recover. He is indeed a fortunate man. If I had not traveled the lane tonight I fear, by the morning, he would surely be dead."

"Has Samuel told you about him?" I asked, feeling no remorse for the man whatsoever.

"I know he is Elijah's son, Robert, and he has been a guest here since before my father left."

"Nothing more?"

"What else is there to tell?" I could think of plenty, but I did not want to burden John with our experiences of this man in the short time he had been with us—and certainly not with mine. I would have two deaths on my hands if either of them knew what had happened in the lane earlier today. To defend my honor was one thing, but to die in the process was inconceivable. Robert was capable of murder. I had no doubt about that.

"So…tell me about the children. Are they happy? When will they return home?" I asked, changing the subject and putting on a cheerful expression that was only partly sincere. John informed me that they were well, and that Miss

Isabelle had taken it upon herself to teach the children to read and write. I was pleased, but thought that I could do a much better job of it. There was so much these children could learn from me, given the chance, but for the time being they were safer out of the way in Edgebarton.

Samuel descended the stairs. I got up to prepare a plate of stew for John, from the small portion remaining.

"Feeling better, are we?" he enquired sarcastically, before going outside to put the horses away in the barn for the night. John smiled and took a spoonful of stew.

"I see nothing has changed in my absence."

"What do you mean?" I asked innocently.

"You and Samuel, still as argumentative as ever, I see. I thought by now you both might have put aside your differences and tried to be more sociable."

"We are," I replied defensively, "now and again."

"This I must see!" exclaimed John, laughing. I playfully ruffled his hair. It might be sooner rather than later, I thought, depending on whether he stayed tonight. With Robert back, it was more likely, although I doubted he would be in any fit state to be a threat tonight. There were a few questions I would have liked to ask John, but they could wait until the morning. Now it was late, and I was physically exhausted. My ankle was throbbing like mad again. The two painkillers I had taken earlier had now worn off. Samuel came back in, covered in snow, and I could see through the window it was falling heavily again. He discarded his cloak and sat on a chair to remove his boots. John looked on, puzzled by his behavior, thinking surely, that he would need his boots to return to the barn for the night as usual. Samuel, on the other hand, was well aware of John's bemused look and avoided eye contact with his brother, should he decide to ask any awkward questions. I said nothing, and waiting apprehensively for his next move.

"Goodnight, John. It is good to have you home," he said, quickly rising to his feet and taking a candle from the table. "Emily, I will no doubt see you shortly?" With that incriminating statement swiftly delivered, he disappeared up the stairs, leaving me to explain to a stunned John why he was sleeping with a woman he found it hard to make civil conversation with, let alone anything else. John sat there with his mouth open in amazement, completely speechless.

"It's *not* what you think," I began. "I just didn't want to be alone here with Robert." John burst out laughing at what he thought was a pathetic excuse. "It's true! Ask Samuel yourself," I cried.

"Do you love him?" asked John excitedly, "Does he love you?" I groaned and raised my eyes to the ceiling in exasperation.

"I don't know," I replied, getting up. "I'm tired and want to go to bed. So, if you will excuse me?" John broke into an enormous grin, obviously enjoying thoughts of his brother bedding me. I was too exhausted to debate this topic of conversation any further tonight. A blast of icy wind blew in from the door as he opened it, bringing with it a shower of snow. I felt guilty, casting him out into a cold barn. He should have had Robert's bed, and that scoundrel upstairs should have been deported to a bed of rat-infested straw instead. "Will you be warm enough?" I asked anxiously. "I have another blanket you could use."

"I will be fine," replied John, "Unless, of course, you require *two* men to guard your chastity?" I handed him a lantern and playfully pushed him out the door. It was good to have him home again. After making sure the fire was safe for the night, I took the other candle and crept slowly upstairs, hesitating momentarily outside of Robert's room. The door was slightly ajar, and I peered in cautiously. By the sound of the heavy snoring coming from the bed, he was asleep. I pulled the door shut quietly. I dreaded the morning coming, but thought it unlikely that he would name me as his attacker without revealing the motive behind it.

It was dark in my room—or, should I say, *our* room now? Samuel had already extinguished his candle and lay precariously on the edge of the bed, facing the window. Undressing quickly, I slid under the cover and lay there, shivering with the cold. His breathing was quiet, and I wondered if he was asleep or just feigning it. There was only one way to find out.

"Samuel, are you asleep?" I whispered towards him. He stirred slightly and moaned. Taking a deep breath, I moved gingerly over to his side and lay up against his warm body.

"What are you doing?" said Samuel suddenly.

"I thought you were asleep," I replied softly, close behind him.

"Even if I was, you have no right to take advantage of me."

"I'm not taking advantage of you. I'm just really *cold*!" I said lightly, putting my arm around him. I could feel his body stiffen to my touch, but he didn't push me away. "Do you think Robert will recover?" I said quietly, my face buried in a mass of soft black curls.

"I'm sure, by tomorrow, he will be up causing more mayhem. It is regrettable that his assailant did not deliver a *fatal* blow to the head."

"But then you would not have a job?"

"To work under such a man would be more of a *penance* than a pleasure, but necessary. Are you going to snuff that candle, Emily? I would like to sleep before dawn," he added harshly, turning onto his back. I reluctantly moved across the bed and blew out the candle. "Are you still cold?" he whispered, after a moment's silence.

"Freezing," I replied truthfully. I heard him move across the bed towards me, and I held my breath as he put his arm around me and drew me close to his body.

"I am also cold," he murmured, close to my ear. I smiled contentedly and snuggled up to him. The harrowing events of the day melted away into a sea of ecstasy. This was *Emily* he held in his arms tonight, not some ghost from the past.

We awoke the following morning still entwined with one another. My nightshirt clung to me with perspiration from our bodies, and Samuel's hair lay damp upon my neck. I trembled as his hand moved sensually over my body, coming to rest on my thigh. My heart beating rapidly, I responded to his touch by running my fingers through his hair and down his back. He moaned quietly and rolled over, away from the temptation he so desired—but fought gallantly to evade—for his own morality. I felt it wouldn't be long before he succumbed to his needs—no man was that invincible—and we would finally become one.

There was movement from the room next door, and all the bad memories of yesterday came flooding back. Samuel hastily dressed and left to see to our wounded guest, who, despite his injuries, had managed to get out of bed and was making his way downstairs. I flopped back onto the pillow. The burden that had been momentarily lifted was once more resting heavily upon my shoulders, as the dreaded day drew nearer by the hour, by the minute.

When I eventually found the courage to go downstairs, I encountered Robert, his head swathed in cloth, talking to John at the table. The gullible lad was enthralled, as we once were, with his seafaring tales. Robert glanced in my direction briefly as I entered the room, and then carried on with his conversation as if nothing had happened.

"Where's Samuel?" I asked, directing my question at John.

"He is outside, chopping firewood, I believe," replied John. "Did you sleep well?" He added with a twinkle in his eye, "You look somewhat tired." I ignored the cheeky innuendo and started to prepare the breakfast.

"I am also well, apart from a throbbing headache, but thank you for your concern," said Robert contemptuously.

"Good," I replied without turning. "I feel so much better for knowing that."

Samuel came back in, lightly touching my waist as he passed by me to sit at the table, sending a pleasurable tingle up my spine.

"What's that?" asked Samuel, pointing to the tankard above the fireplace as I started to pour the porridge. I set down the jug and reached for the letter.

"It came yesterday for Robert. I forgot all about it for some reason." I said, throwing it down in front of him. "If you cannot read it, I will be happy to oblige," I said sarcastically. Robert picked up the letter angrily and tore away the wax seal. Samuel and John waited apprehensively for him to reveal the contents of the letter. I had no need.

"I am to go to Greenham today at three for the reading of my father's Will," he informed us before folding up the letter. "I would be grateful if one of your horses could be at my disposal?"

"Take mine," said John without hesitation, "Samuel's is too temperamental and strong-willed." *Just like it's owner,* I thought, smiling.

With breakfast out of the way, Samuel decided, to my dismay, to take John into the woods with him to shoot a few wild fowl for tonight's meal. My frantic efforts to deter them went unheeded—even by Samuel, who didn't think Robert posed a threat in his present condition. It was with growing unease that I watched them disappear through the trees. I went back inside, trying to appear calm, but inside I was terrified and ready to bolt for the door at the slightest provocation. I silently collected the bowls from the table, purposely avoiding any eye contact or close proximity with Robert.

"You need not worry your pretty little head. Your secret is safe with me…for the time being," said Robert menacingly as he watched me, like a fox might a frightened rabbit.

"What makes you think I won't tell them what you tried to do to me?" I cried, trembling with rage and fear.

"You won't, if you know what's good for you. Unfortunately, Charlotte did not." I stared at him in horror.

"So you *did* know Samuel's Charlotte!" I cried.

"I would like to consider her as *my* Charlotte. Samuel was never fortunate enough to have had the pleasure of her body as I have. Too much of a gentleman for his own good," he sneered, wiping his sweaty palms along his trousers. Suddenly feeling light-headed, I sat down on the bench and tried to recall what Hannah had told me about Charlotte.

"The baby.... Charlotte was carrying *your* child? Oh, God, no! Tell me it isn't so?" The smug expression on his face confirmed my fears. *Robert had raped Samuel's fiancée.* I put my head in my hands in despair, as Robert insisted on telling me every sordid detail.

"She kept her condition from Samuel, too ashamed to tell him the truth," he began. "As her belly became swollen, the guilt became too much for her to bear and she sought my help as the wedding day approached. I suggested that she should come away with me to London and become my wife. She did not love me—in fact, she despised me for the wrong I had done her—but she agreed to my request as I was a man of means, and I could provide adequately for her and the child. Arrangements were secretly made for our journey to London, but her love for Samuel was too strong. On the day of the wedding, she foolishly took it upon herself to return to Mill Cottage with the intention of telling Samuel everything, in the hope that he would *still* marry her. By the time she arrived, everyone had left for the church...everyone except I, who waited patiently among the trees, anticipating her intentions." He stopped to take a sip of mead before he continued, while I sat staring out of the window, not wanting to hear where this was going. "She was so like you in many ways—not only in appearances, but she also had your strong will and fiery temper, making her impetuous and untrustworthy."

"You said '*was*'... what happened to her Robert? What did you do to her to prevent her arriving at the church that day?" I asked, turning to face the man that had caused so much heartbreak in Samuel's life.

"She put up a brave fight. Samuel would have been proud of her." I gasped and edged nervously over towards the door, as I realized that I was alone in this cottage with not only a rapist, but also a murderer. Robert sprang to his feet and reached the door just ahead of me, his hand holding the latch firmly shut. I froze with fear as his face came close to mine. "You are most probably thinking in that inquisitive, but dangerous, mind of yours, 'why is he telling me all this?' Let this be a warning, Miss Emily, of what happens to silly little girls who cannot keep their mouths firmly closed…I do not want to have to dig a further grave," he said in a low rasping tone, his hand caressing the side of my face, before dropping down and gently seizing my neck in his large hand. "Your neck is as dainty and frail as Charlotte's and would snap just as easily." I let out a whimpering cry and pressed myself up against the door as I visualized Charlotte's slumped and lifeless head. He released his hand, laughing like someone manic, and walked back to sit at the table.

With my heart thumping wildly, I unlatched the door and ran out into the cold, with tears streaming down my face. Through the still air, I could hear the distant voices of Samuel and John returning from their hunt, completely oblivious to the drama that had unfolded in their absence. They couldn't possibly see me in this state. They would want to know what was wrong. With this thought in mind, I ran around to the barn and hid among the bales of straw, desperately trying to pull myself together and calm down before I faced them again with a false, cheery disposition. Robert was controlling me now as he had Charlotte. Only, this time; history was *not* going to repeat itself.

John came into the barn to saddle his horse for Robert's trip to Greenham. I waited until he had taken the horse around to the front of the cottage before venturing out, relieved that he would soon be leaving, and I wouldn't have to face him again until he returned, later in the day, delivering his good news.

"Where have you been?" inquired Samuel, after watching Robert gallop off down the track.

"I went into the village," I lied. "We needed more bread."

"You really must learn to make it yourself. It is money recklessly spent, and we can ill afford it at present," said Samuel sternly. The reprimand cut deep, and I felt myself weakening. With no one to turn to, the burden of knowing

Charlotte's demise only added to the weight already carried on my fragile shoulders.

I went inside and started to pluck the feathers off of the pheasants they had shot. My mind was all over the place, as I tried to surmise the events that could lead to Samuel's death tomorrow. *Does he find out from Robert what had happened to Charlotte? It couldn't have been from me, I wasn't here! Was I?* This was very confusing. *Does a fight break out, and Samuel comes off the worst?* Try as I might, I couldn't put my finger on the spark that might ignite a confrontation between Robert and Samuel. I felt sure that I was missing something. Having prepared the birds, I took the carcasses, feathers and entrails outside to dispose of down the pit; a deep hole into which was thrown a variety of rubbish and waste, and was conveniently sited a good distance from the cottage. I stood on the edge, looking down. *Could Robert have thrown Charlotte's corpse down here? No. He said he had dug a grave. If he killed her in, or by, the cottage, then her grave must be somewhere nearby.* I shuddered at the thought of Charlotte's remains lying close by, her spirit watching me resentfully as I took *her* place in Samuel's heart. *Perhaps she has a hand in Samuel's death?* Now I was becoming delusional!

Warming some of the freshly collected sheep's milk, I sat next to Samuel on the bench and watched him clean his gun. An old boyfriend of mine had been a gun fanatic. He often took me to the ranges with him and taught me how to fire the gun at distant ringed targets. This eventually led to the break-up of our relationship, as I became quite gifted at the sport, and he could not stand to be beaten by a woman. I asked Samuel to show me how it was loaded and explain the firing mechanism. He was happy to oblige, but thought it strange for a woman to have an interest in such things. This gun was, of course, a more inferior weapon by modern-day standards, but the end result was the same. It fired...*and it could kill.* I felt uneasy that he always kept it loaded, but I would have to learn to live with that potential hazard in the home.

Darkness fell, and there was still no sign of Robert. John became restless and sat by the window. I was hoping it was his horse that gave him cause for concern, rather than the monster that rode it. By eight o'clock we decided to eat. Everyone was a little anxious for their own individual reasons, and Samuel tried to lighten the mood.

"Maybe his assailant from yesterday decided to finish him off?" He laughed, taking a chunk of bread and mopping up the juices on his plate.

"Maybe my horse is injured?" said John, biting his nail nervously.

"Or *maybe* he is celebrating his good fortune in The Red Lion and has *over-indulged*...as one does," I said, glancing over at Samuel, who developed a sudden fit of coughing. I had to thump him on the back to dislodge a lump of bread.

After our meal, we all moved to the bench by the fire to keep warm. The temperature outside had dropped to below freezing, and even the fire struggled to provide adequate warmth. I sat close to Samuel and, to my surprise, he responded by putting a comforting arm around me, allowing me to rest my head on his shoulder. My thoughts drifted to Robert's confession. At least there was no chance now of Charlotte returning and rekindling their love affair, something that had played on my mind quite a lot recently. It would have been good for Samuel to know what happened to his lost love—to know that she did not desert him, as he believed, and she loved him to the very end. It would have enabled him to move on with his life—a kind of closure, but it would also be a death sentence.

There was no way I could tell him at this moment in time, and I hated having to keep such a terrible secret to myself when he deserved to know the truth. I cuddled up closer to him, my eyes glistening over, when I realized that this could be our last evening together—*our last night.* Tomorrow I wasn't going to let him out of my sight. Although no imminent danger appeared to be threatening his life, I wasn't going to take any chances. I loved him with all my heart, and no one was going to take him from me—not without one hell of a fight.

"Listen!" said John suddenly, springing from his seat and rushing over to the window. We both sat up at the sound of an approaching horse, and I immediately felt unsettled and agitated again. John opened the door, letting in the freezing night air, and went out to greet Robert. There was a scuffle and raised voices before Robert staggered in through the doorway. His face was red and he had a wild, angry appearance about him that denoted all was not well. He stood there swaying, looking from me to Samuel, with an expression that could not be described as anything else but pure hatred.

"What is wrong?" Samuel asked warily. "The Will was as expected, was it not?"

"No. It was precisely what I did *not* expect," growled Robert. "I hope my father rots in hell for dishonoring the promise he made to me!" he cried angrily, slowly approaching Samuel across the room. I moved closer to him, like a guardian angel, ready to defend him with my life should the need arise. "No one stands in the way of Robert William Spedding…*no one,"* he spat venomously into his face, causing him to recoil with alarm. Robert then closed his eyes, the drink finally getting the better of him, and he fell backwards onto the table before slumping to the floor in an undignified heap.

"John, your help is required in removing him to his room," said Samuel, taking command of the situation.

"What did he mean?" asked John, taking hold of Robert's arm and positioning it around his neck.

"I am as bewildered as you as to the nature of his abuse. I have done the man no wrong, and I am therefore not worthy of such threats," replied Samuel. I watched the two men struggle with Robert's heavy frame up the narrow staircase. *Was this the beginning of the end? Was this the unknown spark between Samuel and Robert, which had so far eluded me?* I picked up the fallen chairs and placed them back around the table. In doing so I noticed a piece of parchment, tied with a ribbon, which must have fallen from Robert's cloak as they tried to lift him. It could be a copy of the Will. *Dare I take a look?* It might explain Robert's wrath and give me a clearer picture of what I was up against.

I sat down at the table and untied the thin red ribbon. My hand started to shake as I gingerly unfolded it. The writing was in black ink. Some of the words and spellings were in old English and unfamiliar to me, but it *was* Elijah's Will. I read it slowly, to try and understand what could have incensed Robert so much in his father's final wishes.

'In the name of God Amen. I, Elijah George Jacob Spedding of Weaver House, Littleham, in the County of Kent, being weak in body but of perfect mind and memory—thanks be to God—doe make and ordaine this my Last Will and Testament in manner and form following Imprimis I bequeath my soule into the hands of Almighty God, my body to the earth to be buried decently. I appoint Walter Penbury of Greenham my sole executor as I hereby bequeath my entire Estate, parcels of land, houses, outbuildings and all my mony goods and chattels to my only grandson, Samuel Thomas Spedding, known as Samuel Thomas Howerd of Mill Cottage, Littleham. In witness whereof I have hereunto sett my hand and seale, Dated the 6th and 20th day of November in the year of our Lord God 1695.'

The parchment slipped from my hand as I fainted onto the floor. The realization of Robert's true identity was too much to bear.

Chapter Sixteen

When I came to, I found I was lying on my bed with a dark, threatening shape looming over me. I panicked and began to thrash around with my arms beating off the alleged attacker who, in return, fought to subdue me by gently, but firmly, holding down my arms.

"Emily…it is I, Samuel!" he cried. I stopped struggling, stared up at the worried face before me and dissolved into tears. Releasing my arms, he pulled me close to him, holding me tight against his pounding chest. His hand stroked my hair with the lightest of touches imaginable. He held me in his arms, silently, until I had calmed down and gained control of my emotions again.

"Where's Robert?" I asked anxiously, pulling away from him and drying my eyes on the cover.

"Asleep in his room. You will not be troubled with him until the morning," replied Samuel as he moved a damp lock of hair out of my eyes tenderly.

"And John?"

"He has returned to the barn for the night, only after I assured him that you were comfortable and out of danger." I looked around the room, and my eyes came to rest on the large clothes chest against the wall.

"Quick! Help me drag that chest up against the door so Robert cannot enter!" I cried, scrambling off the bed. Samuel watched me, bewildered for a moment, as I tried to haul the heavy chest across the floor by myself.

"Emily, stop it! What are you doing?" he said, pulling my hand off of the iron ring attached to the chest.

"Your life is in danger, Samuel. You have to protect yourself…you *have* to!" I pleaded with him desperately. He reached into his pocket to retrieve a roll of parchment paper and held it out to me.

"Is there something written here that troubles you? I fear it could be grave enough to have given you a turn. Tell me, Emily. Tell me what is written here." I slowly took the piece of parchment and sat back down on the bed, reading again the line that had brought dread into my heart. *My grandson…Samuel Thomas Howerd of Mill Cottage, Littleham.*

"It is Elijah's Will," I began, my head bowed. "He has left his entire estate to you, all his money—everything he owns." There was a long moment of silence.

"To me?" repeated Samuel quietly. "Why has he left it to *me*? I am no one. Robert is his son." I didn't answer and continued to look at the paper. "The old man had always shown favor towards me. He gave me the job at the mill and paid for a doctor when I was sick once…but to leave me *everything*? I cannot begin to understand the reason behind such an extravagant gesture," said Samuel, taking the Will from me and looking at the words that meant nothing to him. I was thankful, at that moment in time, that he never had the opportunity to become more educated.

"I think that maybe Robert will want to do you harm. He will not let this go without a fight, Samuel. Can you not go to your father in Edgebarton?"

"What? Run away from what is rightfully mine. Certainly not!" cried Samuel, shocked that I should even think of such a preposterous idea. "If Robert thinks that he can dispose of me so readily, then he is mistaken."

"I think that you judge Robert Spedding far too hastily. There may be more to his character than he makes us believe," I said as I looked up into his trusting brown eyes. Samuel smiled and gently took hold of my hand.

"Do you know what this means to me, Emily? I am now a man of means; I *own* the very mill at which I worked. My family will no longer go hungry and wear wretched garments fit for a pauper. I can change all that. I, Samuel Howerd, the illegitimate child of a gypsy!" I squeezed his hand and smiled weakly. I thought about that poor guiltless gypsy boy that was shot for a crime he didn't commit. It would have been so easy to blame him. No amount of pleading his innocence would have counted against the word of a gentleman. I wondered about Samuel's swarthy appearance. There were still a few unanswered questions that I needed to piece together, but one thing was for certain—this was the spark that was to lead to Samuel's death tomorrow, I was sure of it.

My heart was heavy as I undressed and slipped under the cover; I had so much on my mind that sleep tonight would be an impossible task. Samuel was, understandably, in high spirits and lay close to me whilst talking about his newly acquired wealth, which was to be so short-lived. I found it difficult to share his enthusiasm, instead lying there and staring up at the ceiling with glistening eyes. Midnight passed, and the morning of the 16th December 1696 dawned.

I must have eventually slept, because I remember waking some time later and it was daylight. Samuel lay on his stomach, his arm stretched across my body protectively, and his face nestled into my neck. I turned my head and lightly kissed the top of his unruly mop of hair, not unlike his father's in many ways. I wished that we could stay here all day, just as we were, safe in each other's arms. I closed my eyes as a tear trickled down my cheek and mingled with his dark curls, followed by another. I tried to stem the flow, but failed miserably. Samuel was my soul mate. Never before had I felt such passion and love towards a man. I wanted to be with him forever. He stirred from his sleep, his arm tightening its grip around my body. Turning his head, he gazed up at me. There was a softness in his eyes that I hadn't seen before.

"Emily," he whispered. My heart racing, I turned to face him and lost myself in the deep, dark pools of his eyes. "Emily, I think—and pardon me if I am being discourteous—but I feel that my affection towards you is becoming more—" The door of the bedroom burst open just then, and John appeared beside the bed, preventing Samuel from continuing. "What is it, John?" cried Samuel angrily.

"Pardon the intrusion, but Mr Spedding desires to know when you will be joining him for breakfast, as he wishes to apologize for his behaviour last night." Samuel flopped back onto the pillow, exasperated, while I looked from him to John anxiously.

"His wishes are not sincere, but tell him we shall be down shortly," I replied. John nodded, but continued to stand there a moment longer, taking pleasure in the unusual sight before him, until Samuel threw a pillow at him. He ran off down the stairs, laughing. "Don't trust Robert!" I pleaded, as he got up to dress. "Make sure you are not alone with him today, and stay near the cottage."

"Hush, Emily! There is no need for concern. You worry so unnecessarily."

"Perhaps I have reason," I said as I slipped off my nightshirt, hurriedly replacing it with the heavy green woollen dress. He came over to me and placed his hands upon my shoulders.

"I will be quite safe, dear Emily, although I find your anxiety somewhat pleasing that you should care for my wellbeing to such an extent." He leaned forward and placed an affectionate kiss upon my forehead, as one might a sister. I don't know what possessed me, but I caught hold of him around the neck and pulled him to me, my lips pressing down onto his with mounting passion and a need that left me breathless. He pulled away, startled by my sudden show of over-amorous affection, and his expression resembled that of a young adolescent encountering his first kiss behind the bike sheds at school. His naivety in such matters was endearing, and I doubted his experience with the opposite sex ever got beyond the kissing stage. The tantalizing thought that he was still a virgin aroused me all the more.

"Ah! Good morning!" said Robert cheerily as we came into the room. "I have made the fire and prepared the breakfast—the very least I could do, considering my atrocious conduct last night, for which I beg your forgiveness most ardently." I was lost for words and sat down at the table, wondering what other rubbish would spill from that foul mouth of his.

"Your apology is accepted," said Samuel, nodding politely and taking a seat next to his father. His *father*...if only he knew. I surveyed the two men furtively, their similarities were quite apparent, and I don't know why I hadn't noticed the likeness before. The same unruly hair, the same dark eyes that could change so swiftly from soft brown to piecing black in seconds. There the similarities ended. Robert was stout and thick set, Samuel tall and slim, an attribute from his mother's side, for certain. I thanked God that dear Hannah was no longer with us. The humiliation of having to face her attacker yet again, after all those years, would have been a nightmare.

I took a spoonful of porridge from the bowls that Robert had prepared for us and decided to test out his honesty.

"So, I understand that your father's Will was not to your satisfaction?" I questioned casually. His face changed to a more serious demeanor, but he struggled to keep his composure.

"It appears that my father entrusted his wealth to an employee—an action that was instigated by a foolish argument between my father and I some years back, which I had hoped had been resolved," said Robert, choosing his words carefully.

"Does this *employee* know of his fortune?" asked Samuel, giving me a quick glance across the table.

"He will be informed in due course," said Robert bluntly, his eyes firmly fixed upon his bowl.

"Lucky bugger, whoever he is," said John innocently. Robert rose from the table and went over to his cloak, which hung from a hook behind the door, and rummaged through the pockets of the garment.

"Looking for this?" said Samuel, holding up the piece of parchment. Robert's face froze, and his eyes drifted to mine nervously.

"Yes, it must have fallen from my pocket last night," he muttered warily, taking the Will from Samuel's hand.

"I have not been fortunate enough, or indeed had any desire to acquire knowledge of the written word, so rest assured, I have not intruded upon your privacy," declared Samuel, anticipating his unease.

"Miss Emily is a much acclaimed reader and writer, so father informed us!" exclaimed John proudly; entirely ignorant of the dilemma he had just put me in.

"Indeed," said Robert thoughtfully. "Did you also refrain from intruding upon my privacy?"

"What do you think?" I replied sarcastically. He stared at me, trying to read my mind and was in no doubt that I *had* read the contents of the Will. Judging by Samuel's reactions, he doubted that I had told Samuel that he was his father, but was unsure about whether he knew the identity of the Will's beneficiary. It felt good to turn the tables on him, but I also knew I was playing a dangerous game with a lethal competitor.

I left the men to talk in the other room and went into the kitchen to clean the breakfast bowls. Whilst pumping water into the sink from the well, I began to feel tired. Last night's disturbed sleep was beginning to have an effect on me, but I carried on, fighting the urge to go upstairs and lie down. Returning to the fireside, I saw John receiving some money from Robert, and I inquired what it was for.

"John has graciously consented to run an errand for me into Greenham," Robert informed me. "I owe money to Mr. Walter Penbury for the Will formalities." I looked across at John, who was happy and eager to please—he was also in possession of a shiny shilling piece for his trouble. The carefree lad went off to bring his horse around to the front. Samuel stepped outside, under my watchful eye, to chop some firewood. I sat down at the table and contemplated going to feed the animals, but my energy for such chores was considerably lacking. I sipped some more warmed milk from a jug, which Robert had set on the table. "Are you going to tell him?" asked Robert quietly in my ear as he passed behind me.

"What? The fact that your father has left everything to him, or that you raped his mother?" I retorted.

"Either," replied Robert, going to the window to observe Samuel.

"He knows he is now a wealthy man, thanks to your father…the fact that he is your son, I thought, was better not disclosed for the time being."

"A wise move. You learn quickly, Miss Emily," sneered Robert as he moved away from the window.

"Was that why you went away to sea? Some kind of pact with your father?" I asked as he came and sat at the table opposite me.

"A pact that he did not keep. Arrangements were made for me to join the crew on the *Redoubt*—to remain at sea indefinitely, and to refrain from contacting my father as long as he lived. In return, he promised to leave his fortune to me as was intended. He knew that *I* was the true father of Hannah's child. He saw me, that fateful day in the woods, but could not bring it upon himself to betray his only son to the authorities."

"But why is Samuel's complexion so *dark*?" I asked, curious to know his heritage.

"My mother—his grandmother—was of gypsy blood. I escaped the swarthy looks, praise be to God, but Samuel inherited them, which thankfully upheld the gypsy boy story that I cunningly concocted at the time and bore witness to at the unfortunate boy's trial." He continued on about the fact that the world was rid of one more gypsy scum, thanks to him. I was listening, but only just. My eyelids grew heavy, and my concentration was diminishing.

John came in to say he was departing for Greenham now, and that Samuel's horse was found without a shoe, of which John had informed him, and Samuel would be riding into Offenham to the blacksmith's forthwith. The room began to spin, and I could hardly keep my eyes open as I watched, through the window, John mount his horse and ride away. Robert watched me intently as I fought to stay awake. It never occurred to me, at the time, that he had slipped a sedative into my porridge and milk and had cleverly removed the two men from the vicinity without my suspicion.

"Perhaps you had better take some rest? Allow me to assist you to your room," suggested Robert obligingly. I got up unsteadily, my mind no longer capable of rational thought. His strong arm encircled my waist and led me up the staircase to my room—an action, in my right frame of mind, I would never have instigated. But I was not in my right mind—far from it, as Robert laid me down upon the bed. I closed my eyes, welcoming the soft bed on which to sleep. I remembered little as Robert tied my hands with a length of rope and attached the ends to the bedposts on either side. I felt my ankles being fastened together and struggled weakly, moaning Samuel's name as I visualized his face close to mine, his soft lips tracing a line down my neck to my breasts. "You want me now, do you not?" came a whispered voice.

"Samuel, I love you. I want you," I responded huskily, slowly opening my eyes. It took a moment for my brain to register the image of the man's face so close to mine, and in doing so, I started to panic, my hands twisting in their bonds until they bled. Panting for breath from the fruitless effort to free myself, I lay still, trying to understand the reason behind my capture. *If he wanted to take me, he would hardly tie my legs together* I thought.

"This is going to be *such* a pleasure," he smirked. "I want to take my time with you, but first I have another matter to attend to…something I should have done a long time ago."

"Samuel!" I sputtered. "Please don't hurt Samuel! PLEASE, I *BEG* OF YOU, DON'T KILL MY SAMUEL!"

"Save your begging and pleading for later, when I take you. Your screams for mercy will go unheeded, your cries of pain unheard. Then, when I am done with you…*really* done with you, you will join Charlotte in the shallow grave beneath the newly planted pear trees." Robert rose from the bed, extracting from his pocket a dirty rag, which he rammed into my mouth. I gagged on the stench. "We do not want you calling out and warning Samuel, now, do we? He should be arriving back soon, and I will be waiting for him in the barn—to put a shot through that arrogant head of his." I closed my eyes. *Is this how it was to end? Is this how it was meant to be?* I felt so helpless as Robert disappeared from the room, leaving me lying there with tears streaming down my face, and my beloved Samuel's last moments on earth soon to be finalized with one single shot.

I could hear Jas barking out front somewhere. *Could he hear Samuel approaching up the track?* My heart was pounding with the anxiety, my stress levels going through the roof as I lay there, waiting…waiting for the sound of gunfire. Waiting for the end. The barking became more frantic, and then a gun was fired, just outside of the cottage. My heart stopped beating for an instant, until I heard the wretched whimpering cries as Jas yelped in pain…and then there was silence. *Poor faithful Jas. What harm did he ever do to anyone?* Then I heard it. The sound of Samuel's horse as it approached the cottage. I heard him dismount and his footsteps come into the doorway downstairs.

"Emily?" he shouted. "Are you here?" I struggled like crazy, but the ropes just bit deeper into my flesh, causing me to wince with the pain. I tried to call out, but no sound was audible. I heard him leave. I heard him set off to the barn with his horse, to face his father—his executioner.

I cannot begin to describe my feelings as I lay there, waiting for the final gunshot. I wanted to die too. I didn't want to live anymore. I had failed. In my traumatized state I almost missed the sounds of a second horse approaching, the rider stopping just outside. I turned my head towards the window, my eyes wide and staring, as I waited with baited breath for the caller to enter.

"Miss Emily, are you here? Samuel?" came the frantic voice. John's frantic voice. I felt as if I had been given a second chance and looked about me for a way to attract his attention. The bedside table was just in reach, and I swung my legs up and tried to touch the table with my feet, but the angle was all wrong, and I badly twisted the muscles in my back as I attempted the near impossible maneuver. By some fluke, my last effort caught the edge of the table. It teetered on its side before crashing down onto the floor, with the candlestick holder adding to the resonating sound on the bare floorboards. "Who's up there?" yelled John from the bottom of the stairs. *Please come up. PLEASE COME UP,* I pleaded silently. Footsteps on the staircase answered my prayers.

I shall never forget the look on John's face as he entered the room and saw me tied up on the bed. Whatever he expected, it wasn't that. I thrashed about, making muffled grunting noises to get him to untie me, instead of just standing there, looking shocked. He regained his composure and set about releasing me from my bonds, the rag in my mouth being the first to go.

"Quickly, John!" I cried. "Robert is going to shoot Samuel."

"I knew he was in danger. The man to whom I gave the money read the Will to me, and advised me to warn Samuel of a possible attempt upon his life. I rode home as fast as I could."

I tore the last remaining ropes from my hands and fled from the room, with John close behind me. Picking up the loaded gun by the fireplace, I turned to him.

"Stay here. Don't leave the cottage...promise me?"

"I promise," said John, shaking with emotion. "Take care, Miss Emily!" I ran as fast as I could around to the barn. Voices could be heard within, and I peered through a knot in the wood of the barn door. I could just make out Robert standing there, with his back to me, at the far end of the barn—the gun in his hand pointed at Samuel's head. Robert was calmly telling him the awful truth about Charlotte's sudden disappearance, and he went on to tell him who he really was—a final confession before he pulled the trigger.

I wanted to hold Samuel in my arms as he received the dreadful news, and now faced being killed in cold blood—by his own father. I waited. I wanted Samuel to hear everything from Robert so there would be no more secrets between us. As Robert neared the end of his declaration of guilt, his thumb cocked the gun, and he aimed it at Samuel's forehead. I moved fast and pulled open the barn door.

"ROBERT SPEDDING!" I yelled, lifting up the heavy gun and taking aim. He spun round to face me, a look of disbelief on his face as I pulled the trigger, crying out, "GO TO HELL!"

There was a yellow flash of light, followed by a loud blast that threw me backwards. A thick cloud arose with the acrid smell of gunpowder; and a deathly silence fell over the barn. The choking fog began to clear, and I could see Robert sprawled out on the ground at Samuel's feet, unmoving. I began to shake. The shock of what I had just done started to hit me. I collapsed onto a pile of straw. John chose that moment to come bursting into the barn, his panic-stricken face trying to comprehend what had happened and who was injured…or dead.

"I heard the shot. Are you alright, Miss Emily?" He said as he knelt down beside me, almost in tears. He looked across at Samuel, who was standing there traumatized, staring down at the body of his father. "My God, Emily! You killed Mr Spedding! You killed Samuel's father…why?" he cried in despair.

"Because I *had* to…because, today, the 16th of December, you would have lost a brother, and I would have lost the man I love."

Chapter Seventeen

John looked over towards Samuel, who had now dropped to his knees and was sobbing like a baby. I knew his tears were not for his father, but for Charlotte, and I felt he needed some space to vent his emotions. I guess, to be honest, I was also nervous as to how he felt about me now. *Would he be angry and turn me in? Would he understand my motives and have killed Robert himself, given the chance? Or would finding out the truth about Charlotte destroy all our chances of happiness, just as we were beginning to make headway?*

I took John outside and sat him down on a tree stump. As simply as I could, I explained Robert's involvement in Charlotte's disappearance. He was shocked and saw, now, why I didn't hesitate in firing the gun. He was, however, more concerned with how Samuel would cope, knowing the truth, and the affect it would have on us.

"Try not to worry," I told him. "What is to be will be…I really don't know what will happen next." *This is now uncharted territory,* I thought, *history rewritten.*

"What made you so certain Samuel would die today?" asked John, curiously. I smiled and took hold of his hand.

"I had a dream," I lied. "In this dream I saw a gravestone with Samuel's name on it and today's date."

"You are able to see into the future?"

"I saw into the past." I replied quietly, in deep thought.

"I do not understand, Miss Emily."

"I know. Sometimes I don't either, but I believe what I did today will enable Charlotte to rest in peace. Her death has been avenged through me," I said as I turned towards the barn door. I could no longer hear Samuel crying within. "Go and be with your brother. He needs comforting, and I am not sure if I am the one he desires it from right now. If he wants me, he knows where to find me," I said as I stood up. John went inside the barn, and I wandered off in the direction of Jasmine Cottage.

I stood gazing down at the little pear trees, neatly planted in rows above Charlotte's grave. At least I knew now where she lay, if that was any consolation. I found myself speaking to her in low whispers, telling her that it was all over, and she could now rest in peace. I also promised her that I would take care of Samuel, and hoped that she would find it in her heart to wish us well without prejudice. I didn't really believe she could hear me. It made me feel better though; having asked her permission, if anything should ever come of our relationship, just in case she bore a grudge and came back to haunt me. The huge pear tree under which I found the locket was the only surviving tree from these young saplings—the only marker of Charlotte's grave. I began to wonder how the locket came to be buried under the tree. *Who put it there? Was it Robert? My Uncle James. What part did he play in all of this?* He knew where the locket was and that it possessed magical powers. *Had he also traveled back in time to Mill Cottage?* If only I could have spoken to him before he died. Sighing, I looked over my shoulder wistfully, to see if Samuel would come to me…but there was no sign of him. If he now hated me for whatever reason, I could just return to the future, forget all about him, and carry on my life where I left off. *Could I forget him?* He had been so much a part of my life—his family had become mine—I thought of Charles as my own father and I adored Samuel so much. I couldn't live in the future, or the past, without his love.

Mill Cottage was quiet and empty when I returned, as was the barn. Robert's body had been removed, leaving a blood splattered trail across the dusty floor of the barn and out through the door. The gun still lay where I had dropped it. A tear trickled down my cheek. *I had saved his life, but for what?* I suddenly realized that the cart was missing. *Maybe they took his body somewhere to dispose of it?* He would return soon. *Wait! I can hear him now…footsteps coming this way.* My heart pounding, I turned and stared towards the barn door. *What would he say?*

"There you are! I have been looking for you," said John on entering. He appeared a bit disheveled, with a reddened face, and smears of blood soiled the front of his jacket.

"Where's Samuel?" I asked warily.

"He's gone…departed for Edgebarton, as soon as we disposed of that dreadful man's body in the rubbish pit. No one will find him there. The stench from his rotting corpse will mingle with the other putrid smells," explained John, taking off his jacket and handing it to me to wash.

"Why has he gone to Edgebarton? Did he say anything before he went?" I cried in dismay.

"Only that he had arrangements to make, regarding his future with the woman he loves." My heart sank. He had gone to be with Isabelle. *I just know it. I've lost him.*

As I washed John's jacket in the sink, I sobbed my heart out. I had been so close to getting him to love me, and now he was in Isabelle's arms, seeking the comfort *I* so desperately wanted to give him. *Why, oh why, didn't I go to him in the barn after, instead of sending in John?* It was too late now. I couldn't stay here and watch Isabelle and Samuel marry. I had to return to the future and let them get on with it. I burst into tears again—unable to control my emotions—and cried until there were no tears left to cry.

Exhausted from the turmoil, I went outside and hung the jacket out to dry on a tree branch. There was a keen wind, but it was sunny. John was not far from the cottage, digging a hole in the ground in which to bury poor Jas. I could hear him crying quietly to himself as he dug. I didn't want to tell him I was leaving. He wouldn't want me to go, and I couldn't cope with him begging me to stay, for fear I would give in. It was better this way. I could just slip away unnoticed…never to return.

My mind was made up, and I quickly packed my few belongings into the carryall and went back downstairs. I was going to take some photos, but I couldn't bring myself to do it. Every time I looked at them I would be reminded of my days with Samuel, and the heartache would continue. I didn't need to prove anything to Sam. I couldn't care less if he didn't believe me now. I wasn't going back, *so what is the point?* I wanted to leave Samuel one final message, and took down the parchment and quill from the box. I knew *he* couldn't read it, but someone would for him, and that someone would probably be Isabelle. I put quill to parchment and scratched a few simple words... '*I loved you, Samuel Howerd, and will do so for all eternity. Yours forever, Emily.*' After folding the parchment and sealing it with wax, I went over to the fireplace and removed one of the large bricks towards the back. This was the family's secret hiding place that Charles had told me about when he left—the place he had left some money in case we were in urgent need. The money lay there untouched, wrapped in brown paper, and on the top I placed my note. Samuel would find it one day, when I was long gone.

Leaving the cottage I went over to the barn area, placing the carryall on the ground for a moment, while I undid the zip and extracted the locket. I held it unopened in my hand for a while and looked around one last time, my eyes misting over with tears as the vision of Mill Cottage blurred before me.

"Goodbye, everyone," I whispered. "I love you all dearly, but it wasn't to be…please forgive me." I wouldn't be using my one last chance to return here. I had made my decision to remain in the future. The locket sprang open and immediately I was engulfed in a blinding white light, as the sunlight struck it and I spiraled back through time, to where I belonged.

As I opened my eyes, I felt cold and very wet. It was pouring heavily with rain, and a loud rumble of thunder overhead made me jump. I scrambled to my feet awkwardly in the heavy sodden dress and hurried over to the ruins of Mill Cottage to seek shelter from the downpour. I stood there, alone in the empty desolate room, as the rain dripped steadily through a gaping hole in the roof onto the bare stone floor. The rusted fireplace lay cold and long dead like the inhabitants in the ground outside. I shuddered as a feeling of utter despair swept over me. I swore I heard Samuel's voice calling out to me.

I ran outside into the rain, desperate to escape the ghost that tortured my mind and soul across time. I found Betsy where I had left her, up on the verge by the roadside looking extremely dirty, and with a police notice covered in plastic attached to the front screen. I ripped it off as I ran around to the driver's door and hurriedly inserted the key into the lock. By the time I got inside and slammed the door, I was dripping from head to foot, and shaking like a leaf. The notice informed me that I had 30 days in which to remove the car, or it would be taken away and scrapped. The 30 days obviously weren't up, as it was still here, but I had no idea how long I had been gone.

It took several tries in turning over the engine before she spluttered into life, and I drove her gingerly off the verge onto the asphalt road. A car passed me coming the other way at a high speed, and I slammed on my brakes nervously, feeling like a learner driver on her first lesson. It was all so different. I had grown accustomed to the slow, easy-going way of life, and the horse and cart mode of transport. I imagined how terrifying it would be for a person from the 17th century if they were brought into the future. Turning into the village, I could still see the ladies in their bonnets walking along the straw-covered street in my mind, the smell of manure around the horses tethered at various posts along the way, and the dirty urchins begging for food or money from the more respectable folk. With a heavy heart, I took the road out of the village that led to the motorway, and away from the place where I felt I truly belonged.

My journey home took longer than before, due to the fact that I had to pull over and stop on three occasions, when I broke down in tears and couldn't see to drive. I couldn't have felt worse if he had died. It was going to take a long time to get over him, and I knew that no one would ever, *ever* take his place in my heart.

It was dark by the time I arrived home and parked the car outside of the garage. No one saw the miserable and dejected figure of a woman dressed in a long woollen dress ascend the stairs and enter flat number 12 on the third floor. Stepping over the large pile of post and junk mail on the mat, I went to make myself a coffee as if in a dream, but there was no milk. The little food I had left in the fridge had all gone bad, and the smell hit me like a sledgehammer as I opened the fridge door. It didn't matter, really. I could do without a drink, and I had no appetite. Instead, I discarded the dress—a last reminder of my other life—in a heap on the floor and took a shower to wash away the memories. It didn't work. I collapsed onto my bed after and cried myself to sleep, not caring if I ever woke again.

Unfortunately, I did—to the sound of frantic banging on my front door—sometime early the next morning. Dragging myself out of the bed, I shuffled to the front door and undid the latch. Sam stood there, wide-eyed and bewildered.

"Emily! Thank God you're okay!" he cried. "I saw your car outside. Where have you been? I tried to contact you, but your cell phone was off. I even reported you missing to the police! Are you all right? You look dreadful." Overwhelmed by all the questions, I just turned and went back inside, leaving the door open for Sam to enter if he wanted. He followed me inside, stopping to pick up the assortment of post from the mat, where it still lay untouched. He set it on the coffee table. "God! What's that awful smell?" he asked, screwing up his nose in disgust.

"Food's gone bad in the fridge. Can't offer you a coffee—no milk," I said bluntly, and without emotion, as I sat down on the sofa and stared into space.

"Emily, what happened?" Sam asked, gently taking hold of my hand. I snatched it back. It reminded me of Samuel's touch. "Did you go back to the past again?" he asked tentatively.

"I thought you didn't believe in all that?" I retorted. "Or are you just trying to patronize me?"

"Do you want to talk about it?" he urged, worried at how troubled I was.

"No."

"Okay. How about some breakfast at my place?"

"Not hungry."

"Coffee, then?"

"No." Sam thought for a moment. I could feel him watching me intently. I wished he would just go and leave me alone.

"Is it something to do with that Samuel guy you said you met?" he asked finally.

"I don't want to talk about it!" I shouted, the tears so near the surface.

"I take that as a '*yes*,' then," he said sarcastically, "Did he dump you? Or however they referred to it in those days." I turned towards him, my eyes blazing with fury. "I'll go, shall I?" Sam suggested, before standing up and edging towards the door. "You might want to open some of those," he said, pointing towards the letters. "Some have '*final notice*' in red on them." I heard the door click shut behind him, and I buried my head in my hands, the tears rolling down my cheeks. I couldn't cope.

A couple of hours passed and I was still there, curled up in a ball on the sofa in my nightgown, hugging a damp floral cushion. My eyes were red and puffy, through constant crying, and I felt sick. I understood now how people could die of a broken heart. I heard what sounded like a key turn in the lock of my front door, and I looked towards it fearfully as it opened. Sam stepped inside.

"Hope you don't mind. I borrowed your key so I could get back in," he said nervously. "I bought you some milk, bread, butter and eggs—just something to get by on until you feel up to going out."

"Thanks." I muttered unappreciatively.

"How you feeling?" he asked, going into the kitchen and filling the kettle with water. I didn't answer. "I'll make you some scrambled eggs, shall I? You have to eat, Emily, or you'll fade away." *Good,* I thought to myself, *and then it will all be over.*

"I see you haven't opened your post yet," he called out from the kitchen. "I'll give you a hand in a minute." I groaned and closed my eyes. *Why can't he just let me be?* Sam brought in a large plate of scrambled eggs, toast, and a mug of coffee. He placed it down on the table with the cutlery and sat beside me. "Now, you eat that up like a good girl while I sort out all the junk mail."

"I told you I wasn't hungry. You eat it." I said, pushing the plate away.

"Come on, Emily. Stop all this nonsense and eat. If you don't, I'll have to seriously think about calling your doctor and telling him about your delusions of time travel."

"So he can put me in a mental asylum? Whatever. I don't care." I replied, hugging the pillow closer. Sam sighed loudly and picked up a few of the letters.

"I do care about you, Emily, but I just can't believe all this stuff without any kind of evidence to support it. You *are* very convincing, though, I'll give you that!"

"I was going to take some photos," I mumbled, "but I didn't want any reminders."

"Reminders of what? Something or someone? Help me out here. I'm struggling." I looked at Sam over the edge of the cushion.

"I shot and killed a man," I said directly. Sam dropped the letter in his hand and stared at me wide-eyed, not knowing if this was a product of my imagination in this fantasy world of mine, or if I really had killed someone in cold blood. I could see the unease in his face as he tried to contemplate the possibilities. *Was I capable of murder in my disturbed mental state?*

"Who was he?" he inquired casually, trying to appear unperturbed by my confession.

"Samuel's father." Sam frowned and thought for a moment.

"Hang on. Didn't you say some time ago his father was a gypsy boy, who was later shot by someone?"

"It wasn't him. He was innocent. This man killed Charlotte too."

"Who's Charlotte?"

"Samuel's fiancée." Sam ran his hand through his hair, totally bewildered.

"So, let me get this straight—you shot your boyfriend's dad, because he killed his fiancée?"

"Not exactly. I shot him because he was going to kill Samuel." Sam fell back, exasperated, onto the sofa. He shook his head in disbelief.

"Sorry. This is all too much for me."

"I don't expect you to understand. I'm not ever going back. Samuel's gone to be with Isabelle, and that's it. End of story."

"Who's this Isa—?" Sam began.

"Blonde bimbo," I hissed.

"Ah!"

A long silence followed as Sam sorted the letters into two piles—junk and important-looking. He was deep in thought, trying to work out how he could get me out of this depressed state and back to the Emily he knew. He truly believed that I was *in love* with this guy—this imaginary guy from the past that was causing so much trouble. It was all so bizarre, and now I was in grave danger of damaging my health if I didn't snap out of it. It was no longer a joke.

"These are bills, by the looks of them. These are bank statements, and these two are personal," said Sam, balancing the two letters on the top of my cushion.

"You open them," I said, turning away, devoid of any interest or curiosity.

"Only if you eat something," replied Sam, prodding the fork into the eggs and waving it expectantly in front of me.

"Okay. Fine!" I shouted, as I took a mouthful of cold eggs and swallowed it begrudgingly. Sam took the letters and opened the first one.

"It's from your work, I think," he said as he read the first few lines to himself. "This isn't good…"

"What is it?" I asked, leaning over.

"It says here that '*due to your absence and lack of communication with the company over the past weeks, it is with much regret that we are forced to dismiss you*'. Enclosed is your P45, details of your company pension…" I sighed and shrugged my shoulders. It was only a job. "Aren't you the least bit concerned? Right on top of Christmas, too!" cried Sam. "This can't go on, Emily. You're ruining your life!"

"It's already ruined," I replied miserably. Sam muttered something under his breath and tore open the second letter.

"This is hand written from an…'*Elizabeth Cunningham*'."

"Don't know anybody by that name," I said wearily.

"She seems to know you. Shall I read it?" asked Sam. I shrugged.

"Please yourself."

"'*Dear Emily, I obtained your address through the solicitor dealing with Mill Cottage, and see that he managed to locate you and that the deeds to the cottage have been passed on as per your Uncle James' wishes—and mine. We left the cottage many years ago, when James' health began to fail, and we needed to move nearer to London hospitals for his treatment. As a practicing medium, I had always felt a strong presence at the cottage—a traumatic past involving its former occupants, that was unresolved, causing their troubled souls to forever wander the earth in search of an end to their suffering*'. Told you the place was haunted!" said Sam uneasily, interrupting his reading.

"Go on," I urged. "What else does she say?" Sam sighed, not sure if he should continue. This wasn't helping. "Read it!" I cried. Sam continued hesitantly.

"'*Just before James passed away, I made contact with a young woman who said her name was Charlotte. She was deeply distressed and pleaded with me to help her. From what I could gather, something dreadful happened to her on her wedding day, and the man whom she intended to marry was left at the church not ever knowing what had become of her. She wanted him to know she loved him and the reason behind her sudden departure. At that point, the woman materialized in front of me. She was very beautiful with long auburn hair. In her outstretched hand she held some kind of pendant on a chain. I could not see it clearly. The item of jewelry, she informed me, was buried in the vicinity of a pear tree in the grounds of Mill Cottage. It possessed the power to send a person back into the past in order to discover her fate, and finally tell her beloved the truth. Each person would only have three chances before the magic ceased. Then she was gone. I went down to the cottage several times and searched for the pendant but never found it. Charlotte reminded me so much of you—when I saw you at the funeral of Aunt Clara last year. It was with this in mind that I persuaded James to leave the cottage to you in his Will, in the hope that one day you would perhaps find this lost pendant and lay Charlotte's tortured soul to rest forever. May God bless you. Elizabeth Cunningham.'*" He set the letter down upon the table, struggling to find words to say.

"There's the proof you needed," I said defiantly. Sam looked at me and bit his lip.

"Did you do as Charlotte asked?"

"I did."

"Then all is well. Only, it's not, is it?" said Sam, pulling the cushion from my grasp. "I think you fell in love with this Samuel guy, and maybe the feeling was mutual. Am I right?"

"He left me. After I saved his life, he left me and went to her—to Isabelle!" I cried, getting up and going into the bedroom.

"You don't know that! You didn't stay to find out, did you?" Sam retorted, following me across the room, only to have the bedroom door slammed in his face and the lock shot home.

"Go away!" I screamed from inside.

"Emily, open this door...EMILY! You need to go back and find out if it was true."

"I won't be able to return if I do and will be doomed to spend the rest of my life watching Samuel play happy families with Isabelle. No, I won't do it!"

"And if you were wrong?" Silence. "Emily?"

"Then I would have thrown away my one chance of happiness. I loved him so much, Sam. I really loved him!" I whimpered quietly, sliding down the door into a heap on the floor, the tears brimming over and rolling down my pale face onto my nightgown.

"I have to go now," said Sam apologetically. "Toby will be wondering why I'm so long. I'm taking the key, okay? I'll check in on you later." Sam knew I had heard him, but he received no reply. Picking the letter up from the table, he tucked it into his pocket and was about to leave when a worrying thought crossed his mind.

Entering the bathroom, he stepped over the discarded dress on the floor and clicked open the glass cabinet on the wall. He removed a bottle of painkillers, some aspirin and some sleeping pills from the shelf, just in case I felt the need to end it all. The thought, if truth be told, was present in my mind and growing stronger. Sam was, as always, one step ahead. As he went to leave, he stopped to pick up the dress on the bathroom floor and hang it up behind the door. A tinkling sound caught his attention as an object hit the tiled floor. The gold pendant lay before him, and he gingerly bent to pick it up, holding it in his fingers as if it was going to bite him. He remembered me telling him that it only worked if sunlight struck the picture within, but he didn't attempt to open it and pushed it inside his jeans pocket securely, before returning to his flat.

Toby sat reading through the letter that I had received, his eyes full of excitement and interest at its intriguing contents.

"Wow! This is *so* cool! So, she was telling the truth, after all?" said Toby.

"Maybe," replied Sam dubiously.

"What do you mean *maybe*? This backs up her story. How can you not believe her now? Has she still got that pendant thingy?" asked Toby eagerly.

"No," said Sam. "I have." Reaching into his pocket, he took out the infamous pendant and dangled it in front of Toby. "Don't even think of opening it—just in case."

"I'll pull the curtains!" cried Toby. "It won't work without sunlight, you said." Toby carefully released the catch on the side of the locket, and it sprang open, making the two boys jump with fright and check their surroundings apprehensively. Once they were satisfied that it was still the same room and nothing had changed, they peered at the damaged portrait with curiosity. "It looks a bit like Emily," remarked Toby. "Is it her?"

"No. This is Charlotte, the girl who died on her wedding day," Sam told him, "The one that was in love with Samuel—the guy who is causing all these problems now with Emily. God, if I could get my hands on this moron that Emily is so infatuated with, I would give him a peace of my mind!" Sam angrily snapped the locket closed. "Who the hell does he think he is? If only he knew the pain he was causing poor Emily."

"Then maybe you should tell him…" Toby said slowly. Sam looked up at him, stunned. *Surely he couldn't be serious?* But the look on his face told Sam that he was. *Deadly serious.*

Chapter Eighteen

Sam dropped the locket onto the table. He couldn't believe that Toby was suggesting such a ridiculous idea.

"You expect me to go back in time and sort out Emily's boyfriend?" laughed Sam. "You believe that this locket actually *works*?"

"Only one way to find out." said Toby.

"Then *you* try it," retorted Sam.

"You wouldn't say that if you didn't think there might be some truth in it." Sam turned red. *He was right.* I was living proof of its authenticity. "I can drive you down to the cottage, and once you have… *'gone'*, then I will come back and take care of Emily for you—until you return. You can't be away too long. We have to be back at the university after Christmas."

"I haven't said I was doing it!" cried Sam. "Suppose I can't get back?"

"That's the chance you will have to take."

"Thanks…fill me with confidence, why don't you?" groaned Sam.

"Think of Emily, and how heartbroken she is. Even you are worried that she might do something stupid," said Toby, pointing to the bottles of pills lined up on the table. "Maybe this Samuel guy is also devastated that she has gone? Maybe he had no intention of marrying this other woman? Maybe—"

"Okay, I get the point!" yelled Sam. "But how are we going to get Emily to return, if this is so, without telling her I had a heart-to-heart with Samuel in the meantime?"

"Not sure about that. We need some sort of proof from him, declaring his love for her," pondered Toby. "That's if he *does* feel that way for her."

"I can't just march up to him and say, '*Hey you! Do you want to marry Emily, or not?*' Hang on a minute. I don't even know what he looks like. Knowing my luck, he will be six feet tall with bulging muscles." Toby laughed. Sam was apprehensive and smiled weakly. This could go horribly wrong.

"Anyway, you can't go wearing *that*!" said Toby, going over to the computer. "I'll look up the fashion for those times, and we will have to find you something to wear that won't make you stick out like a sore thumb."

For the next hour, Toby looked up the information and jotted down notes on 17th century country attire, while Sam paced the floor anxiously, trying to find logical reasons why this wasn't such a good idea.

"Right," Toby said finally. "I'm going shopping. Won't be long."

"I'll check on Emily and try to find out a few things… indiscreetly," said Sam, going to the door. "Just in case I do decide to do it."

I was still in my room when Sam returned, although the door was now unbolted from my recent trips to the toilet, where I had been sick. He crept in and sat on the edge of the bed gently, as not to wake me…but I wasn't asleep.

"Back again?" I growled from under the cover. "I don't want any food."

"I'm going to make you a milky drink, and I'm not taking no for an answer," said Sam sternly as he got up. "I need to keep you well."

While Sam was in the kitchen, I crawled out of bed and shuffled into the lounge, falling heavily onto the sofa, exhausted. I felt so weak. I wouldn't have the energy to make any food even if I wanted to.

"There you go," said Sam, placing the drink down in front of me and ignoring my disdainful looks. "Drink that, and you'll feel better."

"Doubt it," I mumbled. There was a brief silence, and I could see Sam fiddling with his hair agitatedly, out of the corner of my eye.

"If Samuel had proposed to you, would you have accepted?" he said suddenly. I looked over at him, wondering why he had asked such a question.

"What do you think? Do you suppose I *want* to be here, feeling this way? I would have given up everything to be his wife."

"Sounds like he captured your heart. What was he like? In *looks*, I mean," asked Sam nervously.

"He was my Heathcliff…and I his Cathy," I said quietly, a faraway look in my eyes.

"Heathcliff?"

"Didn't you ever read *Wuthering Heights*?" I replied, surprised.

"Er—no. Not really my thing."

"Then you will never understand the love we had for one another." Sam took a deep breath. This wasn't getting him anywhere. He tried another approach.

"Who else lives at the cottage with Samuel?"

"Just John, his brother. Why all the questions? I really don't want to talk about it anymore…EVER!" I cried, before taking a sip of the warm milk. Sam mumbled an apology and leaned back on the sofa.

"I might be going away for a few days…to visit my mother," announced Sam. "Toby said he would cook for you and make sure you are okay while I'm gone."

"I'm quite capable of looking after myself!" I cried angrily.

"But you're *not*, are you? Not with this depression."

"Thank you, Dr. Warren, for that insight into my condition. Now, if you don't mind, I want to go back to bed." I said bluntly, finishing up the drink and putting the empty glass down in front of Sam, who looked somewhat relieved at my effort. He left, and I returned to my bed, burying my head in the pillow to shut out recurring visions of Samuel's face. It was a face that haunted me during every waking moment of my forlorn existence.

Toby arrived back home, with a collection of bags, an hour later. He threw them triumphantly down in a pile upon the floor.

"These are cool!" he cried excitedly. "I can't wait to see them on you."

"What's Heathcliff like in *Wuthering Heights*?" Sam asked worriedly as he stepped, without interest, over the second-hand purchases.

"Ah! I've read that book!" said Toby, picking up a carrier bag and emptying out its contents. "Nasty piece of work that guy is! Foul temper, too. You wouldn't want to meet him on a dark night, I can tell you…why?" Sam's face had turned a deathly white. "Why do I get the feeling I shouldn't have said that?" said Toby, cringing.

"THAT'S IT! I'M NOT DOING IT!" Sam yelled. "Are you trying to get me killed or something?"

"Did Emily liken Samuel to Heathcliff, then? I'm sure he isn't *that* bad...he had his good points. Anyway, look at these! Aren't they fantastic?" cried Toby, holding up a pair of moth-eaten, brown woollen trousers.

"I'll look like a right twat in those," Sam whined. "And what the hell is *that*?" he cried, picking up a leather jacket with no sleeves.

"It was all the rage in the 1600s, a kind of 17th century designer label," laughed Toby. "Come on. Try it on. It will look great on you. Promise."

Fifteen minutes later, Sam was standing in front of a long mirror staring back, stunned, at his reflection.

"Wonderful!" remarked Toby. "Beats having to explain to them about denim jeans and a t-shirt with *Hard Rock Café* written across it."

"Oh. My. God." was all that Sam could utter. "I look like some drunken vagrant."

"A very dashing drunken vagrant, if I may say so," replied Toby, smiling.

"Stop trying to butter me up. It won't work!"

"Trust me. You look like the perfect peasant. Now, let's go over the plan again, as to what you are going to say," said Toby, pulling him down onto the sofa. "And then we better have an early night. Big day tomorrow for you."

"This could be my last night on earth," cried Sam, almost in tears.

"You are such a girl sometimes! Maybe that's why I love you so much?" replied Toby as he ruffled Sam's sandy hair affectionately. It didn't help.

It was to be a long, worrying night for Sam. He tossed and turned into the early hours, thinking about what lay ahead of him, and wondering how on earth he had got himself into this situation in the first place. There was no turning back now. He had to go through with it. The two boys came in to make me breakfast quite early that morning, and fussed around me like two very annoying mother hens until I threw them out.

"She hasn't missed the locket yet," said Toby thankfully as they descended the stairs to the car park. "You can be there and back before she realizes it's gone."

The journey down to Littleham was tense and quiet. Sam chewed his nails relentlessly and stared out of the window. Toby, in the meantime, tried to relieve his anxieties by playing soothing music and pointing out how beautiful the frosty fields looked as they sparkled in the early morning sunlight. Nothing seemed to help, and when Toby finally drove into Offenham village, the tension Sam felt increased, along with his heart rate.

"I guess the next time you see this village, it will look a little different," remarked Toby, trying to sound relaxed. "So, where do I turn off?" Sam pointed to the turning that led down the lane to Littleham, and the dreaded cottage of doom. Pulling up onto the grass and into the bushes, as Sam instructed, Toby got out and looked about him. "Where is it, then?" he asked, mystified.

"It's just through there a little way," replied Sam feebly.

"Okay. Change into your clothes, then, while I go and take a look." With that, he marched off through the trees, leaving Sam to change begrudgingly into his new attire.

"I'm doing this for Emily," he told himself out loud. "I mustn't be afraid...I can do it." He looked up the lane and thought seriously about running away. If Toby had not returned just then, there was a high possibility he would have gone.

"I hope the place is in better shape when you get there," laughed Toby. "What a dump!" Sam was not amused and sighed heavily.

"Will I do?" he asked sullenly.

"I think you will pass for a county bumpkin. Give me your watch…and the ring," said Toby. "I'll take care of them for you."

"If I don't return, they are yours—plus everything in my flat, and at Uni, and at—"

"Stop it! You *will* come back all right…Emily did, so why not you?" Sam shrugged his shoulders. He was not so convinced. "Here you are," said Toby, handing him the locket and taking several steps back. "I love you, remember that, and take care."

"Probably doesn't work, anyway," muttered Sam. "Do you *have* to stand so far away? I'm not going to explode!" Toby grinned nervously, staying where he was.

"Go on then…open it," he called, taking another step back.

"Coward!" yelled back Sam, flipping open the locket and turning slowly to face the sun. Within seconds he was engulfed in a brilliant light that caused Toby to shield his eyes from the glare. When he looked again, the place where Sam had been standing was deserted.

"Bloody hell, it worked!" exclaimed Toby in amazement, "Shit! What have I done?" He sat down on the grass, still staring mesmerized at the empty space where Sam once stood. "Look after yourself, Sam!" he cried, as a tear ran down his cheek "Come home soon."

Staggering to his feet, Sam opened his eyes and looked about him. The surroundings were similar to where he was moments before, so he wasn't too sure if he *had* in fact traveled back in time.

"Toby?" he whispered "You there?" There was no reply; only the tweeting birds in the trees seemed to acknowledge his existence. He walked, trembling, in the direction of Mill Cottage.

Before long he could see, through the trees, the outline of a stone cottage with a thatched roof. This might be the other one, he thought, peering out from behind a prickly gorse bush. If it is, then Mill Cottage is just beyond it. His heart started to race as he realized that this was definitely no longer the twenty-first century. He felt alone and frightened at the prospect of meeting these ghosts from the past, which Emily had told him so much about. Sure enough, another cottage came into view, not unlike its neighbor, only this one had smoke coming from a chimney on one side. He could hear voices around the back—male voices—and he stayed crouching down in the undergrowth to secretly observe the occupants. A grey-haired man with a beard came around to the front and entered the cottage. He was quite elderly, and Sam wondered if it could be Charles. Then again, *didn't Emily say Charles was staying with his sister somewhere else—with the children? Maybe it isn't him. Maybe this is Samuel? No...too old, unless Emily preferred the more mature guy.* Another man came around to the front and stopped at the doorway momentarily to wave at someone out of sight. *Ah! This could be him*, thought Sam, standing up to get a better view. As the man turned, Sam could see that he was younger than originally thought; perhaps 17 or 18 years old. He reminded him of himself—the same sandy hair and boyish grin. This could be the younger brother—a little *too* young for Emily. The sound of children playing came to his ears, and a bunch of youngsters raced past his hideout towards the lane, nearly blowing his cover. It didn't look like Samuel was at home. Probably still away visiting his girlfriend and making wedding plans. Sam was relieved. He didn't feel overjoyed at the thought of meeting this man, but he knew he had to face him some time.

Gingerly moving out from behind the tree, he approached the cottage cautiously, rehearsing in his mind what he had to say. The door was open, but he didn't dare enter. Instead, he politely knocked on the wooden door and waited.

"Who's there?" came a deep voice from within.

"Can I speak with you, sir?" called out Sam apprehensively. The grey-haired man came to the door and stared down at the stranger before him. "I am looking for Samuel Howerd…is he here?"

"Who is asking?" said the man warily.

"My name is Sam Warren, and I have news concerning a certain woman by the name of Emily, who I believe you know…er, are *acquainted* with."

"Come inside," said the man, stepping to one side. Sam bent his head and entered the doorway, his eyes taking a moment to adjust to the dark interior of the cottage and its contents. The sandy-haired boy was seated by the fire and smiled at him as he stood awkwardly by the table. "I am Charles Howerd, Samuel's father, and this is my son, John," he said, handing Sam a pewter mug filled with mead and gesturing for him to be seated.

"I understood you and the children were staying with your sister," said Sam, sniffing the contents of the mug and cautiously taking a small sip.

"You appear well-informed about my family," said Charles. "From whom did you receive this information?"

"From Emily," replied Sam, pushing the mug to one side.

"You know of her whereabouts? Is she well?" asked John excitedly.

"She is safe in London, but very distraught. That is why I need to speak with Samuel."

"I am sure Samuel will want to speak with you, also, regarding this rather *delicate* matter." Sam began to feel deflated. *Maybe it was true, and there was this other woman?*

"When will Samuel be returning?" asked Sam innocently. He heard a creak on the floorboard behind him, and noticed that John and Charles were looking over his shoulder at someone, who caused them to catch their breath. Slowly, Sam turned towards the door, his heart pounding loudly. It could only be one person.

A tall man in black stood silhouetted in the doorway. Sam couldn't see his face at first, but he knew that this man demanded respect. He had such a formidable presence. Toby's description of Heathcliff was becoming a reality.

"This man knows where Emily is!" cried John, breaking the unnerving silence. The man didn't reply but walked into the room with slow, deliberate strides that sent shivers down Sam's back. The light from the fire fell upon his face and gave Sam his first glimpse of the infamous Samuel Howerd, the man who was to blame for Emily's downfall. Dark tempestuous eyes burned into Sam's with such loathing that his mouth dried out with fear, and he swallowed rapidly. His long black hair hung about his face, adding to his macabre appearance. *Whatever did Emily see in this man? What kind of hold did he have on her?* In his opinion, she was well rid of him. At that moment, Sam wished he were too.

"Where is she?" Samuel growled. "What have you done with her?"

"She is safe. No harm has come to her, I assure you," replied Sam quickly, backing up against the wall in fright.

"You must have forced her, against her will, to go with you! She would not have left here willingly."

"She came to me on her own free will," said Sam, trembling, wondering why the others didn't intervene and help him out.

"She left me to be with *you*?" yelled Samuel furiously.

"She left you because you didn't *want* her!" retorted Sam angrily. "She really loved you. God only knows why. What else was she to do, when you left her to marry Isabelle?"

"MARRY ISABELLE?" thundered Samuel, "Why the *hell* would I want to marry Isabelle?"

"Because you l*ove* her?" suggested Sam shakily. At that point, Charles stepped in, fearing his son was about to lose control and do something he may regret.

"I am sure there has been some misunderstanding regarding the reason for Emily's sudden departure," offered Charles nervously. "Did you not make your intentions clear to her before you left for Edgebarton?" Samuel ignored his father and looked over at John.

"Did you not give her my message?"

"I did, Samuel. I told her you had gone to make arrangements to be with the woman you loved!" cried John.

"Maybe she did not understand me well?" he added, looking at the floor, confused.

"Did you also inquire, as I instructed you, as to the name of her father and where I could find him? So that I could ask for her hand in marriage?" The room fell silent as John turned bright red and looked pleadingly at his brother.

"Forgive me, Samuel, with Robert being shot, and Jas dying…I forgot. I'm so—"

"YOU FOOLISH BOY!" raged Samuel as he turned on his younger brother, grabbing hold of his collar roughly and throwing him across the room, onto the floor.

"Stop it!" cried Sam. "It wasn't his fault. He was upset."

"Mister Warren is right. Your brother is not to blame… let him be, Samuel," demanded Charles sternly, stepping in between the two feuding brothers.

Feeling sorry for the young lad, Sam went over to help him up off the floor, smiling at him reassuringly as he brushed his long sandy hair out of his eyes tenderly.

"You all right?" whispered Sam. John nodded, blushing slightly at the attention he was receiving from this man, and the questionable looks he was getting from his father and Samuel at that moment.

"Emily left behind this letter," said Charles suddenly, taking from his pocket a small piece of parchment paper and passing it to Sam. He read the short message and looked up at Samuel.

"This shows you how she felt about you. Surely you can see that?" The three men exchanged uneasy glances but said nothing. "It says right *here…"* said Sam, pointing to the words on the paper. "Did you not *read* it?" Charles cleared his throat and looked across at John.

"I tried to read it, but—but the words were difficult," explained John. "We do not know what message is written here."

"Oh!" exclaimed Sam, rather embarrassed. "I'm sorry, I didn't realize. Come outside with me, Samuel," directed Sam, thinking that he would rather hear the words privately than in front of his family.

"You wish to challenge me to a duel for Emily's love? I fear you will fail in your endeavor, if I may be so impertinent...but if this is your desire, then so be it," declared Samuel, taking hold of his gun and marching to the door.

"Emily's love? No, no...you don't understand, I have no desire to—er, *be* with her," Sam stuttered. "You see I'm... *gay,*" he whispered, glancing across at John briefly. Samuel frowned and shook his head in confusion.

"You are happy because you do not have her?"

"No, not *happy*, in that sense of the word...I don't think we are on the same wavelength here," sighed Sam, trying to think of what they were called in the 17th century.

"You are a mariner?" enquired Samuel.

"A Mariner? No. Why do you think that?"

"You speak of the sea and waves," replied Samuel seriously. Sam laughed. This was going to take a long time. He took hold of Samuel's arm and began to lead him outside, but dropped it instantly when he received a glare that could turn him to stone.

The two men walked over towards the river silently before sitting down on a log.

"Have you or have you not taken Emily to your bed?" demanded Samuel.

"No—well, yes, but we won't go there," mumbled Sam incoherently, remembering a certain night they shared not so long ago.

"Go where?" asked Samuel. "You are indeed a strange man, Mister Warren. I am finding it hard to understand what your intentions are in regard to the woman I love."

"Listen," said Sam, taking a deep breath. "I DO NOT LOVE EMILY. SHE IS IN LOVE WITH YOU. SHE WANTS TO BE WITH YOU. SHE WILL RETURN IF YOU CAN PROVE THAT YOU LOVE HER AND WANT TO MARRY HER."

"Do not speak to me as if I were a child!" scowled Samuel. Sam ignored the indignant remark, unfolded the piece of parchment in his hand, and read it out loud to Samuel, who looked around warily, afraid that someone would hear.

"There! Does that sound like someone who doesn't want to be with you?" cried Sam. "Now, she needs to hear it from you. I gather you are not too forward in showing your feelings?"

"Bring her to me, and I will tell her my *feelings*, or I will ride to London myself if you are unwilling." Sam thought about the situation he was now in. *Emily won't use her last chance to return without some concrete evidence from Samuel—but how?*

"If I helped you," began Sam, "would you write her a letter, declaring your love for her?" Samuel stared at Sam, aghast.

"What? Tell *you*, a complete stranger, my innermost thoughts regarding a woman?"

"Look, you are going to have to trust me here, Samuel, if you want her back." Samuel laughed and stood up, running his hand through his hair in exasperation.

"The last time I trusted a man, he tried to murder me!"

"Yes, I know all about that…she saved your life though, didn't she? Surely that deserves a thank you note?" Samuel nodded his head in silent contemplation. "Is that a yes then?" asked Sam.

"You will teach me how to do this *writing*?" inquired Samuel, sitting back down.

"Yes, we will do it together. No one shall know of the words you write, except us, and—of course—Emily," replied Sam.

"I must talk with her father. Do you know where I can find him?" asked Samuel anxiously.

"Emily's parents are both dead, so you will have no one to seek permission from. Someone else will have to give her away—Charles, maybe?" Samuel smiled at Sam. There was something about Sam's innocent demeanor that made Samuel warm to him.

"The answer to that dilemma is close at hand, I believe," he said, giving Sam a knowing look. There was no need for an explanation—Sam understood what he wanted, and was more than happy to oblige. Although, at that point, he hadn't thought it through as to exactly *how* he would be able to attend my wedding. Getting me there in the first place was of utmost importance in his mind, with John being a close second.

Chapter Nineteen

The two men walked back to the cottage, just as the bunch of kids Sam had seen earlier appeared through the trees, rosy-cheeked and laughing from their adventures. They stopped in their tracks upon seeing that a stranger was in their midst, and curiously watched at a distance as Samuel and Sam entered the now empty cottage.

"Those are my brothers and sisters," pointed out Samuel tediously. "I brought them back with me. This is where they belong, as does my father. They thought a lot of Emily—loved her as if she were their own mother."

"I'm sorry about your mother," said Sam respectfully. "It can't have been easy for you, coping with the children's grief."

"The discovery that Emily had gone when we returned was not *easy*, as you say, on us, either." He turned his head and gazed out of the window, his eyes glistening with moisture as he spoke in low, deliberate tones. "It was like a recurring nightmare…my bride-to-be vanishing again before we had the chance to take our vows. I feel sometimes that I am destined to be forever unmarried—that fate intervenes for a reason, *punishing* me for my wrongdoings. Yet, I have tried to be a son that Charles can be proud of. Will I *ever* be able to find contentment in my life?"

"I hope so," replied Sam. "You and Emily were meant for each other. Don't give up now, Samuel. Be strong." Sam could now see that there was another side to Samuel beyond the dark and sullen appearance and threatening demeanour. Here was a man crying out to be loved—a sensitive, caring man that had so much to give. He had put up this impenetrable wall of defense that I had found a loose brick in, and had begun to gradually tear it down. There was no doubt in Sam's mind that Samuel would make me a wonderful husband—a husband that would care and protect me and our future children, with his life, if need be.

A muffled giggle brought their attention to the doorway.

"Come forth, children. I wish you to meet Mister Warren. He has brought us good news," called out Samuel. One by one, the children crept inside and stood in a line, their eyes fixed on the newcomer with mounting anticipation. "Miss Emily will be returning to us," announced Samuel. "With God's blessing, she will agree to a marriage between us."

"Will she be our new mother?" asked Mary, her eyes wide open with excitement.

"When will she come?" asked Joseph, stepping forward eagerly.

"I have a sore finger," whimpered little Ellen, sticking it up in the air. "She will make it better." Samuel laughed and waved the children outside.

"Enough now with the questions. Go and play outside. Mister Warren and I have a matter of the utmost urgency to attend to." The children turned and obediently ran back outside, doubtless in a happier frame of mind on hearing the news. Samuel took down the box containing the writing material and placed in it front of Sam. "I think you will find everything you need in there. Emily has used it on more than one occasion." Sam opened the box and stared at the contents within, a little bewildered, but he was trying hard not to show it.

"Right," said Sam hesitantly, as he took out the inkpot and examined the bottle before placing it carefully down on the table. The quill followed and then a roll of parchment. It was at times like this that the inventor of the commonplace ballpoint pen was much admired and respected. "You had better use this sheet to practice on first," said Sam, passing Samuel a small piece of parchment. "Then you can write the proper letter on this sheet." The look on Samuel's face told him that this was going to be harder than he anticipated. "Shall we start with… *'My dearest Emily'*? I will write the '*My'*, and you copy it down." Samuel nodded and watched

Sam dip the quill into the ink and scratch, with difficulty, strange wiggly shapes onto the paper. This method of writing was as new to him as letters were to Samuel. "Your turn now," said Sam, handing him the quill. "Go on. You can do it." Samuel shakily copied the shape of the letters down onto his practice sheet. Apart from looking like a child of six had written it, it was readable and, in a way, more believable that Samuel had completed the arduous task himself. "Good," said Sam, feeling like he was praising a five-year-old on his first day at school. "Now, the next word. '*Dearest'*..." And so they continued, well into the afternoon, before finally producing a work of art that Samuel deserved to be proud of. Sam sat back in the chair, exhausted, but hopeful that I would act on his request and return, after all his effort.

"Read it to me again," begged Samuel. "I want to hear the words I have written by my own hand."

"Just one more time, then," sighed Sam, picking up the parchment wearily.

My Dearest Emily
PLEASE Come home
I Love you with
ALL my heart and
WAnt you to
consent to be my
wife. I cannot Live
without you here
by My side. I beg
of you, Return to
me. Samuel H.

Samuel smiled contentedly. His part was done.

"There is not a coach to London until the day after tomorrow. Please be our guest until that time. You can sleep here at Mill Cottage, for there is much room now I have inherited old Elijah's house."

"Thank you," replied Sam gratefully. He didn't really need to stay around, but he was intrigued and excited to have this opportunity to see, with his own eyes, what life was like back in the late 17th Century. Toby could wait. This was much more interesting.

Charles and John returned soon after. They had been fishing in the pond by the mill and had captured four decent-sized trout for their meal that evening. While Charles prepared the fish, John built the fire. Samuel chopped more firewood, and Ellen set the table. Joseph ran into the village to buy more bread, and Hannah fetched some milk. William filled the oil lamps, and Mary changed the linen on a bed upstairs. Everyone did their bit—no arguments, no backtalk, and no Playstations or computers to drag them away from! It was all so simple and so uncomplicated.

The children ate first around the table, due to the limited space, while Charles, Samuel, John and Sam sat on the bench by the fire. He heard all about the plans that Samuel had for the mill, the improvements he intended to make to the looms and machinery and, most of all, to the working conditions of the men and women employed there. Sam was horrified to learn of the accidents that had occurred in recent years, due to the lack of safety measures, and the fact that there was no physician on site to deal with any emergencies. Children, as young as seven, were losing fingers and arms, often resulting in their deaths due to blood loss and shock. Sam sighed. They had so much to learn.

He glanced over at John, who was twiddling with the quill and writing invisible words on a scrap of leftover parchment.

"Would you like to learn to read and write John?" Sam asked him suddenly, making him look up, startled.

"I would indeed!" he cried. "It is important for a man to master this ability. Do you not think, Mister Warren?"

"Call me Sam, please. And, yes, it is very important. Not only for a man, but for a woman also."

"Emily could read and write," replied John, thinking deeply. "How is it that she—a woman—can be so educated?"

"Where indeed *did* she obtain such knowledge?" asked Samuel, frowning. Sam began to feel uncomfortable and shook his head.

"I don't know, but it is not impossible for you all to learn." The three men looked at Sam, baffled. Even the two older children at the table, who had been listening, stared over at Sam. "You could use the other cottage—Elijah's place—as a schoolhouse. Emily could teach a small group each day. I'm sure she would love to do that," Sam said calmly. He didn't anticipate that the thought of his idea would be met with such chaotic excitement among the children, and enthusiastic praise from the other men.

"You could also teach at the school," said Samuel, after the initial frenzy had died down. "The mill workers would be eager scholars, given the chance to better themselves—as would I." Charles smiled broadly across at his son at this surprising remark.

"Why the sudden interest to learn to read and write? Do my ears deceive me?" asked Charles, laughing.

"I cannot have a wife more educated than myself. I would be made to look a fool. Besides, I have realized the importance of the written word—and the benefits it can bring forth," said Samuel seriously, swilling down the remainder of his mead.

"I cannot teach at your school," said Sam abruptly, before things got out of hand. "I have to return to my duties…I am a physician in London."

"A *physician*!" cried Samuel. "Indeed, you shall come and work for me. I will pay you well to attend my employees and family, when required."

"I can't—I—" began Sam, wishing he had kept his mouth shut.

"Good! That is settled then," said Samuel as he got up. "Shall we eat now? The children are done."

Sam ate his meal in silence, whilst wondering how on earth he'd managed to get himself employed as a full-time doctor, without so much as an interview! If he came back to attend the wedding, he would just simply disappear after, leaving me—regrettably—to pick up the pieces. He had his own life to lead back home, qualifying to become a proper doctor, maybe even becoming a consultant one day. It was the only thing he had ever wanted to do—to help make sick people better.

"The fish is good, is it not, Mister Warren?" inquired John, looking somewhat concerned. "You have spoken very little of late. Your mind is elsewhere."

"No, the fish is very good, John. Pardon me. I did not intend to appear rude." John smiled across the table at Sam, making his heart skip a beat.

"I can take you fishing tomorrow, if you so desire?" asked John innocently. Sam swallowed hard. Did he have to use the word '*desire*'?

"That would be very nice," replied Sam. "Very nice indeed."

"Have some more mead," insisted Charles, pouring him another mug full of the strange-tasting liquid. Sam cringed inwardly. It had taken him the better part of the mealtime to consume the first mug, and his head was already spinning. He did not feel it was polite to refuse, considering they were giving him board and lodgings for the night.

After he had finished his meal, Charles offered him a clay pipe to smoke, which he *did* refuse, and they retired once more to the bench by the fire. Sam was glad of the warmth from the fire, as he was beginning to shiver with the damp and cold air, which found it's way easily in from the outside through the ill-fitting windows and doors. It couldn't be good for them, but they appeared to be used to the harsh conditions and were, therefore, far more resilient than he was. Being molly-coddled with central heating and fluffy slippers certainly weakens your resistance.

"Where does everyone sleep?" Sam asked curiously, noticing that the children had all disappeared out of the cottage.

"The children all sleep over in the other cottage, and I sleep at Weaver's Cottage, Elijah's old place," replied Charles.

"And you two?" inquired Sam, nodding to Samuel and John.

"We have the two rooms upstairs now. We used to sleep in the barn," explained John, leaning across to refill his mug.

"No! No more. Thank you." Sam cried, covering his mug defensively with his hand.

"Come now, young Mister Warren. It will keep you warm for the cold night ahead," urged Charles.

"Just a little then. So where will *I* be sleeping?" Sam asked casually, taking another reluctant sip from the mug.

"With me!" said John cheerfully. "It is large and of ample size." Sam's mouthful took a sudden wrong turn on its downward passage, resulting in a coughing fit that sprayed mead all over a surprised Samuel, who had fallen asleep.

"I'm *so* sorry," cried Sam, when he eventually recovered and could speak again. "Do you have a cloth thingy?" he added, getting unsteadily to his feet and stumbling over Samuel's in the process, which sent him crashing to the floor.

"Take him upstairs, John, before more damage is done," cried Samuel, jumping up and taking off his wet coat crossly, before stepping over Sam. "I believe Mister Warren has had sufficient to drink for one evening," he slurred, walking erratically over to the table and knocking a chair down as he tried to gain his balance.

"Haven't we all?" noted Charles sleepily. "I will also be on my way, and I bid you all a good night." With that, he staggered out of the door and into the night.

John helped Sam to his feet and steered him towards the staircase.

"I can't see straight!" wailed Sam, falling up the first stair clumsily. "What's in that stuff? It's lethal!" John laughed as he pushed Sam further up the narrow wooden staircase. Samuel stood, swaying unsteadily, at the top. He held a candle out and awaited the arrival of his drunken guest.

"I trust you will sleep well, my friend," said Samuel, handing John the candle.

"Yes. Yes. Thank you. Thank you. I will…I think," mumbled Sam, holding his head. John led him into the bedroom, and Sam flopped down onto the large double bed heavily. That was the last thing he remembered that evening before he passed out. A large *double bed* of ample size. *That's* what he was referring to!

Sam awoke the next morning with a thumping headache. He turned away from the bright light that shone in through the window and came face to face with John, lying asleep on the adjacent pillow.

"Oh my God!" muttered Sam quietly, sitting up in the bed and pushing back the heavy cover to discover he was wearing very little underneath. He thought hard to try and remember what had happened last night, but it was all just a blur.

"You are awake," came a soft voice from behind him. He turned slowly and smiled sheepishly at John. "Did you sleep well, Mister Warren? I had a most pleasant night."

"You *did*?" replied Sam anxiously. "I don't remember anything."

"Your clothes are there, over on the chest. I took the liberty to remove them, as you were—at the time—somewhat indisposed." Sam laughed nervously and slid off of the high mattress onto the cold wooden floorboards.

"It won't happen again," said Sam, shivering and pulling on his heavy woollen trousers quickly. "I'm just not used to that kind of…*drink*."

"I do not drink much, either," replied John, getting out of bed and dressing beside Sam. "We are alike, are we not, Mister Warren?"

"Sam…call me Sam, *please*."

"Very well, but it is not expected of me to be so familiar with a guest."

"And sharing a bed isn't familiar?" asked Sam, surprised. John looked at Sam, bewildered. It obviously was not an unusual occurrence, nor did it apparently signify anything untoward—which, of course, it wasn't. *Maybe it would be better if I were to sleep with Samuel?* Thought Sam briefly, but he dismissed that ludicrous idea immediately. That just *wasn't* right!

When they arrived downstairs, he found a welcome roaring fire in the grate, built by Samuel much earlier that morning, before he went outside to chop more wood. Mary had prepared some porridge, which was bubbling in a black iron pot over the fire. Little Ellen came over and sat down close to Sam on the bench.

"Master Samuel said to show you my finger because you were a phiss…phissyision," said Ellen, trying hard to pronounce the word correctly.

"A physician…call me a *doctor*. It's much easier," laughed Sam, taking hold of the erect finger gently and examining it. "Ah, I see what the problem is…you have a splinter in it."

"A what? Will I die?" whimpered Ellen, starting to cry. Sam laughed.

"No, of course not. Shall I get it out for you? It's just a little piece of wood."

"Will it hurt?" asked Ellen anxiously.

"No. I'll be very gentle. Do you have a needle? From a sewing box, maybe?" asked Sam, looking over at Mary.

"Mother had a sewing box. I will fetch one," said Mary helpfully. Within minutes she returned with a needle, which Sam carefully inserted into the flames of the fire for a few moments to sterilize it.

"Why did you do that?" inquired John, with interest, as he took a seat nearby.

"To make it clean, otherwise I might put germs into the finger, and it will get infected." As soon as he said it, he realized that they wouldn't have a clue what he meant, and he tried to backtrack on his explanation. He had to learn to think and speak differently. "If there is dirt on the needle—tiny little specks that we cannot see—and I put it into Ellen's finger, then that dirt will come off the needle into her finger."

"Then what?" asked John, his big blue eyes opened wide and were immensely distracting.

"Then," continued Sam, taking a deep breath, "the dirt will make the skin go all red and painful. Like it is now."

"But you haven't used the needle yet. How did the dirt get in?" urged John.

"Maybe when Ellen was playing? Dirt is everywhere. You should learn to always wash your hands before you eat and after '*other things*'," he said, pointing downwards. They seemed to understand.

"How will you get the dirt out?" asked Mary, joining the finger discussion party.

"Well, when I have removed the splinter with this *clean* needle, I will wash the wound well in hot water and wrap it in...a cloth, maybe? To keep it clean while it heals...gets better."

"Ooooh," they said in unison. Sam smiled and took hold of her finger firmly as they all peered intently over his shoulder, fascinated—all except for Ellen, who had her eyes tightly shut, preparing for the worst. In no time at all the splinter was carefully removed and, after waiting for some water to heat, Sam cleaned it thoroughly and tied a small piece of white cloth, found by Mary, around the finger. Ellen was so proud of her finger; she ran off happily to show everyone what Mister Warren had done! Looking back, it was that simple task that put the seeds of doubt in Sam's mind as to where he belonged, and with who.

After he had eaten his fill of porridge, he decided to take a stroll into the village. John's proposed fishing trip was postponed until later, as he needed to take a horse to the blacksmith's to have a new shoe put on. Charles arrived, as they were about to depart, and was accosted by Ellen in the doorway, where he was forced to listen to the amazing '*finger story*'.

"You have made a friend for life there, Mister Warren," laughed Charles. "Thank you most kindly for your assistance in this *small* matter."

"You are most welcome," replied Sam, smiling. Charles went over to the fireplace and removed the secret brick at the back. From inside he removed a velvet bag that contained coins. "That's a good hiding place," remarked Sam. "You would never know it was there."

"It is where I discovered Emily's letter. She knew of this place. I would be most grateful if you were to refrain from mentioning this place to anyone outside of the family."

"Of course, sir," replied Sam respectfully.

The door of the cottage was thrust open forcibly, and Samuel strode in, covered in wood chippings and visibly sweating from the exertion. He poured some mead into a mug and swilled it down in one go, wiping his lips across with the back of a dirty hand.

"Wash your hands, Samuel!" cried Ellen, horrified. "Mister Warren said to do it, or you will go all red." Samuel stopped and stared at Sam.

"All red? What nonsense have you been filling this young girl's mind with?" he said irritably.

"She speaks the truth, Samuel. It is most important for you to clean your hands. Mister Warren said—" John was interrupted in mid-speech.

"*Mister Warren* will have a chance to prove to me his worth in the very near future, and I have no doubt he will be a fine physician also, judging by the praise I have received regarding his first patient," said Samuel, nodding over towards an elated Ellen, who waved her bandaged finger proudly in the air. Charles ruffled Ellen's hair affectionately as he walked past her and up to Sam.

"Here is some money. It is not a great deal, but it will enable you to buy some compounds and herbs from the shop in the village. Buy what you require to treat minor ailments. The rest you can purchase later—when you begin your work here permanently, as the mill's physician." A number of large, heavy coins were pressed into Sam's hand gratefully. He didn't know what to say. It seemed to be a foregone conclusion that he would come back, with me, and stay on as the local doctor. He hated the idea of letting this family down. They, and the local community, needed him desperately. It was with a heavy heart that he walked into the village with John and the horse. His mind was all over the place, as he tried to distance himself from this surreal situation. He could see why I got involved with them. It was so hard not to.

John left the horse at the blacksmith's whilst he and Sam strolled around the village. It was absolutely fascinating for Sam, as his eyes took in the many different sights around him, only previously seen in history books. The pungent smells added to the reality that he was *really* here—back in 1696.

"Here is the church where Emily and Samuel will be wed," said John, grabbing hold of his arm affectionately. Sam smiled. He knew this church. It was where it all began. There was the inn where he and I had spent the night—a different name, but still a public house, judging by the smell of the strong ale and pipe smoke that wafted out into the street. He looked across the road, to see if the tearoom was still there. The building was still recognizable, but the shop sold drapery items instead. "Here is where you can purchase the compounds and other such ingredients," explained John, steering him towards a dark little shop with bottles and ancient medical artifacts in the window—enough to scare you half to death! He had no idea what he was supposed to be buying—what herbs treated what ailments, or what strange powders or formulas existed in these times. He would have to go on the Internet and look it all up. *What am I thinking? I have no intention of accepting the position offered by Samuel.*

"I think I will purchase the goods another time, if that is all right? I need to bring my books from London and list down the ingredients required," said Sam, so convincingly that he almost had himself fooled. John appeared to accept his explanation without question, and they returned to the blacksmith's to collect the newly shoed horse.

A large coach driven by six black horses came thundering down the street and pulled over near the inn, the horses snorting out hot steam from their nostrils as the coach rattled to a stop. On the top of the coach were several large trunks and packages, which were swiftly unloaded onto the street and collected by young lads for the coach's occupants. Three gentlemen and a lady alighted from the coach and entered the inn. A man then led the tired horses through to a stable area at the back.

"The coach from London," remarked John, noticing Sam's interest. "Did you not arrive in such a way?"

"Yes, of course! The same one will return tomorrow, I take it?"

"Indeed it will. It would be wise to secure your passage now, as it can get quite full near Christmas." Sam couldn't think of a reason to say why this was unnecessary, and John was more than willing to pay for his journey home. He stood watching as John arranged for his transportation to London and paid the man accordingly. He received, in return, a small white ticket for his fare.

The skies suddenly darkened, and small flakes of snow began to fall silently onto the street, causing people to disappear into shops and inns to escape the flurry.

"Best be getting back," said John, taking hold of the horse's reins and mounting the beast effortlessly. "Our fishing trip will have to wait until you return, for I fear it will be a heavy fall."

"That isn't a problem," replied Sam, beginning to walk off up the street, in the direction of Littleham.

"Where are you going?" cried John. "Come behind me." Sam couldn't help smiling at his choice of words, so innocently delivered.

"If you don't mind, I think I will walk back," called Sam, looking at the height at which he was expected to position himself. John was adamant.

"Give me your hand, and put your foot in the stirrup," demanded John as he brought the horse around. "You do not ride in London?"

"Not much," muttered Sam, remembering that the last time he rode any such animal was when he was five years old. It had been a donkey on the beach. He had fallen off and vowed then never to mount an animal again. "See you back at the cottage!" he called out, running up the street, leaving John staring after him, confused and a little hurt.

The rest of the afternoon was spent following John around as he attended to the chores assigned to him. Feeding the animals, brushing down the horses and disposing of the household waste were but a few of the many things that needed to be done. As Sam stood, mesmerized on the edge of the rubbish pit, looking down into its murky depths, he remembered what I had told him. John glanced across at him anxiously, realizing that he knew about Robert.

"You will not betray us, Sam? He deserved to die, did he not?"

"Your secret is safe with me, I assure you. He was a bad man, John. You need not feel any guilt over disposing of him in such a way." John smiled up at Sam. For a moment, their eyes locked, and a feeling of warmth spread through Sam. It was both pleasurable and not unfamiliar. Without thinking of the consequences, Sam put his arms around him and held him tight in an affectionate embrace that was received willingly by John. This prompted him to kiss Sam lightly on the cheek as he pulled away reluctantly.

"I have feelings for you that I know are wrong," whispered John, his eyes downcast.

"It's all right. I understand. Believe me; I do, although your family may not be so tolerant of your open displays of affection for me."

"I will not displease them, for fear that we will be parted, most assuredly," replied John, alarmed at the prospect of never seeing Sam again.

"I think we had better get back to the cottage," said Sam, trying to change the subject, and avoid showing the guilt over his intention *not* to return. This, however, was proving even more difficult as time went by. The two men walked slowly back through the falling snow, unaware that Samuel had watched the whole scenario intently from the nearby woods. It had crossed Samuel's mind since Sam's arrival that there was something a little *unnatural* about the relationship between the two men. Now his thoughts were confirmed. He smiled to himself as he walked over to the cottage to join them. Sam's affection for John could be used to his advantage, and Sam's position as the mill's physician would be more appealing when he returned, with me, from London.

Chapter Twenty

Sam felt unsettled during the evening meal that night. His emotions were running high with the decisions he was confronted with, and the turmoil he felt within. The sooner he left Mill Cottage and returned home to normality, the better. Samuel had been watching him all evening, with an enigmatic smile upon his face, as if he knew something Sam didn't.

"No mead tonight, Mister Warren?" inquired Samuel, filling his own mug to the brim.

"No, thank you. I need a clear head for my journey to London tomorrow," replied Sam, reaching over for a jug of milk, which had been left by the children.

"Undeniably so. That is very wise of you. Milk will have a more soothing effect and help you to sleep…if, indeed, that is possible." Sam looked up, surprised at the odd remark.

"Why do you say that?" he asked warily.

"I find myself that it is most difficult to sleep on the eve of a long journey," Samuel replied casually, glancing over at John, whose expression had taken on the appearance of a startled rabbit caught in the headlights of a car.

Charles went over to the window and peered out into the darkness. It had stopped snowing, the temperature outside now having dropped to well below freezing, leaving the newly laid snow glistening in the moonlight.

"At what time does the coach depart for London?" he asked, sitting back down by the fire. Sam took out the ticket from his pocket.

"It says thirty minutes past the hour of nine in the morning."

"I will come with you to the village," said John. "To make sure your departure is without any hindrance," he added quickly.

"That won't be necessary," Sam replied nervously.

"But I insist!" urged John, wanting to be with Sam until the last possible moment, to say a proper goodbye. Sam nodded in agreement. A plan was already hatching in his mind as to how he could pull this off.

"When do you think you will return with Emily?" asked Samuel, pulling the leg off of a roasted rabbit on the table, and tearing at the meat with his teeth. "Two days? Maybe three?"

"I'm not sure," replied Sam truthfully. "I have to convince her to come first."

"She is unsure of her feelings for me? Why would she hesitate so?" cried Samuel in alarm.

"She loves you. There is no doubt about that. It's just a big step to take...a really big step." Samuel frowned. He didn't understand the problem. "I will do all I can to persuade her to come, and that letter will help, I am sure," continued Sam, trying to give Samuel a bit of hope.

"Well, I hope you are successful in your endeavour, Mister Warren," said Charles as he rose from the bench. "If not, Samuel will be impossible to live with!" Only John and Sam grinned at the witty remark. Samuel's eyes started to turn black. "I wish you a safe journey, Mister Warren, and God speed," said Charles, shaking his hand firmly. "I will no doubt see you before you depart." The men watched as Charles shuffled unsteadily to the door and unlatched it. It would mean so much for him to see Samuel happily married. *And the sooner the better,* thought Sam. Time was running out for him.

The three remaining men sat silently by the fire, each absorbed in their own thoughts. Sam didn't want to be the one suggesting it was time to go to bed, even though he was finding it hard to stay awake. John didn't either, for similar reasons. Finally, it was Samuel who decided they should call it a night. They all went wearily up the stairs—John first, followed by Sam. Samuel followed up at the rear and discretely caught hold of Sam's arm.

"Be gentle with him," he hissed. "Or you will have me to answer to, without doubt." Sam turned bright red and opened his mouth to speak, but nothing came out. *How does he know? Does Charles know, as well? Oh God! This is so embarrassing.*

"Why do you sleep so far on the edge?" asked John, as they settled down into the bed for the night.

"I don't want to get too '*attached*' to you…so to speak," said Sam, cursing himself for using such explicit words. "Besides, I need my sleep. I have a long day tomorrow."

"You do *like* me, do you not?" whispered John, reaching out and touching his shoulder gently.

"Yes, I do…and that is the problem," replied Sam, giving his hand a reassuring squeeze. "Goodnight, John. See you in the morning."

"Goodnight, Sam," whispered back John as he turned over. "Do not be away too long." Sam closed his eyes, forcing a solitary tear to slowly run down his cheek. He hated himself at that moment.

Sam rose early the next morning, shortly after dawn. He quietly slipped out of bed, so as not to wake John, and dressed hurriedly in the corner of the room. All was quiet within the cottage. He assumed Samuel was still asleep, as he tiptoed down the creaky staircase in his socks.

"You have risen early this morning, Mister Warren?" called a familiar voice from the kitchen area. Sam turned and saw Samuel enter the room, half-shaven, with a blade in his hand.

"Oh! I didn't think you were awake yet," said Sam, biting his lip anxiously.

"Did you think you could just slip away unnoticed?" asked Samuel, who returned to the stone sink to complete his shave.

"No, of course not," replied Sam, his voice wavering. For that was *precisely* what he intended to do. *Why is it that Samuel always seems to know what I'm thinking?*

"Bring in some of the firewood from outside, so I can get the fire going...unless you have something better to do?"

called out Samuel. Sam opened the cottage door and stepped out onto the crisp white snow. It was freezing, and the logs were frozen solidly together in the pile. He managed to separate three or four before his fingers went numb, and he went back inside with the wood, his nose and cheeks flushed red with a healthy glow. Sam stood there, rigid, with his arms wrapped around himself as he watched Samuel build the fire and light it. *Imagine having to do that every morning,* he thought. *Give me central heating any day!*

Mary arrived. She appeared to have taken on the role of mother temporarily—a great burden for her young years, but one she endured without any objection. He had great admiration for this family. Modern-day kids had no idea what they were missing. They might have more luxuries in the future and life was a whole lot more comfortable, but they had lost that family bond—that *unity*—which was so strong here. Sam helped Mary prepare the breakfast. His plans to '*disappear'* were put aside momentarily, as he carried the heavy iron pot and fastened it onto a hook above the fire. John came down, which shelved his strategy for any unnoticeable exit. Plan B was therefore put into operation.

Breakfast was an uncomfortable affair. Everywhere he looked, John's pleading puppy dog eyes, Samuel's risqué remarks, or the children's over-the-top admiration confronted him. Even Charles constantly praised him for enlightening his children's minds with his knowledge, making him feel like some kind of Guardian Angel sent from a higher domain. He wasn't too far off the mark there. Charles took out his pocket watch and peered intently at the face for several moments, trying to focus on the figures with his fading eyesight.

"You best be on your way, young man. You wouldn't want to miss the coach's departure," he said, inserting the timepiece back into his pocket. John jumped up and reached for his cloak behind the door, indicating that he was ready to walk to the village with Sam. There was no escape. After some emotional goodbyes from the children, and a '*don't let me down, or else'* threat from Samuel, he and John made their way along the snowy track to the village. He looked back—just once. Little Ellen was still waving frantically outside of the cottage. With a lump in his throat, he walked on.

The coach was already on the street, prepared for its long journey to London—the horses fidgeting excitedly in their leather harnesses, eager to be on their way. It was 9:15am. There were to be three more passengers—all men, all respectfully dressed in garments of good quality. They nodded politely to Sam and bid him a good morning, as he handed the coachman his ticket.

"Don't hug me," whispered Sam to John. "I have to travel with these people after." John laughed. He understood the implications, but hiding his feelings was going to be difficult as they said their goodbyes. It was soon time, and the three men boarded the coach and took up their seats. "Guess I had better get on," said Sam begrudgingly. "Take good care of everyone for me."

"I shall do that," said John, his voice weak and tearful. "Come back soon. I will miss you dreadfully." Sam held out his hand and grasped John's tightly.

"Take care, my friend," said Sam. Tears started to run down John's face in abundance, as Sam turned quickly to board the coach before he, too, gave way to his emotions. Taking up a seat next to the window, he stared out, blinded with tears, at the figure of John standing forlornly on the street. The coach swayed to one side as the coachmen climbed up on top, and the horses jerked forward unsteadily, as he took up the reins to begin the long journey.

There wasn't much to see, apart from miles of endless woods and fields. The boredom, together with the swaying of the coach, lulled him into a slumber that lasted the good part of two hours. He didn't feel in the mood for polite conversation with the other men and their ongoing discussion concerning sheep rustlers. The coach pulled into an inn after some time, to allow the horses to be changed and the occupants to stretch their legs—perhaps indulging in some light refreshment, if they so wished. Sam still had the money that Charles had given him, so bought some bread and cheese from the innkeeper, which he washed down with some ale.

The original plan was to use the locket nearby the cottage, then walk into the village and phone Toby to come and collect him. He had notes tucked away in his jacket pocket, in case he wanted something to eat at the pub while he waited. Plan B, now in operation, was to go into London, return back to the future discretely, and catch a train home to Banbury, which was a relatively short distance from Central London. It would save Toby driving all the way down to collect him. It sounded good, in theory.

The coach rumbled on, now with a fresh set of horses, over the uneven and slush-covered ground. His fellow passengers had fallen asleep, which was not surprising, considering the amount of ale they had put away when they stopped. Sam wished he could sleep too. It would prevent his mind from thinking about John and the rest of the Howerd family, who he had come to grow so fond of in such a short time. They stopped again, before nightfall, at another inn. This one was far more rowdy and of a dubious nature. It looked like it doubled as a brothel. Various busty women, offering certain services, approached Sam. They appeared surprised when he politely turned them down, and they could be seen gathering in dark corners after, discussing his masculinity, or lack thereof. Sam didn't care what they thought. He just wanted this tedious journey to end so he could return home to Toby.

Back on the road, the scenery had just started to become interesting, as they entered a more built-up area just before darkness fell. The coachman lit a lantern and hung it from a hook inside the coach, offering blankets and cushions for warmth and comfort. He asked the coachman when they were expected to arrive in London, to which he replied,

"Late tomorrow morn, sir, if the weather holds." Sam sighed and pulled the blanket up around his neck. He was cold and uncomfortable. I guess this is what you call *Coach Class*; he thought drearily—a bit different from British Airways, with their movies and drinks trolleys. He smiled to himself at the ludicrous thought and looked across at the sleeping man opposite. They'd never know what a plane is—or a DVD player, or even *electricity*. The world would change so much in 300 years. They couldn't begin to imagine what the future held. Sam laid his head against the propped up cushion on the window ledge and closed his eyes. If he could just get some sleep, then time would pass more quickly. A long night lay ahead of him, as the coach continued on through the darkness on its bumpy ride to London—a London that Sam would not be familiar with. The prospect was daunting.

Hours later he was awoken from his sleep, by the iron wheels of the coach negotiating its way over uneven cobblestones. Looking sleepily out of the window, he was amazed to see crowds of people bustling about in the street, brick buildings of all shapes and sizes, and market stalls. The noise was deafening, as the market traders advertised their wares, each competing against the next stall for customers. Sam looked over at the other men questioningly. He refrained against asking the all-time favorite phrase, '*Are we there yet?*' although the significance of it would be lost to them.

"Covent Garden," remarked one of the men. "We will soon arrive at our destination." No sooner had he uttered those welcoming words than the coach pulled over and stopped abruptly. The door was opened, and the men proceeded to alight the coach, with Sam the last to leave. He stood there on the street, taking in the chaotic scenes around him, as the other men collected their belongings and vanished into the throng. This was vastly different from Offenham village—not just because of the huge number of people milling around. The filth and stench was far worse—utterly stomach churning.

He wasn't sure which way to go. All he wanted to do was find a quiet corner where he could disappear out of this hellhole. Finding such a place was going to prove difficult. He walked slowly down the street, his boots sinking into the muddy pools of excrement that covered the road, together with the steaming horse manure and rotting corpses of dead animals. Sam covered his mouth, terrified of inhaling some airborne disease. A cart rattled by, its wheels spraying putrid urine and stagnant water over his trousers. He stepped back against the side of a badly constructed brick house, which looked like it was about to fall down at any second, to survey the damage. In doing so, he narrowly missed the contents of a chamber pot being emptied from an upstairs window into the street below. *This is awful. How on earth could people live like this?* It was no wonder they didn't reach any great age.

Crossing the street, he tried to find, amongst the rabbit warren of alleys, one that was exposed to the sunlight, but all were dark and enclosed. Suddenly, a woman grabbed hold of his arm as he peered around the back of a shop, thrusting his hand down the front of her dress, into a sea of sweaty flesh.

"Ere, boy. Have a hold of them beauties. Put airs on ya chest, they will," she cackled, her mouth open wide, displaying four rotting teeth. Sam pulled out his hand, horrified, and ran off up the road as he ignored the vile obscenities that spewed forth from the woman's mouth. A young leper boy, covered in sores, held out his hand pitifully to Sam as he rounded the corner, only to be pushed cruelly to the ground by a bunch of lice-infested children as they raced past.

Finally, by chance, he saw a narrow passageway between two houses. At the end, a shaft of sunlight filtered down through the dense, smoky air. Coughing badly as the black, suffocating smoke filled his lungs; Sam reached into his pocket and quickly took out the locket. As he flipped it open and exposed it to the weak sunlight, it never occurred to Sam *where* he would reappear in modern-day London. As long as it had a toilet nearby, he was happy...he was bursting to go!

Now they say, '*be careful what you wish for because it might come true,*' which, in Sam's case, was precisely so. Having made the transition back, he staggered unsteadily against something hard and opened his eyes. His head was still spinning, but he breathed a sigh of relief as he realized he was back in the future. There was no mistaking the modern-day sink units, the soap dispensers and hand dryers on the tiled walls—and the distinct lack of urinals!

"Shit! I'm in a ladies' toilet!" he cried, diving for the nearest stall and locking the door firmly behind him. After relieving himself, he sat on the closed lid and contemplated his next move. He couldn't stay in there. He had to go out, into whatever lie on the other side of the door, and get home.

"My God, I stink!" he said, looking down at his soiled trousers. It was at this point that it suddenly dawned on him what he was wearing. "No!" he cried, burying his head in his hands in despair. "You stupid idiot, Sam!" He couldn't believe he hadn't thought this through properly before he decided to alter his plans. His mind had been in such turmoil, what with leaving John and Mill Cottage, and then there was the unscheduled trip to London. He had forgotten that Toby wouldn't be there to give him his change of clothes. *Now what?*

He heard the outside door click open and someone, presumably a woman, entered the toilet. He listened as her footsteps went into the stall next to his and the bolt shot home. He had an idea. The woman flushed the toilet and unbolted the door. Sam took a deep breath and unlocked his door as the woman washed her hands at the sink.

"Excuse me. I wondered if you could do something for me?" he said nervously. The woman jumped and spun around, her mouth open in surprise. "If I gave you some money, could you…" Sam was unable to finish the sentence as the woman let out a piecing scream and ran for the door, pulling it open frantically. Then she was gone. "…buy me some jeans and a shirt?" continued Sam. He stared at the stranger, whose reflection he saw in the mirror, and banged his fist into the tiled wall in frustration. "Damn it!" he cried, almost in tears. There was only one thing for it. He had to go outside and face the world. As he approached the door, it swung back sharply, and two burly security men entered. They each took a hold of Sam's arms as the woman stood, petrified, in the doorway.

"Is this the man?" asked one of them. The woman nodded and disappeared from view.

"What's that awful smell?" cried the other man as he dragged Sam towards the door. "You've got some explaining to do."

"It's not what you think!" yelled Sam, struggling. "I just wanted some clothes."

"Tell it to the officer down the station, mate." Sam was marched through the bedding section of a department store, amid staring shoppers. The humiliation of it would remain with him for years to come.

Outside of the store, a police car was waiting, and he was shoved inside it in an undignified manner. The officer in the back was sitting as far away as possible from him. His pleas of innocence fell on deaf ears as the car drove speedily to the nearest police station, which happened to be quite near.

"Empty your pockets," said the officer behind the counter, wrinkling his nose in disgust as the smell reached his nostrils. Sam hesitated. There were things in his pockets that he would rather not disclose. "DO…YOU…SPEAK…ENGLISH?" shouted the officer.

"Yes," replied Sam quietly.

"So what part of 'empty your pockets' don't you understand?" Sam still hesitated, his mind one step ahead, trying to think up plausible explanations for the objects in his pockets. "If you don't empty them, I will be forced to do so myself, and I'd rather not," continued the officer, folding his arms. "So what's it to be?" Sam begrudgingly took the items from his pockets. Some notes to the value of £30, a handful of large coins of unknown value, a piece of parchment paper with some childish writing on, and a locket. The officer wrote down a description of the items, in the best way he knew how, and asked Sam to sign for them before inserting the unusual collection into a plastic bag.

"I'll get them back, won't I?" asked Sam anxiously.

"All in good time," he replied. "Now…your name and address, please?" Sam gave him the relevant information and was taken to a small room containing a desk, recording equipment, and three chairs. He sat dejectedly on one of the chairs with his head in his hands. He was so tired. All he wanted to do was go home.

The door opened, and two plain-clothed men entered the room and sat down opposite him. One switched on the tape, while the other opened up a file with blank pages.

"My name is Detective Inspector Michael Evans, and this is my colleague, PC Jack Wood. Could you state your name, please?"

"You already know my name," said Sam despairingly, sitting back on the chair.

"For the benefit of the tape, would you please state your name?"

"Samuel James Warren."

"Thank you. It does help if you co-operate, Mr Warren," replied the inspector, moving his chair back, away from the table. "It appears you approached a woman in the ladies' toilet of a certain department store at 11:55 this morning and offered her money in return for a certain *favor*?"

"I wanted her to buy me some *clothes*…I offered her the money as payment for them. Nothing else," pleaded Sam.

"Why were you loitering in the ladies' toilet?" he continued, while scribbling some notes onto a sheet of paper.

"I went in the wrong door."

"So why didn't you come out again?"

"I was just about to when the security guys came in."

"Funny that…the woman says you appeared from a stall."

"I was desperate to go." The two officers exchanged looks. Sam bit his lip nervously.

"Can you tell me why you are dressed in such soiled and odd clothing?"

"I went to a fancy dress party last night and got a bit drunk," replied Sam, saying the first thing that entered his head.

"As a *what,* precisely?" inquired the Inspector, casting a disgusted eye over his attire.

"A 17th Century peasant."

"Is the smell for realistic effect? Seems a bit over the top for a party. I hope you weren't expecting to get laid?" Sam was not amused by the Inspector's coarse remark. "So, can you give me a name and address, where this *so-called* party was held?" Sam's face dropped. If he gave a false name and address, they would no doubt check it out and find he was lying.

"I can't remember," Sam muttered before looking away. The inspector sighed and reached for the plastic bag containing his confiscated items. Sam started to feel sick.

"Interesting little collection we have here, is it not?"

"If you say so." The contents were emptied out onto the desk in front of him.

"These coins. More realistic effects, I take it?"

"Obviously."

"A piece of paper—parchment, if I am not mistaken?" said the inspector, waving it in the air. "With a love letter written on it, by a somewhat *uneducated* individual." Sam didn't reply. "This brings me to the last item—this rather antique-looking locket." His heart stopped beating as the inspector prised the locket apart and peered at the faded and water-stained picture within. "Someone you know? Your mother, perhaps? Or grandmother?"

"No. No one I know," replied Sam truthfully. The inspector snapped the locket shut impatiently and banged it down upon the table.

"Mr Warren, is there *anyone* who could vouch for you?"

"Yes, my partner, Toby. He will speak for me."

"Your partner?"

"Do the maths," said Sam wearily. The inspector shot a knowing glance at his colleague, who had turned rather pink. Giving Sam his phone, he proceeded to dial his home number. After three minutes of waiting for an answer, Sam clicked the phone off. "Must be out," he said miserably.

"Mr Warren…" began the Inspector again.

"Actually, when you come to think of it, wouldn't you expect to see me loitering in the *men's* toilet?" volunteered Sam innocently.

"MR WARREN! I think you had better stop right there before you dig yourself into an even bigger hole." Sam stopped, realizing what he was implying. It wasn't helping. The door of the room opened, and an officer handed the inspector a note, which he read immediately. He nodded his thanks. "Look, Mr Warren. Why don't you stop wasting police time and tell me exactly what you were doing in the ladies' toilet, dressed like a smelly peasant? I'm in no hurry to get home. Are you?" The thought of spending the night in the police station was enough to tip Sam over the edge.

"Fine. You want to know? Then I'll tell you! I've travelled back in time—to the 17th century—to sort out a friend's love life. On my return to the future, I reappeared in the ladies' toilet. Not planned, just happened. Okay?" The room fell silent as the two officers looked at one another. Inspector Evans began to laugh.

"I've heard of some excuses in my time, but I have to admit, that's a first!" Sam leaned forward across the desk.

"But it's *true*!" he cried.

"All right, Mr Warren. I'm going to let you off with a caution this time, seeing as you have no criminal record or convictions, according to this report. May I suggest you go and visit your doctor at some point, as I think you may be a little delusional?" Sam breathed a sigh of relief.

"Can I go home now?" he asked, taking the plastic bag off of the inspector and signing for it.

"Where is it you live? Banbury?" the inspector asked, checking the address. "Aren't you going out that way this evening?" he inquired of PC Woods, who nodded his reply rather cautiously. "There you go! Got yourself a lift, too. Who said the police force was uncaring?"

"Thank you," said Sam gratefully. He couldn't begin to think what a nightmare journey home it would have been otherwise.

Sam arrived back at his home around 7pm and trudged wearily up the stairs to his flat. He was exhausted and looked forward to seeing the surprised, but happy face on Toby as he answered the door. Hopefully he was in now. He rang the doorbell and waited excitedly, as he heard footsteps approaching from inside. The door opened and Toby faced Sam in the doorway.

"SURPRISE!" Sam cried joyfully. Toby stared at Sam in utter shock, the color draining from his face.

"Sam, what are doing here? Why didn't you ring me?" he asked anxiously.

"Long story, my friend…*long* story," said Sam, giving Toby a hug, which made him recoil in horror and push him away.

"Yeah, I know. I pong a bit," Sam said, laughing and pushing past him into the lounge. "I *must* get out of these dreadful clothes and have a shower…I've so much to tell you!" With that, Sam made his way towards the bedroom.

"Don't go in there!" cried Toby suddenly. Sam stopped and looked at the panic stricken expression on Toby's face.

"Why?"

"Just don't…I need to talk to you," replied Toby, avoiding his eyes. Sam turned around and threw open the bedroom door. Lying in their bed, looking exceedingly guilty, was a guy Sam recognized from the university—one of his best friends.

Chapter Twenty-One

Toby came up behind Sam and gently took hold of his arm.

"Oliver came over to keep me company while you were away," Toby said weakly.

"You don't say!" cried Sam. "Seems like he was doing rather a good job of it." Thrusting open the wardrobe door angrily, Sam pulled out some clean shirts, jeans and underwear, hastily discarding the soiled clothes on the floor. He dressed and stuffed the rest into a shopping bag, along with two very important items. "No wonder you were in such a hurry to get shot of me!" yelled Sam. "Hoping I wouldn't make it back, were you?"

"No, Sam. That isn't true," wailed Toby, blocking his exit.

"Forget it, Toby. I just don't care anymore! As for you, Oliver," he said, turning to the cowering guy in the bed. "You deserve one another."

"Please, Sam. It wasn't meant to be like this," pleaded Toby.

"No! I wasn't meant to come back unexpectedly and catch you in bed with my best friend," Sam yelled, pushing past him roughly. "How's Emily, by the way?" asked Sam as he filled a glass with water and drank thirstily.

"She's fine. I think she went into town today, but she's back now. Sam, listen..."

"I'm surprised you noticed," cut in Sam bluntly.

"Sam! I still *love* you," cried Toby pathetically as Sam headed for the door.

"I'm going to see Emily…don't wait up for me." With that parting remark Sam slammed the door shut and headed down the corridor, fuming.

I had just sat down with a mug of chocolate when I heard loud banging on my front door. Presuming it was Toby, yet again; I got up wearily and answered it, ready to decline another of his constant offers of help. I was surprised to see a very red-faced Sam standing in the doorway, clutching a large bag.

"Hi," I said, taken aback. "Didn't expect to see you back yet."

"Can I come in?" muttered Sam. "Slight problem on the home front." I stepped back to allow him to enter, wrinkling my nose in disgust at the smell as he passed. It looked serious, whatever it was.

"Coffee?" I offered anxiously as Sam flopped down onto the sofa, exhausted.

"Love one," he replied. I went into the kitchen to refill the kettle, and returned to find Sam fidgeting about with the cushions on the sofa, as if he was looking for something.

"You okay? You look a bit dishevelled."

"Yeah, fine…could do with a shower later, if I may?"

"Yours not working, then?" I asked, a little puzzled.

"Probably…look Emily, could I crash out here tonight?"

"Why?" I asked warily.

"Let's just say Toby has a friend over—my friend, actually. Well, he *was*."

"You're not making any sense," I said frowning. Sam sighed and lay back on the sofa, his eyes drooping as he fought to stay awake.

"I came home to find Toby in bed with my best friend."

"You're joking?" I cried. "Toby thought the world of you."

"Well, there you go…nothing is certain in this world, is it? Or in any other."

"You don't seem too upset by it," I said as I went into the kitchen to make his coffee.

"No, not really. What is to be will be, as they say."

"How's your mum?" I called out from the kitchen, changing the subject. "You didn't stay long."

"My mum?" he replied, baffled. "Oh! My *mum*…yeah, she's okay, I guess. Two days is quite enough, though."

"That bad?" Sam smiled up at me and took the mug from my hand. I watched him as he sipped the hot coffee, an expression of sheer pleasure on his somewhat grubby face. His hair was matted and greasy, which was unusual for Sam, and I wondered how he had come to let himself go so much.

"Couldn't do me a sandwich, could you?" he asked, finishing off the coffee.

"Doesn't your mum feed you?" I said laughing. Sam just smiled apologetically, and I returned to the kitchen. "Cheese or ham?" I called out

"Ham, please…with pickle."

"Yes, *Master*," I replied jokily, and set about preparing the snack. Five minutes later I returned with the sandwich to find Sam sound asleep on the sofa. I didn't have the heart to wake him, so fetched a blanket from the bedroom to throw over him. "Sleep tight," I whispered, leaning over and kissing the top of his head lightly. "God, Sam! You really *do* need a shower!" Taking the sandwich to nibble in bed, I closed my bedroom door. I felt there was something Sam wasn't telling me, but that would have to wait until morning now.

I awoke the following morning to the sound of the water running in the shower. Turning over, I looked at the clock. It was not even eight yet. Slipping on my robe and slippers, I padded out into the lounge and gathered up the blanket. *Would he want to stay tonight, too?* I wondered, before storing it away in the cupboard. By the time I had prepared the morning coffee, Sam had emerged clean and damp from the bathroom, wrapped in a soft blue towel.

"That's better," he said, rubbing his hair dry with a hand towel. "Sorry about last night…what happened to my sandwich?"

"I ate it!" I replied, laughing, "You fell asleep." Sam smiled and pulled a face. "Shall we try again with breakfast?" I suggested. "Cereal and toast okay?"

"Marvelous," replied Sam. "I'll go and dress."

Half an hour later we were sitting around the kitchen table tucking into our breakfast. Sam had a third helping of Fruit Loops. It looked like he hadn't eaten for a week.

"I must say, you seem a bit happier than when I left," said Sam, swilling down his second cup of coffee.

"I'm trying. Really, I am. Toby was a good help, actually. We talked a lot. He said I had to move on and forget the past…and Samuel." Sam stopped in mid-mouthful, and an anxious expression crossed his face. "I have to accept what happened. I can't change it, can I?"

"Suppose you were wrong about Samuel…suppose he really *did* love you?" said Sam nervously.

"That's something I will never know…still, life goes on, and so must I. I realize that now," I said, collecting up the plates.

"You can't!" cried Sam.

"Can't what?"

"Move on…"

"Why not? Do you want to see me miserable all the time?"

"You don't need to be…do you still love him?"

"What kind of crazy question is that?"

"If I had proof that he loved you…would it change things?"

"Sam? What are you going on about?"

"When I went to see my '*mum*'," began Sam cautiously, "I stopped by Littleham on the way home."

"You didn't say your mum lived near Littleham," I interrupted.

"Just moved there...anyway, I had a look around the cottage and found this secret hiding place behind a brick by the fireplace."

"I know of it. I left a letter there for Samuel just before I departed. It was a stupid letter, but I wanted him to know that I would always love him," I said, sitting down at the table as all the memories came flooding back.

"Well, I guess he found the note," continued Sam.

"How would you know that?"

"Because he replied..." I stared at Sam as if he had gone mad.

"Don't talk daft!" I cried. "He can't even read, let alone write." Sam took from his pocket a small piece of parchment and unfolded it before me. My heart started to pound loudly as he handed it over for me to read, which I did. "You wrote this!" I cried, close to tears. "What kind of cruel joke are you playing on me, Sam?"

"Emily...I *swear* to you, I never wrote this letter," pleaded Sam. "You wanted proof, and there it is. He loves you, Emily. He wants to *marry* you. You have to believe me." The tears started to roll down my face, as my world was turned upside down—yet again.

"I...I don't know," I stammered. "I couldn't come back home anymore. It's a lot to think about."

"You wouldn't want to come home, Emily. You would be so happy...and, just think, you could start a little school and teach all the local children to read and write," rambled on Sam excitedly.

"You seem very sure about all this..." I said suspiciously.

"I have a feeling it will all work out well...trust me." I reread the letter again.

"I wonder who helped him to write this." I pondered. "It's very good."

"Someone with a vested interest in your happiness, no doubt," replied Sam.

"It couldn't be Isabelle. She wants him for herself. I can't think of anyone else who *knows* me and can read and write well enough to have helped in this."

"Does it *really* matter?" said Sam, slightly irritated.

"No, not really," I replied, surprised at Sam's tone of voice. "In any case, there is a slight problem...well, a big problem, actually."

"What's that?" asked Sam, concerned.

"I can't find the locket. I thought I had left it in my dress pocket, but it's not there. I've searched the house out, but I can't seem to find it."

"Oh…" said Sam, glancing over towards the sofa. "I expect it's somewhere around—slid down a little gap between something…have you looked under the cushions on the sofa and the armchair?"

"Of course I have, I tell you. It's nowhere to be found." Sam jumped up and started frantically searching the house, while I sat and watched, bemused. "Maybe it's trying to tell me something," I called out as Sam started to throw the cushions off of the sofa erratically. "Like I'm not *meant* to return." Sighing, I got up and started to wash the breakfast plates, leaving Sam to his fruitless search.

"FOUND IT!" yelled out Sam, rushing into the kitchen clutching the locket. "It was down the side of the sofa, like I suspected."

"Great," I muttered unenthusiastically. In a way, I wished he hadn't found it. Then I wouldn't have been forced into making a decision—a decision that would affect my whole life. My future. Sam stood there expectantly, waiting for a response. *What did he expect me to say? 'Okay. I'm off now—back to marry Samuel. Nice knowing you?' There is so much to think about—my flat, my car, my belongings, and my money, to name but a few.* Sam realized he was pushing me too hard and backed off a little.

"I know it's a big step. Take your time and think about it," he said, sitting back down at the table and fiddling with his hair. Something, I noticed, he always did when he was agitated.

"I *really* can't think about it right now," I said, leaning up against the cupboards and folding my arms. "Talking of relationships, though…what are you going to do about Toby?"

"Toby who?" replied Sam, smiling mischievously.

"You know what I mean."

"Dunno...don't care much, either."

"You sound like you have found someone else?" I asked cautiously. Sam looked up at me startled, confirming my suspicion. "Well…who is he, then? Someone I know?"

"Could be…" He replied guardedly. "But this isn't about *me*, is it?"

"Why are you so adamant about me returning? You don't know anything about this family—what they are like… whether I would be safe there?"

"From what you have told me, they seem a decent lot," said Sam, looking away, out of the window.

"Samuel could be a little *unpredictable,"* I told him, remembering back to a certain cart ride home. "But underneath he was a pussy cat; really...you would have liked him."

"Indeed I would have," said Sam, forgetting himself, and using terminology that he had grown accustomed to in the past two days.

"Indeed I would have?" I repeated back, amused. "That sounds like something they would have said."

"Who?" said Sam, trying to bluff his way out of a tricky situation. Fortunately, he was saved by the bell…well, a knock in this case, on my front door. "I know who that is," said Sam, drearily.

"Shall I let him in?"

"If you *must*." I opened the door to find a sheepish looking Toby standing there, his big brown mournful eyes pleading forgiveness.

"It's not *me* you have to convince," I said bluntly, walking back into the lounge. Sam stood up and glared at Toby. "Would you two like to take this discussion back to *your* flat? I really don't want to be involved in this dispute."

"Sorry, Emily. Yes, of course," Sam said apologetically and he walked out, closely followed by Toby, who looked like he was walking to the gallows. I had a feeling Sam already knew this particular relationship was finished.

It was good to be on my own. It gave me time to think, without Sam pressing me for answers. I picked up the note and read it again, pressing it to my lips, as thoughts of my lost love washed over me in a warm embrace.

"He wants to *marry* me!" I said out loud. *Mrs Samuel Howerd, the wife of a wealthy mill owner. I like the sound of that.* After a moment's thought, I picked up a chair and took it over to a cupboard on the far wall. Standing up on it,

I could just about reach the small top section. I pulled out a large cardboard box covered in dust. Setting it down on the table, I carefully undid the yellowed string and slid it off. Lifting up the lid and removing the tissue paper, I stared down at the contents wistfully. My mother's wedding dress. I had kept it all these years in the hope that one day I would have the chance to wear it. Carefully lifting it from the box, I held it up against me and gasped. It was beautiful! I was very young when I last glimpsed it—not old enough to appreciate its simple, yet elegant, design. I ran my hand around the sweetheart neckline and down the long lace sleeves that matched the fine laced bodice, which fitted tightly into the waist. The rest of the gown, in heavy satin, flowed to the floor, spreading out at the back into a train edged with pink satin roses. I imagined Samuel's face as I walked down the aisle towards him. It was perfect…*he was perfect.*

The sudden shrill of the telephone made me jump, and I dropped the dress to answer it. Mr. Jenkins, my landlord, was on the other end demanding last month's rent in no uncertain terms. I had fallen behind with the payments since losing my job and, unless I could find the money to cover the shortfall in the next five days, he would have to serve me notice to vacate the premises. Something else for me to worry over—I decided that I needed to get out of the flat for a while. It was all closing in on me, and I felt claustrophobic.

Taking the bus into town, I alighted near the Shopping Mall and wandered aimlessly along the pedestrian precinct, looking into shop windows. I had neither the money nor the inclination to buy anything, and felt even more depressed. I wished my mum was still alive. I needed someone to talk to—someone who understood a woman's feelings, and could advise me as to what to do for the best. Then again, she wouldn't have let me go—*would she? To lose her only daughter and never see her again?* My fate was decided. But I didn't have a mother, or a father—no one to confide in and talk me out of this surreal situation. Except Sam…and he, for some reason, *wanted* me to go. *So, what was stopping me?*

I sat down on a bench and watched the people come and go, with their shopping bags and moaning kids in tow. I could end up like one of these desperate housewives in a few years. Husband in a boring nine to five job, a couple of kids demanding the latest game console, just because Jake down the road has one. A holiday once a year to Spain because it was the '*thing to do*', despite not having the money to pay for it and adding to the ever increasing debt on the credit card. A mortgage that never seemed to reduce. A nagging mother-in-law, perhaps. Endless arguments leading to divorce. Lonely old age, ending in death in a nursing home, because you were too much of a burden for your children to care for. *Did I really want all this?* They didn't have an alternative…I do. I have the chance to lead a peaceful life in the idyllic countryside—no debts, no mortgage around my neck, and no pressure from the children to buy the latest gadgets. My tasks would be simple—keep the house clean, feed the animals, cook one decent meal a day, make sure the children were clean and healthy, and support my husband… Samuel Howerd. The man I loved so desperately. What would *you* choose?

A breeze got up suddenly, and swirled around some candy wrappers and a sheet of newspaper, the latter getting entangled around my legs. Bending down, I pulled away the offending item and noticed it was the horoscope page of the local rag. I don't know what made me look at it, but I did, to absorb the words written under my star sign of Virgo.

"Hey, Emily! How're you doing?" said a male voice close to me. I looked up, startled to see Adrian, a workmate from my old office. "We all miss you at work, you know…so, what you been up to lately? Haven't seen you about."

"Oh! This and that," I said, smiling forcibly. *Like hell they missed me!* I thought. *Probably half of them never realized I had gone.*

"No hot-blooded male whisked you off your feet, then?" he continued sarcastically. My shackles began to rise, and the words were out of my mouth before I could stop them.

"Actually, now you come to ask, I'm getting married very soon."

"Oh!" replied Adrian, not expecting that particular response. "Who is it? Not Patrick, the nerd from Accounts?"

"No."

"Is it Jason? He always had the hots for you."

"NO!"

"I know…it's Russell Wainright, at the other branch!"

"NO! You don't know him…and are never likely to either, so stop trying to guess."

"Must get back to the office and tell Gloria!" said Adrian, excitedly. "She swore no one would want a stuck-up frigid cow like you…her words, not mine," he added quickly, before running off up the road, eager to share the news with his colleagues.

I arrived back home a little after two, noticing as I walked through the parking lot, the absence of Toby's car. Thinking Sam would be in need of some TLC after the break-up, I stopped at his flat and rang the bell.

"You okay?" I said caringly as he opened the door. He smiled feebly, and I put my arms around him to give him a big, reassuring hug. "You'll soon get over him." I said sympathetically.

"I'm just making a coffee. Want one?" said Sam cheerfully, prising himself away from my embrace and heading for the kitchen.

"Sure," I replied, making myself comfortable on the worn sofa. "So, when do I get to meet this new '*acquaintance*' of yours?" I called out. "What's his name?" Sam didn't answer, and I waited until he returned with the coffee, thinking he hadn't heard me. "What's your new friend's name?" I asked again as he put down the mugs onto the table. Sam hesitated for a moment.

"John…his name is John," he replied cautiously.

"Nice name," I said, taking a ginger biscuit from the tin. "If he is as good-natured as Samuel's brother is, you will be very happy together." Sam began to play with his hair. "Why don't you invite him here for Christmas?" I asked casually.

"I can't...he's away at the moment."

"Anywhere nice?"

"Down in the country somewhere...with his family."

"Oh, that's a pity. Still, it won't be for long. I feel better knowing you have someone special here, and won't be alone when I return to Samuel." Sam stared at me, his mouth gaping open in surprise.

"You mean, you're going to do it? You're *really* going to go back and marry Samuel?" I nodded my head, smiling, and took a sip of coffee. "That's fantastic! Oh, Emily. I'm *so* pleased for you! What made you decide to go?"

"There's nothing here for me, Sam. I just feel I belong there, with Samuel, and then I saw this...and I knew what I had to do," I said, handing Sam the piece of torn newspaper. "Read under Virgo."

'Virgo August 24th—September 22nd

You are entering the most adventurous part of your chart, and a life-changing decision, that has up to now eluded you, is now crystal clear. The answer is simple...just follow your heart.'

Chapter Twenty-Two

Sam looked at me and laughed.

"Is this what made you decide to go? A cryptic message from *Madam Mystic*?"

"No! Well, *yes*, kind of, but not just that. There were other contributing factors."

"Like what?" asked Sam, trying hard to be serious.

"Would you say I was *frigid*?" I asked guardedly. Sam couldn't contain himself any longer and collapsed into uncontrollable laughter. I knew I shouldn't have asked.

"Honey," he spluttered, after finally gaining control. "You're asking the wrong guy here, aren't you?" I smiled, realizing the error of my words.

"I'm going to miss you so much, Sam," I said, taking hold of his hand affectionately. *He is my best friend, my rock and he is always, always there for me…come what may.*

"Hey, don't get all sentimental on me, or you'll start me crying," said Sam as he gave me a big hug. I could feel the tears starting to prick the backs of my eyes.

"It's just so *final*," I wailed. "I can't ring you now and again and tell you my news… or send you a postcard." Sam hugged me tighter. "You will never know if I'm happy, if I *did* marry Samuel, and how many children I had!"

"You're not having second thoughts, are you?" asked Sam anxiously.

"I don't know...maybe." I replied half-heartedly.

"Come on, young lady, enough of these melancholy thoughts," said Sam as he jumped up. "We have work to do."

"I don't know where to start!" I cried. "There's so much to sort out." Sam went over to a drawer and took out some paper and a pen.

"Just as well that I'm here to help then, isn't it?" I smiled weakly as Sam scribbled down the first item on the list—my car, Betsy.

"I want you to have her," I said without hesitation. "You need some means of transport for university, visiting your mum, and for you and John to go on days out together." Sam appeared slightly uncomfortable and didn't respond. "Please, say you'll take her. I know you will look after her," I pleaded.

"Okay, if you insist," he replied reluctantly, marking down the name, *'Sam'* next to the car. We moved on to the next item—my furniture. If I sold it, I would gain quite a bit of cash, *but what would I do with the cash?* It would be of no use to me there. Sam suggested buying some old coins from that era with the money, and we checked out the availability of such coins on the Internet. What few were around fetched quite considerable sums at auctions. It was not an option, so we discarded it as a bad idea. My bank account held just under £100, with a further £500 in a building society account. Then there was my jewelry, not much of any real value, but in need of a home. Clothes and personal effects came next. There was very little I could actually take with me, without rousing suspicion. I decided to donate my clothes to a charity shop, as well as some personal items.

"You take the money, Sam," I said, getting tired of all these formalities. "Put it to good use for your future. I can't think of a more deserving person."

"I couldn't possibly!" cried Sam, horrified at the thought. "Why don't you give it to a charity, like Cancer Research, or the Red Cross?" I was a bit surprised at Sam's refusal of an extra £600 in his bank account, but he was adamant, and I decided to split the money between my favourite charities. "You won't go before Christmas, will you?" Sam asked suddenly. "You can stay here in my flat, if you like, bearing in mind most of your stuff will soon be sold, including your bed." I hadn't realized how close it was to Christmas, with it being the 22nd of December already. It would take me a few days to clear everything out and close my accounts.

"Thanks, Sam. I would love to spend Christmas Day with you," I replied, swallowing hard. *My last Christmas Day, as I knew it.* "I shall leave on the 26th December, though." That feeling of doubt began to wash over me again. It was as if I was going to *die* that day. I would cease to be Emily Howard—forever erased from existence.

The next two days were a whirlwind of frantic organization, with numerous trips into town with Betsy, filled to the brim with my belongings. The landlord was informed of my departure, and he advertized my flat the same day, confident that it would be snapped up quickly, thus ensuring his continued income. Everything I owned was gradually being stripped away. My life was fading into a mere shadow of what it once was. Whenever Sam saw that look of anxiety cross my face, he would remind me why I was doing this, and for whom. I would think of Samuel, and my spirits lifted. I would be all right once I was there…it was just the '*going*' bit.

On the evening of Christmas Eve, I watched as the last remaining items of furniture were removed from my flat, and I was left standing in an empty room. My only possessions were a large brown paper parcel containing three woollen dresses, some pieces of old jewelry…and a wedding dress. The blue silk dress I had saved for a special occasion lay on top of the parcel, together with some boots and a shawl. These I would wear when I departed this life.

"I've just made some dinner," said Sam quietly, as he entered the vacant flat. "It's your favorite." I turned and faced him, tears streaming down my pale face. "Oh, Emily," he whispered, taking me in his arms, "It will be all right. I promise you."

"I know, I know…" I sobbed as I laid my head on his shoulder. "I'll be all right, Sam."

Returning to Sam's flat, I sat down at his kitchen table and picked around with my meal, whilst watching a solitary candle flicker in its brass holder.

"Just to get you acclimatized," Sam said, smiling and pointing his fork at the centerpiece, "You know, there is something very romantic about candlelight. Don't you think?" I nodded my head in agreement, and continued to push the sweet and sour chicken around on my plate. "You don't want that, do you?" said Sam, after watching my futile efforts. I looked up and felt guilty; he had gone to so much effort.

"I'm sorry, Sam. It's lovely. Really it is…"

"Just no appetite?" he replied, knowingly. I smiled apologetically and pushed the plate away. Sam stared at me in deep thought for a moment, choosing his words carefully. "You know what, Emily? I think you should go tomorrow instead."

"It's Christmas Day, Sam! I said I would spend it with you here!" I cried.

"It would be the best Christmas present yet, to know you are happy and with the one you love. Don't worry about me. This will be your day...yours and Samuel's. Can you imagine what a wonderful surprise it will be for them? To receive *you* on Christmas Day!" I laughed as I visualized the children's faces and the look of total shock upon Samuel's, as I stood there in my blue silk dress before him. "Besides," continued Sam, "I couldn't cope with you moping about the place and not eating for another day." We laughed together. He was right. It was the best thing to do. Delaying my departure another day was torture for all concerned.

Sam and I spent the evening reflecting on life—what we wanted out of it, and what we were prepared to give up for the sake of love and inner happiness. By 11pm I was totally shattered. It had been a long day—physically, as well as emotionally—and I felt myself drifting off to Sam's soothing voice.

"Come on, sleepy. Let's get you to bed," said Sam, gently removing his arm from around my shoulder. I got up stiffly and followed him into the bedroom, half asleep. "Don't worry. I've changed the sheets," he told me as he pulled open the covers. I stood and stared at the bed for a moment, gathering my thoughts.

"Where are you going to sleep?" I asked, looking around.

"Well, I was going to share a bed with you, but if that's a problem, then…"

"NO! No, that's okay, Sam. I mean, it's not the first time, is it?" Sam smiled and started to undress.

"Just don't tell Samuel, will you?" he joked. "He might not understand."

Minutes later, I lay there in the darkness, staring up at the ceiling. For some reason, I no longer felt tired. The street lamp outside cast a faint glow across Sam's face, and I could see that beneath that irritating fringe, his eyes were also open, and he was busy thinking.

"When you return tomorrow, they are going to want to know where you have been," he began, and I could sense that an explanation to my disappearance was forthcoming. "Tell them you have been staying with an acquaintance in London, who is a physician. You could use my real name—Sam Warren. They won't know any different." I listened while Sam rambled on. He seemed to have it all well thought out. "If they should ask why I had not travelled back with you, just say… just say I was '*unavoidably detained*' and hoped to make the journey from London later, to attend the wedding."

"And when you don't show?" I asked, turning to face him.

"Then they will think I was unable to come after all, and I will soon be forgotten." I lay there, thinking over his convincing account of where I had been. It all sounded pretty feasible, and true, to a certain extent.

"How will I know what date I will marry?" I asked suddenly. "For you to '*attend*' this wedding." Sam was quick with a reply. "I know the perfect date for your wedding," he told me, propping himself up on one elbow.

"When?"

"The first day of January, of course." I stared at him blankly, unable to see the significance of that date. He moved closer. "The start of a new year…*a new life*. Get it?"

"Oh, right…yeah, I guess that would be apt, in a way." Sam smiled to himself and flopped back down on the pillow.

"Now get some sleep, Emily. Tomorrow is Christmas Day." I leaned over and kissed Sam on the forehead tenderly.

"Goodnight, Sam…I'll *never* forget you," I said huskily, as my eyes filled to the brim with tears, which overflowed onto my pillow. I dreaded tomorrow, but deep down, my heart beat loud and strong in anticipation of once again being with my Samuel. This time it was going to be forever. Sam wrapped his comforting arms around me and held me close. He knew how I was feeling. What I didn't see was the relieved expression on his face and the secretive smile that played upon his lips.

Sam awoke early the following morning and was sitting, dressed, on the side of the bed with a mug of steaming hot coffee in his hand when I opened my eyes.

"Morning, sleepy. Happy Christmas," he whispered, planting a brotherly kiss on my forehead. I stretched and moaned softly, adjusting my eyes to the light.

"Happy Christmas, Sam," I replied sleepily, turning over onto my back. Suddenly, the realization of what was happening today hit me like a ton of bricks.

"What would you like for your last *futuristic* breakfast?" joked Sam. "I have bacon, eggs, mushrooms, tomatoes…?" I stared at him. *How could he be so jovial?* He didn't appear too concerned that he would never see me again after today.

"Just cereal will be fine," I replied, rather disconcerted. Sam picked up on my negative vibes and went over to a drawer, extracting something small from within.

"I bought this for you," he said, handing me a small velvet bag. I was taken aback.

"I haven't got you anything!" I cried in dismay.

"It doesn't matter. I don't want anything."

"Oh, Sam," I whispered, pulling the little drawstring on the bag and opening it up. I pulled out a gold chain and gasped, for attached on the end, was a beautiful golden locket.

"I'm afraid this one isn't magical, but I thought you could have a miniature portrait painted of Samuel and place it inside. To be worn close to your heart."

"It's beautiful, Sam," I cried, flipping it open. "Thank you so much. I will treasure it always." I closed the locket and placed it beside the bed, feeling guilty for not having bought him a gift in return.

I found it hard to eat any breakfast. Every spoonful felt like a brick in my throat, and I eventually gave up and pushed it aside.

"I'm going to have a shower, if that's okay?" I said, getting up. "Then I will change into my dress."

"Sure. Go ahead...make the most of it," replied Sam, clearing away the plates.

Forty-five minutes later, I emerged from the bathroom, my long, damp auburn hair cascading over my bare shoulders, contrasting beautifully with the deep blue of the silk dress.

"Wow!" said Sam as I glided into the room. "You're going to knock his socks off with that. I can see his face now!" I laughed coyly and sat down on the sofa.

"Let's get this over with, Sam. I'm ready to leave."

"Okay. I'll get my coat. Don't forget your parcel and the locket…both of them!" As we walked down to the car, I handed Sam the keys.

"You drive. My mind isn't really '*with it'* at the moment." Sam took the keys without question and got into the car. He understood the effect this was having on me. The engine roared into life, and I looked up at my flat window one last time. *This is the right thing to do,* I kept telling myself, as Betsy turned out of the parking lot into the busy street, and began the final journey to Littleham.

Sam and I spoke very little on the way down. I didn't know what to say. *What is there to say?* I was very close to tears as it was, and feared the slightest reference to our last few hours together would upset the already fragile balance. I looked out of the window at the houses, the cars, and the shops as we passed them—soon to be only memories of a past life.

We arrived in Offenham just after one, and drove slowly through the village. Sam pulled over to gaze thoughtfully along the row of shops.

"Why have we stopped?" I asked after a moment. Sam smiled furtively over at me and drove on to the end of the street, before turning right into the lane that led to Littleham. He parked the car up onto the grass verge and shut off the engine.

"You're home, Emily," he said, stealing me a sideways glance. I felt the tears start to well up and fought them back courageously, but I knew it wouldn't be long before the floodgates would open. Collecting my parcel from the back seat, I took a deep breath and got out of the car. "I wouldn't do it too near the cottage. Someone might see you materialize," Sam said as we walked through the undergrowth a few yards. "About *here* should be all right." I stood still, my eyes fixed firmly on my black boots. "Well, this is it then," said Sam, trying to sound cheerful, but there was an edge to his voice. I couldn't hold out much longer. "Will you do something for me?" he asked, flicking his fringe back out of his eyes, as if to give me one last reminder.

"What's that?"

"When you begin to disappear, will you throw the locket to the ground? I would like to keep it as a memento. Besides, you won't have any use for it now." I nodded my head. It would be better to eliminate the chance of Samuel ever finding it on me. I reached into my pocket and took out the pendant, fingering it nervously in my hand. "Good job the sun's shining," chirped Sam, looking up into the trees rather than at me. That was it. I flung myself at Sam, causing him to stagger backwards in surprise. The tears flowed in torrents down my face.

"Take care," I sobbed. "Be happy."

"I will…now, for God's sake, just *go*, will you? Before I start crying, too. Remember what I told you to say," reminded

Sam, stepping back. I wiped away the tears to enable me to see what I was doing with the locket, and flipped it open, securing my heavy parcel under my arm. Without looking back at Sam, I stepped forward into the sunlight…*forward into my future*. As the blinding light erupted around me, I released the locket from my grasp. My time had expired. I had made my choice, and I prayed it was the right one.

Sam opened his eyes and looked about him. On the ground near where I had once stood, something bright caught his eye. He walked over and stared down at the locket lying on the muddy ground. Smiling, he picked it up and held it tightly in his hand. "Goodbye, Emily," he whispered. "Give my love to John." He walked back to the car and sat there for a while, deep in thought, before starting the engine and beginning the long, lonely drive back home to Banbury.

The first thing that hit me was the cold. The silk dress was pretty, but not ideal for this inclement weather. Unwrapping a corner of the brown paper parcel, I extracted my woollen shawl and covered my bare shoulders. All was quiet as I made my way along the track to Mill Cottage. No sign of the children playing outside, just a few scraggly chickens wandering aimlessly about in search of food on the frozen ground. I could now see the smoke from the chimney rising straight and steady, up into the still air. As I drew nearer, faint voices could be heard from within the cottage. I stopped just outside of the door and listened. The children were inside, chattering excitedly—maybe about their presents? *Did they have presents, then?* I expected so, though nothing like on the grand scale of kids in the future. John spoke. I could recognize his soft, gentle voice anywhere. Charles replied in a muffled tone. My heart started to beat faster as I strained my ears for the one voice I wanted to hear. I did not have to wait long before I heard Samuel's voice, loud and clear, scolding one of the children for spilling their drink. The mere sound of his voice sent quivers down my spine. After straightening my dress and smoothing down my hair, I took a deep breath and opened the latch on the door, letting it swing open.

The conversation in the room came to an abrupt halt as all heads turned towards the door. I looked around the room quickly, and my eyes came to rest on a tall dark man, leaning up against the fireplace. Taking a step towards him, I did a slow and respectful curtsy, looking straight into his stunned, dark eyes.

"I gratefully accept your proposal of marriage, Samuel Howerd, if you still want me? Oh, and…Merry Christmas, everyone!"

~ Chapter Twenty-Three ~

After a moment of complete silence, the room erupted into complete chaos. Ellen took a flying leap and flung herself at me.

"Miss Emily! I knew you would return to us! I just knew it!" Everyone seemed to be talking at once, as they all crowded around me. I was quite overwhelmed by the welcome I was receiving from this family.

"Let the poor girl sit down," said Charles, laughing. "She must be weary."

"Yes, I am rather. It is a long journey from London," I said, taking a seat at the table where the family had now gathered, the smaller children seated upon the laps of their older brothers and sisters.

"Indeed it is," replied Charles as he poured me some wine. I glanced over to the fireplace, where one solitary person still stood, his gaze averted towards the fire. I felt that maybe I should elaborate on a few finer points concerning my absence.

"I have been staying with a physician friend of mine, by the name of Mister Sam Warren...until I had reason to return," I explained, stealing another glance over to the fireplace. I began to feel anxious, as if an icy hand was gripping my heart. *Why does he ignore me?*

"How is Mister Warren? I trust he is well, having not escorted you from London himself," said John suddenly.

"Yes, he is quite well," I replied, wondering why he should be concerned about the welfare of someone he didn't know. Then again, they were courteous people, and any acquaintance of mine would warrant polite inquiries concerning their well-being.

"He will travel down for the wedding, I trust?" urged John.

"He will do his utmost to attend," I lied. *That is, if there is going to be any wedding*, I thought dismally. My mournful looks in Samuel's direction didn't go unnoticed by Charles, who followed my gaze across the room.

"Come, children. Let us go outside and leave Miss Emily and Samuel with some privacy, to discuss matters of the heart," said Charles, rising slowly from his chair.

"No!" came Samuel's loud, commanding voice. My heart came to a stop. "Miss Emily and I shall venture outside. It is far too cold to expect that of you." Samuel went over to the door and took down his mother's cape. With trembling hands, he placed it over my shoulders and ushered me towards the door. I went silently, unsure of what to expect. He had given me no reason to feel jubilant up until now. Closing the door firmly shut behind him, he led me towards the stream. "You, no doubt, received my letter?" he inquired of me as we came upon the frozen stream, and followed its path slowly through the woodland.

"It is the reason why I am here...to accept your proposal. Although, I am not altogether sure now, from your demeanor, it is what you want?" Samuel came to an abrupt halt and stared at me in disbelief.

"My God, Emily! I have thought of nothing else since that fateful day in which you saved my life. I shall be forever in your debt. I knew, then, that I wanted to be with you for the rest of my life—a life that would have tragically ended that day, if it had not been for you." His hand rose and gently brushed my hair away from my face. "When I returned from my aunt's and found you gone, it was as if my heart had been ripped from my body—my bride to be taken from me yet again. Can you not imagine how my tortured soul suffered so? Or maybe you did not care?"

"I thought you had gone back to Isabelle. *Truly* I did," I cried. "I would never have left if I had known of your real intentions. I am so sorry, Samuel. Can you ever forgive me?"

"Your acceptance to be my betrothed is forgiveness enough. Speak no more of it, for you are here now," he replied, moving his hand around to the nape of my neck, sending my heart racing. "When I saw you standing there in the doorway, it was as much as I could do to withhold my feelings," he continued. I could feel his warm breath upon my face, his fingers moving up through my hair and grasping the back of my head. My lips parted as he lowered his head and gently—oh so gently—brushed his lips against mine.

"Samuel…" I whispered, pulling him hard against me. His lips traveled down the side of my neck, and I pulled open the cape to allow him access to my bare shoulders. I heard him moan softly, his long black locks of hair falling forward onto my breast. Drunk with desire, I instinctively moved my hand under his cloak and down his thigh. I came to rest on a hard mound that pulsated through the thick cloth of his trousers.

"Emily...Emily, pray withdraw your hand, for I fear I will take you here and now if you do not."

"Would that be so bad?" I asked, smiling seductively up at him.

"It would not be appropriate for you to give yourself to me before our wedding night, or I to take advantage of being alone with you." I dropped my hand away reluctantly.

"It is rather cold, too," I said, pulling my cape back up around my shoulders again. "Tell me you *love* me," I demanded, grasping hold of his arm.

"I would not have proposed to you if I did not."

"I want to hear you say it!" I pleaded. Samuel looked about him nervously for signs of company. Expressing his innermost feelings openly was not his strong point, and he struggled to mouth the words. I raised my eyebrows expectantly and waited. I needed to hear the words spoken from his lips.

"We have many arrangements to make regarding the wedding," he continued, changing the subject.

"SAY IT!" I cried. He realized he was not going to be released until he had succumbed to my wishes. He took a deep breath.

"I love you, Emily…I love you with all my body and soul. You are everything a man could ever desire. I promise to be true to you always. My heart will never stray…it is forever yours." His eyes glistened over as he bent forward and kissed my lips tenderly. I would have been happy with just three little words.

"Thank you," I whispered, wrapping my arms around his waist. "You do not know what that means to me—to hear you say that."

Crunching footsteps were suddenly heard approaching on the frozen ground.

"Father says if you don't come in soon, you will catch your death, and there will be no wedding!" cried Mary, appearing through the bare trees, clutching her shawl tightly around her. We both laughed, and Samuel put his arm around his shivering sister.

"We cannot have that now, can we? To deprive you of being a flower maiden at our wedding would be inconceivable, would it not, young Mary?" The three of us made our way back to the warmth of Mill Cottage, my hand tightly entwined with Samuel's. I was so blissfully happy I could burst. There was only one person missing to share in my happiness—but that could never be.

A good deal of the wedding arrangements had already been roughly planned, when Samuel had returned earlier to his aunt's house. I couldn't help wondering how dear Isabelle took the news—probably sobbed uncontrollably into her delicate lace handkerchief for days! A message was dispatched by horseback to Edgebarton, summoning Aunt Elizabeth and Isabelle to Littleham in preparation for our wedding, without further delay.

"Can I ask but one thing?" I said, after listening to the already decided agenda. "I want the wedding date to be the first day of January." Everyone exchanged blank looks with one another, and Samuel shrugged his shoulders.

"If that is what you wish, then the first of January it shall be."

"Thank you, Samuel." I replied, smiling. No one asked *why* I wanted that day.

"My father, John and I will reside at Weaver's Cottage forthwith until the day of the wedding. The children will stay at the other cottage, and you, Emily, will reside here with Aunt Elizabeth and Isabelle." Samuel noticed my startled expression and added quickly, "If that meets with your approval, my dear Emily?"

"I suppose so." I replied, a little hesitantly. The thought of being under the same roof as a jilted Isabelle was somewhat daunting, and I hoped she would have the maturity to accept defeat graciously. I guess Charles and Samuel had the matters all in hand, given the fact that they both had a practice run of it with Charlotte. A cold chill crept up my back, and I wondered what *she* might be thinking about all this. This, in turn, provoked another question. "Who will be staying with me here *tonight*? I have no wish to be alone." Judging by their bewildered response, this was one item of meticulous planning that they had not accounted for.

"I will sleep with Miss Emily tonight," volunteered Mary.

"Can I too?" piped up Ellen, excitedly. I gratefully accepted their offer of company for the night, although there was only one person I *really* wanted in my bed.

A roasted pig, that Charles had slaughtered earlier, had turned slowly on a spit above the fire all day and was finally ready. We all tucked in hungrily. It was delicious, and was by far the best *Christmas dinner* I had ever eaten. The wine flowed freely, and I felt relaxed and warm as I laid my head on Samuel's shoulder by the fire. His fingers gently caressed the back of my neck, sending tingling sensations down my back and a yearning in my groin that grew more intense as the evening wore on. *The next seven days were going to be hell.* Hannah, William and Joseph bid me goodnight around eight and walked the short distance to Jasmine Cottage. Mary and Ellen went upstairs shortly after, leaving just Charles, John, Samuel and I on the bench, finishing off the remainder of a third bottle of wine. *Or was it the fourth?*

I can't remember. My mind drifted to Sam, all alone in his flat in Banbury at Christmas. It was a pity his new friend John could not be with him. I wanted him to be as happy and content as I was right now.

"I think it is time to depart to Weaver's for the night, while we are still capable of walking," slurred Charles, putting down his empty wine goblet. "Come, John. Let us leave and let Samuel bid Emily goodnight." John took hold of his father's arm and threw a cloak around his shoulders before lighting the one remaining lantern on a hook by the door. The bitter cold night air blew in fiercely through the open door, fanning the flames of the fire momentarily as they staggered out together into the inky blackness.

"I wish you didn't have to go," I whispered; putting my arms around his strong, firm body. I felt his muscles go tense at my touch, and he pulled away.

"I can wait and so must you, however hard it may seem," he said, tilting my head to look into my eyes. "What we have will be worth the wait, my dearest. Trust me." I didn't doubt that for one second. I just had to control my impulsive urge to rip his clothes off whenever I saw him. *How could he be so composed?* Then again, if he had never indulged in any sexual activity before, he would find it easier to handle, unlike me. I was almost *certain* Samuel was a virgin, which somehow aroused my passionate instincts even more. I bolted the door after he left and, taking a candle from the table, I slowly ascended the creaking staircase to my room.

The girls were already fast asleep as I silently undressed and quickly slid underneath the covers. Moving Ellen gently over a few inches to enable me to lie down, I let out a long and contented sigh. *Well, girl,* I thought to myself, *you've done it now. No running back to the future anymore when times get bad. Whatever happens from now on, I will have to stay and see it through, for better or for worse.* I had a responsibility now to these children, in the role of their *new* mother, and I wasn't going to let them down. I leaned over and blew out the candle. It had been a long day, and

I fell asleep almost immediately. My last thoughts were of Samuel, lying naked in my arms, a contented smile upon his face.

Sleeping with children has its disadvantages. They wake up incredibly early in the morning! After waking me up, they tried unsuccessfully to get me out of the warm bed and finally scampered off downstairs, leaving me in peace. It was still dark outside, for heaven's sake! Sometime later I stirred from my sleep again and sensed someone was watching me. Samuel stood silently in the doorway, with his arms folded.

"How long have you been there?" I asked, brushing my tangled hair back behind my ears. He smiled and took a step further into the room.

"You are truly beautiful while you sleep," he said huskily. "But…" he continued, "breakfast is prepared, and it is time for you to rise."

"I'll be down shortly. Do I not get a good morning kiss?"

"I think not, whilst you reside in your bed. It would be unwise to give cause for temptation," he replied, a faint smile upon his lips. With that, he turned and was gone, leaving me to dress alone.

This morning I put on my thick woollen brown dress. It was more sensible against the cold for one, and I would not be accused of enticing erotic thoughts, in one so determined to avoid any intimate contact. By the time I arrived downstairs, the place was all but deserted, the children having eaten and gone into the woods to play. Charles had gone into the village to discuss the marriage with the curate, John was feeding the animals, and Samuel was brushing down his horse by the barn. I hurriedly ate some breakfast and put on my cape before wandering around to the barn.

"Are you going somewhere?" I asked casually, as he threw the saddle over the horses back effortlessly.

"To the mill. I have to prepare some things before the workers return tomorrow."

"Can I come?" I blurted out. "I have not seen this mill, as yet, and as you are the owner of the business *and* my future husband, I have a vested interest in it, do I not?" Samuel stared at me, surprised that I should want to observe his place of work, but he nodded in agreement.

"I will fetch John to accompany us," he said, striding off. I laughed to myself. *Was this in case I made a move on him in the empty premises?* I found this all rather amusing, but positively charming as well.

Samuel returned with John before he mounted his black horse, signaling for me to climb up behind him.

"If it's all the same to you, I would rather walk." I said anxiously, watching his agitated horse turning in circles, snorting noisily.

"I will walk with you, Miss Emily. It is not far, and if we walk briskly, we will not feel the cold so keenly," said John, offering his arm politely.

"Very well…I shall ride ahead and meet you there, if that is your desire." With that, Samuel dug his heels into the highly-strung beast and galloped off down the track. John and I followed the stream, along a well-trodden narrow path, unsuitable for horses or larger means of transport. He informed me this was a quicker route, and by far prettier than the muddy track.

Although now, being winter, it was not at its most attractive. I knew from past experience how lovely it looked with the trees in full leaf, and the woodland flowers carpeting the ground. I remembered the soothing trickle of water as the stream wound its way downwards through the wood, tumbling over the mossy rocks as it went. For now, though, it was still—the movement of the water frozen solid and awaiting the time when it would once again be released from its icy grip, and could continue its relentless journey.

"Is there not a young lady that catches your eye, John?" I asked nonchalantly, stopping to observe a robin that had perched on a nearby holly bush, and was pecking hungrily at the red berries.

"Indeed, there is not," replied John quietly.

"That's a pity…never mind. You are young and handsome—a fine catch for any fair maiden, I am sure." John smiled and walked on. "You know, you remind me of my friend, Sam Warren, in a way. You have the same mannerisms and the same gentle nature. You would have got on well together."

"Would have?" said John, stopping to look at me. "Am I to assume he will not be attending the wedding?"

"I'm not sure." I replied, feeling that an outright, 'N*o, he definitely won't be'* answer would not be received too well. Why he should be so concerned whether my friend came or not was beyond me. *Maybe he thought of him as someone educated he could talk to and learn from?*

The pathway widened out and forked to the left and right. John took the right hand one, which was the more used of the two. The stream became a small river, which in turn, became an outlet from a large lake.

"It's beautiful!" I said to John as I stood, clutching his arm, on the steep bank. Most of it was frozen over, apart from a small section in the middle that was dark and still.

"There are many fish within these deep waters. Samuel is a far better fisherman than I," laughed John, urging me on. "The mill is just around this corner." I don't know what I was expecting to see, but I was taken by surprise as I laid my eyes, for the first time, on the much talked about mill.

The three-story stone Mill House rose before me, its walls covered in ivy that reached up high onto the roof and tall chimney. Filthy windows adorned the building and high doorways, from which thick rope pulleys hung motionless, down to the ground. Primitive was an understatement, and I cringed openly as I stepped inside the dirty, dark building. Several wooden looms were scattered haphazardly on the stone floor, on which were littered the remnants of cloth and discarded textiles. The dust in the air was suffocating, and I coughed spasmodically to clear my throat. Other iron contraptions and archaic items of machinery filled the large room, with numerous long wooden cutting tables. On the wall, to one side, was attached a storage unit for the bolts of completed cloth. Large pigeonholes were stuffed full of heavy materials, awaiting dispatch by cart to nearby towns and villages. At the end of the room was a large desk, rather like a schoolteacher's in front of a class. At the desk in a large winged chair, sat Samuel, who watched me intently as I approached.

"Welcome to my mill," he announced, in a superior tone, as I drew near. "You appear a little dismayed. Does what you see displease you?"

"No! I am just a little overwhelmed. I have never seen the inside of a mill before." *At least not one in working order, like this*, I thought. Samuel raised his eyebrow and rose from the chair majestically. Again, that urge arose within me to throw him down on the table and have my wicked way with him. Thank God John was here!

"Pray, let me enlighten you as to the workings of this establishment," he said, gesturing forward. John followed a respectful three paces behind as Samuel gave me a tour of his mill, and explained in great detail how thc cloth was manufactured from start to finish. By the time he had finished, I felt I had been on a museum tour of a 17th century woollen mill, and half expected to proceed through a door into a bright modern-day gift shop, in order to buy souvenirs of my visit—but this was real, and I had to stop making comparisons in my mind.

"How many workers do you have here?" I inquired as we returned to his desk.

"Around thirty. I cannot be precise, as the children come and go."

"Children?"

"There are several, mainly belonging to the women workers employed here."

"How old?"

"From eight upward. Any younger and their strength is too weak to operate the looms." I gasped. "You disapprove?"

"I hope none of your brothers and sisters are made to toil here?"

"No one is *made* to work here. They come of their own free will...and no, I will not allow any of my family to work for me."

"Glad to hear it!" I cried, relieved that he had some respect left. "I should like to return when the mill is working, if I may?"

"You may not like what you see."

"Then I can suggest changes to improve the conditions."

"I already have improvements in motion, particularly regarding the safety of my employees…and I do not like my competence being questioned by a *woman*." For a moment we both stood there, glaring at one another. Samuel's eyes had turned black as night, and it was just like old times! Only, this time it did not last long, as I apologized almost immediately for my disrespect of his authority. Something else I had to adhere to and learn to live with—women these days were not considered worthy of an opinion. If I wanted to assert my initiative in the future, I would have to do it in a way that did not undermine his position, but where I could still get my own way! That shouldn't be difficult. I was good at that.

"We should return soon," said John, anxiously looking out of the grimy window at the grey leaden skies.

"Indeed we should. I assume the proposal of a ride home would be, again, declined?" said Samuel, coming to my side.

"No, I shall not decline this time. I am quite tired from all the walking about," I said truthfully.

"I will make haste back to Mill Cottage," called out John, already starting to walk back on his own. Samuel put his strong hands around my waist and lifted me up with ease into the saddle, mounting the horse himself, behind me, this time. I leaned back against his warm body as he held me tightly around the waist with one hand, the other grasping the horse's reins, keeping it at a steady walking pace. Large snowflakes began to fall from the sky as we approached the last part of the track when, in the distance, we could hear the sound of a carriage traveling in our direction.

As it drew nearer, Samuel maneuvered the horse off of the track into the woodland, to allow sufficient room for the travelers to pass. Seconds later, a carriage driven by four white horses thundered past us, flinging up mud and debris from the track. The occupants did not go unnoticed by Samuel.

"Aunt Elizabeth and Isabelle have arrived," he informed me. It was with great trepidation that I rode the last quarter-mile home.

They had already entered the cottage when we came to a halt outside, and Samuel lifted me down.

"I shall take the horse to the barn. Go in, out of the cold, and warm yourself by the fire," said Samuel, touching my shoulder as if I were fragile porcelain china. "I will return shortly to greet our company," he added, seeing my look of alarm. Pushing open the cottage door, I peered around the edge nervously and saw that the whole family was gathered to welcome our wedding guests. Aunt Elizabeth spotted me immediately.

"Emily! My *dear* girl," she cried, coming towards me with outstretched arms and crushing me to her bosom in an affectionate embrace. "How wonderful to see you again, and what delightful circumstances in which to meet—your marriage to Samuel Howerd! Oh, I do adore a wedding... pray tell, where *is* the fortunate young man?"

"Just taking his horse to the barn," I replied, scanning the room for signs of a mass of blonde ringlets. The staircase door opened suddenly and Isabelle, in all her glory, stepped down daintily into the room.

"Mother!" she whinged pathetically. "There is nowhere to hang my dresses. I cannot abide creases in my garments. Something will have to be done!"

"Later, Isabelle dear. Remember, you are a guest in this house, and you should show some respect. Now come and greet Emily. I am sure you have much to talk about." Isabelle shot a contemptuous look in my direction and forced a weak smile.

"Miss Emily," she said sweetly, bobbing down in a short curtsy. "How *lovely* to see you again."

"Likewise," I replied, returning her curtsy. "I trust you had a pleasant journey?" To be honest, I couldn't give a damn about her journey down, but for the sake of appearing polite, I forced myself to ask.

"It was uncomfortable and dreadfully tiring, but thank you for asking," she replied with a hint of sarcasm.

The cottage door swung open, and Samuel entered.

"Aunt Elizabeth," he said, bowing respectfully. "It is a pleasure to welcome you into our humble abode."

"Samuel, my *dear* boy. I am so happy for you!" she cried, kissing his cheek. "She is positively delightful, and I wish you much happiness together." Isabelle stepped forward and held out her hand to be kissed.

"Miss Isabelle," said Samuel curtly, ignoring her outstretched hand. "So glad you could come." He then turned to speak with his father, leaving Isabelle seething in his wake. I bit my lip, in an effort to control a smug smile, which quivered on my lips. These next few days would be most entertaining.

Aunt Elizabeth came into the kitchen, while I was preparing a large pot of stewed rabbit for our evening meal, and offered to help.

"Isabelle has taken it sorely upon herself that Samuel has chosen you to be his intended, but she will no doubt in time recover and accept his decision amiably."

"I understand her feelings," I replied sincerely. "She has known Samuel since childhood and thought, although incorrectly, that it was a foregone conclusion that they would eventually wed."

"Indeed it was so," said Elizabeth, scraping the remainder of the rabbit into the iron cauldron. "It was a surprise at first, when I learned from Charles that Samuel's affection had lain with you for some time."

"I had no idea until recently that he harbored such amorous feelings for me. His proposal of marriage was as much a shock to me as it was to you."

"Do you love him?" asked Elizabeth, taking hold of my hand.

*"Yes, I do…*more than life itself."

"Then you have my blessing, dear child," she replied, squeezing my hand warmly. "Now…I do believe I saw some bottles of wine under here."

The lunchtime meal was a noisy, cramped and excitable occasion. Somehow, with chairs borrowed from the other cottage and a strategically placed bench, we managed to fit eleven of us around the table. Isabelle and her mother were placed opposite Samuel and I, which enabled Isabelle to watch his every movement with unnerving precision. Every time he spoke to me, her hands would clench her wine goblet with such rigidity, her knuckles turned white. I found great satisfaction in winding her up, and would purposely lean close to Samuel and whisper in his ear, touching his hand tenderly for more dramatic effect. He responded affectionately, safe in the knowledge we were not alone, and I could only go so far. With her meal almost untouched and pushed back across the table, she sat there, her rosy red lips moving seductively around the rim of her wine goblet. Her eyes transfixed on her prey. The children gave up trying to make conversation with the usually bubbly and talkative Isabelle, and went upstairs to play with the Christmas gifts that Aunt Elizabeth had so generously brought for them.

With the meal eaten and the bottles of wine standing empty, Samuel and John proceeded to rearrange the furniture and ferry the additional chairs back from whence they came.

"Why do you and Emily not take a turn outside before darkness falls?" said Elizabeth to her daughter. "Charles and I will clear away here. It will give us time to discuss arrangements." I smiled across at Isabelle, who could have quite happily throttled her mother by the look on her face.

"Certainly, mother," she replied through clenched teeth. "We have much to talk about." With that, she picked up her cape and flounced past me, out of the door.

The air was decidedly frosty, for two reasons, as we walked over to the stream in silence and followed a footpath downwards.

"I'm sorry, Isabelle," I said, trying to break the tension. "I know you loved him, and it must be hard for you to see him with me."

"You have no idea!" she cried, turning to face me, her face red with rage. "All the time you were at Edgebarton, I *trusted* you. I opened my heart to you and told you my innermost desires."

"I know," I replied quietly.

"And all the time, you were scheming to take him from me, *knowing* it would break my heart."

"No! That isn't so, Isabelle," I cried, appalled that she could think me so heartless. "I had no intention of *purposely* stealing him away. I thought he hated me at the time."

"Hated you? What gave you cause to think he hated you, when you bore such a striking resemblance to Charlotte?"

"Maybe that was the reason."

"So what happened to change his mind, pray tell?" insisted Isabelle, determined to get to the truth behind her rejection. "Did you take him to your bed and seduce him?"

"No!"

"What then?"

"He just came to realize how much he loved me when I went away…back to London."

"Ah yes! I remember it well. He came to arrange the wedding and returned to find you had '*run away'…*"

"I had my reasons," I replied, not wanting to go into detail.

"Hardly a foundation for a good marriage, with such doubts in your mind?"

"It was purely a misunderstanding that has now been resolved." Isabelle gave a cynical laugh and folded her arms defiantly.

"It's *me* he loves. He always has and always will. You delude yourself, Miss Emily."

"So why did he want to marry Charlotte? He could have chosen *you*, if that were his desire."

"Samuel is easily distracted by a beautiful face. He didn't know what he was doing until it was almost too late…it was fortunate that I was here."

"Fortunate?" I repeated, puzzled. Isabelle looked alarmed and turned away from me.

"Yes…to comfort him after Charlotte disappeared, so suddenly, on their wedding day." There was something in the tone of her voice that made me feel uneasy, but I couldn't quite put my finger on it.

"You must have been delighted, when Charlotte didn't show up at the church?" I said warily, moving over to her side to observe her expression. "Now you have another contender. Only, this time, I am not going to '*disappear*', so you had better get used to the fact that I shall become Mrs Samuel Howerd, and get over this insane obsession you have with him."

"That will *never* happen. I shall not rest until I wear his wedding ring…whatever it takes." Isabelle turned and looked at me, her eyes filled with hate and malice. I watched, dazed, as she gathered up her dress and returned to the cottage. *Just how far will this woman go to get her wish?*

~ Chapter Twenty-Four ~

I stood there for some time after, gathering my thoughts. *What did she mean by that? Does she intend to wreak havoc at my wedding?* I had to speak to someone about Isabelle's threatening behavior. I made my way over to Jasmine Cottage to see Samuel. He was on the way back when we met, and I took hold of his arm and turned him around.

"Emily! Whatever is the matter? You are quite ashen in the face," he said, genuinely concerned.

"It's Isabelle," I spluttered, biting my lip, "You will have to talk to her. Tell her you don't love her."

"I do *not* love her," he replied, bewildered.

"*I* know that, but she is infatuated with you, to the extent that I fear she will do something to prevent our marriage taking place." Samuel stared at me for a moment and then began to laugh.

"Isabelle does not have the shrewdness or the capability to do such a thing. It is merely jealously that provokes her… she is quite harmless, I assure you."

"I am not convinced, Samuel. She worries me. You did not see the look in her eyes. It was as if she were possessed by the devil himself." He sighed and pulled me close to him, kissing the top of my head tenderly.

"I will speak with her when a moment arises and put an end to all this foolishness," he said, taking hold of my hand and leading me back to Mill Cottage.

I was relieved to see that Isabelle had gone to bed early when we returned. Aunt Elizabeth told us she had developed a bad headache, probably brought on by the stress of traveling. The evening meal was a much more relaxed affair without Isabelle's incessant scrutiny, but I still felt a little on edge, and kept going over in my mind what she had said.

When the men had left for the night, and Elizabeth and I were clearing up after, I decided to ask a few casual questions, regarding Isabelle's involvement in Charlotte's wedding day.

"She was *so* excited to be the main Flower Maiden!" cried the aunt. "No one had ever asked her before."

"What did she have to do?" I inquired, stacking the dirty plates.

"She stayed with the bride after we had all departed for the church and made sure she was prepared. Then she came to the church before the carriage arrived to await her arrival outside and escort her in." An icy cold shiver went down my back.

"So Charlotte disappeared after Isabelle left for the church?"

"Indeed, that is so. She never arrived at the church, and the carriage driver never saw her when he arrived at Jasmine Cottage. Isabelle was *so* distraught, the poor girl."

"I bet she was," I mumbled under my breath. My mind was in turmoil as I tried to fit together pieces of the jigsaw. *So where did Robert Spedding fit into all this? Did Isabelle know Robert? Surely not!*

"That is why," continued Elizabeth, unaware of my anxieties, "Isabelle has *insisted* that she be your Flower Maiden—to try and banish the nightmares she has endured ever since."

"What?" I cried, horrified. "I really don't think that is a good idea, Aunt Elizabeth."

"Why ever not, dear child? Unless, you are also thinking of eloping before the wedding, like Charlotte?"

"Certainly not!"

"Then, forgive me, but I see no reason why my daughter would not be acceptable as your Flower Maiden," said Elizabeth bluntly, plainly put out by my objection.

"Then it is only fair to have *all* the Flower Maidens with me beforehand, and for them to travel to the church with me in my carriage," I demanded. There was no way I was going to be left alone with Isabelle. Goodness knows what she might do to prevent me marrying the love of her life! I was beginning to get paranoid!

"That is not the tradition, but if that is your wish, then so be it," said Elizabeth curtly. I was relieved. If I could eliminate any chances of Isabelle doing me harm, then the day should proceed without any calamities. I didn't want to end up buried under a pear tree, like unfortunate Charlotte.

Sleep that night did not come easily; I tossed and turned and finally got out to position the bedside table against the door, to alert me to any intruders. I didn't think Isabelle would try anything with her mother in close proximity, but it made me feel more secure. It reminded me of the times when Robert slept across the landing, and I started to think about him and Isabelle. *Was it possible that somehow both she and Robert were involved in Charlotte's murder?* I groaned and turned over towards the window, as my eyelids became heavy. The black skeletal branches of the trees outside cast eerie shadows on the walls, as they danced up and down in the wind. If only Samuel were here to comfort me. I had another five harrowing days ahead of me, and five sleepless nights had to be endured before he was finally mine.

The bedside table grated noisily against the floor, as it was pushed back forcibly by the door opening. I sat up in bed, startled and confused, with my heart beating rapidly. I looked over towards the door.

"Breakfast is prepared, Emily," came Elizabeth's familiar voice.

"Breakfast? What time is it?" I asked, looking towards the window and the darkness that still prevailed outside.

"A little after seven," the aunt replied. "Do not take long in dressing, or the porridge will go cold." The door clicked shut on the latch, and I listened as her heavy footsteps descended the staircase. I got dressed quickly, not wanting to aggravate the aunt further after last night, and came downstairs yawning. I *had* to get more sleep tonight.

Isabelle was already up and sitting at the table, devouring her porridge.

"Good morning, Isabelle," I said cheerfully. I needed to keep on her good side, and then she might think twice about any intended sabotage. She looked up at me swiftly and dropped her gaze.

"Is it?" she muttered. Aunt Elizabeth came in from the kitchen with some milk and set it down on the table, before being seated herself.

"There now," she announced, smiling. "Eat your fill, and then we can go into Greenham and purchase some fine material for your wedding gown, Emily."

"I already have one." I replied, hoping that I would not appear ungrateful for her offer.

"You do? Good heavens, child, you *are* well prepared. Can we see it?"

"No, I would rather it be a surprise. I bought it in London…last week," I lied, taking my first spoonful of porridge and swallowing it nervously, as the thought occurred to me that Isabelle may have poisoned or drugged it, like Robert had. *This is ridiculous! I can't starve myself until the wedding.*

"Then we shall purchase cloth for the Flower Maidens frocks. You *can* sew?"

"A little…I can replace a button," I said, ignoring Isabelle's callous laugh.

"Very well," sighed Elizabeth. "I can see that it will be down to my daughter and I to make the four garments. Isabelle is an excellent seamstress. Is that not so, dear?" Isabelle pushed away her empty bowl and sneered at me across the table.

"Samuel will expect his wife to be able to cook, sew, and produce fine children. He will be disappointed to find you are sorely lacking in two of these necessities…the other remains to be seen, if you are together long enough!"

"Isabelle!" cried Elizabeth "That is *most* discourteous of you. Please forgive my daughter for her outburst, Emily. I fear the wedding is bringing forth bad memories that are causing her to act out of character."

"It's all right. I understand, Aunt Elizabeth." I said, trying to pretend the cruel jibe had not affected me. "It will take more than a spoiled meal or an unpatched hole to sever the love that Samuel and I have together. As for children, I am sure we will have no problems in producing strong, healthy offspring, for *many* years to come." Isabelle glared at me, before getting up and going upstairs in a huff, much to her mother's exasperation. Mary came in with Hannah just then, both wearing thick capes and bonnets.

"I have asked the eldest girls to accompany us to town. Their opinion will be sought after, regarding the choice of cloth for their garments…ah, I hear Charles with the cart now!"

I had hoped it might have been Samuel, and inquired after his whereabouts to his father, as we climbed up on the cart. He informed me that Samuel was up at the mill with John, and was likely to remain there for most of the day. Excitable women discussing cloths and wedding preparations were not his forte, he had told Charles, and it was best for him to keep out of our way as much as possible. *Typical man*, I thought, smiling. Three hundred years later, and they still hated being dragged around shops by their other halves. Isabelle joined us reluctantly, and complained bitterly about the hard bench that her delicate posterior had to be seated on. I went back inside and collected the cushion from the bench to stop her whining, and threw it at her with more force than intended.

We arrived in Greenham just after 9:30am. The town was already bustling with people, and I had forgotten how busy it was compared to Offenham. We visited several shops that sold cloth before we found one that had a material that everyone agreed upon—a rich, dark red. Elizabeth had in mind to add a fur trim, which I thought would look lovely, and I persuaded her to purchase extra cloth to make me a cape to wear over my wedding gown. It would be far too cold just to wear the dress to and from the church. With the bolts of cloth stored away on the cart, and a farthing given to a young lad to watch over it, we all went into a coffee house for a hot drink, which Charles insisted on paying for. Isabelle had a tea, declaring that this new drink of coffee was positively vulgar, and it would never last. I grinned. *How wrong you are dear*, I thought, sipping the hot dark liquid from a cup. Not exactly your cappuccino, but palatable, nonetheless.

Mary and Hannah had chocolate and sat up the corner by the window, impeccably behaved, compared to the spoilt brat with golden ringlets pouting in the other chair, demanding to go home before she froze to death. I felt like giving her a good slap. *The patience that Elizabeth must have to tolerate her incessant moaning!* She had my utmost admiration. As we returned to the cart, it started to rain heavily. I thought Isabelle was about to throw a fit, until Charles managed to calm her down, by covering her with an old blanket he kept under the bench.

"I hope it hasn't got *fleas*!" she cried, inspecting the blanket gingerly.

"Most likely *infested* with them," I whispered in her ear, as I passed by her to sit down. She started to scratch herself frantically, declaring that she would be eaten alive before arriving home. No one appeared to be bothered.

By the time we got back to Mill Cottage we were wet through. I ushered the girls inside and stripped off their wet clothing immediately, before they caught a chill. I also changed my dress and dried my hair by the fire. Isabelle ran off upstairs to change. Her immaculate ringlets turned into dripping wet tendrils that stuck to her face. Elizabeth brought in some cheese and bread from the kitchen and heated some milk above the fire. The other children joined us, and Ellen was thrilled with the cloth for her Flower Maiden frock, insisting hers was to be made first. The cloth for the frocks and all the sewing accessories were taken over to the other cottage, where there would be more room to lay them out and work upon them. No time was wasted, although Isabelle had to be dragged over there by her mother to commence measuring and sewing. I stayed with them and helped a little, until I heard Samuel and John return home from the mill later that afternoon. Isabelle heard them too, and stabbed herself with the needle in frustration as I left the cottage.

On seeing me, Samuel's face lit up, and he held open his arms to embrace me warmly.

"I've missed you," I whispered, holding him tightly.

"I, too, have been distracted in my thoughts all day. I must learn to not let my heart rule my head whilst working."

"We found some beautiful cloth for the Flower Maidens," I said excitedly, pouring him some mead from an earthenware jug.

"Indeed, I am without doubt they will look enchanting… as will you."

"You will not be disappointed when you see me. My gown is quite beautiful."

"The gown is of no significance. The person who wears it is deemed more worthy," he replied, kissing my lips gently. I responded, and the pressure of his mouth over mine increased. I let out a soft moan as the passion arose within me, and we fell against the table in a rapacious embrace. "Emily…" he whispered huskily, his moist lips tasting the soft skin of my heaving breasts as they strained against the fabric of my dress, yearning to be released in their entirety. I lay down on the table, his body covered mine, devouring any resistance to his touch. I parted my legs and yanked my dress up around my waist, pulling him hard against me.

"Take me," I breathed. "I want you so much." I truly believe he would have, if the sound of Aunt Elizabeth and Isabelle talking outside had not disturbed us. We scrambled off the table, like two naughty schoolchildren, my face red and hair in disarray. Inside, my heart beat rapidly, as I tried to compose myself. Samuel looked as guilty as hell, with his hair damp with sweat, and his shirt partly unfastened. The door opened, and they entered.

"Emily, my dear, you look a little flushed. I do hope the drenching we received this morning has not given you a fever?"

"No, I am quite well, Aunt Elizabeth," I replied, still shaking. Isabelle knew exactly what had caused my rise in temperature, and threw Samuel a disdainful look. He responded by going outside to chop some firewood and cool down.

"It is fortunate that we arrived when we did," hissed Isabelle, as her mother disappeared upstairs. "Or your chastity might have been under threat."

"What makes you think it hasn't already been taken?" I retorted.

"How interesting. Does Samuel know of this?" she smirked.

"By Samuel, you stupid woman!" I cried, losing my temper. Isabelle look startled for a moment by my blatant insult, but was not deterred in her verbal abuse.

"He is too much of a gentleman to take a woman to bed before her wedding night. You cannot fool me!"

"Ask him about the three nights he spent with me in my bed, then!"

"You lie! You devious witch!" yelled Isabelle, launching herself at me across the room in a fit of fury. Grabbing hold of a handful of my hair, she pulled me downwards onto the floor and proceeded to lay into me with her fists. I was taken off-guard by the sudden onslaught, and the strength of one so fragile-looking. I took some painful blows, before I managed to gain the upper hand, and stopped her from reaching for the knife on the edge of the table. The commotion brought Aunt Elizabeth hurtling down the stairs and Samuel in from outside, wielding an axe. It took both of them to pull the demented Isabelle off of me and restrain her.

"Whatever is going on here?" cried Elizabeth, looking from one to the other of us in bewilderment. "Explain your conduct this instant!"

"Ask *her*! She started it!" I yelled, sitting upright on the floor, holding my head.

"You should never have returned, then Samuel would have been free to marry *me*...you've ruined everything now!" screamed Isabelle, struggling to free herself from her captors. "But you will regret this, as God is my witness, you will surely pay tenfold."

"Get her out of here, Samuel! I don't want her anywhere near me, and you can forget about being my Flower Maiden!"

"Tell them, Samuel…tell them you love me and always have," Isabelle pleaded, flinging her arms around Samuel's neck. He rejected the embrace with contempt.

"Is this true?" said Elizabeth to Samuel.

"No. It is most certainly not! I have *never* told her I loved her. My feelings for Isabelle have always been no more than brotherly affection. Unfortunately, I cannot deem her affection for me as that of the same fraternal nature. I do *not* love your daughter, Aunt Elizabeth. You must believe in me, for I speak the truth." Samuel bent down and helped me to my feet, wiping away the blood that trickled down from a cut above my eye.

"Isabelle and I will reside in the other cottage from tonight. It is best for all concerned. That will give Isabelle the opportunity to reflect on her behavior and make amends before the wedding," said Elizabeth, as she firmly took hold of her daughter's arm, and marched a sobbing Isabelle out of the door. I felt sorry for the aunt. It must have been humiliating to have her daughter behave in such an unladylike manner, and I hoped she would be able to knock some sense into her, before she lost the plot completely.

Mary and Hannah gave up their bed for the unexpected visitors at Jasmine Cottage, and took the room upstairs, next to mine. They were eager to know what had transpired to warrant such an exchange, but Samuel told them they were too young to understand the complexities of love, and packed them off to bed with a bowl of soup each and a bread roll. Charles and John remained at Weaver's that evening and knew nothing of the drama that had unfolded here. Samuel wanted it to remain so, as he didn't wish to burden his father with his sister's problematic daughter.

Samuel and I later sat by the fire, with our bowls of soup. Neither of us felt like eating, but we needed something warm inside us for the cold night ahead, which we would face alone in our separate bedrooms. Our ardor had been completely extinguished, and the earlier flames of passion were now a distant memory. Isabelle had seen to that, and I began to wonder if we would ultimately make it to the altar to become husband and wife. The more I thought about it, the more hopeless it seemed. Samuel grasped my hand tightly, as if sensing my anxieties.

"Do not fret so, my love. It *will* come to pass that you and I shall be bound together in the sanctity of marriage...I promise you." I squeezed his hand, comforted by his words of reassurance. As I kissed him goodnight, and locked the door behind him, I could not shake off a feeling of unease within me, as if something bad was about to happen.

The next few days followed a similar pattern. I would get up, light the fire, make the breakfast, feed the animals, fetch groceries from the village, and entertain the children with exciting stories of far off lands. I even began to teach them a few letters of the alphabet, and my mind drifted to Sam's suggestion of a school for the youngsters of the parish. It was a brilliant idea, but I had far too much on my mind at present to plan ahead.

Aunt Elizabeth came and went frequently, updating me on the work completed on the Flower Maiden frocks. She also collected food to cook for her daughter and the children. I had not laid eyes on Isabelle for days, and began to wonder if her mother had her chained to the bedpost for her punishment. She appeared reluctant to talk about her wayward daughter, and changed the subject whenever I inquired after her. Samuel, John and Charles also paid me regular visits during the day, and I couldn't help noticing that John was particularly jubilant on one occasion, for a reason I could not fathom. Now I come to think of it, Charles and Samuel had a certain enigmatic ambience about them, and I put it down to the excitement of the forthcoming wedding.

On the eve of our wedding, the family gathered together at Mill Cottage to welcome in the New Year. Isabelle came out of hiding and joined her mother for the celebration. She was extremely quiet and subdued, and kept her eyes constantly downcast to the floor. It was difficult to ascertain if she was genuinely sorry for her behavior, or if she was just preoccupied with contemplating her next move. I didn't trust her. Charles raised his goblet and toasted Samuel and I on a happy and fruitful life together, after which everyone cheered ecstatically and hugged us—all except Isabelle, who left during the toast and returned to Jasmine Cottage alone.

"I do wish you would reconsider and have Isabelle as your Flower Maiden," said Elizabeth, taking hold of my arm and steering me to a quiet corner. "She is *truly* sorry for her offensive behavior."

"I still fear that she may do something reckless tomorrow. I cannot take that chance, Aunt Elizabeth. I'm so sorry," I replied.

"Then *I* shall have to dress you tomorrow morn instead. Be sure to rise early, for there is much to do before the service at eleven."

"I will, Aunt Elizabeth…and thank you so much for all your help."

"Thank *you* for allowing my brother to give you away."

"He has always been like a father to me, as I have no one else." Elizabeth smiled and laid her hand on my shoulder.

"Now, off to bed with you, young lady. You appear to be in need of a good night's rest." Everyone started to leave. Ellen was already sound asleep on the bench. John picked her up gently and took her back home. Samuel was the last to leave and took hold of my hands tenderly.

"Tomorrow night, you will be mine in body and soul. We shall consummate the marriage as one should, in holy wedlock." My mind went back to the quick fumble on the dining table earlier, and I was *glad* we had been disturbed. It just wasn't right. He smiled at me intently, as if he wanted to say something, but held back.

"I will see you at the church, then?" I asked, kissing him lightly on the cheek. His expression suddenly changed to that of a more solemn demeanor, and I knew what he was thinking. "I shall be there, Samuel…this time, your bride *will* come."

"Miss Emily, wake up!" cried Mary and Hannah excitedly, bouncing up and down on my bed. I stirred, dazed, and opened my eyes.

"What's the matter? What's happened?" I asked anxiously, struggling to sit up.

"It's your wedding day! Oh, do wake up and come down. Aunt Elizabeth is here with our frocks and your cape."

"Is it morning already? I feel I have just gone to sleep."

"Yes, it is, and what a beautiful morning it will be, once the sun has risen… Emily, do *please* get up!" cried Mary, pulling off the covers impatiently.

"All right! All right. I'm getting up." I laughed, pulling the covers back over me. "Tell Aunt Elizabeth I will be down shortly." The girls shrieked with joy and ran downstairs. I wished I felt as confident that the day ahead would be as beautiful as they envisaged. I wanted it to be, more than anything. So why did I have this premonition that something untoward was looming?

"Ah, you are finally up," said Elizabeth, as I came downstairs and shuffled over to the table, before flopping down heavily into a chair. "Did you sleep at all last night? You look positively worn out, my dear girl." I couldn't help smiling broadly. Now that was a question she should be asking me *tomorrow* morning. "Something amuses you?" said Elizabeth, pouring me a mug of warm milk.

"No, nothing…I'm just happy." Ellen rushed in through the door, followed by her brothers.

"I could not restrain her any longer. She is so eager," laughed William.

"I want to see your wedding gown, Miss Emily! Where is it? Is it upstairs?" cried Ellen, jumping onto my lap like an excitable puppy.

"All in good time, little one. First we have to dress all the Flower Maidens and do their hair."

"I want to be dressed *first!*" cried Ellen, going over to the pile of red garments edged with white fur. "Is this mine?" She picked up the first one she saw.

"That's far too big for you, Ellen," laughed Hannah. "That would fit Miss Isabelle." I looked over at Elizabeth inquiringly.

"I thought, maybe, you would reconsider your decision? The poor girl is inconsolable," said Elizabeth, hoping I would change my mind.

"It is not the fact that she cannot be my Flower Maiden that upsets her. It is the fact that Samuel is marrying me and not *her.* I still stand by my decision…I DON'T WANT HER THERE."

"Not even in the church?"

"No!"

"Very well, then *I* shall wait outside with her also…you really are quite stubborn Emily, over such a petty matter." With that, she flounced off through the door, slamming it shut behind her. I could see now where Isabelle got her temper.

"Right! It's just you and me girls…shall we get you dressed?"

It took a great deal longer than anticipated to dress three highly-strung girls and attend to their hair. The end result was worth the effort. They looked absolutely delightful, like little Christmas Santas! Each held a posy of holly, with red berries and snowdrops, secured on a white ribbon. Elizabeth and Isabelle had done a marvelous job.

I rushed upstairs with a pitcher of water to wash and change, with a little under an hour to prepare myself. I pulled the large, brown paper parcel out from under the bed, where I had hidden it these past few days, and unwrapped the dress. Getting into it was difficult, and I kept getting my foot tangled within the layers of underskirt in my haste to get ready. Finally, it was on. I cursed that I could not check if it looked all right in a full-length mirror. I would just have to ask the girls later. Among the small selection of jewelry

I had brought with me was a dainty diamante tiara, which I positioned across my head, after I had secured my hair up into a bun. Again, without a mirror, I had no idea if it looked okay. It was so frustrating.

"Miss Emily, the carriage is here!" Mary shouted up the staircase, "Are you ready?"

"Just coming!" I called back. *Well, this is it.* I was *finally* getting married, but never in my wildest dreams did I imagine it would be to someone that lived 300 years ago, and who died before I was born.

Holding up the heavy satin gown and train, I negotiated the narrow staircase slowly and carefully, afraid that I would snag the dress on some protruding splinters of wood on the way down. As I stepped down into the room, three faces stared, mesmerized at the vision before them, their jaws dropping open in awe. For the first time that day, they were rendcred speechless.

"Will I do?" I asked, smiling.

"Oh, Miss Emily!" cried Mary, stepping forward and touching the satin dress cautiously. "I have never seen such material. It is *truly* beautiful." Tears welled up in her eyes as she walked around me in wonder.

"Are they real roses?" asked Ellen, pointing to the train. "They *look* like real roses."

"No, they are made of silk," I replied, laughing, "These will live forever." Hannah handed me my cape of red cloth, again edged with a matching white fur trim, even on the hood. I slipped it on over my dress, but left it open. I was surprised that Aunt Elizabeth had not returned to check if I was all right. This whole Flower Maiden thing with Isabelle had infuriated her, and she called *me* petty!

Someone had gone to a lot of trouble and decorated the open carriage with holly, Christmas roses and ribbons for me. I needed the girls' help to get me up the high step into the carriage, scrunching my dress up close to me, to allow them room to sit down. For a moment, I forgot where I was, and wondered if the photographer had been arranged for the church. Then, with a touch of sadness, I remembered. It was a pity I would have no record of my wedding day to look back on in years to come—all I would have would be memories. It didn't take long to arrive at the church. Many people in the village stopped and stared, as my carriage passed through, and they gathered at the entrance to watch me alight with my Flower Maidens in attendance. Gasps of admiration arose from the women as they jostled one another to get a better view, and the gentlemen nodded to one another in approval. I held my dress up off of the muddy pathway as we walked towards the church entrance, while Hannah and Mary carried the train between them. Little Ellen walked ahead, swinging her posy, enjoying all the attention.

As we approached the huge wooden doors, I caught sight of Aunt Elizabeth and Isabelle standing among the gravestones, looking thoroughly miserable.

"Maybe they could stand at the *back* of the church?" suggested Mary. *Perhaps I went a bit too far in forbidding them to attend—after all the hard work they put into the frocks?*

"You can come in and sit at the back, if you so wish," I called across to the two solitary figures. "Just make sure Isabelle shows some respect."

I entered the church porch, took off my cape, and dropped my dress to the floor, while the girls straightened it out and set the train. Charles came out through the door, and stopped in his tracks upon seeing me.

"My dear Emily…" he said, choked with emotion. "You look positively radiant. Samuel is a very fortunate man indeed." He offered his arm, and I took it affectionately, as Hannah handed me my bouquet of matching holly and snowdrops, bound in a red ribbon.

"Thank you, father." I said quietly, and he beamed with pride at his new daughter. The door swung open, and organ music began to play from somewhere within the church. Ellen walked forward on her own, followed a few steps behind by Mary and Hannah. Charles and I began the slow walk down to the altar, smiling and nodding to the congregation that stood between the pews, which were decorated with winter flowers and ribbons. Many people were unknown to me, but all were there for one purpose—to celebrate the marriage of Emily and Samuel Howerd.

As we drew nearer, I could see the smiling faces of John and his brothers to the left, and the curate waiting with the Bible in his hand. My eyes searched for Samuel among the line of heads in the row to the right, coming to rest on a mop of black curls. He turned and stepped out from the pew to face me, and my heart gave an enormous leap in my chest. Charles took my hand and placed it into Samuel's, as I stood and stared at the man before me.

He was simply dressed, in tight black trousers with a long shirt frilled down the front, with matching cuffs. The top was unfastened at the neck, revealing the dark hairs on his chest, and his long black curls cascaded down over his shoulders, contrasting with the brilliant white of his shirt. He was equally stunned by my appearance, and neither of us were taking in what the curate was saying at first.

"I love you…" I whispered, and he responded likewise. The curate gave a discrete cough, to gain our attention, before continuing. The bit that I was dreading—'"*Does anyone here know of any lawful impediment why these two people should not be joined in holy matrimony?*"'—passed without hindrance. I breathed a sigh of relief that Isabelle had kept her mouth shut and hadn't made a scene. Samuel tore his eyes away from mine for a moment and glanced over at his father, a mischievous smile spread over his face, as the curate asked,

"Who giveth this woman to be married to this man?" I waited for Charles to respond.

"I DO!" A loud, clear voice said from the back of the church. I recognized it immediately and spun round.

"Sam? Is that really you?" I cried, as a sandy-haired man with a floppy fringe stepped out from the shadows.

৵ Chapter Twenty-Five ৵

Everyone in the congregation turned around to see who this '*Sam'* person was, as he walked down the aisle towards me, grinning like a Cheshire cat.

"I do," he repeated, taking my hand and gently kissing it. "*I,* Samuel Warren, giveth this woman to be married to this man."

"Sam, what are you *doing* here?" I whispered loudly, looking about me in a panic.

"Well, that's a nice welcome!" he said, laughing.

"You know what I mean! Of course I'm pleased to see you, but…" Ellen came up to us and showed Sam her finger.

"Look, it's all better now!" she said, smiling up at him in adoration. I stared at her.

"What does she mean?" I asked bewildered. Then I suddenly remembered Samuel. *Oh my God!* I thought. *He is going to think I have a secret lover!* I turned to face him, expecting his eyes to be black and filled with anger at the unexpected arrival of this strange man at our wedding. "This is Mister Sam Warren…the physician I stayed with in London," I explained nervously, surprised at Samuel's serene and smiling expression.

"We are already acquainted," replied Samuel, bowing respectfully to Sam.

"You can't be!" I cried. "It isn't possible." The curate stepped forward and politely intervened, calming the scandalous gossiping among the guests.

"I beg your pardon, but could we continue with the service and keep the joyful reunions for afterwards?"

"I'll tell you later," said Sam, stepping aside and taking a seat next to John. I turned back to face Samuel, totally stunned. There were so many questions in my mind, but they had to be put aside until after. Isabelle must be overjoyed at this turn of events, thinking that my marriage is *already* in jeopardy.

The service continued, and John came forward to place a thin gold band on a white velvet cushion. This was subsequently blessed, and Samuel slid the ring gently onto my finger, repeating the words spoken by the curate. I was shaking like a leaf with emotion and had to fight back the tears. Sam's arrival was the icing on the cake. No one in the world could have been happier than I was at that moment in time. I repeated my vows to Samuel, as he held my hands tightly in his, his eyes never leaving mine as I spoke in a soft whisper. Every word was said with sincerity—with truth and undying love.

A hymn was then sung, and more prayers followed, before the curate came to the end of the short service, and with God's blessing, finally pronounced us husband and wife. The tears that I had held back so gallantly now flowed freely, as I kissed my husband amid cheers of delight from the congregation. We turned to face everyone as Mary gave me back my bouquet, and the church organ sprang into life once more, its jubilant melody resounding around the bare stone walls. I held onto Samuel's arm proudly, and we walked slowly back up the aisle, followed by our three Flower Maidens who, henceforth, were our adopted children.

Before we ventured out into the cold, Samuel put my red and white cape around my shoulders lovingly. There was no sign of Isabelle and her mother, but with so many people crowding around, I could have overlooked them. The one person I *was* looking for was Sam. *That guy has some explaining to do!* He appeared through the church door, and before I had a chance to catch his attention, Samuel had put his arm around Sam's shoulder and led him off down the path, talking to him in low undertones.

"I don't believe it!" I cried to John. "You would think they were old friends."

"Well, in a way, they are indeed good friends, as are we," said John, taking my arm and walking with me down the pathway to the church gate. I smiled and nodded to the crowd as I went, and we caught up with them at the gate.

"Do you *know* him?" I asked Samuel, pointing my finger at Sam.

"Indeed. I am indebted to Mister Warren, for if he had not brought it to my attention the reason why you had left me so unexpectedly, then we would not be standing here today as man and wife." Samuel smiled across at Sam. "The letter was *his* design. Were you not impressed with my efforts under such a fine tutor?"

"You helped him write the letter?" I said to Sam in disbelief. Samuel laughed.

"I can see that you both have *much* to discuss, but first we have to greet our guests in the tavern and join in the celebrations." Samuel took my arm, and we walked the short distance to the tavern, where Charles had arranged a small reception.

Inside, a huge roaring fire at one end supplied the heat and subsequent roasting of a large boar that turned on a spit above it. Wine, ale, and mead were amply supplied, together with an abundance of freshly baked bread, cheese, cold meats and other less recognizable offerings.

My dress stirred much commenting among the women. It was touched, examined and admired by many of the village folk, who had never in their lives set their eyes upon such a fine garment before. I was not familiar with many of the guests, but I accepted their good wishes for a happy future cheerfully. After the initial excitement had died down, I took Sam to one side and made him explain to me *how* and *when* he had gone back in time, and subsequently took it upon himself to arrange my future. The visit to his mother, the disappearance of my locket, the letter, and the desperate attempt to get me to return, all started to make sense.

"Why didn't you *tell* me?" I cried. "You knew how upset I was at leaving you behind, and all the time you were planning to return for my wedding!"

"I knew what your reaction would have been, if I told you I was intending to go back and sort out your love life."

"Too right!"

"So…I decided to do it without you knowing. As for the wedding, I couldn't let the fruits of my labor pass without my presence, could I?" Sam said, smiling cheekily. *How can I be angry with him?* I thought, giving him a hug. John came over and stood beside Sam, and a certain look passed between them, which didn't go unnoticed. It was my turn to laugh.

"This is *'John'*, isn't it? This is the John you spoke about?" I said, recalling his past conversations regarding his new acquaintance. Sam nodded, blushing slightly. "I didn't realise he was—you were—together?"

"Neither my father nor my younger siblings are aware of my preferences, and I would be grateful for you to abide by my wishes, and for it to remain so," said John, looking around anxiously.

"What about Samuel?" I asked.

"He knows and has accepted the arrangement without malice." I was surprised to learn that, but I was pleased that he looked kindly upon them. John excused himself and went to refill his plate.

Aunt Elizabeth and Isabelle appeared out of nowhere and approached me tentatively.

"I would like you to meet a good friend of mine. Mister Sam Warren. He is a physician in London." I said happily, more for Isabelle's sake than the aunt's.

"Delighted to make your acquaintance, sir," said Elizabeth, curtsying gracefully. "May I present my daughter? Miss Isabelle."

"Ah! The enchanting Isabelle. Emily has told me much about you," said Sam, bowing and taking her hand, on which to bestow a kiss.

"I trust, although I doubt, that you have heard good things about me," purred Isabelle, giving me a sly sideways glare.

"Undeniably," replied Sam, lying through his teeth, but smiling sweetly.

"You look beautiful, my dear," said Elizabeth. "That dress is exquisite. Truly it is."

"Thank you so much, aunt. I am sorry for my behaviour earlier. Please forgive me, for I do not want to appear ungrateful for all the hard work you put into making the lovely Flower Maiden frocks."

"Nonsense, child. It is all forgotten," said Elizabeth, gesturing with a wave of her hand. Samuel came up behind me and encircled his arm around my waist.

"Aunt Elizabeth, I trust you are enjoying the celebrations…Miss Isabelle?"

"Oh yes! It is positively divine. Is it not, dear daughter?" Isabelle fixed her eyes upon Samuel like a stalking lion, unsmiling, unemotional, and likened in demeanor to someone slightly insane. The hairs on my arms bristled upright in response. Samuel was equally as affected, and left abruptly to talk to a group of women, eager for his attention. Aunt Elizabeth caught sight of a woman she knew and dragged Isabelle over to meet her.

"My God!" said Sam after she left. "That's a bunny boiler if ever I saw one!"

"A what?"

"You *know*. Didn't you ever see that film *Fatal Attraction*?" asked Sam, shuddering. I nodded, remembering.

"She hasn't done anything as yet, although I have had a really bad feeling for a few days now."

"It's the quiet ones you have to watch out for. They're the worst."

"Shut up, Sam. You're scaring me!" I whispered loudly.

"Just *saying*," said Sam, picking up another goblet of wine from a passing wench.

The afternoon wore on, and soon people started to leave. Samuel was over in the far corner, talking to some men he obviously knew, throwing his head back in laughter at some joke. It was wonderful to see him so happy and relaxed. I was so proud of him. Samuel Howerd, my *husband*, and I, Emily Howerd, his *wife*. John and Sam had disappeared outside somewhere for some privacy, and Charles was talking to his sister. I looked out of the window. The children had been banished outside for making too much noise, and they now played in the street, the girl's dresses soaking up the mud around the hems as they raced up and down. It didn't matter, as long as they were happy. I sipped my wine and picked up the last remaining scraps of some dark meat on a plate. Someone said it was pigeon. Whatever it was, it tasted nice. It suddenly occurred to me that Isabelle was not in the room. She had been intently watching Samuel all afternoon...and now she was gone. Probably skulked off home in a mood, no doubt.

A young boy entered the tavern and called out Samuel's name. He turned and summoned the boy over. A letter was delivered to him, which he unsealed, and after frowning at the contents, gave it to one of the men who could read. Sam came back in and followed my gaze to see what had captured my attention so ardently. Samuel placed the letter hurriedly into his pocket, a worried expression upon his face.

"What is it, my love?" I asked anxiously as he came over to me.

"There are some problems up at the mill with the machinery. It is probably the loom that has given me cause for concern all week. I will not be long, my love"

"It's our wedding day, for goodness sake! Can no one else deal with it?" I cried in dismay. He kissed my cheek tenderly.

"Take care of my wife, Mister Warren," he said, turning to Sam. "I will hasten back." With that, he strode out of the door to attend to his dilemma at the mill.

"He's passionate about his work, isn't he?" said Sam, laughing. "Not that that's a bad thing. Here, have you tried these things? They're delicious."

That *'feeling'* I had harbored all week returned with a vengeance, and I couldn't stop myself from asking Aunt Elizabeth where Isabelle had absconded to.

"Oh! The poor girl had a terrible headache. She tried to remain, for fear of appearing unsociable, but she was almost in tears. I sent her home to rest in bed. The best thing to do, do you not agree, Mrs. Howerd?"

"Of course. I hope she recovers soon," I replied, smiling at the first use of my married name. "Isabelle has a headache, and has gone home." I told Sam, making a face.

"Ah! Poor love. Probably plotting her revenge, more like." I stared at Sam.

"You don't think she has a headache, then? Maybe she isn't at home at all?" My mind went into overdrive. *The letter from the mill—was it genuine? Or was it a trap, to get him away?* My heart started to race, and I worked myself into a panic. "Is the carriage still outside?" I said, rushing over to the window.

"Think so…why?" asked Sam, puzzled.

"I want to go back to the cottage and check if she's there!" I cried, heading towards the door. Sam followed me out, trying in vain to calm me down.

"Emily! Hold on a minute!" he called, as I hitched up my dress and clambered inside the carriage.

"Take me back to Mill Cottage, please…quickly!" I shouted to the driver. "You coming or what?" I asked Sam, just as John came out of the tavern, a puzzled look upon his face.

"Where are you going, Sam?" he called out from the doorway.

"Back to Mill Cottage. Emily's worried that Isabelle is up to something."

"Isabelle?"

"I'll explain later…tell Charles where we have gone!" yelled Sam, taking a seat next to me.

The carriage set off at a fast pace, the horses galloping along the street, throwing us violently from side to side.

"I hope you're right about this," said Sam.

"Trust me for once, won't you? I know something is wrong." I told the driver to stop as we approached Jasmine Cottage, and flung open the door before it had halted.

"For goodness sake, Emily, take it easy!" cried Sam. I ignored his concern and scrambled down the high step of the carriage, inevitably catching my foot in the dress. I was sent, sprawling, onto the dirty ground. The driver and Sam hauled me to my feet, and I pushed them away recklessly in my haste to get into the cottage and allay my fears.

"ISABELLE!" I screamed out. "ARE YOU HERE?" My call was met by an icy silence.

"Perhaps she's asleep upstairs?" suggested Sam, coming to my side.

"Well, don't just stand there, go up and see!" I yelled at him. "I can't in this dress very well!" Sam obeyed and ran up the stairs to the bedrooms. I waited with baited breath below.

"She's not here!" he called down. I was out of the door and on my way to Mill Cottage on foot before he got back down, beckoning the driver to follow with the carriage. Again, Sam ascended the staircase to search for the elusive Isabelle, but this time he came back down slowly.

"What is it? Is she there?" I shouted at him, almost in tears.

"No, but this is…" he replied, holding a sheet of parchment in his hand. The look on his face unnerved me, and I snatched the paper from his hand. "I haven't read it all—just the first few lines—but I think you may be right," he said. With trembling hands, I read the first lines of the long letter.

'By the time you read this, it will all be over. Samuel and I are together where no mortal soul can touch us or tear us apart. He is now mine for all eternity…'

"No! This can't be happening!" I sobbed as Sam pulled me outside.

"Take us to the mill, as fast as you can!" yelled Sam to the driver. "Come on, Emily. We might get there in time."

As I sat in the carriage with Sam, I just felt sick. Nothing seemed real, and it was as if I was looking down on myself from above, like in a dream.

"Samuel can look after himself. Try not to worry," said Sam, putting a comforting arm around me. "I'm sure he's okay."

"The last words he said to you were, '*take care of my wife'*," I said, turning to face him, as the tears cascaded down my face. "He *knew* Sam…he knew something might happen." Sam didn't reply.

We arrived at the mill, and Sam helped me down. Outside were some men loading a cart with bolts of cloth, and Sam walked up to them purposefully while I stayed near the carriage, almost afraid to hear what I feared.

"Is Samuel Howerd here?" he demanded.

"No…he be at his wedding today, to Miss Emily. We do not expect to see him until the morn to be sure…or later," he replied, smiling impishly.

"Do you have a loom that is broken?" urged Sam.

"Aye, we had one that was working nought a few days back, but Mister Howerd be a-repairing it himself, and a fine job, too, he made of it."

"So, no one sent for him to come here?"

"No. No one here, sir. It would be more than we dare, this being his wedding day and all," replied the man, turning to untie another batch of cloth lowered from above.

"What about a young woman with long fair hair. Have you seen anyone like that?"

"Neither, sir. Sorry I could not be helping you more." Sam thanked the man and came back over to me.

"The letter was definitely fake," he said anxiously. "No one has seen him or Isabelle around here." Sam thought for a moment as an idea came to him.

"*What*?" I cried, "What are you thinking?"

"You don't think…you don't think it's possible that Samuel and Isabelle could have eloped together?" The shocked look on my face made him rethink his assumption quickly. "No…that was a *stupid* suggestion, I'm sorry—been watching too many films."

"We have to search the area. He must be around here somewhere. He *must* be," I said, taking a step forward and catching my dress in a bramble. "Damn dress!" I yelled and started to unfasten the side buttons.

"What are you doing?" asked Sam, confused.

"What does it look like? I'm taking it off! Don't *worry,* it has an underslip." As I frantically scrambled out of the cumbersome dress, we heard the sound of approaching horses. Charles and John cantered to a halt in front of us, looking worried.

"What is happening, Emily? John told me you and Mister Warren had gone to the mill to find Samuel. I do not understand. Is there concern for his well-being?"

"We believe Isabelle intends to harm him," cried Sam, throwing my cape around me to stop me from shaking violently. "Only we cannot find him...or Isabelle. Will you help us search the area?"

They didn't need asking twice, and set off in opposite directions along the bridle paths. Sam and I followed a direct path leading to the lake, where Charles and John would eventually end up. Without the dress, I was able to run more quickly. The horrible feeling in the pit of my stomach persisted—so many emotions, and fears, were all swamping my mind at once. We found nothing—no sign of my husband anywhere. I was close to breaking point as we arrived at the lake.

We stood silently on the banks of the lake, looking out over the frozen, still water. Everything was quiet and bathed in twilight, as the night descended upon us rapidly.

"Where *is* he, Sam?" I whispered, choking back the tears. "What has she done with him?" Sam put his arms around me and held me close. Words were useless. Charles and John appeared through the trees, and looked at Sam inquiringly.

"Any sign of him?" asked Charles anxiously. Sam shook his head. All four of us stood huddled together, shivering with the cold. No one knew what to do next.

"What's *that*?" said John suddenly, pointing out across the lake. We all turned and followed his gaze, straining our eyes in the fading light to see what had caught his attention. "Look, there! In the middle of the lake, where the ice recedes...something white." cried John, moving along the bank to get a better view. Sam joined him, his eyes fixed on the small patch of brilliant white.

"Is it him?" I sobbed. "Sam, is it *HIM*?"

"I don't know…I'm not sure," replied Sam, turning towards the horses. "Fetch me that rope from your saddle, Charles, and tie it around my waist." I gasped in horror as I realized what Sam intended to do.

"Oh God! Be careful, Sam! I couldn't bear to lose you, too." John clung to my arm, trembling, as Sam stepped onto the frozen lake and made his way gingerly across the surface towards the center, with Charles feeding the rope slowly from the bank. The further he went, the more difficult it was to see him, and I kept calling to him to make sure he was okay. Eventually, he disappeared into the gloom, with only his muffled voice floating on the night air to comfort us. Eventually the rope came to a stop, and silence prevailed. "SAM?" I screamed across the lake. "HAVE YOU FOUND HIM?" We waited for a reply for what seemed like an eternity. There was nothing.

"IT'S SAMUEL!" he finally called back. My heart leapt for a moment, but the tone of his voice frightened me.

"Is he all right, Sam? SAM?"

"I'M TYING THE ROPE AROUND HIM. WHEN I SAY PULL…*PULL*!" John and I rushed over and took hold of the end of the rope with Charles. On Sam's command, we all pulled the weight on the other end. Sam made it back to shore, just as we were hauling Samuel up the steep bank, and helped us in those final moments.

Charles rolled Samuel over, and I stepped back in horror, my hand flying to my mouth to muffle the screams. Gently, Charles moved his dripping black hair, encrusted with mud, away from his face. His eyes were closed, and his complexion bluish, with dark purple lips. Sam felt the pulse in his neck and looked up at us in despair.

"I fear we are too late," he whispered. "He's dead!"

Chapter Twenty-Six

"NO! He's not dead…he can't be!" I screamed hysterically, dropping to my knees. "Sam, *do* something! You're a doctor, for Christ's sake, do something!"

"I don't think I can…he's been in the icy water too long."

"That can help, can't it? The cold water, I read about it once. You've *got* to try, Sam. Please—*for me.* I beg you!" The desperation in my voice spurred Sam into action. He tilted Samuel's head back and covered his mouth with his, gently blowing air into his lungs. My husband's chest rose and fell, as Sam repeatedly blew in more air, and pumped his chest with his hands in between. I held his cold limp hand in mine, pleading for him not to leave me.

"What is he *doing*?" cried John, on the verge of tears. "Why is he kissing him?" Now was not the time to explain the technique of resuscitation, and my full attention was on Sam, praying that God would answer my prayers—praying for a miracle.

Three minutes passed, and Sam was growing tired. I wouldn't let him stop. I urged him on. Despite his pleas that it was no use. Suddenly Samuel lurched upwards, spewing water from his mouth and coughing violently. Sam immediately stopped and rolled him onto his side into the recovery position.

"He's alive!" I cried, "You *did* it, Sam!" I screamed, throwing my arms around him and knocking him off balance. "SAMUEL! Samuel, can you hear me? It's me, Emily…your wife," I said, stroking his face, which had now turned a deathly white. But he looked decidedly healthier than before. "Why doesn't he answer me?" I cried, looking up at Sam in dismay.

"He will take a while to recover from this. Hopefully no long-term damage was sustained. He's breathing on his own now, so that's a promising sign," explained Sam, sounding just like a doctor giving his prognosis.

"How can that be?" asked Charles, bewildered. "He was dead…and you brought him back to life, by this '*kissing'* thing?"

"No time to explain now. We have to get him home and warmed up fast, or all my efforts could be in vain," replied Sam. The thought that my Samuel was still in danger, and could still die, made me take command of the situation.

"Quick! Get him onto a horse and back to the mill. The carriage is there waiting. We can take him home in that. HURRY! THERE'S NO TIME TO LOSE!" I screamed.

Charles, John and Sam carried him over to one of the horses and laid him carefully across the saddle. His father led his horse back up the path to the mill. From there, his dripping wet body was transferred into the carriage with Sam and me for the short trip back to Mill Cottage. John and Charles followed behind on horseback and arrived with us. He was *so* cold, and I took off my cape to wrap around him, willing him to hold on and fight for his life. I had no concern for my own well-being. My flimsy underslip was saturated with freezing, muddy water. My hair hung down in matted strands, and I shook uncontrollably from the shock. I cradled his head on my lap, and my tears started to fall onto his face, as I realized just how close I had become to being widowed on my wedding day.

Arriving at Mill Cottage, Sam and the driver of the coach carried him upstairs to my bed and undressed him. Charles was exhausted from the trauma and collapsed in a chair, whilst John ran back to Weaver's Cottage to collect dry clothes for the men. I hurriedly tried to heat some milk up in a pot over the fire, throwing on more firewood in an effort to rekindle the dying embers from our long absence.

"The children." moaned Charles, struggling to his feet. "They are still at the tavern."

"Stay seated, Charles," I said, helping him back down. "Someone will fetch them home later. It's better that they remain there for a while. Your sister will be sure to care for them in the meantime." Sam came back down with the carriage driver. "Is he all right?" I asked anxiously. Sam nodded.

"I have some brandy in the carriage," interrupted the driver, heading for the door. "You will do well to put some in the milk to warm him when he is able to drink."

"I have put on some extra blankets from the other room," added Sam. "He is still unconscious… all we can do now is wait."

"I will go and sit with him," I said quietly.

"Get those wet clothes off first, Emily, for goodness sake!" cried Sam. "You will be of no use when sick with a fever. Samuel needs you most."

He was right. I went upstairs, with the candle shaking in its holder, to change out of my wet things and into a dry woollen dress. Samuel showed no signs of stirring, and I lay down on the bed next to him, my arm draped over his body. This was meant to be our wedding night—when finally we could become one together. Even if he did regain consciousness, he would be in no fit state to make love. *There will be plenty of other nights,* I thought, moving a damp lock of hair from his face and kissing his cheek tenderly.

Sometime later, the bedroom door opened, and Sam came in quietly with a mug of brandy milk.

"Is he still asleep?" he asked, sitting down carefully on the edge of the bed and passing me the drink.

"Yes…you don't think he is in a coma, do you? Maybe he will sleep for weeks…or months!"

"I don't know, Emily. Without modern equipment there is no way of telling," replied Sam, sighing heavily. "Just talk to him. Let him know you are here."

"I will. I'm not leaving his side until he wakes."

"What do you think happened to him? I noticed some blood on the back of his head earlier. Perhaps Isabelle smashed him over the head with something hard?" Sam said, carefully checking the pillow for fresh bloodstains.

"Isabelle! I had forgotten all about her. Where do you think she is?" I whispered across the bed.

"I think she killed herself, after trying to do Samuel in, judging by what she wrote in the letter," whispered back Sam.

"Where is that letter?" I asked.

"Not sure. I think it's still in the carriage with your dress… I'll get them later." I sipped the warm milk gratefully. The touch of brandy did add some extra warmth. If only Samuel would take some.

We sat quietly for a while, watching Samuel's chest rise and fall steadily. I suddenly thought, *what would have happened if Sam had not returned for the wedding*? Samuel would most certainly have died tonight.

"Sam…" I said quietly. He looked up at me through his fringe and smiled. "I don't know how to repay you for what you did today. You saved his life. Thank God you came back."

"I told you that I would *always* be here for you, didn't I?" he said, taking my hand. "And I meant every word." I was about to ask him what he and Samuel were talking about, outside of the church, when we heard the cottage door open and raised voices coming from downstairs. Aunt Elizabeth's unmistakable voice resounded loudly up the staircase.

"Charles! What in heaven's name is going on? You all disappeared, leaving me with five dreadfully tiresome children to bring home, with no explanation!" she cried angrily. I leapt off the bed, fuming, and ran downstairs. Sam was close behind me, telling me to try and keep calm. "And *where* is my daughter? She is not at the cottage." She ranted on. I burst through the door into the room and confronted Elizabeth.

"Your precious daughter tried to kill my husband this evening…no, wait! She *did* succeed in killing him!" I screamed at her.

"What do you mean? Samuel's *dead*?" She replied, taken aback by my aggressive onslaught.

"If it wasn't for Sam, he would be—no thanks to that murdering, jealous bitch of a daughter of yours!"

"How *dare* you speak of Isabelle in that manner!" yelled Elizabeth, stepping nearer to me. "Where is she? I want to speak with her."

"Hopefully that won't be possible. With a bit of luck, she's dead, and I hope she rots in hell!" I seethed venomously. Elizabeth raised her hand and slapped me hard across the face. If it weren't for Sam stepping in just then, I would have done her some serious harm.

"Go back upstairs, Emily. *I'll* speak with her," urged Sam, steering me towards the stairs. "This isn't doing anyone any good—especially Charles."

I went back upstairs reluctantly. Someone had to pay for this, and Elizabeth was the object of my wrath. Sitting on the edge of the bed, I listened to the heated argument that continued below, finally finishing with a slam of the cottage door as she left. Shortly after, Sam came back up.

"You okay?" he asked, "How's the face?"

"Smarting," I replied dolefully.

"Mary and Hannah are downstairs. They want to see their brother."

"Did you tell them what happened?" I asked anxiously.

"I told them that Samuel had fallen from his horse, hurting his head, and that he was, at the moment, unconscious. I didn't want to frighten them with all the grisly details."

"That was thoughtful of you. Bring them in for a moment, will you?" Sam went to fetch the girls, who came around the door, looking scared stiff. "It's all right. Come here and sit down," I said, beckoning them over. They both perched on the edge of the bed, staring at their brother in concern.

"Will he wake up?" asked Mary, close to tears.

"Is he breathing?" added Hannah, leaning over.

"He will be fine in a few days," I assured them. "He just needs to rest now, and recover." I put my arms around the girls and hugged them. "Please don't worry. Run along to bed now, both of you, and sleep well." Mary leaned towards me and kissed my cheek lightly.

"Goodnight, *mother*," she whispered. Hannah followed suit, and my eyes filled with tears of joy as they left the room.

"Do you want me to stay here tonight?" asked Sam.

"No. I'll be fine. You and John take Charles home. I'll see you in the morning." Sam suddenly laughed and shook his head disbelievingly.

"I was just about to say, 'Give me a ring, if you need me in the night!'"

"It takes some getting used to doesn't it? I have bitten my tongue on many occasions to prevent myself from saying something I shouldn't," I said, laughing. Sam's expression changed, and he took my hand.

"It's good to see you laugh again, Emily. Everything's going to work out fine, I promise you. Your future will be filled with much laughter and happiness, mark my words." I smiled at his words of comfort, as he closed the bedroom door quietly after him. *I hope so Sam...I really do.* Blowing out the candle, I slipped under the covers, wrapping my arms around Samuel as he slept on into the night. I listened to him breathing, I prayed for him to awaken soon, and I told him how much I loved him...over and over again, until I too finally slept.

I must have been exhausted, for it was already light when Sam gently shook me awake the following morning. I sat up with a start.

"What time is it?" I cried. "I have to light the fire...I have to do breakfast."

"It's all taken care of. Don't worry. I did the fire, and John prepared the breakfast." My eyes wandered to Samuel. His complexion was pinker now, but still he slept. "Stay there. I'll bring you breakfast in bed!" said Sam, smiling. "But don't make a habit of it!" Sam scurried off downstairs, and I leaned over and kissed Samuel's forehead.

"Please wake up soon, darling," I whispered. "I need you."

After breakfast, Sam suggested that I take it in turns with Mary to watch Samuel, enabling me to have a break and do any necessary chores. Charles had stayed up at Weaver's, as yesterday had taken its toll on his failing health, and he needed to rest. He demanded, though, that he be told immediately when his son regained consciousness. John and Sam had visited the mill earlier that morning and informed the workers about their master's plight. They were also told to be on the look out for the missing Isabelle, whether she be dead or alive.

My tiara and wedding dress were returned to me—the latter being in dire need of a wash—but there was no sign of the incriminating letter. As for Aunt Elizabeth, she decided to instigate her own search for her daughter, refusing to believe that she had anything to do with Samuel's unfortunate accident. Without the letter, it was difficult to *prove* her involvement, but we all knew it was her.

Early that afternoon, a young man on horseback came to the cottage. I had just come downstairs from sitting with Samuel for the past two hours. He hadn't woken yet, but he had made several small movements and moaned on one occasion. It was a good sign, Sam had informed me, and this kept my spirits up.

"Come quickly, to the mill pond…they have found something!" cried the young mill worker before he galloped off at speed.

"I want to come!" I demanded as John untied his horse.

"You're not going without me," said Sam. "You go with John on horseback, and I'll run up there. I know the way."

"Tell Mary what's happening." I yelled, as I stood on a log and pulled myself up behind John. I held on for dear life as John rode fast along the track to the mill. *What have they found? Is it Isabelle?*

When we arrived at the '*pond',* as the lad called it, there was a small group of men huddled together on the banks. I literally fell off of the horse in my hurry to get over to them.

"What have you found?" I cried, pushing a man out of the way to get a better view. I stared down at the sodden heap on the ground. It was difficult to see what it was at first... an animal? A human? "What is it? Is it her...is it Isabelle?" One of the men produced a large pole and turned the mass over. It plopped down heavily, water running off it in all directions. There was a face of some description—a bloated and purple face. Sam arrived and came up behind me, peering over my shoulder.

"It's her, all right," he said, taking a closer look. "I recognise that brooch on her dress from the reception." I couldn't believe that the once dainty and immaculate Isabelle was reduced to this hideous lump of pulp. I suddenly felt nauseous and turned away. "By the looks of her, she has been in the water since yesterday," continued Sam, as I threw up in some nearby bushes. "She obviously committed suicide after supposedly killing Samuel. You okay, Emily? Not a pretty sight, is it?"

"We have to take her back to the cottage." called out John, who had stayed by his horse throughout, not wanting to be subjected to such a ghastly spectacle. He was right. Her mother would want to know of her daughter's demise, and deal with it accordingly. If I had my way, she deserved to be thrown down the pit to join Robert Spedding. A cart was brought from the mill, and her body was heaved up onto the back. A dirty blanket was laid over her, disguising the image of her face, which haunted me. "I'll drive the cart back," offered John," if someone can take my horse?"

"I WILL!" cried Sam and I in unison, neither of us wanting to join John alongside Isabelle's lifeless body.

We both walked slowly back along the track, leading John's horse.

"I bet she is one *very* pissed off ghost!" said Sam, laughing and trying to lift the sombre mood. "I bet you are not her favorite person right now...not that you ever were!" *Great!* I thought. *Now I have Charlotte, Robert and Isabelle baying for my blood.* "Hey! She can't harm you now," Sam said, noticing my pained expression and putting his arm around my shoulder affectionately. "It's all over."

"I still have Aunt Elizabeth to deal with," I reminded him.

"I don't think you will have much trouble from her...if only I could find that blasted letter!"

When we arrived back at the cottage, there seemed to be some commotion outside. Mary was talking excitedly to John and, on seeing me, she shrieked out loud.

"It's Samuel! He's waking up! Come quickly!" Handing Sam the reins of John's horse, I hitched up my dress, ran into the cottage and up the stairs into the bedroom.

"Samuel, my love. I'm here!" I cried, falling onto the bed beside him. He slowly opened his eyes and turned his head towards me, his eyelids fighting to stay open.

"Emily?" he croaked. "Emily, is that you?"

"Yes, darling. It's me—Emily—your wife," I whispered softly, stroking his black hair.

"My wife?" he said, frowning. "I am married?"

"Yes, my love. We were married yesterday...do you not remember?" He turned away from me and closed his eyes. "I'll fetch you a drink. I won't be long," I promised, standing up.

"How is he?" asked Sam as I came downstairs, looking concerned.

"He doesn't remember getting married."

"I'm not surprised! He took quite a hefty whack on the head, but I'm sure the memory will return in time. I doubt, though, that he will recall Isabelle attacking him. The mind tends to blot out the bad stuff." I nodded and reheated some broth in a pot over the fire. "If not, then you will have to get married all over again!" laughed Sam, as John came in the door looking worried.

"I have sent Mary over to fetch Aunt Elizabeth...this is going to be unpleasant." In my excitement, I had forgotten about Isabelle outside on the cart. I stepped outside to see Elizabeth approaching hurriedly along the path.

"Mary asked me to come. Have you found Isabelle? Is she safe?" she cried, all flustered. Sam looked at me, and then at John.

"Come in and sit down, aunt," said John, taking her arm. She went inside reluctantly, glaring at me as she passed. I turned to Mary.

"Go to Weaver's Cottage, and tell your father that Samuel is awake and well, and keep the children away from here for a while."

"Why?" she asked, puzzled.

"I'll tell you later…now go!" Mary ran off, confused. I wondered how upset the children would be to find out their cousin, Isabelle, was dead.

"For goodness sake, John! Stop standing there like a stuffed goose and tell me why you brought me over here," she wailed, impatient to get on.

"Isabelle's dead," I said bluntly from the doorway. "They found her body this afternoon in the mill's lake, and if you don't believe me, take a look outside on the back of the cart." Aunt Elizabeth just stared at me, the words I had just spoken obviously taking time to sink in. I walked over to the fire and poured some hot broth into a bowl for Samuel. Subtlety was not my speciality, particularly where Elizabeth was concerned.

"Is this true?" she asked John, the color draining from her face. Both Sam and John nodded. Letting out a long moan, Elizabeth teetered towards a chair, and Sam only just made it over in time to catch her before she fell to the floor. I went upstairs, leaving Sam in charge of bringing her round from the faint. After all, he was the expert.

Samuel was lying there with his eyes open, staring blankly at the ceiling. I sat on the bed and stirred the broth carefully. His eyes never left the ceiling.

"Here, darling. Have some of this broth," I said, leaning over.

"I could hear Aunt Elizabeth downstairs…why is she here and not in Edgebarton?" said Samuel, turning to face me.

"She came down for the wedding," I replied, biting my lip.

"Wedding? What wedding is this that you constantly speak of? Charlotte has gone. There was no wedding." Tears started to well up in my eyes. *Have all those precious moments from our wedding been wiped from his memory? Is this Isabelle's way of getting the last laugh?* "Why are *you* here with me? Feeding me broth like a child, and not downstairs with your mother?"

"My *mother*? I said confused."

"Isabelle, do not play games with me. I have the most awful headache," said Samuel, irritably.

"Samuel I'm *not* Isabelle. I am Emily! You called me Emily, just a little while ago. Don't you remember?" Samuel buried his head in his hands in despair.

"Just go away, will you? GET OUT OF MY ROOM!" he yelled, throwing a pillow at me angrily. I picked it up off the floor, and carefully laid it on the bottom of the bed, before leaving.

Outside of the room, I burst into tears and sat down on the top stair, hugging my knees and rocking back and forth. Sam came to the bottom of the staircase and looked up.

"The undertaker has taken Isabelle's body away, and Charles is here comforting Elizab—Emily, what's the matter?" he asked, coming up the stairs, "Why are you crying? Is Samuel all right?"

"No, he bloody well isn't!" I cried in between sobs. "One minute he knows me, and the next he thinks I'm Isabelle… and now he's thrown me out of my *own* room!"

"Give it time, Emily," said Sam softly. "He's had a terrible ordeal. You can't expect everything to be as it was."

"But I *want* it to be!" I cried. "I want us to be a proper married couple."

"And you *will be*. You have to be patient with him until he regains his memory." I sighed heavily and, wiping away the tears, went downstairs.

Elizabeth was still crying, her head on Charles's shoulder as he rubbed her back soothingly. I felt no compassion for the mother, whose daughter had deliberately set out to ruin everything I held so dear.

"Is my son well?" Charles asked worriedly, over the top of her head.

"As well as can be expected," I replied, "although his memory is affected, and he may appear somewhat… confused." Charles nodded despairingly. He had hoped for better news in these troubled times.

John and Sam had taken over the kitchen and were preparing a meal for us all. They were so compatible. Sam had found his soul mate. This would present a problem when Sam had to return home. He had his university studies commencing soon, and I wondered how he would cope with leaving John. It was all such a mess.

I opened the cottage door and went outside to get some air. Darkness was already falling, but I noticed some of the children, over by the stream, sitting dolefully on a log. I had neglected them, whilst dealing with my own problems, and went over to make it up.

"Is Cousin Isabelle really dead?" asked Joseph, his eyes wide and frightened.

"I heard John talking to father earlier. He said that Isabelle tried to kill Samuel…does he speak the truth?" cried William. Hannah started to cry, and I put my arms around the scared little girl. I tried to explain to them in simple language what had happened to Samuel and their cousin Isabelle, and how her love for their brother had led to this dreadful conclusion.

"Where are Mary and Ellen?" I asked, standing up. "The meal will soon be ready."

"Mary is in the cottage, removing the bed linen on Aunt Elizabeth's bed. It reeks of Isabelle's perfume, and she thought it wise to change the sheets, said William soulfully." Mary had maturity far beyond her years. She would make someone a wonderful wife and caring mother one day.

"And little Ellen?"

"She is in the woods playing—over by the mill somewhere," replied William, unconcerned that one so small should be playing all alone in the dark woods. I was horrified at the thought, and was about to race off and find her when she appeared, singing merrily to herself through the trees.

"ELLEN!" I cried, relieved. "You mustn't go off on your own like that!"

"I wasn't alone. I had my little birdie friend with me," she said happily.

"Your what?" I asked, puzzled.

"I found him stuck in a bush, and I got him out. Poor birdie," she replied, producing a piece of partially screwed up parchment. "Look how he flies, mother. He is all better now, and I shall keep him!" With that, she threw the '*birdie*' into the air and we watched, mesmerized, as it sailed on the wind momentarily, before dropping down onto the ground at my feet. I picked up the fallen '*bird*' and carefully started to unwrap the parchment, my heart racing as I recognized Isabelle's writing and the words.

'By the time you read this, it will all be over.'

Chapter Twenty-Seven

"I need to keep this, Ellen," I told her, smoothing out the page. "It's important."

"No! You cannot take it. Give me back my birdie!" she screamed, launching herself at me in an angry tantrum. "It's mine. Give it back!"

"Look…listen to me. How about if I get you an even *better* birdie—one that flies really well—as high as the tree tops?" She stopped thrashing about, and her tear filled eyes sparkled with renewed excitement.

"Show me," she demanded. I told her to wait there while I went to find it, as it was very '*shy*', and ran back into the cottage, clutching the letter, straight through into the kitchen.

"Sam!" I whispered loudly. "I've got the letter."

"Brilliant. Where was it?" replied Sam, wiping his hands down his woollen trousers.

"Ellen found it…long story. Now I need you to do something for me," I said, fetching the writing box from the other room and extracting a sheet of parchment. "Here. Make me a paper airplane," I whispered, shoving him back into the kitchen.

"A *what*?"

"Make a paper airplane for Ellen...only it's a *bird*, okay?"

"Okay…" said Sam, slowly taking the parchment from me and laying it on the table, ready to fold. "I take it you know what you're doing?" I smiled in reply, as he quickly folded it into the standard paper airplane design, tried and tested by millions of school kids over the years.

"That's pretty impressive!" I said as he finished his masterpiece. "Ellen is outside. Go and show her how the bird flies." Sam knew better than to question me, and he went outside to test his creation.

Charles stood up as I came back into the room, helping an unsteady Elizabeth to her feet.

"I shall be taking my sister back to Weaver's cottage until the funeral," he said. The very mention of the word *'funeral'* sent Elizabeth into another wailing fit. *Charles will have his hands full,* I thought, as they walked slowly from the cottage, both supporting one another for different reasons. I was eager for them to depart, so that I could read the rest of Isabelle's suicide note in peace. As soon as the latch clicked shut, I hurriedly unfolded the parchment. It was still readable, although somewhat crumpled and grimy.

'By the time you read this, it will all be over. Samuel and I are together where no mortal soul can touch us or tear us apart. He is now mine for all eternity.

Charlotte's marriage to Samuel Howerd was forestalled with the assistance of Elijah's son, Robert Spedding, who harbored his own reasons for preventing such a union taking place, which he never disclosed. The gratification of my body was given willingly, and taken readily, by the said gentleman in return for the deed I requested. Her body now lieth under the young pear trees, should you desire to rebury her remains in hallowed ground.

Emily, you betrayed my trust and henceforth sealed your fate, however hard you endeavoured to outwit me. You may have succeeded in marrying the man I love, but the thought of you having the pleasure of his body on your wedding night, and thereafter, was intolerable. To take Samuel's life and subsequently mine, would put an end to this torture within my soul, and it was with a clear conscious that I have done what I truly deemed necessary.

Mother, dear, do not weep tears of sorrow at my grave, for I only shed tears of joy. It is my wish—and I beg of you to grant me this—that I be buried by Samuel's side to rest in eternal happiness and contentment. It is all that I beseech thee.

Forgive me, Isabelle.'

I felt a great satisfaction in knowing that her final wishes would not be adhered to, and that I *had* outwitted her in the end. Sam came back in, rosy-cheeked from playing with the children, closely followed by John.

"She *knew* Robert Spedding," I declared, handing him the letter. "I had a feeling they were both involved in Charlotte's murder, and this proves it." John sat down, looking somewhat shaken, as Sam read the letter out loud to him, one hand resting reassuringly on his shoulder.

"Well," said Sam, giving a low whistle. "She has confessed to everything here. It's just as well she did drown herself, or she would have been hung, for sure."

"I cannot believe Cousin Isabelle has done such terrible things. She was always so sweet and demure," said John, shaking his head in dismay.

A noise upstairs caught my attention, and I presumed Samuel was awake again.

"I'll see if he will take a little food," I told Sam, as he went over to the fire to check if the rabbit stew was cooked sufficiently. Samuel was not only awake, but also intent on getting out of bed, by the time I entered the bedroom. I steadied him as he swayed precariously by the bed, trying to regain his balance. "Maybe you should remain in bed a while longer, my love," I suggested nervously.

"This is *not* my bed…I have to return to—to—DAMN IT! I cannot recall the name," he cried, sitting back down on the edge of the bed in despair. "Why can I not remember? What has happened to me? I cannot even name the woman that stands before me." I bent down and took his hands in mine, the tears starting to brim over, but I held them back.

"My name is Emily," I said gently. "You are in love with me, and we are married. I am your *wife*, Samuel, and this is our room…our bed." I half expected him to have another go at me, but to my surprise, he just held on to my hands tightly, his head bowed in silence. "Just let me take care of you, and we will get through this together…but you have to trust me." He nodded his head, resigning himself to the fact that he was rendered helpless, and in need of my help, until he could once more remember sufficiently to be able to cope. "Do you think you can make it downstairs for something to eat?" I asked, standing up.

"It is not my legs that I have the problem with, woman!" he scolded, refusing my hand. "If I do remember anything, it is the ability to walk unaided." I stepped aside and let him go forward, ready to grab him should he show signs of falling. Fortunately, he made it safely to the bottom of the stairs and into the room.

Everyone, except Charles and Aunt Elizabeth, was gathered together around the table and on the bench, cradling steaming bowls of Sam and John's delicious stew. The conversation ceased abruptly as Samuel entered, and everyone stared over at him. William immediately gave up his chair to enable his brother to sit down, the strain already showing on Samuel's pale face. John ladled some stew into a bowl and fetched a spoon, placing it carefully on the table in front of him.

"Take care, for it is hot," cautioned John thoughtfully. He was met by an icy stare.

"John, fetch your *brother* a drink, would you?" I asked, emphasizing his name and status in case Samuel didn't recall who he was.

We all ate in silence, afraid to venture into familiar conversation or discuss recent issues. I could see that Ellen was getting increasingly disturbed by her brother's behavior and, as usual, didn't think before saying what was on her mind.

"I *hate* Cousin Isabelle!" She cried, throwing down her spoon. "I'm *glad* she's dead!" With that epic declaration she went over to Samuel and threw her arms around his neck, before bursting into tears. "Hasten and get better, brother, for I want to show you my new birdie," she sobbed. Samuel looked up at me, frowning, before pushing her to one side. I volunteered the information I thought he required.

"That is Ellen, your sister, and her birdie is—"

"I KNOW WHO SHE IS, GOD DAMN IT!" he yelled angrily. "Why, I want to know, was I not informed that Isabelle is dead? Did you all intend to keep this from me for some reason?" I was taken aback for a moment, and Sam stepped in to rescue me.

"Samuel, when was the last time you recall seeing Isabelle?"

"At Edgebarton, when I went to arrange Charlotte's—or was it Emily's—wedding?" he replied uncertainly.

"You don't remember seeing her by the mill pond recently?" I nudged Sam discretely, afraid that he was overstepping the mark.

"The mill pond? Why would she be up at the mill pond?" Sam looked at me and whispered under his breath,

"Take him up to the mill pond tomorrow and see if he can remember what happened."

"You think that's a good idea?"

"It may jog his memory. Tell him what happened anyway...he needs to know."

"ENOUGH OF THIS WHISPERING!" thundered Samuel, pushing Sam away from me. "*Who* are you, anyway?"

"Mister Sam Warren, a physician from London," he replied, so importantly it made me smile.

"I am not so sick as to require the assistance of a *physician*. You have had a wasted journey, sir, I fear." The children were becoming alarmed and upset by their brother's irrational behavior, and I needed to get them out.

"I am going to get the children to bed over at the other cottage. When I return, I think it best that you and John go back to Weavers." I said to Sam, whilst gathering up the children like a mother hen would her chicks, "Try and get Samuel upstairs and in bed while I'm gone." Sam made a face. He obviously hadn't much faith in his ability to handle my wayward husband now that he was *alive*.

When I returned, about half an hour later, I could hear Samuel protesting loudly in the upstairs bedroom, long before I reached the door of Mill Cottage. John was sitting downstairs, visibly distraught, and in tears.

"Hey. Come on now," I said softly, putting my arm around his shoulder. "It's going to be all right. Your brother's going to recover and be back to himself again soon."

"I hate to see him so wretched. He is like a stranger in our midst, and I cannot bear it, Emily." I kissed the top of his head affectionately. This was affecting the whole family, one catastrophe after another. *When will it all end?*

"TAKE YOUR HANDS OFF OF ME!" I heard Samuel yell from upstairs, and I hurried up the staircase to sort the two men out before things came to blows.

"Thank God! You're back!" cried Sam, clearly relieved by my presence. "He won't do *anything* I say."

"It's all right, Sam. I'll take over from here. There's a very unhappy lad downstairs that really needs you right now. Go back to Weaver's, and I'll see you tomorrow." Sam looked worried. "I'll be fine. Go on," I urged, shooing him out the door.

"That man...that '*person*' was trying to disrobe me and get me into bed!" protested Samuel. "There's something about his manner that vexes me." I smiled to myself and handed him the clean nightshirt that Sam had been trying to get on him to no avail. "You, as I am told, are my wife, and therefore my body is not unfamiliar to you."

"No, it is not," I replied rather weakly, as he pulled the soiled nightshirt off over his head and stood before me, completely naked, in the candlelight. I tried to appear unperturbed by the sight my eyes refused to stray from, but as hard as I tried—and I really *did* try—I could not stop myself from glancing downwards momentarily. My heart was racing. I passed my tongue over my dry lips and watched as he picked up the clean nightshirt and quickly covered up his magnificent body.

"How long, exactly, have we been wed?" he asked casually, slipping beneath the covers.

"Since yesterday," I replied slowly, unbuttoning my dress.

"Have I taken you yet? I have no recollection that we have consummated our marriage." There was no emotion in his voice, no feeling, and no love. It just didn't feel right. I stopped and turned to him.

"Samuel, who am I?"

"Your name, I believe, is Emily."

"Do you love me?"

"I am told that I married you, so I must have had some feelings of love for you."

"But do you love me now?"

"I don't know…maybe, although by some means, it feels like we have only just been acquainted. I cannot feel *love* for a woman I hardly know." I made a decision right there and then, as much as I wanted him, there was no way I was letting him touch me until Samuel …*my* Samuel, returned. This man was as much a stranger to me, as I was to him. I continued undressing and slipped in beside him.

"Samuel, I will sleep with you, but until you regain your memory, I ask that you refrain from touching me. I have waited this long for us to be as one, I can wait until you remember the love that we shared, and you can *feel* it within your heart."

"I understand," he replied coldly. Turning over, he bid me a simple, "Goodnight." I blew out the candle and lay back down on my pillow. The tears fell thick and fast as I entered the second night of this loveless marriage. I *had* to make him remember me. Tomorrow, I would take him to the lake and tell him how Isabelle intended to kill him.

The night did not pass without incident. Sometime in the early hours, Samuel awoke, screaming and bathed in sweat.

"What are you doing? Isabelle, no! ISABELLE! Emily, help me. Where are you? Oh God, no…please God, no."

"Samuel, it's all right. I'm here, my darling. It was just a bad dream," I whispered soothingly, sitting up next to him. "She can't harm you now." He lay back down, his eyes staring widely around the moonlit room. I put my arms around him and held him tight until the shaking subsided, and he once again fell asleep. *Is this a good sign?* I wondered. To recover, he needed to confront his demons, even those from beyond the grave.

Samuel was still asleep when I rose early the following morning. It was still dark outside as I went to gather some logs for the fire. The freezing temperatures from the night before made the ice on the ground sparkle, in the waning light of the moon, which was now slowly dipping down as dawn began to break. The hot underlying embers in the grate soon sparked into life and took hold of the fresh wood with renewed vigor. I warmed my cold hands for a few moments to get the feeling back in them before attempting to prepare breakfast. With the porridge warming above the fire, I went back outside to feed the animals. One of the old hens had died in the night from the cold, and lay stiff and frozen on the ground. I picked up the poor unfortunate bird and took it inside. Nothing ever got wasted here. When Samuel was well again, I would get him to build a hen house, so that they could keep warm on such bitter nights.

Lighting a second candle, I placed it on the table and sat down. In the mesmerizing flicker of the flame I recalled, with clarity, the vision of Samuel standing there before me naked last night. A warmth spread over me as, in my mind's eye, I ran my hand over his masculine chest, tracing the line of thick dark hair down over his stomach, to where it ended in a forest of black curls, partly obscuring his manhood that, for now, hung limp and unresponsive. This was torture, and I didn't know how long I could refrain from distancing myself from him.

The cottage door flew open, and John came in with an armful of clean clothes for Samuel, which he dumped on the table without a word as he slumped down onto the bench. I could tell by his expression that he was in a bad mood, and I was just about to ask him what was wrong when Sam came in, looking equally depressed.

"What's up with you two?" I asked, looking at their miserable faces. "Had a bit of a tiff, have we?" Sam took hold of my arm and propelled me into the kitchen.

"I'm going to have to return home soon; university starts next week, and I have an assignment to finish."

"You can't leave me with all these problems!" I cried. "Can't you stay a while longer, at least until Samuel is better?"

"I only intended to come for the wedding, Emily, and then return. It could be months before Samuel regains his memory…I can't stay around that long!"

"Why not?" I pleaded. "You could find a job here and help me set up that school you were always on about."

"Actually…I already have a job here. Samuel wants—*wanted*—to employ me as the mill's physician."

"Is that what he was talking to you about outside of the church?" I inquired.

"Yes, he wanted to know if I had decided to accept his offer."

"And *have* you?"

"It could be a bit difficult, considering he isn't aware he even made me the offer in the first place. But then, if he *does* remember, I would have to give up my chance of getting a degree and becoming a fully-fledged doctor. It's all I ever wanted to do." I nodded my head, understanding his dilemma, but my mind was racing ahead.

"Think of the *reasons* why you wanted to become a doctor, Sam," I said thoughtfully. He looked at me and contemplated his answer.

"Because…because I wanted to help people who were sick, to give aid to the injured and to make people better, so they could live long and prosperous lives."

"Exactly!" I cried. "And you could do that in a sterile glass-fronted hospital building with several floors and fancy lifts…*or* you could do it here, in 17th century rural England. You may not have the medicines or the technology, but you could save lives and treat the sick with your knowledge. Sam, you could make such a difference to these people's lives, and think how so much more fulfilling that would be?" I could see that my words were having an impact. He was thinking long and hard about what I had just said. "What have you told John?" I asked. "You have obviously said something to him."

"I mentioned that I was going back to London soon to resume my practice."

"He doesn't want you to go either...that's two against one!" Sam started to get irritated, as he battled with his conscience, and pushed past me back into the room.

"Stop it, Emily. I can't think straight!" I decided to let it be, for now, and give it time to sink in, but I was optimistic that I had made an impression.

Gathering up Samuel's clothes, I went back upstairs to see if he had awakened. As I entered the room, he turned and looked at me.

"Are those my clothes?"

"They are," I replied, laying them down on the bed. "Get dressed and come down when you're ready." I had no desire to subject myself to another floorshow, and hurried from the room before he removed his nightshirt, disintegrating my rapidly fading will power.

Samuel ate his breakfast in silence, occasionally stealing sideways glances at Sam and John, and then shaking his head, bewildered and confused. He had not brought up the topic again of Isabelle's death. Ellen's declaration yesterday was evidently forgotten, along with everything else.

"How is your father?" I asked John, trying to make conversation.

"His health is very poor, and I am doubtful he will be able to attend Isab—" A sharp kick directed at John's shin from Sam silenced him immediately, and produced further scowls in his direction.

"More bread, Samuel?" I asked quickly, passing him a basket of freshly baked bread, which Mary had collected from the village baker's just after dawn. He shook his head and pushed the basket away. "I was thinking," I continued. "I would like to take a walk up to the lake some time today, Samuel. The fresh air would do you good and assist in your recovery. We could call in at the mill too, and ensure that all is well. What do you think?"

"I *think* that it is far too cold outside to venture any distance. The ice can be treacherous underfoot."

"We can wrap up warm and wear sturdy boots," I urged, looking over at Sam for support.

"Emily is right. You should go, Samuel. I believe you will find the walk '*enlightening'.*" Samuel looked from Sam to John, and then to me, as we all held our breath in anticipation of his reply.

"Very well. I shall take a turn around the lake with you, but I would rather not take it upon myself to visit the mill… not at present."

"Of course. Whatever you want, my love," I cried, relieved that he had agreed to go.

We both dressed warmly for our January stroll through the woods up to the lake. Samuel wore his thick black cloak, and I chose to wear my red cape with the white fur that I had worn at our wedding. I thought he might recognize it, but he didn't even give it a second glance. As I went to shut the cottage door, I looked back in at Sam.

"You *will* be here when I get back, won't you?" I asked anxiously.

"I want to hear how you got on, and if it helped at all…of course I'll be here!"

"Think about what I said…" I called out as I closed the door.

"I haven't done anything but!" he shouted back.

Linking my arm through Samuel's, in case I slipped on the ice, we made our way carefully along the narrow pathway. He wasn't in a very talkative mood, and I found it hard to engage in any kind of conversation that didn't require a simple yes or no in reply. There was a distant air between us, and he held my arm out of sheer politeness, rather than affection.

Further on, I stopped to look at some snowdrops that were pushing through the hard ground. As I took hold of his arm again, he was staring at me with a smile upon his lips and a faraway look in his eyes.

"What is it?" I asked curiously.

"I do not know, but just for a moment then, as I watched you, I felt something…a feeling that quite overwhelmed me, and then it was gone."

"Was it love?"

"It was too fleeting to pass judgment on, but let us continue to walk and keep warm…it is not far now to the lake?"

"No, Samuel. Not far."

Arriving at the lake brought back to me the horrific memories of finding Samuel in the water, and the fight to bring him back to life. I shook with emotion as we stopped for a moment, gazing out across the frozen expanse.

"Why have you brought me here? Did this place contribute to my illness?" he asked, looking around bewildered.

"This is where it happened," I said softly. "This is where you died." Samuel looked at me as if I were demented. "It all began with you receiving a letter in the tavern. Just after our wedding."

I proceeded to tell him the story of the false letter to lure him away, how we found him in the lake some time later, and how Sam brought him back from the dead, with his knowledge of a '*recently discovered*' method of breathing air into the lungs. He listened intently, almost disbelievingly, to a story he had no recollection of. I went on to tell him about Isabelle's fate and the letter she left behind, which I had in my pocket, and read to him out loud. He put his hand up and rubbed the back of his head several times as I recounted the tale, recalling perhaps the pain of being struck.

"Is there *nothing* you can recall, Samuel?" I asked, feeling despondent that it hadn't jogged his memory as anticipated.

"Only fleeting visions that are in disarray, and therefore have no meaning," he replied, unlinking my arm from his purposefully, and walking along the bank on his own. I sighed heavily as I watched him walk aimlessly along, a lost soul trapped in a misty world of ghostly images and forgotten realities.

I was looking the other way when it happened. One minute he was there, the next…gone. He had slipped on the ice and shot down the bank into the icy water, breaking through the thin ice near the shore. His cries for help were frantic and hysterical as he thrashed about in the shallow water, trying to get a grip of the slippery bank. His cumbersome, heavy cloak dragged him down and thwarting his efforts to get out. I ran over to him, sliding down the bank into the water myself to grab hold of his hand. The look of terror in his eyes gave me a surge of strength, enabling me to pull him clear of the water and back up the bank.

We lay there, exhausted, soaking wet and trembling, until our rapid breathing slowed to a more regular pace. Samuel was the first to speak, his eyes taking on a softer appearance as he leaned over and gently touched my arm.

"Emily," he whispered. "It *is* Emily, is it not? I am starting to recall what happened with Isabelle. I can remember our wedding, Emily. I can see you in your wedding gown... you looked so beautiful." I pulled away and stared at him, stunned.

"You can remember our wedding, Samuel?" He nodded, pulling me back again.

"All the good memories...*and* all the bad," he replied, lifting my head and cupping my wet face in his large hands. "I remember how much I love you, Emily. My dear sweet Emily. My *wife*." I was too choked with emotion to reply. The shock of the icy water and the horror associated with it must have had an effect on him. My prayers had been answered.

"Come on. Let's get home and out of these wet clothes. I don't want to lose you to a fever. Not now—not after all this." He smiled and helped me to my feet.

"You will never lose me, my darling. Three times I have nearly died, and three times you were there to save me."

All I knew was that life was looking a whole lot brighter than when I awoke this morning. Everyone would be *so* relieved to hear he had regained his memory. This was indeed something to celebrate, with the best part saved until last, in the confines of our bedroom.

Chapter Twenty-Eight

As we walked back along the pathway to Mill Cottage, shivering with the cold, Samuel relayed to me what had happened when he arrived at the mill, in response to the urgent letter. Isabelle had been waiting outside, and took him to the lake on the pretence that there was also a problem there. Here she begged and pleaded with him to leave me, declaring her perpetual love for him and promising that they could be so happy together. Samuel would have none of it, and a fierce argument broke out, in which he pushed her to the ground in a rage. As he turned to retrace his steps to the mill, Isabelle must have picked up a large rock. He felt a sharp pain to the back of his head, and then everything went black. The next thing he knew, he was coughing up water on the bank and could hear distant voices before he lost consciousness again. The days that followed were nothing more than a hazy blur of unrecognizable faces and utter loneliness, from which he was now thankfully released.

Sam and John heard our voices as we approached and came out to meet us.

"Good God!" cried Sam in horror, upon seeing our dripping clothing, "What were you trying to *do*, Emily? Drown him again in the hope he remembered something?"

"She is not to blame for my appearance, Mister Warren. An unfortunate slip of the foot upon the ice caused me to fall into the water. Although '*unfortunate*' is perhaps the wrong description, for the cold water has awakened my memory, and I can once more remember your faces and that of my beloved wife."

"I am so pleased for you, brother," said John, hugging Samuel briefly. "I feared your condition would remain indefinitely. We must hasten to tell father, as soon as you have both acquired some dry clothing."

"How is father?" asked Samuel, going inside and taking off his sodden cloak.

"He is very weak and struggles to breathe. I think it is his heart," replied Sam, biting his lip. I stared at him for a moment, thinking how readily Sam had responded to a question directed at John, as if he were his own father.

"Can you relieve his condition?" inquired Samuel, removing his jacket.

"I can make him comfortable, but I cannot cure the ailment…regrettably."

"You must accompany us to Weaver's then, and do what you consider necessary." He unfastened his shirt slowly, each button exposing more of his flesh, after which his hand moved quickly down to undo his trousers. I could not take anymore. With a quiet moan, I ran upstairs to change my own clothing. This was going to be a *very* long day.

The children arrived and were delighted to hear that their brother was well again, especially Ellen, who dragged Samuel outside to show him her paper bird. When I first suggested that they also come with us to visit their ailing father, Samuel disapproved and thought that it would prove too much for them. I explained to him the severity of his condition and that, according to Sam, he might not be with us much longer. His children had a right to see their father before it was too late. Reluctantly, he agreed, but only for a few minutes.

Isabelle's funeral was to take place tomorrow morning. Aunt Elizabeth would no doubt attend, and I dreaded the whole event. *Perhaps I can stay behind with Samuel?* Who, I should imagine, would have no desire to attend the funeral of his would-be assassin. John and Sam could take the children, if they wished to go, and also accompany Elizabeth.

After a small meal, we all ambled along the footpath, well wrapped up against the cold, to Weaver's Cottage. Mary held on to my hand on one side, and Hannah on the other, while Samuel carried little Ellen ahead of us. William and Joseph walked alongside Sam and John. There was a melancholy cloud overshadowing all of us. Our jubilation at Samuel's recovery had been short lived, and was replaced by the impending prospect of another death soon within the family. I vowed that, when this inevitable event had passed, there would be no more tears at Mill Cottage—only laughter and happiness.

I had not seen Weaver's Cottage as yet and was surprised at how drab and rundown the place was. Old Elijah had not done any repairs for years, by the look of the crumbling stone brickwork, and the badly deteriorated thatched roof, I doubted whether it was worth spending money on repairs. The door was unlatched, and we all entered into the dark and musty interior. An indescribable smell reached my nostrils, that of which I could not fathom, and by Sam's expression, I could tell that he too had encountered the pungent aroma, but seemed unperturbed by it.

"What's that *awful* smell?" I whispered. He shrugged his shoulders and followed Samuel carefully up the half-rotten staircase. Something furry brushed past my leg on the way up, and I let out a little scream, clutching hold of Sam's arm in terror, much to his amusement. Aunt Elizabeth poked her head warily around one of the doors, as we arrived at the top of the stairs, and breathed a sigh of relief.

"Samuel, it is you…and the children also. Is this wise?"

"They have come to see their father, before it is too late," I whispered loudly, giving her a scowl and adding sarcastically, "*if* that meets with your approval?" Samuel took hold of my arm firmly and pulled me in the direction of his father's room, before I said something else inappropriate. The others waited outside while Samuel and I went in first.

A pale, gaunt-looking man laid upon the pillow of a large carved bed, a mere shadow of his former self. His breathing was laboured, as Sam had mentioned earlier, and I could hear the fluid on his lungs gurgling as he inhaled. He recognised Samuel and held out his hand for him to approach.

"You are well again, son?" he whispered weakly, grasping hold of his hand and pulling him down onto the bed.

"Yes, father, I am well. My memory has returned once more, thank the Lord." Charles looked over his shoulder at me and beckoned me over to sit by his side, taking hold of my hand also. His blue eyes filled with tears as he looked at both of us.

"I am deeply saddened, for I will not see my first grandchild, but I know you will both have many healthy sons to carry on the Howerd name—and beautiful daughters that will marry well into money." He stopped for a moment, to catch his breath, and we waited patiently for him to continue. "Samuel, I shall not be able to attend Isabelle's funeral tomorrow, and I ask that you escort my sister to the church, and burial thereafter, for me. I know it is a lot to ask of you. Believe me, I would not subject you to this ordeal unless it was truly necessary. She is not to blame for her daughter's insanity, and I beseech thee to hold your tongue and let the service pass without impediment."

"I will do as you ask, father. You need not worry that I will discredit you, for I am a changed man now, with a wife and family to support." I smiled across at Samuel, who returned it lovingly, melting my heart.

"I will come and sit with you tomorrow, while the others are at the church." I told Charles, squeezing his hand, "You can tell me stories of what Samuel was like as a child." Charles rolled his eyes and Samuel looked away embarrassed. It was not a time in his life he was proud of, evidently.

"My brothers and sisters are outside and wish to see you, but if you are too tired, then I will send them away forthwith?" said Samuel, standing up.

"Pray, let them enter. I am never too tired for my children," he replied, smiling. I kissed the old man tenderly on his forehead and bid him goodbye until tomorrow. A lump rose in my throat as I hurriedly exited the room.

"Think I've found the source of that smell. It was in the bread oven by the fire," announced Sam, cringing.

"What was it?"

"THIS!" he cried, holding up by the tail a huge rat that had obviously been dead some time, and was subsequently writhing with maggots. Some dropped down onto the wooden floor and wiggled down between the cracks, as I recoiled in horror.

"Oh God, Sam! Get rid of it! It's disgusting!" The stench from the decomposed rodent was overwhelming, and I ran down the stairs to escape the putrid smell. "I think we should get your father back to Mill Cottage after tomorrow. This place is not fit for one so gravely ill, and I could care for him easier there," I told Samuel as we waited outside for the children. Samuel nodded vaguely in agreement, his mind dwelling on tomorrow's funeral. "You all right about going tomorrow?" I asked, gently touching his arm. "I will understand if you'd rather not go."

"I will respect my father's wishes. I have not been, as you are aware, the most amiable son to him in the past, and this is my way of rectifying my guilt."

"I'm *so* proud of you," I purred, leaning over and kissing his cheek. Samuel turned his face towards me. His lips sought mine, gently at first, and then with a passion that left me breathless with desire.

"GET A ROOM!" laughed Sam, as he came out the door with John. We broke apart immediately, blushing profusely.

"What does he mean by '*get a room?*'" Samuel asked, puzzled. "I have a room. In fact, I have several."

"Take no notice of Mister Warren. His sense of humor leaves much to be desired at the best of times…ah! Here come the children," I added, on hearing them descend the staircase. Their little faces were etched with grief, after seeing their once robust and masterful father reduced to such a pitifully weak man. I put my arms around the girls and hugged them close, wiping away the tears from Hannah's face. "It's all right, my darlings. I'm here, and so is Samuel." I whispered. "We will take care of you, I promise."

"Why does everyone we love have to die?" sobbed Mary into my cape. "You and Samuel will most probably die next, and then we will have no one!"

"I'm not going to die, Mary—not for a *very* long time," I told her, cupping her tear-stained face in my hands. I could say that with the utmost sincerity, for I had seen the proof. Samuel went back in, reluctantly, to speak to his aunt about collecting her tomorrow, and asked her whether she needed any food for tonight. "There are plenty of rats around if she's peckish," I muttered under my breath as we left.

A bitter wind had got up as we walked back along the pathway. By the time we reached home, it was dusk, and the temperature had dropped dramatically. The children were cold and tired, and it was some time before we got the fire going to heat some chicken broth.

"Can I sleep with you tonight?" asked Ellen, cuddling up to me on the bench. Samuel glanced up at me anxiously, and I knew what he was thinking. My own thoughts were not dissimilar to his.

"No, not tonight, little one," I replied, kissing her head. "Not *tonight*."

When they had all eaten their fill, John and I walked with them back to Jasmine Cottage, and made up a fire to heat the cottage for the night. He was concerned about Sam, and asked me if he proposed to leave him soon and return to London. I told him that I could not be certain of his intentions, and the final decision was up to him—we could only try and persuade him otherwise. I promised that, after tomorrow's funeral, I would speak with him again.

With the children safely tucked up in bed, we lit a lantern and returned the short distance back along the path. Sam was lingering in the doorway when we arrived, ready to go back to Weaver's with John for the night. How they could sleep in that deplorable place was beyond me. It made me itch just to think of what might lurk in the beds. Aunt Elizabeth was eager to return to Edgebarton as soon as possible, and would have stayed in the village inn had it not been for her brother's deteriorating health.

"Well, have a pleasant night," said Sam, grinning widely. "You have the place to yourselves, so you can make as much n–"

"Okay, thank you, Sam!" I interrupted quickly, handing him the lantern and pushing him purposefully on his way. I was nervous enough as it was. Silly, I know, but this was a long-awaited moment in my life, and I didn't want to stuff it up...if you'll pardon the expression!

When I went back inside, Samuel had disappeared upstairs, but I was surprised to see my wedding dress carefully laid out across the table. The mud had dried and flaked off, and it was difficult to see the water stains in the candlelight. There was a note tucked under one of the roses, with just one line scrawled in Sam's writing. *Samuel wants you to put this on. He's waiting for you.* I smiled and ran my hand over the smooth satin sensuously. It would be so romantic, like a bride on her wedding night. Well, *almost*, give or take a few unexpected disruptions along the way. I slipped off my dress and underwear, trembling with anticipation of what was to come, pulled the wedding gown up and over my naked body. The cold material against my hot body felt soothing and strangely erotic. I went over and latched the door. Then, taking the candle from the table, I ascended the stairs slowly, one hand holding a bunch of the dress, to clear my steps as I went.

The bedroom door was slightly ajar, and the light from the candle within flickered on the walls. I took a deep breath and entered. Samuel was laying on the bed, fully dressed, his head raised upon the pillow, the white shirt now gaping open down at the waist. A warm surge spread through my body as I glanced down the length of his body. My heart quickened in pace, for finally I could abandon myself to him, the man that had lain in wait for me, for over 300 years.

He looked over at me as I stood in the doorway, his eyes smoldering with desire and longing. I approached the bed nervously and stopped a foot or so away, my own eyes never straying from his. Without speaking, he rose from the bed and stood before me, tall and virile, his long, dark hair falling into curls over his shoulders. My legs started to buckle as he stared intently into my eyes for a moment, before lowering his head and kissing me lovingly upon the lips. I closed my eyes, drinking in the softness of his lips as they glided across mine and onto my cheek like a summer breeze. I trembled, the pounding of the pulse in my groin growing stronger by the second. Bending quickly, he effortlessly scooped me up into his arms and laid me down upon the bed, sinking down beside me into a deep cushion of rumpled satin and underskirts. His large hand roamed over the dress and down to the bottom hem, urgently seeking a way in past the fabric that kept us momentarily apart. My heart was thudding wildly as he made contact with the warm flesh of my leg and followed it upwards. I gave a soft moan as his hand reached the moistness of my inner thigh… and then he stopped. Withdrawing his hand, he hurriedly unfastened his trousers, scrambling out of them as if there wasn't a moment to lose, his inexperience making it impossible for him to hold back any longer. I pulled up my dress and took hold of his hardened shaft in my hand, guiding him quickly to the area he sought so feverishly. All the time, I was aware that the slightest kiss, or further caress from me, would have tipped him over the edge before he had reached his goal. For his benefit, I refrained from spoiling this special moment for him.

He slid swiftly into the wet depths of my body, with a powerful lunge that made me gasp with rapturous pleasure, for he was to discover a place he had not ventured before. A place that aroused within him such immense feelings of passion, love and desire that were, for now, beyond his control. On the second thrust, he reached his climax, with a cry of such intensity, it was as if he had released all those years of pent-up emotion in one single outburst. It was only now that I dared to touch him, as he lay spent and drenched with perspiration, within me.

"Emily…I love you," he whispered huskily, his breathing coming in rapid and uneven bursts. I ran my fingers through the damp locks of his long hair, down over his broad back, to his muscular cheeks and strong thighs. He moaned and pressed into me again with the little strength he had left.

"And I love you too, Samuel. I always have...and always will," I answered back, with tears in my eyes. I did not mind that he had taken me so quickly this first time. It was understandable. I looked forward to teaching him the art of lovemaking '*21st century style*', where the wife was no longer expected to lay back and think of England, but actively participated in making it an enjoyable, and lengthy, experience for both concerned. It would blow his mind! I managed to pull up the blanket to cover Samuel as he slept, still deep inside me, until the early hours. I lay there awake, long after he had fallen asleep; his cheek nestled close to mine as a feeling of warm contentment spread over me. I had never felt like this before. This was so different to any other man I had slept with in the past—or, should I say, the future? This was *love*...true and pure.

Samuel woke up just before dawn, our bodies parting as he rolled over onto his back. I was glad he had not uttered the feeble apologies I usually received of, '*Sorry I was a bit quick,*' or '*I shouldn't have had that last beer.*' Or my personal favourite: '*Did we do anything? I can't remember.*' This was all so innocent and unspoilt by the brash society of the future. I slipped off of the bed and unfastened my gown, dropping it to the floor in a heap, before hastily climbing back in under the cover and out of the cold.

Samuel's face was illuminated in the moonlight, which penetrated the window, and I could see he was wide awake. I moved over, on top of him, my hair falling forward over my face, as I watched his expression change to one of mounting desire. I kissed his lips, his ears, and his neck before moving down to gently tease his nipples with my tongue until they stood stiff and erect. His hands responded by grasping hold of my breasts firmly in his strong hands. Then he hesitated, not knowing quite what he was meant to do with them! So I brushed my breast over his lips tantalizingly, until he opened his mouth and closed it around the nipple, sucking in the soft flesh. It was now my turn to fight for control of my composure, which I desperately tried to hold on to, as I felt his hardening manhood pressing urgently against my bare stomach.

"Samuel..." I whispered, taking hold of him in my hand and running my fingers lightly over the wet tip, until he was near to climaxing. I stopped in time and withdrew my hand. He was totally at my mercy, as I entwined my hands in his and pressed them down onto the pillow. I noticed, for the first time, several healed scars on his arms, resulting, I should imagine, from the hard labor he had endured over the years. I kissed them tenderly, and he flinched as if they still troubled him. Then I maneuvered my body expertly in line with his, as he closed his eyes and became lost in a world of drunken ecstasy. I only allowed him to penetrate me slightly, rising and falling with each gentle thrust until he cried out, *begging* me, *pleading* for me to let him take me completely. When I knew he could take no more, and only then, did I release my weight onto him, enabling us to reach a crescendo together that I feared those at Jasmine Cottage would surely hear!

"My God, Emily!" cried Samuel, after several minutes had passed; "There is no doubt that tonight you *will* be with child."

"If not, then we will have to try harder," I said, smiling mischievously. Samuel groaned and flopped back on the pillow. I laughed and snuggled up to him, as he pondered on how many children he would eventually father, and whether he would die of exhaustion in the process. He never envisioned it could all be so tiring.

"Do all women possess such knowledge of how to please a man in bed? Or has my virginity been taken by one already deflowered?" asked Samuel suddenly.

"I have read books that explain a husband's needs. Where else would I obtain such knowledge?" I lied convincingly.

"They write books about *fornication*?" cried Samuel disbelievingly.

"Most certainly."

"Is there one for men also?"

"I expect so…but as you cannot read, I will endeavor to teach you myself."

"I am sure it will be a pleasurable experience, one for which I am most grateful," he replied innocently. Ignorance in this instance, was indeed, bliss.

Daylight came all too quickly, and we were both awoken by the sound of banging on the door of the cottage.

"I will go," said Samuel, getting out of bed and pulling on his trousers. "We have slept late, and nothing is prepared."

"I'm sure they will understand…given the circumstances," I replied, smiling. He returned to the bed and kissed me passionately, before breaking off suddenly and stepping back.

"A fire burns within me now that I cannot douse. I cannot touch you without rekindling that flame, whether it be day or night."

"You will learn to master that need quite quickly, I assure you." I replied. "I think taking me on the table during mealtime could prove a little embarrassing for all concerned, do you not agree?" Samuel stared at me, shocked, before realizing that I was only teasing. He had much to learn about me.

"Samuel, open the door!" cried John loudly, from below our window, "We have father here in the cart. Also Aunt Elizabeth." Samuel and I threw one another a concerned look, before he hurriedly left the room and ran down the stairs to unlock the door. I quickly reached for my old dress, the sweet aroma of Samuel's bodily fluids still strong upon my skin. I had no time to wash, and hoped that only *I* would be aware of the lingering scent, which would serve as a pleasurable reminder of our passion throughout the day. Sam met me halfway down the stairs, his eyes sparkling with anticipation.

"So, how was it?" he whispered, smiling. "Did he live up to your expectations?" I laughed and blushed slightly at the directness of his question.

"Sam!" I hissed back, stopping opposite him on the stair. "Some things are best kept to oneself."

"Was he a virgin?" urged Sam excitedly, blocking my way. I nodded my reply. "I knew it! Wow! I bet you taught

him a thing or two. Poor guy, he looks totally shattered…a bit like John did, the first time we—"

"Don't even go there!" I cried, screwing up my face in mock disgust, and pushed past him down the stairs. I could hear Sam's laughter behind me as I entered the room below.

Charles was sitting on the bench, wrapped in a thick blanket, intently watching John attend to the fire. He was lost in his own little world, and was hardly aware of my presence as I knelt before him.

"Good morning, father," I said softly, taking his hand in mine. His tired blue eyes turned towards me, and he smiled wearily.

"Emily, my child," he breathed quietly, gripping my hand weakly, before his attention once more returned to the fire. At the table behind us sat Aunt Elizabeth, crying silently. She shook her head in despair, the pain etched in deep furrows upon her brow.

"I cannot take much more of this incessant grief," she wailed, burying her face in a black handkerchief. I sighed heavily, the anger and resentment melting away as I looked down at the broken woman, feeling nothing now but sorrow. Samuel put a comforting arm around my shoulder, sensing my sadness.

"Go and see to the children," he whispered, kissing my cheek tenderly. Taking my cape down from behind the door, I slipped it over my woollen dress and left the cottage.

Once outside, I broke down in tears and cried all the way along the path to Jasmine Cottage, my emotions all over the place. Tears were shed for Charles, for Elizabeth, and even for poor Isabelle. I understood her now, but I would *never* forgive her for what she did. True love is intoxicating, its power potent enough to drive you to the brink of insanity and beyond, in order to keep the man you love. If any woman ever dared come between Samuel and I, she would not live to fulfil her objective, for that I am certain.

Breakfast was a solemn affair that morning. Even the children ate in silence, which was a rare occurrence. Samuel's eyes burned into mine across the table, as I leaned forward and ladled more porridge into his bowl. The sexual tension between us was strong, and I kept visualizing what I had joked about earlier, regarding the table. After we had finished eating, I took some of the bowls into the kitchen, and as I stood pumping water into the stone sink, two firm hands encircled my waist.

"Samuel!" I said, laughing. "We have more pressing matters, this morning, to attend to." His hands moved around to my breasts.

"I have a matter also that is pressing most urgently...*feel*," he whispered loudly, taking hold of my hand and holding it against his bulging crotch. We giggled like lovesick teenagers, embracing passionately against the sink, unaware that Aunt Elizabeth was watching us from the doorway.

"SAMUEL HOWERD!" she shouted, her face like thunder. I could feel Samuel's body tense as she approached. "Your conduct is disgraceful. Have you *no* respect?"

"Please forgive me, Aunt Elizabeth," replied Samuel meekly, stepping away from me nervously, as if he were a naughty child.

"He was only kissing his wife!" I cried, annoyed at her attitude.

"Such uncouth behavior should be reserved for the privacy of your bedroom. Public displays of affection are considered ill-mannered and vulgar. I am not altogether sure, Samuel, that your choice of a wife is befitting your status as a mill owner." I looked at my husband, awaiting his reply. He just stood there rigid, unable to respond, an expression of fear upon his face that I had not seen before.

"How *dare* you stand there and accuse—" I yelled at Elizabeth, stepping forward, but I was interrupted by a shout from Sam before I could continue my tirade.

"The carriage is here with Isabelle's coffin." Elizabeth spun around with a startled cry.

"My precious daughter...your mother is coming, my darling!" she cried, rushing through the room in tears.

"I shall return the moment I have sent my aunt back to Edgebarton on the afternoon coach, and for *me*, it is not a moment too soon," said Samuel quietly, stroking my hair. "Let not her words trouble you, for she has a cruel tongue, but her grief is much to blame on this occasion. You are *more* than worthy to be my wife, and the way we show our love is not to be considered dishonorable in any way." I smiled and pressed my lips to his, before he picked up his cloak and ushered the children outside to join Sam, John and Elizabeth behind the carriage, leaving me to wonder about the way he had reacted towards his aunt's abuse.

Charles staggered to the door, with my help, to see off the cortège, the single black horse with a feathered plume, walking slowly with its head bowed along the track to the lane. Isabelle was to be buried next to her father—her mother's choice, as hers was no longer conceivable. Sam turned to look at me as they rounded the corner. I was too far away to see his pained expression or the tears that welled in his eyes as he silently bid me goodbye.

Having got Charles once more settled on the bench with a mug of warm broth, I tentatively asked him about Samuel's childhood, of which he appeared reluctant to fill me in. After some gentle persuading, he began to open up, and I had a feeling that there were unresolved issues in his past regarding Samuel, which he had kept secret from me.

"He has *always* been a loner, as far back as I can remember, preferring to roam the woods on his own, rather than play games with his adopted brothers and sisters, despite constant encouragement." Charles stopped to catch his breath. "As he got older," he continued, "he became more subdued and difficult, never more so than when they returned from Edgebarton after summer visits with Elizabeth and Isabelle." Charles sighed heavily and shook his head in despair. "I thought it was because he had returned home. The children loved to play with Isabelle and complained bitterly when they had to come home. All except Samuel, who came willingly but remained withdrawn and unresponsive, even becoming violent in response to my subtle enquiries regarding his sullen mood. I *should* have known…"

"Known what?" I asked, puzzled, my heart starting to race with anxiety.

"I should have known what my sister was doing to him. It wasn't until years later that I discovered the truth, when he returned one time from Edgebarton and collapsed. It was then, as I undressed him to put him to bed, that I saw the terrible scars on his arms. Delirious with fever, he broke down and told me the truth. She was very clever in covering her tracks. I never thought for one moment that she was capable of such cruelty. My love and respect for my sister died at that moment." I remembered the marks I had seen last night in bed, and how he had recoiled away from my caring touch.

"She beat him?" I asked quietly, biting my lip.

"She loathed the boy and frequently took a studded belt to him, always inflicting the damage in a place covered by clothing so as not to draw attention. Then she would tie him up and torture him in the cellar below while the others played happily outside. She would burn his arms with hot irons until he confessed to being the bastard child that he unfortunately was—the devil's spawn with a heart as black as his eyes." His blue eyes filled with tears, and he lowered his head. I was stunned and stared into the fire as Charles continued. "When he became an adult, the abuse continued, but in a more emotional way, until he deemed himself not worthy to walk this earth, or to find someone to love him for who he was. He responded to Isabelle's affection, hungry for love and kindness. Elizabeth encouraged the union, waiting for the time when he would propose to her daughter. At the last minute, she intended—I discovered later—to send Isabelle far away, spiralling Samuel into the depths of despair as retribution for his existence. He blamed his mother and me for *apparently* condoning his plight—a cross that we have had to bear, despite our ignorance. Then you came to us one day—an unexpected visitor that saved him from eternal damnation, for I believe he would surely have taken his own life soon had you not arrived when you did." Charles stopped and took a sip of the broth, his hands trembling as they grasped the mug. Tears were streaming down my face as I pulled the blanket up around him. I couldn't speak at first. My mouth felt dry, and I thought I was going to be sick.

"You should have *told* me this before she left," I said finally, shaking with rage.

"She has already been punished for her wrongdoing. God does not pay his debts with money, my child. Her daughter has been taken from her; by the very man she sought to destroy…justice has been done."

Chapter Twenty-Nine

The only thing I wanted to do at that moment was to hold Samuel in my arms, to tell him how much I loved him and that no one—*no one*—was ever going to hurt him again. Charles looked dreadfully tired and deathly white, so I suggested that he go upstairs to lie down for a while. The revelation of Samuel's abuse had exhausted him, but I felt he was relieved that I now knew the whole sordid story and would forgive Samuel for his past misdemeanors. I came back downstairs after settling Charles and peered expectantly out of the window, awaiting their return, but there was no sign as of yet. I couldn't settle and went outside to check the animals, before sitting down on a log by the door, anxiously looking up the track for them to return.

It seemed like an eternity before I heard the sound of distant voices, resounding among the trees in the rapidly fading afternoon light. Samuel's deep masculine tone was unmistakeable, and I ran a little way down the track to greet them. The children appeared first, with Ellen skipping merrily in front in her dark woollen dress and bonnet. The black-cloaked figures of the men followed at a slower pace some way behind. William spotted me first, his face changing to one of concern, as to why I had come to meet them.

"Is father worse?" he asked, drawing level with me.

"Do not worry. Your father is resting peacefully upstairs," I replied, putting my arm affectionately around his shoulder. "How was the funeral? Did many people attend?"

"The church was indeed full, with acquaintances of Aunt Elizabeth mainly. Isabelle had few friends to speak of outside of the family," said John, walking rapidly past me into the cottage, frowning.

"Run along inside, children—out of the cold. I will be in shortly to prepare a meal," I instructed them, as my brimming eyes rested on Samuel, who was approaching me up the path.

"My love, you tremble so with the cold," he said, throwing his cloak around my shoulders, as I flung my arms around his neck in a tight embrace, the tears running down my flushed cheeks as I clung on to him desperately.

"Oh, Samuel!" I sobbed. "You're safe now, my darling. She's gone, and I won't ever let her set foot inside Mill Cottage again, I promise you." I felt his body stiffen, and his hands firmly took hold of my shoulders.

"What do you mean by that remark?" he inquired, the tone in his voice turning more serious as he distanced himself from me.

"She cannot hurt you anymore, Samuel…it's over," I cried, stroking the side of his face. His eyes changed instantly to a foreboding black, and he pushed my hand away.

"You know? Who told you?" he shouted angrily.

"It's all right, my love. I understand. You have nothing to be ashamed of."

"It was father, wasn't it? It *has* to be." I grabbed hold of his shirt, in a futile effort to halt his progress into the cottage, and was left holding a piece of torn white cotton.

"Samuel, *don't!"* I screamed after him. "Let him be, please. I beg of you!" My frantic cries fell upon deaf ears. He was a man on a mission, and there was no stopping him. John came back out of the door, seemingly unperturbed by Samuel's rapid ascent up the stairs. He had other things on his mind.

"Where's Sam?" he asked, mystified.

"What?" I replied, trying to gather my thoughts. "He went with you to the church."

"He did indeed, and stayed for the service, but then he left to return here while Samuel and I went with Aunt Elizabeth to the coach." He now had my full attention.

"I haven't seen him…" I said quietly. "Have you tried the other cottage?"

"I am just going there now," said John, anxiously setting off down the track. *He can't be far away*; I thought to myself, and went back into the cottage to see what traumas Samuel had caused inside.

"I have prepared the chicken, mother," called out Mary, as I hurriedly passed by.

"Thank you, darling…I will be with you in a short while. I just need to see your father."

I went cautiously up the stairs, noticing that everything was quiet. I could hear no voices. Pushing open the door to Charles's bedroom, I saw that Samuel was sitting on the side of the bed with his back to me. I waited a moment before I spoke.

"Do not stand in the doorway, Emily. Pray enter, and sit with me," said Samuel, sensing that I was there, without turning around. As I approached the bed, Charles came into view. At first I thought he was sleeping, but soon realized he was not, and I let out a muffed gasp. "He had already passed away when I came into the room…in case you were wondering," he said, turning to look at me.

"I never thought for one second that you—"

"I was *angry*, Emily!" he interrupted. "Angry and ashamed that you, my wife, would now think so lowly of me."

"No, Samuel!" I cried, grasping his hand. "It wasn't your fault! I love and respect you even more for what you endured so courageously all those years. Your father died at peace with himself. Now it is a time to move on and forget the past, because the future of *our* family depends on it." Samuel gave me a faint smile and returned his gaze to his father, lying serenely on the pillow. "He was a good man, Samuel." I whispered. "I am proud to have known him." He squeezed my hand, acknowledging my statement as his eyes glistened over, and he broke down in oceans of tears.

Footsteps on the stairs had me on my feet and heading for the door, in order to stop whomever it was from entering. John at the top of the stairs, waving a piece of paper, confronted me.

"He was not there, but I found this letter with writing on it…read it to me, Emily," commanded John. I steered him away from the room purposefully.

"John..." I began. "There's something I have to…"

"Sam's gone, has he not? Tell me it is not true, Emily. Read it…READ IT!" I stared at him thoughtfully for a moment. This was not the time to tell him such sad news. I sat down on the top of the stairs, sighing heavily as I begrudgingly read the short letter in Sam's handwriting, fearing more upset was to follow.

'Emily,

as I sat in the church, looking at the glistening cross on the altar, suddenly everything became clear. I don't know why we didn't think of it before. The solution to the problem, and the very thing that was holding me back, was staring me in the face. The answer, my dear Emily, can be found at the end of the rainbow.

Sam'

John looked at me, confused, as I folded up the letter slowly and handed it to him.

"What does it mean?" he pleaded; his large blue eyes open wide. "Is he coming back? Where has he gone? *What* can be found at the end of a rainbow, Emily?" I smiled and kissed his cheek lightly.

"A pot of gold lies at the end of a rainbow, John, and I do believe that Sam will bring it back home with him… have faith." I could tell, by the look on John's face as he descended the stairs, that he had no idea what I was talking about. I only hoped that I was right. Samuel came out of his father's room, his eyes red and swollen, and took hold of my hand tenderly.

"Gather our family around the table, Emily. After today, there will be no more weeping at Mill Cottage. A new era has begun."

As Samuel stood proudly at the table, as head of the household, he informed his brothers and sisters compassionately of their father's death. I expected there to be lots of tears, but they had all steeled themselves inwardly for this dreaded announcement. They all knew that the end was not too far away and was, ultimately, inevitable. Death was not an unfamiliar visitor to Mill Cottage. They had lost so many of those closest to them in such a short time, but these brave little soldiers of misfortune had battled on regardless.

While I busied myself in the kitchen, trying to hold it together, Samuel took each child upstairs to pay his or her last respects to their father. I was feeling very emotional as it was. I knew, without a doubt, that the sight of these grief-stricken children kissing their father's cheek for the last time would have reduced me into a blubbering wreck. John rode into town to summon the undertaker, who arrived just as we finished our meal. Ellen clung to my dress, as the plain wooden box was taken from the cottage, and loaded unceremoniously onto the waiting cart. We all stood silently outside and watched as Charles's body was taken away down the track in the twilight.

"Goodbye, father," called out Ellen as the cart disappeared around the bend. "Give mother a kiss from me when you reach heaven." Samuel held me close as I sobbed uncontrollably against his shoulder. *Goodbye, father.*

Charles was buried the following afternoon, with his beloved wife, Hannah. As the first shovel of earth landed, with a dull thud on top of the coffin, my eyes wandered to the nearby graves of those we had lost before. Mary, Elizabeth, Sarah, and little Eliza, robbed of life before it had barely begun. A small hand took hold of mine and clasped it tightly. Looking down, I smiled lovingly at the child beside me.

"Today, Ellen, is the start of new beginnings for us," I said, bending down to her level. "Father would not want us to be sad. He would want us to be happy, would he not?" She turned her pale, tear-stained face towards me and nodded uncertainly.

"When will Mister Warren come back? Father liked him. He said Mister Warren would make a school for us, and you would teach us. Father wanted us to become edicu—educted—"

"Educated, darling. It means that you will be able to read and write, and know about the world in which we live. When Sam returns—and I know he will—then we can make those wishes come true, I promise you," I told her before standing up.

"Promise what?" asked Samuel, stepping nearer and putting a comforting arm around our shoulders.

"I have a promise to fulfil to your father, Samuel, and God willing, the Howerd family name will go down in history, as being the founders of the first village school. Every man, woman and child has the right to be educated, to prosper, and to lead the way forward into the future." Samuel smiled proudly and pulled me close.

"Whatever would I have done without you, dearest Emily?" I couldn't even *begin* to answer that question.

The old Samuel Howerd died along with his father. It was replaced by a warm, caring family man that never again raised his hand in anger or lost his temper. A man that listened without prejudice to any suggestions, worked from dawn to dusk to ensure his family never went hungry, and became the best lover that any woman could ever wish for.

As I predicted, and much to John's delight, Sam returned two weeks later, to stay for good. He was laden with two heavy carryalls, and clutching the locket tightly. One was stuffed full of medical books, covering all aspects of treatments conventional or otherwise, 18th century diseases, compounds and homeopathic remedies. He had sold my car and all of his belongings. And this, together with his savings, had purchased the one thing that never went out-of-date, the universal currency of all time—GOLD. Part of our newfound wealth was used to buy the very latest machinery for the mill, which enabled us to increase the export of textiles and improve the safety of employees, which no longer exploited child labor. Samuel Howerd became a well-respected, considerate and successful businessman in the process.

Aunt Elizabeth died three months after her brother Charles. Racked with guilt, she left her entire estate to

Samuel. A trust was set up with the money to care for orphaned and abused children, which would be run by William, Hannah and Joseph in later years, blissfully unaware of the truth behind Samuel's choice. Little Ellen wants to become a teacher today. Yesterday, she wanted to be an artist. Tomorrow? Who knows? As long as she is happy, it doesn't really matter.

Weaver's Cottage was torn down and a new house built on the site, which was to become '*Sam's Surgery*'. This housed a consultation room, patient waiting area, a small operating room, and a larger room accommodating four beds for the more seriously ill. Sam lived upstairs with John in clean and comfortable surroundings, always available should he be needed—day or night. He was not a fully qualified doctor, but with his basic knowledge and dedication, he learned through his books to be able to treat and cure the local community of many ailments, that would have otherwise subjected the sufferer to many years of unnecessary pain. He grew blue and green mold on bread, and carefully extracted the yellow liquid from it, with which he could make rudimentary penicillin, saving countless lives from death through infection. John took a great interest in his work and learned from Sam how to mix compounds and mixtures, relieving Sam of the more mundane jobs, enabling him to attend to the sick. Together, they were a great team. Even young Mary helped out, by making beds and fetching drinks for the patients on the ward—a proper little Florence Nightingale, more than a century before the good lady was born.

Sam's reputation grew, and people would come from far and wide to be treated by him. Although he never charged for his services, donations were always gratefully received, and the richer clientele were more than generous in contributing towards the costs of medicines and supplies. There was always the nagging fear in my mind that he would be seen as some kind of charlatan or witch doctor, bearing in mind the era in which we now lived. Sam always said that this kind of hysteria was born out of ignorance and fear of the unknown. To safeguard himself, and teach valuable lessons to the community, he held regular talks in the village inn, explaining the importance of hygiene, well-being, and the prevention of spreading diseases. Questions were readily answered in basic easy-to-understand language. They had nothing to fear, and much to learn, about a world they knew so little about.

Mary, Hannah and Ellen moved in with Samuel and I at Mill Cottage, and the two boys lived upstairs at Jasmine Cottage. The downstairs area was converted into a small classroom with two long benches and chairs, seating a maximum of ten pupils. Every morning, I laid out a sheet of parchment paper, a quill and a little clay pot of ink in front of each chair. The places were filled rapidly with eager individuals from the village and mill. There was even a waiting list drawn up in case of cancellations, of which there were none. Finally, due to demand, we had to create another larger classroom in the barn, and I split the day into two sessions—the younger ones in the morning at the cottage, the older ones in the afternoon at the barn. It was hard work, but it was so rewarding to see their captivated expressions as they added together simple numbers by themselves, and I was delighted as I watched them read the words they had written.

It was difficult, at first, to hold back from telling them of the world that I once knew—the world of the future, where fast cars raced along concreted roads, jet airliners that carried people through the skies to distant lands and space rockets landing people on the moon. It was a world in which I no longer existed in, and I didn't want to. *This* was my life. My world was here, with all the people I loved. I wouldn't have it any other way.

Emily Ann Howerd.'

I stopped writing and set the quill down upon my desk. The rain had ceased now, but the skies grew darker, as night came upon us once more. The baby in the cot beside me stirred momentarily, and I gently pushed a lock of black curly hair away from my son's eyes. *James John Howerd,* born exactly nine months to the day after Samuel and I first made love, and delivered by a triumphant Sam. I pulled open the desk drawer quietly and picked up the locket that lay within, running my fingers over the gold casing that held Charlotte's picture, as my mind drifted back to where it all began.

Placing the locket on the desk, I reached into the drawer once again and removed a color photo, which Sam had taken just before he returned to me—a photo of my gravestone in the village churchyard.

'Here lieth the body of Emily Ann Howerd of this parish. Born February 21st 1987, who dyed 7th October 1752 aged 87. Also of her beloved husband, Samuel Howerd, who departed this life on the same day, consumed with grief. May they rest in peace.'

Sam had etched my date of birth upon my headstone as an everlasting epitaph to our extraordinary journey through time, and a challenging riddle to anyone who took a moment to stop and read the ancient stone. I smiled at his sense of humor, as I folded up the sheets of parchment and tied them with a red ribbon. Together with the locket and the photo, I placed the items in an iron box and buried it in the ground, at the entrance to Mill Cottage. Someday, in the not-so-distant future, another visitor would surely come. Until then…we waited.

Epilogue

Jack Howard tucked a strand of curly black hair behind his ear, as he stood in Offenham village churchyard, with his wife Ann.

"It says here," he announced, eagerly reading from an information leaflet, which he had picked up in the village tearoom, "that my distant ancestor, Emily Ann Howerd, founded in 1697 what is known today as '*The Howard Grammar School for Boys and Girls*'. The same year that '*The Warren Memorial Hospital*' down the road was also founded, by a guy called Sam Warren."

Ann wasn't listening. She was bored to tears by all this, and had only agreed to accompany her husband on a drive down to Offenham to get out of the house for a while. Now she was seriously regretting it. Their solicitors, *Messers W. Thornton and Co.,* had asked Jack to call into their offices at his convenience. He was given possession of a box found on the site of a derelict cottage nearby, as bulldozers cleared the area to build the school. They had spent years trying to trace any surviving relatives of the said Emily Howerd, and eventually found Jack. The faded sheets of parchment, together with a scrap of disintegrated paper within, had prompted the visit to Offenham that day.

His fingers reached into his pocket, and anxiously caressed the tarnished pendant that he had also found in the box, and hidden from his wife. He had to know the truth.

"You don't believe in all this rubbish?" asked Ann, looking at her watch impatiently. Jack shrugged his shoulders as he walked over to a gravestone that stood up against the church wall.

"Look at this inscription, Ann," he said, brushing aside the invasive ivy. "Born 1987, died 1752...what's that all about?"

"Obviously the work of some vandal with a warped sense of humor," muttered Ann. "You don't honestly believe that she *was* from the future?" The look on Jack's face gave her the answer. "I'm sorry, but without proof, I refuse to believe in this nonsense…now, *come on*, I'm starving. Let's go and eat at that inn we saw in the High Street."

Ann set off back through the churchyard and down the path to the gate. Ten minutes had passed, and Jack still had not joined her. She retraced her steps back to the churchyard.

"Hey! Jack, where are you?" she called out nervously. "JACK?" There was no sign of her husband.

It was as if he had, quite literally, vanished off the face of the earth…

Milton Keynes UK
Ingram Content Group UK Ltd.
UKHW011327080823
426529UK00001B/102